JANNA MACGREGOR

A Simple Seduction

To Lenora Bell
for letting Honoria borrow your name.

You're simply the best.

A Simple Seduction

JANNA MACGREGOR

Prologue

rdeerton House
London
Home of the Fourth Duke of Pelham

"A whore begets a whore."

Liquid gurgled, followed by a splash. Seconds later, the noise repeated. He had poured another glass.

Her father was drinking again.

At the rapier-sharp anger in her father's voice, eight-year-old Lady Honoria Davies Ardeerton, the eldest daughter of the Duke of Pelham, slid farther into the darkened alcove. A dull, off-rhythm thud pounded in her chest, much like her performances at the pianoforte. She hated the instrument almost as much as her father despised her.

"Are you calling me a whore?" The chill in her mother's voice would have frozen the water in the courtyard fountain in the middle of July. "Must we do this? First, it was weekly, now it's become daily."

The second-floor bookcases in her father's lair, otherwise known as his study, hid Honoria from view. The enclosed space held the advantage of flawless acoustics, which amplified every word and subtle nuance uttered in the room.

When her mother had received the summons to attend the duke, Honoria had followed. Of course, she'd stayed a respectable distance behind. Such was her secret power. Everyone thought her a docile child with no outstanding characteristics. She had hardly any artistic vision, negligible athletic prowess, and her appearance favored a newborn filly, all legs, and scarcely any grace.

Little did they know, she could hide in plain sight. In the midst of a party, no one knew her whereabouts.

Because no one noticed her.

Quiet as a cat on the hunt, Honoria could follow most people who lived and worked at her father's ducal estate. None of them had a clue she was there. That included her seven-year-old sister, Philippa, whom everyone affectionately called Pippa. She was Honoria's closest confidante, but even Pippa didn't know Honoria's unique talent for listening to conversations she wasn't supposed to hear.

The only person she couldn't successfully trail was her brother, Dane Ardeerton, the Marquess of Meyrick, their father's heir. At four and ten, Dane had finished his term at Eton and had returned to the ducal seat in Amesbury with a new habit. In the early evenings, he'd meet one of the young women who worked at the village tavern.

Honoria had made it a practice to follow him. She really couldn't have cared less where he went or what he did, but if she could follow Dane undetected, she could follow anyone. But alas, Dane was devilishly good at hiding himself. When she'd lost sight of him and returned for home, that's when he'd surprised her by jumping out from some tree or bush. He always lectured how it wasn't proper to follow him, then threatened to tell their mother.

Dane never threatened to tell their father. Her brother would never lay such an unspeakable burden upon her.

At one point, Honoria had thought it would be a blessing if she could excel at something—anything. Ridiculously, she'd believed her father would then be pleased with her. Try as she might, she had never succeeded. Besides his blond hair, broad shoulders, and piercing blue eyes, which her siblings had all inherited, her father's most defining feature was the constant sneer he wore in her presence.

She'd once prayed for an entire month that if he'd just give her one smile, she'd forgo all her Christmas presents. It had not succeeded.

Her father had never hit her, but he had other ways of punishing her. One year, he'd banished her from taking singing lessons. Truthfully, it had been a boon. She hadn't much of a voice, and even the French voice instructor was aware of that simple fact. He'd cringed every time she tried to reach a high note.

Her father had decreed that she had no talent at painting. He'd instructed the staff at their London home of Ardeerton House to throw out her art box.

That had hurt. It had been her second most prized possession. Her maternal Aunt Harriet had given it to her for her eighth birthday.

But what had finally proven his irrefutable anger was the day he'd ordered her darling pony, Elsbeth, be taken away. The piebald had been her pride and joy. The pony had never sat in judgment of Honoria and her lack of talents. Every day, she'd gone to the stables with some treat for her beloved Elsbeth. With every carrot, apple, or bag of oats, Elsbeth had nuzzled her velvet nose against Honoria. She had listened to Honoria for hours as she'd told her stories of magical kingdoms where little girls were loved and cherished. And such acceptance from the mare had given her confidence. Yet, it had turned into a double-edged sword.

One day, Honoria had done the unthinkable. She'd dishonored her father by directly defying him. He'd criticized her at the dinner table for her lack of conversation skills and her lack of grace. She'd delivered an impudent rejoinder. She had pointed out that if he wouldn't talk so much, then perhaps she could contribute to the conversation. At the complete shock on his face, she'd grown bolder. She'd then reminded him that if he hadn't prohibited her from dance lessons, perhaps she could have learned to move with enough grace to please him.

As soon as the last words had slipped from her mouth, he had slapped both hands onto the table. She'd known immediately that her life would change but didn't realize how much. The words still haunted her.

"Since you can't master the simple skill of riding a meek pony, I'll give

it to someone who can put the pony to better use." He arched an arrogant eyebrow.

"But, Father," she pleaded with tears in her eyes. She couldn't lose Elsbeth. "I'm sorry. Please, don't."

He sneered at her in revulsion. "I'll send the animal to the glue factory."

It was one of the few times her mother had tried to defend her.

The next day, Elsbeth was gone, and Honoria had never had the chance to say goodbye since she'd been sent to her room. She had cried for a week.

Honoria startled slightly at her father's voice when he broke her reverie.

"I've come to several decisions."

"Oh, please tell me I'm to be banished." The boredom in her mother's voice floated in the air.

"Not you. But let this be a lesson to stay away from Frawley." Honoria's father slammed the glass down.

"It was a mistake. I slept in his bed once." Honoria's mother sniffed. "You, on the other hand, have never been without a mistress. The day your heir was born, you were nowhere to be found. You were with *her*."

"Sally?" Her father chuckled. "She's a hell of a lot warmer than you, *my dear*. If you look up the word frigid in the dictionary, there's a picture of your bed."

Her parents had always argued, but she'd always attributed it to both being hard-headed and hard-hearted. Bile rose in her throat. She'd never once considered that they'd been unfaithful to one another.

"You're foxed," her mother retorted. "You won't remember this conversation tomorrow."

"I didn't call you here to compare bed partners," he retorted. "It's *your* daughter."

"She's yours, too." Her mother huffed. "She looks just like you!"

"Half the children of the aristocracy have blond hair and blue eyes," her father drawled. "She's not mine. Honoria's complete ineptitude at anything that defines a young lady is proof. I can't stand to look at her another day." The crinkle of paper filled the air. "This is a letter denying she's mine. One of my solicitors will deliver it to her groom before her marriage. We'll see who claims her then."

"She's a child," her mother pleaded. "You can't be so cruel."

"The truth hurts."

"What about Pippa?" her mother said softly.

"She stays. My heir and youngest child are mine. You weren't with him then."

Honoria locked her knees to keep upright and bit her lip to keep from crying out. Scalding tears cascaded down her face, leaving a hot trail of bitterness.

"Damn you for putting me in this position," her father bellowed. "Though she has my protection, and I provide for her, I will not tolerate her under my roof anymore. I'll not have the taint of her around me or *my children*. She's not of my blood. Therefore, I'm sending her away to a finishing school in York."

York? Her hands started to shake.

"No, please don't send her away," her mother begged.

Without Dane or Pippa, she'd be utterly lost. While she'd accepted her mother's indifference and her father's hatred, she'd always had her siblings. They'd always been by her side after their father had punished her.

But banishment because she wasn't her father's child? What kind of horrid trickery was this? Did that mean that Dane and Pippa would forsake her, too?

She brought a trembling hand to her mouth as she felt every bit of hope she'd clung to over the years slip through her fingers. All those wasted hours trying to please the duke could never be reclaimed. She wobbled slightly as she tried to make sense of what was happening.

Suddenly, strong arms surrounded her from nowhere.

"Shhh," Dane whispered into her ear. "I'll protect you."

"What was that?" their father barked.

Dane pulled her from the alcove and through the servants' hallway. Honoria stumbled since her tears wouldn't stop, and she couldn't see in front of her.

Dane kept his arm around her shoulder and pulled her into another room. When he shut the door and twisted the lock, they were in the silver closet.

"Honor," he said softly as he pulled her into his embrace. Though he was a young man, he'd always been the one who'd comforted her. When Elsbeth had been taken from her, it was Dane who'd held her as she'd cried uncontrollably.

"You can't protect me. You're leaving..." Unable to catch her breath, she hiccupped.

"University starts next week." He patted her back. "I'll think of something."

For a moment, she felt about as strong as a pile of ash. It was hopeless.

The next morning confirmed it. One of the upstairs maids woke her and advised her that her trunks were packed for the journey to Mrs. Rutland's Finishing School for Young Ladies.

The sullen maid said that she'd been assigned the dismal task of escorting her north. Within fifteen minutes, Honoria had dressed and descended the stairs from the family floor to the entry. No one waited for her. No one met her to say goodbye.

The desperation that had haunted her last night rose in conjunction with the morning sunrise. She stepped outside, and with every ounce of dignity she possessed, she took the stairs to the waiting carriage. The maid assigned to travel with her stood next to a liveried footman who held the carriage door open for her.

Honoria paused, then glanced at her mother's apartments. The curtains were still drawn. Even her own mother hadn't bothered to see her off to a place she'd never visited before.

A motion drew her attention to her brother's bedroom window. A movement of sorts had disturbed the curtains. Slowly, they settled into place.

The coachman, the footman, and the maid wouldn't look at her. Never had she felt so worthless and abandoned. The duke controlled every aspect of her life, and he didn't want her. Obviously, he'd made certain that none of the family would say goodbye.

Her chest ached, but she would survive this on her own. She refused to shed a tear. Not now, and never again for her parents. Whatever she felt for them died in that instant. She'd never claim them as family.

It made little difference that they didn't claim her.

Honoria lifted a foot to climb the carriage steps.

"Stop," Dane demanded. Everyone paused at her brother's voice. Once he was beside her, he turned his arrogant gaze to the servants. "I shall have a private moment with my sister."

At his commanding tone, they scurried down the gravel drive like mice caught in the kitchen pantry.

Dane helped her into the carriage and took her hands in his. "I'll come for you. I have enough money to hire a governess and rent an apartment."

"Don't," she said quietly so no one would overhear. "I'm not worth his wrath."

Dane frowned. "You're worth everything. You're my eldest sister." He put a coin purse into her hands. "There's a hundred pounds."

Her eyes widened at the amount. "That's a fortune."

He smirked slightly. "It's nothing. I won it before I came home for my holiday. It's yours."

Tears welled in her eyes. When she gazed at her brother, he had difficulty swallowing.

"I'll never forget you or Pippa." She smiled slightly. "If Father has his way, we'll never see each other again."

"Don't say that." He squeezed her hand. "Father is intolerant of me, you, and Pippa if he believes we're less than perfect. That's how he treats family. You're just his latest victim."

As of yesterday, she wasn't even family. But did her brother know that? "What did you hear him say yesterday?"

Dane shrugged slightly. "Enough to know that he was sending you away. I tried to reach you as soon as I could when I saw mother go into his study. I knew you wouldn't be far behind."

"Do you know why?" A small sob escaped.

"No." He hugged her just like he'd done so many times in the past when she was upset. "Honor, it doesn't matter."

Perhaps if she held the secret close, her brother and sister would never discover the truth or the shame she carried that she wasn't an Ardeerton. They wouldn't know the taint in her blood.

Perhaps they'd never forsake her.

Finally, he pulled away and reached into his coat pocket. "This is from Pippa." He pulled out another bag.

When she opened it, she gasped. "These are grandmother's jewels, the ones that Mother gave Pippa."

Dane smiled affectionally. "She said sell them if you need the money."

A single tear slid down her cheek. "Tell her thank you for me."

He nodded.

"You're brave to be here with me." She swiped at another tear. "You should go before he becomes angry with you."

"I don't care." He leaned forward, and with his thumb, brushed away another wayward tear.

"I hate living here. I hate London," she whispered.

"Then you'll never live here again if you don't want to."

"Promise?" she asked.

He made an X over his heart. "Promise. We'll all be together. You, me, and Pippa." He glanced out the window. "I must go, but say this after me, 'I am an Ardeerton.'"

"I can't."

"Honor, say it," he cajoled softly.

She turned away as flames of heat licked her cheeks. She refused to say that she wasn't the duke's daughter. Her flayed heart couldn't bear much more. "He doesn't want me."

"I want you."

The conviction in his voice shocked her. He grabbed her arms and shook her gently. "Look at me. I'll be the Duke of Pelham one day. What I say will become law. Everything he has ever spewed will be forgotten and buried just like he will be." His eyes glistened with emotion. "You are my sister. Now, say it. 'I am an Ardeerton. Nothing will defeat me.'"

"I am an Ardeerton," she said softly. "Nothing will defeat me."

"Good but tip your nose in the air like Mother." He mimicked their parent. "If you ever feel weak or scared, saying it will give you strength. You're my sister, and I love—"

Honoria put her hand to his mouth. "Don't. It's safer that way. Anyone or anything I cherish, he destroys. So, I shan't say it either."

A flash of hurt reflected in Dane's eyes. He nodded, then looked away. "Take care of yourself," he answered gruffly, then descended the carriage. As she watched, he called for the servants to return. Without a look back, he returned to the house.

The maid climbed into the carriage, and within seconds, they were off.

She vowed then that she'd never tell anyone, "I love you."

It was the only way to guard what little remained of her pride.

And her heart.

One

leven years later
E   *Pelham Hall, Family Seat of the Duke of Pelham, Amesbury*

"My lady?"

Honoria raised her gaze to discover Winston, the Pelham Hall butler, standing in her doorway. Circumspect and loyal to a fault, he'd been with the family for over forty years.

"Has the post arrived?" she asked.

"Indeed." Before stepping into her study, he surveyed the hallway without his usual silver salver. "I'm afraid nothing for you, my lady." A sympathetic grin pulled at his thin lips. Though he was in his sixth decade, he'd been more of a father to her than anyone else.

Honoria glanced at the calendar on her desk. "It's been three weeks since I hired that investigator. How long do you suppose it would take to find out if the old duke's letter exists?"

"It would depend upon how many solicitors he used." Winston rocked back on his heels slightly and clasped his hands in front of him. "I don't mean to complicate matters or distress you, but have you considered that the old duke might have solicitors in Scotland? Or else-where? The Pelham dukedom owns several business ventures throughout the British Isles. His Grace didn't sell a single one when he inherited the title."

Her brother was now the Duke of Pelham. When the old duke had died from a stroke, Dane had immediately sent a carriage to the finishing school in York. Thankfully, she had arrived at Pelham Hall after the funeral and burial. Pippa had a governess, so she had been there to mourn her father. As usual, her siblings had greeted her warmly, but her mother had acted as if she were a stranger. Within the month, their mother had died in her sleep. The doctor had said she'd died of a broken heart.

Honoria always thought the doctor had had the wrong diagnosis. She believed the old duke had shattered her mother's heart years before. He'd indeed done the same with Honoria's.

Thankfully, she'd had Winston. After her mother's death, the butler had told Honoria that he'd been in the servants' hallway that fateful day when her father had disposed of her and sent her to York. He'd been putting away a few silver pieces and had overheard the old duke rant that he didn't claim her and had written that hateful letter.

"I believe the solicitor is someone in London." Honoria walked around the desk and stood before Winston. "The old duke wouldn't put forth much effort on my behalf. He would have planned on me having a Season and making a match in London. It would have made sense to leave the letter in the care of a solicitor there."

"Sounds logical, my lady," Winston agreed.

Her heart slogged at a sudden thought. "You don't suppose it could still be at Ardeerton House?"

Winston shook his head. "Most definitely not, Lady Honoria. I went through every drawer, nook, and cranny. When I worked there, I was the under butler, so I had access to your father's...the old duke's keys. Remember, when you left Ardeerton House for the last time, I had a month to investigate the whole house before I was promoted to head butler and moved to Pelham Hall." He chuckled slightly. "I'll never forget when the new duke found me in his study and asked what the devil I was doing in his desk drawer."

Honoria's hand flew to her mouth in shock. "You never told me my brother caught you."

He nodded, never upsetting his silvery white hair that was always perfectly combed. "Indeed. I explained to His Grace that I was checking all the old duke's keys to ensure everything was in order. His Grace was genuinely thankful for my efforts. Told me he trusted and needed me at Pelham Hall. I'm privileged to serve him." His forehead crinkled into neat lines resembling the perfectly furrowed fields surrounding the estate. "Perhaps you should tell His Grace and Lady Pippa. They would help find the letter."

"*No.*" Honoria blinked. She hadn't meant to sound so gruff. "I apologize, but I don't want to distress them with this."

"Don't you think they'd want to share your burden, my lady? They're your family. Family helps family."

Even before she'd hired a private investigator to locate the letter, Winston had gently and consistently urged her to tell her brother. She'd always declined but never shared her reasons. She'd already lost her mother, and her hopes and dreams for a husband and a family of her own, because of the old duke's black heart. She couldn't bear to lose her brother and sister also. Though they had their own lives, she and her two siblings were still close. Pippa would soon find a suitable match and marry. That would mean the same was expected of Honoria. She couldn't marry. Not until she had that damnable letter in her hands. If Society knew Honoria was not the old duke's child, it would demand that her siblings not accept her. Of course, her siblings loved her and would stand by her, but at what cost? What was her tainted blood worth? She didn't want to hazard a guess.

Months ago, she'd decided they'd never have to face such a quandary. She had put into motion a plan and recruited Winston to help her. She had hired a private investigator to ferret out the whereabouts of the duke's written censure. If that letter existed, it would be delivered to her.

The threat it represented had cast all her aspirations for marriage into the garbage. Now, she was taking control of her life.

When she found the letter, all her problems would be solved. The letter would be in her possession, and no one would be any wiser.

She'd never have to worry again about losing her siblings, or ruining their reputation, or hers.

Just then, a knock sounded. Alice Roberts, the lady's maid she and Pippa shared, entered the room. "My lady, His Grace and Lady Pippa are waiting for you to join them in the family dining room."

Honoria stole a glance at the ormolu clock setting on the fireplace mantle. "I'm late."

"Allow me to escort you to them." Without a hair falling out of place, Winston gracefully bowed.

As soon as they had passed the doorway, Alice called out, "Good luck."

Honoria stopped and turned to her. "Why would I need luck?"

Alice shrugged slightly. "I have that feeling again." She pointed to her elbow. "It only pains me when something is stirring in the air. It's not a good omen."

Winston slowly turned to Honoria. "Alice is usually right when her elbow hurts."

Honoria smiled. "Pray that it's only a change in weather."

Honoria entered the small dining room where she and her family usually ate their meals, Dane stood, then walked around the table to greet her.

"There you are, darling." He wrapped her arm around hers, then turned to Winston. "Thank you for escorting Lady Honoria down. It saves me the trouble of hiring a Bow Street runner to find her."

"I didn't realize I was that important." Honoria tightened her grip around her brother's arm, then tilted her gaze to his. Though she was tall, Dane was a good five inches taller. Tucked into his cravat, a ruby-encrusted gold stick pin winked at her. The gold perfectly matched the warm hue of his hair.

"You're my sister. You and Pippa are more important than anything else in the world," Dane answered.

"Brilliantly said, brother." Pippa clapped.

"Thank you. I can be eloquently sentimental when the appropriate time arises." Laughing, Dane executed a perfect bow before turning back to Honoria. "You look lovely in that dress."

With mischief in her eyes, she playfully slapped his arm. "You always say that."

"I always mean it."

Dane always commented when she wore the ivory silk dress that he'd bought for her in London. It was one of her favorites because of the diagonal garland of red flowers embroidered on the dress. Always thoughtful, her brother brought her gifts when he returned from his London trips. Sometimes, he'd bring her jewelry, books, and even reticules. Honoria suspected it was a way to entice her to travel with him to London. She appreciated the thought, but London would never interest her.

"Your Grace, I'm afraid it was me who kept Lady Honoria." Winston bowed to Lady Pippa. "My lady, my deepest apologies."

Pippa smiled and waved a hand in dismissal. "We all know how you two love to discuss the latest Gothics." Her mouth puckered slightly. "I wish I could join in the conversations when you discuss the books, but they're just so..."

"Gothic?" Dane offered unhelpfully.

Winston's shoulders bobbled up and down as he tried to hide his laughter.

Pippa rolled her eyes, but a smile lit her face. "I was looking for a more dramatic word than scary."

"Gothic, it is," Dane said as he escorted Honoria to the table.

After Honoria had taken her place opposite Pippa, Dane sat in between them. This was one of Honoria's favorite things in the world. She and her siblings would share their days. It was ordinary conversation, but Honoria found such routines comforting. This was her world, and she cherished it.

"I'll have the footmen serve." Winston bowed again, then departed the room.

A flurry of activity commenced when the three footmen entered. Each had a serving tray made from the finest silver sterling engraved with the duchy's herald, two eagles guarding a lion. Dane had proclaimed that the birds represented him and Pippa guarding Honoria.

As a child, she'd always said she was the lion guarding her two siblings. Such playfulness had made Honoria feel safe until her father had sent her away. How things had changed since then. She called her brother Pelham in front of others to honor him and his title. But in her heart, he would always be Dane, her champion and defender.

While the footmen served the food, they settled into the meal where they dined on fish soup with capers, grilled salmon with truffle garnish, and sauteed potatoes with butter. Once the dishes were cleared from the table, Dane motioned for the door to be closed.

He never abided by the "accustomed rules of society." That meant he never sent Pippa and Honoria away while he enjoyed a brandy after dinner. He always served them one as well. But when the footmen were dismissed before dessert, that only meant one thing.

Their conversation would turn to private matters.

As soon as they were alone, both Pelham and Pippa turned their full attention to Honoria. She stiffened at the determined looks on each of their faces. Once again, they wanted her to go to London and planned to present their best arguments.

It never worked.

"I must go to the city as soon as possible for business. Pippa is joining me." Dane leaned closer to Honoria. "I know you hate to leave Pelham Hall, but I want you to come." He reached across the table and took her hand in his. "Honor, I think it would do you some good to leave here." He waggled his eyebrows. "You can see the world."

"London is not the world."

"Neither is Amesbury." Dane squeezed her hand, then released it. He took a sip of brandy and studied her. "Hear me out. I can't force you to come with us, but I can badger and beg until you relent." His face turned solemn. "Don't make me do that, Honor. Please."

By then, Honoria was shaking her head.

"Please," Pippa pleaded. "There's so much that I want to show you. So many wonderful people I want you to meet."

While she loved the nickname her siblings used when they were in private, she hated the topic of discussion. They'd been through this at least a thousand times before. She would never step foot in London again unless she was kidnapped, blindfolded, with her hands tied behind her back, and thrown into a carriage.

"You both are too kind." She smiled her best-consoling smile. "But what you are asking is out of the question. The Middletons' baby will be born within the next two weeks, according to the midwife." She turned a level gaze to her brother. "It's my responsibility to ensure the welfare of your tenants when you're away. Besides, it's my pleasure to attend the family. Someone from Pelham Hall should be here if there's an emergency."

"I agree." Dane nodded. "I asked Winston to do it. He'll represent our family, and Pelham Hall, when he takes a basket to congratulate the Middleton family on the new baby." Obviously, pleased with himself, a ghost of a smile tugged at his lips. "I've already arranged for the midwife to attend Mrs. Middleton every day until the baby arrives. Your argument is moot."

"It's settled," Pippa said triumphantly. "We'll go to my favorite modiste, Mademoiselle Mignon. You can order a new wardrobe. Pelham will pay."

"Gladly," Dane said.

"It is not settled," Honoria reasoned. "I have a gorgeous wardrobe Pippa designed for me." She turned to her sister. "You're so talented. You've created apparel for me that others would be envious of."

"Excellent point." Dane rested his chin in his hand as he regarded her. "But no one sees those dresses because you won't leave Amesbury."

"That reasoning won't work, my dear brother." Honoria defiantly folded her arms across her chest. "You see, when Pippa goes to town, she wears her own creations. Besides, I have other responsibilities. I call on Mr. Chasity every Thursday. I need to know who in the parish might require assistance."

"The vicar is more than capable of tending to the needs of his flock without your generosity and guidance for a month." He waited, challenging her with an arch of one perfect aristocratic eyebrow. "We shall leave tomorrow."

"You're staying a month?" Honoria cried. "That's an eternity." She shook her head vehemently as she tried to find another argument.

In two days, it was her brother's annual masquerade ball at the Jolly Rooster, a coaching inn and gambling hell less than two miles from Pelham Hall. Her brother had bought the Jolly Rooster and turned it into his very own playground of sorts.

For the first time ever, Honoria would attend without her brother's knowledge. She would shortly turn the age of twenty-five, and she wanted to find a lover for one night. It'd be her birthday present to herself. She wanted someone discreet who would give her pleasure but expect nothing from her in return.

People came from all over the British Isles to attend the event. Surely, she'd be able to find a perfect lover, someone she didn't know, and more importantly, someone who didn't know her. While Dane welcomed his closest friends for visits at Pelham Hall, and Honoria had been introduced to some of them, her brother had many other acquaintances whom he routinely met in London. She planned to find one of those men and have a night that she'd never forget. Afterward, she'd pay a handsome sum for the man's services in thanks for her experiencing a new world of passion, then walk away.

Her skin prickled as she thought of such a night. Most women of her social status would be horrified at the idea of acquiring a lover. But Honoria knew her own mind and wasn't afraid of new experiences. For heaven's sake, she was familiar with the animals on the estate's farm. Secretly, she'd watched the horses breed. In finishing school, she'd even collected erotic books from her favorite York bookstore. She knew what to expect from a man and wanted to experience it.

Which made it all the more important that her brother did not cancel his annual masquerade.

"What about your masquerade?" Honoria's gaze skated between Pippa and her brother.

Dane examined her with an intensity that made it impossible to steady her erratic pulse. "I'm canceling it. The inn will run smoothly with Harry in charge."

Loyal and intelligent, Harry Bergeron was Dane's majordomo.

"You can't leave Harry with all the responsibility. You can't cancel a party with only two days notice. You have guests that are already traveling." She was practically shouting.

He narrowed his eyes. "You sound as if you don't want to miss it. Need I remind you that my masquerades are not an appropriate venue for either of you."

Pippa rolled her eyes. "Don't act like such a governess. I wager I've seen more risqué behavior in the dark walkways of Vauxhall than what happens at the Jolly Rooster." She turned to Honoria. "I'd love to take you to Vauxhall."

For a moment, she struggled with how to respond. "Maybe someday." She turned her attention back to their brother. "You enjoy hosting that party. It's a chance to meet with all your friends at the Jolly Rooster. I'd hate for you to have to miss it."

He smiled gently. "You're very kind to be concerned. But if you come to London, there's no place I'd rather be. Besides, in a week, I'll be able to see them there and introduce them to you."

Pippa nodded vehemently. "That's right, Honor. I'd love to introduce you to my London friends. Plus, you can visit your friends from finishing school."

This was the worst time for her siblings to bring up London. She had to remain here in case her investigator found the letter and sent it to her. If that happened, she'd go wherever she wanted, including London. She'd never stay at Ardeerton House, the family residence in the city. She still had nightmares about the day she was dismissed by her father.

At that moment, Winston knocked on the open door and stepped into the salon. "I beg your pardon, my ladies." He turned to Pelham. "Your Grace, one of the footmen from the Jolly Rooster has arrived. Apparently, your presence is needed immediately."

Dane raked a large hand through his blond tresses. Pippa was the one who most favored their brother. They both possessed light blond hair and light blue eyes that almost appeared gray, features that came from their father.

Honoria possessed blonde hair that had darkened with hints of red. She'd inherited her mother's eyes that were more the color of sapphires.

But she favored her brother in her stature. She was almost a veritable giant compared to other women. Her lithe form differed from the beautiful Pippa, who had endless curves.

"The chef must be threatening to quit again. Fussy Frenchmen are the bane of my existence." Dane rose from his chair. "Thank you, Winston." He returned his attention to Honoria, who now stood beside him. "I'll return as quickly as I can. We'll continue our discussion later." He pressed a kiss to her forehead, then grasped Honoria's shoulders gently. His voice softened. "I thought perhaps you might consider marrying if you went to town. I'll ensure you find a good man, one who isn't after your fortune or wants favors from me." He turned to Pippa. "That applies to you also."

"No," Honoria said firmly. "I don't want any man." Her cheeks heated at her outburst.

"Oh, darling," He pulled her into his embrace and held her like he had all those times when she'd relied on him for comfort. "If you truly don't want marriage, I won't force you. But know this—you're a prize." He bent slightly until his eyes met hers. "I just want you to be happy."

When tears threatened at his kind words, Honoria stepped out of her brother's arms. Her brother would know immediately that she was weakening. For heaven's sake, he was the best brother ever. She tightened her stomach, then cleared her throat. "I haven't changed my mind. I will not marry."

As Pippa and Pelham started to protest, Honoria held up her hand. "My trust says that I'm in control of that money on my next birthday. I've decided that I'd rather do something productive with my life. I need to find fulfillment outside of being someone's dutiful wife."

"Will you at least think about London for my sake?" Dane bowed as he took his leave. The sound of his bootheels clipped across the marble hallway until silence reigned.

"And for my sake?" Pippa pleaded.

Honoria didn't want to go to London. She just wanted something new in her life—the destruction of that damnable letter.

And a lover.

Pippa studied her. It was the look she always wore when working on a puzzle or sewing a difficult dress pattern. "Hmm," she said softly. "I always believe that with the right clothes, a person opens like a bloom, revealing everything they are so others can see their true self." She stood and took Honoria's hands in hers and squeezed. "You need to visit Mademoiselle Mignon. You've been hiding for so long that you've forgotten who you are."

"What nonsense. But I can tell you this"—Honoria squeezed her sister's hands in return—"I haven't forgotten how wonderful you are."

Pippa gently tucked a loose curl behind Honoria's ear. "Nor have I forgotten that you're a beautiful bird who should leave the nest and fly high above the clouds."

Two

"It's mine." Marcus Kirkland, the sixth Earl of Trafford, held out his arms and slowly turned in a circle. "All mine."

The Duke of Pelham and Hugh Calthorpe, the Marquess of Ravenscroft, the two men he'd grown up with at Eton, hefted their glasses in salute, then downed the rare whiskey that Marcus had served to celebrate the momentous occasion.

"I can't believe this is the reason for my urgent summons to the Jolly Rooster." Small lines around Pelham's eyes crinkled in obvious fondness. "You purchased Woodbury Park without me even having a hint that it was for sale."

"I'm taken by complete surprise myself." Ravenscroft swung his gaze from Pelham to Marcus. "Why did you keep it a secret?" A wide grin grew across his face. "Not that I'm displeased, but I would have never thought you'd purchase an estate this far from London."

"It felt right. Particularly, since both of you have estates so close to here." Marcus sat at his desk while his two friends settled into the pair of club chairs that faced him. "I didn't tell you because I didn't know if I'd be the lucky one to purchase it."

"Why not?" Pelham asked. "I'm from here and know most of what is going on in the county."

Marcus folded his hands on the desk. The Robert Allen desk was a handsome piece. He'd purchased the estate, complete with all the furnishings. "When Mr. McBride died last year, the rest of the family hadn't decided whether to sell the estate."

"It is a massive house, and the farmlands go on for miles and miles. It practically rivals Pelham Hall in size." Ravenscroft stood and refilled their glasses.

"What are you going to do with it?" Pelham swirled the amber liquid in the leaded cut glass tumbler.

"That's what I wanted to share today." Marcus leaned back in his chair and regarded his friends. "It's for my charity, the Earl and Countess of Trafford's Foundling Society." Just saying the name made him sit a little taller and feel closer to his deceased parents. "I decided this is my calling. I want to help children of deceased peers understand their place in the world and hopefully provide them with role models. Heaven knows, my years at school would have been smoother if I'd had an adult take an interest in me."

Marcus had entered Eton a year after he'd lost both of his parents. His father had died in a carriage accident, and his mother had passed not three months later from a fever. Because he was an only child, Marcus's world had been torn asunder.

He stood and faced Pelham and Ravenscroft. "When you're both in London next, I want to introduce you to some of the children I'm helping."

Pelham nodded firmly. "It'd be my pleasure. I'll lend financial assistance if you need it."

"I'll contribute as well," Ravenscroft volunteered.

"Thank you, but I don't need money. I need your time. I plan to invite several of the children here during the summer and winter holidays. I hope it becomes like a home away from home for them. I want them to develop friendships with the other children who come here. It's my wish that they'll become like family."

"A commendable idea." Pelham rested one long leg across his other knee. "Since I spend the majority of my time here, I'll lend assistance anytime you need me."

"Same for me," Ravenscroft said.

Marcus cleared the sudden lump in his throat and smiled. "If it hadn't been for you both becoming my friends at Eton, I don't know what would have become of me."

After his parents had passed, he had never felt comfortable with his own company and had done the unthinkable. At the age of fourteen, Marcus had done his best to become the most profligate, dissolute, and debauched student in the history of Eton. He had drunk to excess, had hosted gambling games in his room, and had his first sexual experience with a recent widow, all by the time he was fifteen.

Ravenscroft tipped his head back and stared at the ceiling for a moment. His chest shook, but he was silent. It was the only indication that he was trying to keep his laughter contained. Once it was under control, he turned to Pelham. "Remember when the brother of that widow marched into school to speak with the headmaster."

Pelham nodded, then addressed Marcus. "If recollection serves me correctly, the headmaster called you into his office and threatened to expel you." Pelham shook his head, but there was a ghost of a smile on his lips. "Then he called Ravenscroft and me into his office."

Ravenscroft smirked. "He pleaded with us to do something with that 'hooligan.'"

"Please don't remind me of those days." Marcus smiled, but he was still haunted by the matter. His father and mother would have been aghast at his behavior if they'd known what had happened.

Yet, they must have still been looking out for his well-being from heaven, as shortly after his confrontation with the headmaster, Pelham and Ravenscroft had decided to take him under their wing. No questions were asked. His friends had protected him and kept him out of trouble, but more importantly, they had allowed him to share his grief.

The three had been inseparable, and they'd become what every other young man attending the school wanted to be—the unofficial influencers of the institution. Not a decision or an activity took place without their approval or opinion. Even the school's administration sought their advice on multiple occasions.

"Perhaps my sisters could entertain the girls who visit." Pelham's eyes narrowed in concentration. "It's not just for boys, is it?"

"No. It's for all children who need a sense of family." Marcus didn't add it was as much for him as the children.

"This may be indelicate, but pray indulge me." Ravenscroft settled back into his chair. The pose was intended to give the appearance of ease, but Marcus knew better. This was when his friend could cut you in two without even showing you the blade. "What guardian in their right mind would send innocents to your home."

"Meaning?" Pelham asked.

"For God's sake, Duke." Ravenscroft shook his head slowly. "He's not married. His previous exploits are well-known around society."

Pelham's brow furrowed into deep lines that were reminiscent of the neatly plowed fields of Woodbury Park. "It's been years since Trafford acted like an idiot."

Marcus held up his hand to stop any further arguments around this topic. "I'm aware society's opinion of me is slow to change. I've been working hard to polish my reputation over the last several years. I volunteer at several charities."

"You're trying to become a darling of the *ton*," Ravenscroft teased.

"Those are your words. Not mine," Marcus said wryly before he took a deep breath. It was only recently that he'd considered the need to marry. To make his charity a success, he needed to find a wife who valued the same things that he did. He needed someone who would give their heart to these children who'd lost so much.

That was the perfect woman for him, and he meant to find her.

"It's time I marry."

Ravenscroft choked on his sip of whiskey.

The color drained from Pelham's face.

"Marry?" Ravenscroft managed to wheeze the single word in a whisper.

"Not all of us are afraid of the word or the institution." Marcus tilted his chin, challenging his friends. "I want a wife, and there is nothing wrong with that. She can help me entertain the children and keep me company on cold nights."

"Can't a dog do that?" Ravenscroft asked earnestly.

Marcus ignored him, but Pelham didn't.

"Don't be an arse. All three of us will have to face this decision sooner rather than later." The duke turned to Marcus. "I understand. I hope this doesn't sound presumptuous, but I have two sisters."

"Not a good idea to offer up your sisters," Ravenscroft announced.

"Why the bloody hell not?" Pelham's voice had deepened into a rasp much like a snake's hiss of warning before it struck. "They're beautiful, well-mannered, and heiresses."

"I didn't mean anything offensive." Ravenscroft sighed in disgruntlement. He stood and walked to the fireplace to stir the fire back to life. "You can't offer them up like a haunch of venison in a butcher's shop without asking them if they're interested. The last time I saw Lady Pippa, she didn't seem to be in any hurry to marry."

"And how would you know?" Pelham asked.

"I've chatted with her in London a few times when you escorted her to events. I noticed she spent most of her time with the ladies who were in attendance," Ravenscroft offered. "She didn't seem very interested in any of the men who asked for a dance or came to chat with her."

Pelham chuckled. "That's because she's an artist of sorts. She designs and sews gowns. She loves to study the various dresses and accessories at those events. Hence, her preference to spend time with women versus men."

"Well, she is widely popular," Ravenscroft murmured under his breath.

Since Marcus spent most of his time in London, he had met Lady Pippa several times as well when she'd traveled with her brother. She was pleasant and kind and well-liked by her peers. Of course, being a duke's daughter and sister made her the crème de la crème of society. The fact that her brother was one of the few millionaires in London made her even more desirable to the men of the *ton*.

Funny, but he'd never met Pelham's oldest sister, Lady Honoria. The duke had mentioned that she avoided London because she didn't like the city. That had caused gossip to spread like wildfire. Rumors had swirled when Lady Pippa had participated in her first Season, and her older sister had been nowhere in attendance. It was the normal custom that the eldest female entered society at least for a year before any other females of the family could enjoy their first Season. It gave time for the oldest to make a match.

Rumors had erupted that Pelham's oldest sister shied away from society because some terrible accident had disfigured her face after she'd left finishing school. If he recalled correctly, someone had joked that she'd grown another head. Naturally, he'd defended her. She was his best friend's sister.

Pelham cleared his throat. "When my sister...Honoria turns twenty-five next month, she'll come into a large fortune. Perhaps she'd be of interest to you."

Marcus studied his friend for a long moment. The flush above the duke's collar crept up to his cheeks. It was obvious this was painful for him to discuss.

"I wouldn't be interested in her fortune," he said gently. Like Pelham and, for that matter, Ravenscroft, Marcus was also a millionaire.

"I know that about you." Pelham cleared his throat and faced Marcus. "She's kind, resourceful, and a joy to be around." The sincere affection in the duke's eyes when he discussed his sisters was on display this evening.

It never grew tiresome to Marcus.

"I'll be honest, I don't know if she'll ever marry. However, I'd like for her to have a chance if she wants it." Pelham gazed at his glass for a moment. "I don't want her to be alone."

"I would feel the same about my sister if I was fortunate to have one," Marcus said diplomatically. He didn't want his friend to think that he wasn't interested. But he needed a woman who had a sterling reputation. She must possess unbreakable confidence but with a heart big enough to shower affection on the various children who might come in and out of their lives. A woman, who didn't venture into society and was an enigma to most of the people in London, might not make the perfect wife Marcus needed.

"I've never met Lady Honoria either," Ravenscroft said in agreement. "She's always gone from Pelham Hall when I've visited."

The duke shook his head. "Every time you or Trafford have visited, she's been at her cottage I gave her last year that is next to the estate. It's close to a school she started for the Pelham Hall tenants' children. She stays there on occasion when she's working with the school staff or the children."

"A school, you say?" Marcus was interested in Lady Honoria now.

Pelham nodded. "Farming is changing rapidly. The men and women who work the fields need to learn their letters and numbers. Honoria believes they need to be able to read the latest literature on the matter and incorporate it into their crops and livestock management."

"That's forward-thinking," Ravenscroft volunteered.

"That describes both of my sisters," Pelham said proudly.

"So, Lady Honoria would welcome living in Amesbury?" Marcus asked, trying to be nonchalant.

"It would be her preference." Pelham's smile broadened. "If she was married to you, I'm certain of it." His gaze darted between Ravenscroft and Marcus. "I'd always hoped one of you would marry one of my sisters."

Marcus smiled at his friend. It was quite the compliment that Pelham felt that way about Ravenscroft and himself. However, it was best to take it slow and steady in his hunt for a proper and well-respected wife.

He would not jeopardize his charity with a rash choice.

"I would welcome the opportunity to meet Lady Honoria." Marcus gave his most convincing smile.

"Well, it will have to wait for a day or two." Ravenscroft waggled his eyebrows. "There is the matter of Pelham's masquerade."

"I was going to cancel the party and travel to London, but now that you're here, you must come. I won't take no for an answer," Pelham drawled.

Marcus should have said no.

Now, thirty-six hours later, he was in hell.

Actually, he was in the Jolly Rooster.

The masquerade was fully underway. Pelham had arranged for a bevy of lovely ladies from the demi-monde to attend and entertain his guests throughout the night. The masquerade was a highly sought-after invitation. The proverbial rafters of the coaching inn, that was also served as a gambling hell, were filled with drunk peers and wealthy men attempting to land one of the beautiful doves for an evening of entertainment and excess.

Feminine and masculine peals of laughter rang louder than the Sunday church bells. The room seemed to swirl with the vivid colors of the guests' costumes. Servants who were carrying trays of champagne and stronger spirits packed the room. It was thrilling but mundane at the same time. He should be joining in the entertainment, but he kept close to Pelham and Ravenscroft. Besides the two men Marcus stood next to, his closest companion was boredom. Resting his elbows on the balustrade of the second floor overlooking the main gambling room, he glanced at the festive crowd below.

He hated masquerades. All the machinations of deception were his idea of misery.

Marcus surveyed the crowd once more. There was a time when he'd reveled in entertainments like masquerades. Not anymore.

Then he saw *her*.

A siren dressed in a flesh-colored gown that hugged her slight curves. For a moment, he thought her dressed in a mermaid costume until he saw the shells strategically covering her breasts. As she stood at the entrance of the room that had been turned into a dance floor and dining area, his breath caught. The costume seemed to shimmer with the reflection of water drops just like Venus when she'd risen from the sea. Her turquoise mask hid her eyes, but its shape emphasized her heart-shaped face. She bit her full bottom lip, and her brow furrowed in contemplation as she gazed about the room.

Please don't have an escort.

For the first time in months, something was amiss in the middle of Marcus's chest. The thud of a heartbeat expressing interest in a woman? Whatever it was, it was a sign that he'd best grab the beauty before someone else did.

What was he doing? He was supposed to be focusing on finding a wife. Not salivating over some unknown woman. But for some singular reason, she called to him. Surely, there wouldn't be any harm in chatting with her.

"Is that *Lady Godiva*?" Ravenscroft asked.

Marcus shook his head. "Look at the shells. She's Botticelli's *Venus*."

Pelham scoffed. "A bit too cultured for this affair. Besides, she's late. She didn't arrive with the other ladies of the demi-monde." He tsked slightly. "There's always one that wants to make a grand entrance." He clasped his hands behind his back and stared at the floor below as if he were king of all he surveyed. "Ten to one odds, she's looking for a new protector."

Ravenscroft chuckled. "Aren't all women looking for a new protector?"

"Who turned you into a cynical cow?" Pelham retorted with a grin.

In his black domino, the Marquess of Ravenscroft was a formidable man. The same height as Pelham, but at least two stone heavier, he could have been the twin brother of Lucifer with his black hair and matching black eyes that gleamed through his mask. Standing next to Pelham, who had dressed as the golden Adonis, the marquess and the duke looked like true opposites.

Marcus stood a scant inch shorter than the other two men. What little he lacked in height, he gained in speed. No one could outmaneuver or outrun him when he set his mind on catching something.

Or someone.

Like Venus.

For the first time in her life, Honoria felt beautiful. Concealed behind the mask and the burnished blonde hair that fell to her waist, she straightened her back and studied the crowd. Men stopped their conversations and stared at her. Their appreciation for her costume made their eyes glint.

As Honoria surveyed the room, more and more men turned her way. Even the women who were attending took notice. Most of the men wore simple black cloaks with a traditional black domino mask, but some were dressed as clowns, jesters, medieval warriors, and even priests.

The women were far more colorful in their dress. Shepherds, nuns, and queens of yesterday were all represented at her brother's masquerade party.

She'd changed her simple gown for the costume behind a copse of trees. When she first put it on, she'd felt exposed. With a silk that perfectly matched her skin, Honoria's gown made everyone take a second glance to ensure that she wasn't naked. Golden gauze netting with strategically sewn brilliants and beads covered the gown. Her every breath made the ensemble twinkle like water drops clinging to her skin.

And there was no one else dressed like her.

Honoria glanced up at the second floor balcony where her brother stood in all his glory, dressed as some Greek god. The pale sheen of his blond hair was unmistakable. Two men flanked him.

She took a breath to summon the fortitude to step into the masquerade. Not a single soul would know her identity. Including her brother. All anyone saw was Venus. A smile creased her crimson-colored lips. Never in her life had she worn rouge on her lips, but her disguise emboldened her. Such confidence gave her the courage to find a lover.

A footman dressed as one of Robin Hood's merry men took her hand and helped her onto the dancefloor. "May I offer something to drink?"

When she shook her head, the footman bowed then left.

As she surveyed the people gaily dancing, the crowd parted, and a man strode toward her. He'd been one of the men standing by her brother. The man's height allowed him to see over the crowd. From afar, he walked with confidence. The closer he came, the more defined his features. His gaze locked with hers. His expression was terrifyingly determined and self-assured. His mask didn't hide his square jaw and chiseled cheekbones.

He was the one she would pick tonight.

Her heart pounded in her chest as another idea took hold.

What if Pelham had recognized her and sent the man to escort her to him? In that instant, her best-laid plans of hiding behind a costume seemed outrageous.

The stranger's gaze never left hers as he approached. With his every step, her heart pounded harder and faster. Quickly, she scanned the room for an exit. She would not allow herself to be discovered and face the humiliation of confessing to Pelham.

He'd not understand why she wanted one night of passion and affection before she turned her back on the possibility of marriage. Though Pelham had constantly argued that she was hardly a spinster and highly desirable as a potential marriage candidate for the male paragons of the *ton*, she wasn't for them.

Several couples danced across the floor and blocked the veritable giant from continuing his resolute stride to reach her. Honoria took the opportunity and hurried through a door on the left that led out to a passageway. Once out of the ballroom, she took the first left and found a library of sorts. As her heartbeat galloped in her chest, she tucked herself into a darkened corner next to a bookshelf and waited. Old habits never died. She still had the ability to hide in plain sight.

Slowly, she brought her hand to her heart and breathed as quietly as she could, praying her runaway heartbeat would slow down before it burst through her ribs.

No footsteps followed her.

She relaxed her shoulders. Immediately, she inhaled the scent of oranges and spices. The pleasant fragrance was layered with something darker, and without a sound, she gulped another breath.

She leaned her head against the bookshelf and closed her eyes. She could taste the disappointment that quickly replaced her giddy excitement for a pleasure-filled evening of fun. She wagered the man would be looking for her all night. Perhaps it was best if she went home and waited for her brother's arrival. No doubt, he'd summon her to his study tomorrow for a proper lecture.

He'd never chastise Honoria for her actions tonight, but he'd be disappointed in her. That would hurt far worse than any punishment he could inflict.

Why was it that men could enjoy the company of a woman without matrimony, yet a woman couldn't enjoy a man's company without being ruined? Honoria glanced out the window at the star-filled sky. It was such a magical night, but now it held no promise of amusement.

Honoria smoothed her hands down the beautiful gown again. Such a waste not to be able to wear it all evening. She hadn't even had the chance to dance or flirt with a handsome man.

Well, there was nothing to be gained by asking the what-ifs and why-couldn'ts of the evening. Yet, Honoria had stood on the edge of the room and commanded attention.

Pushing aside her disappointment, Honoria carefully stepped onto the terrace. Once she'd found the steps that led to the small garden, she carefully gathered up her gown in her hand so she could move at will without the fear of falling.

As she lifted her foot to take the first step, a deep masculine voice chuckled. Then a half growl, half whisper surrounded her. "Venus, I was afraid you'd gone back into your shell."

Three

When Venus whipped around, Marcus instinctively grabbed her arm to keep her from falling.

Her other hand flew to her chest, and her eyes widened behind the mask.

"Careful. I apologize for startling you." Gently, he released her. "I didn't want you to take a tumble." He offered his most charming smile. "I hoped we could spend some time together this evening."

"Do I know you?" Venus asked.

The sweet, silken smoothness of her alto voice sent prickles across his skin. "No. Shall we change that?"

"Perhaps." Her gaze traveled the length of his body then returned to his. "I want..." She shook her head. "Pardon me. I must gather my thoughts. I don't know how to approach the subject, so I'll be direct." A smile creased her lips. "I'd like to spend the night with you. How much does something like that cost? One hundred pounds?"

"You...you want me to pay you a hundred pounds?" Marcus needed a chair before he fell over. Never before had a woman bargained for her favors at such an exorbitant price. But then, he didn't have much practice in this type of negotiation. He didn't have a mistress. Too messy.

Nor did he seek entertainment at bawdy houses. This woman was attractive, but one hundred pounds?

Her eyes widened in horror. "Oh no. I'll pay you. But there are no attachments."

"Meaning?" he asked.

"I'll not marry you."

Marriage? Who thinks of marriage at a gambling hell masquerade party?

He blinked twice, trying to understand what she was saying. Then it dawned on him that Pelham and Ravenscroft must be behind such a farce. "Did my friends put you up to this?"

Venus frowned. "I assure you this is just between us." She tilted her nose in the air. "But I won't proceed until it's understood that there are no attachments."

He slowly released a breath. *What the deuce was she up to?* "You think you'll be forced into marriage if we spend time together?"

She cocked her head. "Isn't that normally what happens?"

"At a masquerade?" He chuckled when her brow crinkled adorably. "I suppose if we're compromised and must marry, one of the priests attending tonight can do the honors."

He bit his lip to keep from laughing again. This was not the type of marriage he should be concentrating on. But it was only for one night. Where was the harm? He could think of real marriage candidates tomorrow. He didn't even have a woman in mind except for perhaps Pelham's odd older sister. The duke hadn't seemed to care that Marcus wanted to talk to Venus.

She laughed, the sound reminding him of the Christmas bells of his youth. "You're teasing me. The evening grows late." She almost curtseyed, then caught herself. "If you'll excuse me?"

"Wait." He placed his hand on her forearm, stopping her from leaving his side. *Was he actually considering her offer?* She was unusual in a way he couldn't explain. Yet, there was something about her that intrigued him. "Before I commit to your request, I want to see how we are together. Have a taste of one another."

She stood there, not moving an inch. With her mask, it was hard to read her expression.

"Wouldn't you agree?" He took a step back and waved a hand in invitation for her to join him on the terrace. "Come, Venus."

Eventually, she took a step closer. Her jasmine scent wafted his way. "You're certain you don't know who I am?"

"No. But I would very much like to change that." He inhaled and held her fragrance for as long as he could. Her floral scent was as unique as she was. She was tall for a woman—extremely so. When he kissed her, he wouldn't have to bend in half to meet her lips with his. Quickly, Marcus allowed his gaze to take in her form. Venus's dress hugged every curve of her lithe body. He'd always preferred women who were voluptuous, but Venus set his pulse pounding.

She studied him as he studied her. After a moment, her brow crinkled. "I've never been to a masquerade before."

"Never fear, Venus. I'll teach you everything you need to know." When she bit her plump lower lip, it took every ounce of fortitude not to lean in and kiss her. His voice lowered of its own accord. "We are all inexperienced at one point in time or another."

Her eyes widened behind her mask. "I—I—"

Damn him to hell. She almost seemed shocked in what he'd said. "I meant as in first-time-to-a-masquerade. My first such party was when I was seventeen and at university."

"How old are you now?" A hint of challenge tinted her voice.

"Thirty. Is that too old?"

She glanced at the steps of the terrace and shook her head. Slowly she lifted her eyes to his, and a broad smile graced her lips. "It's ideal. Like a perfectly aged whisky."

He tilted his head back and laughed. "No one has ever compared me to perfection."

"I didn't say that, good sir." Her lips pursed in a wicked smile. "I believe that no whisky is truly perfection."

Marcus brought his hand to his heart in a mock show of pain. "You wound me, Venus."

"You didn't let me finish," she said softly. "Remember, whisky continues to change in taste as it ages. Just like humans. Perfectly aged is a personal preference, is it not?"

"Oh, Venus, we shall get along very well, I predict." He took a step closer. "You are my ideal of desire."

"How can you know that if you haven't seen me or spent any time with me?" she challenged.

"I know myself," he volleyed. "Therefore, I know what I desire." He slowly reached toward her, then cupped the back of her neck. She inhaled sharply but didn't pull away. "I desire you."

He wanted to tear her mask off and take her into a kiss where they both would lose themselves within one another. He definitely wasn't perfect and never would be. Yet she was interested in him.

"How do we make introductions without revealing who we are?" she asked.

"If you're not comfortable telling me your real name, I can be Adonis to your Venus."

She shook her head. "Their story is sad. Venus begged him not to go hunting because she dreamt that he would be killed. He didn't listen."

"And died when a wild boar attacked him." He'd give anything to see her face at this moment. "Why don't you call me Marcus?"

When she smiled, he felt ten feet tall.

"That's a beautiful name." She cupped his cheek. "Call me...Noria... I mean Nora."

"Nora," he whispered, then lowered his lips to hers.

"It's short for Lenora," she exclaimed softly when he brushed his mouth against hers. It wasn't a kiss per se, but a hello of sorts. He pulled back and studied her gaze. The pounding pulse at the base of her neck drew his attention. God, he wanted to kiss her there. Frankly, there wasn't an inch of her that he didn't want to taste. He leaned in again and angled his mouth to hers. This time, he pressed his lips to hers and stayed there. Slowly, ever so slowly, he took her in his arms and brought her close. Through the thickness of his cloak, the hard shells covering her breasts pressed into his chest.

A whimper escaped her.

"Am I hurting you?" He took a step back.

"Don't you dare pull away," she exclaimed breathlessly, then clutched his cloak in both hands and brought him closer. "Things are just now getting interesting."

Honoria had never acted so brazenly, and it felt wonderful. For the second time in her life, she felt beautiful and desired. Marcus's eyes gleamed with want and what she recognized as desire. Truly, she was Venus, and she wanted everything that he would offer her tonight. One night of magic. One night of bliss.

Boldly, she pressed her lips against his. He pulled her tighter into his arms and groaned slightly as he deepened the kiss. Her mind emptied of all thoughts or concerns except for the man who held her. Wrapping her arms around his neck, she pressed against him, the movement so natural she didn't even second-guess herself. Without warning, he pressed his tongue against the seam of her mouth, begging entrance.

She sighed slightly, then stiffened in his arms. *He put his tongue in my mouth.*

"Relax, darling," he murmured against her lips. "If I didn't know any better, I'd think you've never been kissed."

Honoria swallowed. Somehow, she had hoped to fool him into believing that she had experience kissing a man. He pulled her tighter against the rock-solid plane of his chest. She'd always been a large woman who towered over other women and most men. But in Marcus's arms, she thought of herself as feminine and petite.

Every part of her tingled with a hunger for something more. She could easily melt into him, never wanting to be separated.

Such was the power of his kiss.

As his tongue boldly stroked hers, she did the same to him. He seemed to like it as their kiss grew more frantic.

"Enough," he growled, then pulled away, leaving her stunned.

By then, they both were panting. His dark eyes glowed with a fire that seemed lit from within. She placed a hand on his chest to stop herself from falling into a heap at his feet. Marcus placed his hand over hers, keeping her steady, then wrapped the other against her waist.

"Was I doing it correctly?" she asked.

38

As he opened his mouth to respond, another male voice came from behind them.

"The way you both were participating indicates that you did it more than satisfactorily."

Oh God, that voice. That gravelly voice caused goosebumps to break across her skin. She shivered in response. *Bloody hell, it was Pelham.* Her gaze darted to the steps. She had two options. Stay there and face his wrath or flee. It would be difficult in her narrow skirt. But if she made it to the entrance of the Jolly Rooster, she could then escape.

But one thing Pelham had taught her was that she was an Ardeerton. She didn't run from anything, and that included her own brother. Squaring her shoulders, she prepared herself to face him.

But she didn't have to bear that burden. As soon as she turned around, Marcus moved to stand in front of her, blocking Pelham's view. The man she'd just been kissing herself silly with reached behind him and took her hand. In a move that melted every inch of her heart, he entwined their fingers together.

"Pelham, your ability to sneak up on people never ceases to amaze me," Marcus drawled. "What do you want?"

Honoria peeked over Marcus's shoulder.

Her brother stared straight at Marcus, not sparing her a glance. "A game of vingt-et-un is ready to start."

Marcus shook his head abruptly. "I had a beautiful woman in my arms, and you interrupted us to ask if I wanted to play a game of cards with you? Have you lost your mind?"

Her brother's nostrils flared in annoyance. "I'm the host of this party. Forgive me if I wanted to invite you to a game."

Marcus squeezed her fingers gently. "I'm quite content with what I'm doing this evening."

Pelham's gaze shot to Honoria. She froze when his eyes met hers. As she waited for the dreadful moment when he recognized her, she forced herself to breathe. Pelham's eyes narrowed for a moment, but then he returned his attention to Marcus and grunted.

Her brother actually grunted. She'd never heard such a sound from him before.

Pelham turned to her and bowed gallantly. "Madame, a pleasure. Be sure and pick up your earnings before you return to London on the morrow."

Honoria had no idea what he meant but nodded in acceptance. Why would she have earned any money just by attending?

Her brother walked briskly back into the Jolly Rooster.

Marcus turned on his heel and faced her. "Now, where were we?" He cupped her cheeks. "We've had enough interruptions for this evening."

"So does that mean you'll agree to my terms?" The breathlessness in her voice surprised her. She sounded like a sultry siren and felt like one, too.

"Yes," he said softly, while taking her hand to his lips for a lingering kiss. "Come. I know the perfect place for us."

Carefully, he escorted her down the steps. The mermaid design of her gown made ordinary walking difficult. When they reached the garden, he gave his arm. Together, they crossed the inn's lawn, drawing her farther and farther away from the Jolly Rooster.

Perhaps it wasn't such a grand idea to go with this beautiful stranger without finding out a bit more. "Where are we going?"

"Someplace where I will make you very comfortable."

"Inside the inn?"

"No, darling." Marcus shot her a grin that stole her breath. "Someplace cozy. I was thinking of my home."

Four

Marcus had made the decision as soon as Pelham interrupted them to leave the Jolly Rooster and take Nora with him. It was the only way he'd have privacy with her this evening.

He wrapped his arm around his enchantress's waist as they made their way to the stables. At the gate entrance to the bustling courtyard of the inn, he took her hand to lead her inside to collect her wages, but Nora dug her heels in, and they came to a halt.

"Don't you want to gather the wages you've earned?" he asked.

"I haven't earned anything. Are all the guests paid for attending?"

He smiled. Such an innocent in so many ways. "It's a stipend for your time and travel from London. Don't worry. Tomorrow, I'll ensure that you make it back to the city." He'd already decided that he'd pay her well for the evening.

"London? I didn't travel from there." Through her mask, her eyes widened. "You think me part of the demi-monde?"

"Aren't you?"

She shook her head.

Then who was she? "I take it you're from around here?"

"Yes," she said somewhat curtly. "And you?"

"Several counties to the north, but I like to spend time here and in

London." He didn't share that his ancestral seat was in Bedford, and he rarely traveled there.

"That's perfect," she purred with a contented smile.

This woman was full of contradictions, and he never quite knew what she was thinking, but he quite liked her stalwart independence.

In the soft moonlight, she was even more ethereal. Her skin glistened as if relishing the kisses granted from the delightful celestial rays. His gut tightened at the sight. Never had a woman been more alluring and tempting to him in his entire life. He could have sworn that the moon had enchanted him in such fashion, making him almost—dare he think it?—lovesick.

She leaned in slightly and lowered her voice. "May I tell you a secret?" Without waiting for him to agree, she continued, "I wasn't invited. I've always wanted to attend a masquerade as someone else. When I discovered there was one here, I decided to join the revelry."

"How fortunate for me." Nora's delicate scent teased the night air, and he drew in a deep breath. He was charmed. Like a magical being, she'd woven a spell around him, and he was in no hurry to escape. Everything about his Venus seemed to draw him closer to her.

He held out his hand again, and she studied it. If her lovemaking was anything like her sweet kisses, they both would enjoy the evening. She was like a breath of fresh air, and how he needed to purge the stench and grime of the city from his thoughts.

Slowly, she placed her hand in his, and he squeezed it gently. "I shall take you to my house."

"In Bedford?" Her hand flew to her chest.

He chuckled. "No. I have a residence here."

"I have a horse and a cart that I can't leave," Nora said. "I'll follow you. Where do you live?" She placed her gloved hand against his mouth and smiled. "I apologize. Don't tell me. It's best if we don't share the rest of our names or homes with one another. I wouldn't feel comfortable otherwise."

She was definitely a conundrum. Which fired his curiosity to find out more about her. He nodded slowly. "I have an idea. We could stay here for the night. In the morning, I could send for a carriage to take you home. Someone from the Jolly Rooster could take your cart and horse home tonight." He leaned closer, and unable to resist, he pressed his lips to her cool cheek. "Or someplace else. I have access to a hunting lodge."

He wouldn't take her to Woodbury Park, but he could take her to his hunting lodge that lay on the northern boundary of his estate.

"No hunting lodges either." She dipped her head. "Though it's tempting."

He'd follow her to the moon and back just as long as he could spend the night with her. What was it about her that he couldn't resist? Perhaps it was her beauty or her innocence and honesty. Maybe it was because she didn't care who he was.

"Let's stay here in the inn," she said after a long moment of silence. Without hesitation, she stood on her tiptoes, then pressed her lips to his. "I want to be with you."

Honoria wanted to purr like a satisfied cat lounging in the rays of the midday sun. It had been an easy choice whether to stay at the inn or travel with Marcus. She'd meant what she'd said earlier. She didn't want any attachments to a man. But truthfully, she didn't want the night to end either.

He entwined their fingers once again, then led her back inside. The walls echoed with masculine chortles, perfectly mixed with feminine laughter.

Instead of taking her into the main room to join the others, he pulled her to a staircase to the left of the building. He leaned close so she could hear him over the ruckus, his breath tickling her ear. "I have rooms upstairs. It's not my favorite place. It's quite drafty and the noise carries." He smiled apologetically. "At least, we'll be alone."

She nodded. How many other women had he taken to his rooms during one of these parties? She scolded herself for such nonsensical thinking. This was exactly what she wanted. An experienced lover who would have no expectations for anything more.

One night. No strings.

Once they had arrived on the second floor, he walked beside her. They came upon a couple desperate for one another, embracing in a passionate kiss. She slowed her steps when the man gently squeezed one of the woman's breasts. The woman moaned. Whether with pain or pleasure, it was hard to tell.

She should have been horrified, but instead, she couldn't tear her eyes away.

Honoria moved closer to Marcus. Instantly, he lightly rested his hand on the small of her back, the heat of his touch sending more fire through her veins, melting her insides.

"You like to watch other people?" The deep cadence of his voice had softened for her ears only.

Hesitating only a moment, she replied, "I think so."

Now, the man slowly pulled the woman's gown from one shoulder, revealing her breast. He slid his hand across her skin and played with her turgid nipple. Mesmerized, Honoria stared as the man slowly made love to the woman in the hallway. Every muscle inside of her tightened. A dull ache resided in her lower belly, and she grew damp between her thighs. Nothing in her erotic books described watching others.

Slowly, the man's gaze lifted to hers. "Do you want to join us?"

Honoria shook her head and stepped closer to Marcus.

Marcus wrapped an arm around her waist and then pressed his lips against her ear. "Let's leave."

It was such a small gesture, but it proved she'd chosen a suitable man for her first time. This was the outcome she'd sought when attending her brother's fete. A perfect night with a perfect man who would teach her everything.

As they continued toward the end of the hall, Marcus didn't take his eyes from hers. Honoria struggled with something witty to say. She'd never been alone with a man like this heading for his bedroom. Her heart pounded as the hallway seemed to shrink in size. The breadth of his shoulders seemed twice as big as when they'd been alone together in the garden. She bit her lip and glanced out a passing window into the dark night. He'd think her a ninny if she didn't think of some conversation to share with him.

With a painful exhale, she turned slightly. "Will we take off our masks in the room?"

She wanted to cringe at her words. Instead of beguiling and seducing him with phrases and sentiments, she had just asked the obvious.

"Yes. When we're alone, and I can see you in the light," he said softly.

"Oh." She sounded like a neophyte.

Well, that was exactly what she was. An almost twenty-five-year-old virgin who had skated into spinsterhood. But tonight, she was skating on the edges of impropriety. It was exactly where she wanted to be.

"I want to study your face in the firelight. I want to know if you glow there as much as you do in the moonlight."

The roughness in his voice simultaneously sent a chill and flash of heat careening through her insides. It was quite disconcerting. With each step, her gown brushed against her nipples, causing them to stiffen. Between her thighs, an ache resided, and she pushed her legs together in hopes of relieving the discomfort.

"Here we are," he said and opened the door for her.

She studied his eyes behind his mask. If they truly were windows into a person's soul, his promised sin and rapture.

She stepped in, and he followed, closing the door behind him.

Without another word, he carefully cupped her cheeks with his gloveless hands. Somehow, he'd taken off his gloves without her seeing him do it. His roughened skin indicated he'd done manual labor. A tremble resonated through her. *Was she about to kiss a farmer?*

But if he was at her brother's party, then he had to be wealthy. It made sense if Marcus were a gentleman farmer. That explained why his shoulders were broad and his body as hard as iron. He worked the lands.

When his lips touched hers, she leaned into his embrace. It was laughable that she, a duke's sister, was being seduced by a farmer, yet everything about him was irresistible.

His tongue flicked across her lips. On a sigh, she opened for him. With each stroke of his tongue against hers, he pulled her tighter. The hard planes of his chest just heightened her pleasure.

An image of Marcus kissing her there popped into her thoughts.

Would he be gentle like the man in the hall, or would he be voracious, like a man starving and her his sustenance?

"Nora." He said her name like a prayer as he pulled away.

She'd been so lost in their kiss she hadn't realized where they stood. It was a small but elegantly furnished sitting room. Why was she not surprised? Her brother spared no expense for his playground.

With an inherent gracefulness, Marcus walked to a side table where a bottle of wine and brandy stood. He lifted a wine glass in her direction. "A drink?"

"No, thank you," she said. Then it hit her. She was going to do this. "This" meaning bedding a man.

He poured a fingerful of liquid into a tumbler and took a swig. His Adam's apple rippled with the movement. With the black cloak hanging from his shoulders and the mask hiding his face, she should have been scared witless at the sight. He looked like the devil inviting her into his secret den of seduction.

Holding out his hand, he waited for her. After a moment, she placed her hand in his.

"Come sit down."

Light poured from the candles lit around the room, turning it into a golden palace. A soft glow kissed his dark locks. Earlier, she had thought his hair dark brown, but in the candlelight, it turned raven-black, glinting with tints of midnight blue. The long length brushed his shoulders.

Lud, he was breathtaking, the most handsome man she'd ever seen.

She forced herself to look at the four walls. "Beautiful room." Good lord, she sounded ridiculous.

"Not as beautiful as you," he said. "We've waited long enough. Take off your mask."

She turned to face him and challenged him with a smile. "We do it together."

He chuckled, then nodded. "The suspense is killing me."

"What if I disappoint you?" The question slipped out before she could think otherwise.

"How could you?" He tilted his head and regarded her with a gaze so intense she worried he saw her in a different light, one that laid bare

46

all her imperfections that she was so well-acquainted with. "I'm already enchanted with you." He huffed a breath, then smiled like a rogue who'd just claimed himself conqueror of the entire world. "I should be worried that you'll be so disheartened with my appearance that you'll run screaming."

"I never run from anything," she retorted.

"That's what I'm counting on." He smiled, then winked at her through his black mask. "On the count of three, if you please."

They both counted aloud as they reached behind their heads. She was so nervous that, for a moment, her fingers became tangled together. She managed to untie her mask as they both said three, but she held it in place with her hand as she watched him discard his.

Immediately, he lifted his head as he brushed his long hair away from his features. "What sweet relief. Now, I can breathe."

For the love of heaven, he wasn't simply attractive. He was stunning. A slight aquiline nose had been hidden behind the paper-mache, but it matched the shape of his square jaw. His angular cheeks reminded her of a marble statue of Osiris that stood in the informal garden at Pelham Hall. Marcus was uncommonly beautiful, if a man could be considered such.

But it was his eyes that caught her breath. She'd thought them brown, but in the firelight, she could see they were the deepest blue, much like the fathomless depths of an ocean. "You're not what I expected."

"Meaning?" He lifted an eyebrow in mock protest, but the twinkle in his blue orbs gave away his playful attitude.

"I didn't expect you to be so handsome," she answered truthfully. "I hope that's not offensive." She chewed on her lower lip, willing something else to come to mind. "I've never seen many men...who look like you."

He laughed slightly. "Thank you. Now, if memory serves me correctly, we both were going to lower our masks together. Venus had no issue unveiling herself when she rose from the ocean. It's only fair you let me see your face."

She squeezed her legs tighter at the gentle roughness in his voice. Looking down at the carpet, she slowly lowered the blue-green mask. If he found her looks lacking, she didn't want to see the disappointment in his face. She would pay him enough to overlook her flaws.

She continued to stare at the mask as if mesmerized by the brilliant flashing crystals as they caught the light from the candles. In response, the flames flickered in approval. A burning log hissed then collapsed in the fireplace.

It was the only sound in the room. She forced her gaze to his. After an unbearable moment, she broke their silence. "Say something," she whispered.

"Venus was known for many things. Love, beauty, passion, and seduction to name a few. She was also known for victory. Which is appropriate for tonight. You've won me by your beauty and grace." He discarded his cloak on a nearby chair as he made his way to her.

A newly forged heat bludgeoned her cheeks. It was utter nonsense, but it felt divine, particularly to a woman such as her. When she gazed in the mirror, Honoria knew she wasn't ugly. But to be declared beautiful? It was a heady pronouncement to hear.

"God save us both," he murmured.

It was an odd thing to say. "What do you mean?"

By then, he'd reached her side. She'd expected him to kiss her again, but instead he simply held her as he studied her face. While she was certain that a thousand emotions must have flashed in her eyes in time with the pounding of her heartbeat, he stood calm and serene.

Good heavens, a little affection from this man, and she'd fall in love. It would take little for the raw passion to explode between them and bring her to her knees.

"What are we doing here, Venus?" He slowly shook his head, then moved several inches away from her.

It felt like miles.

She studied his face and his eyes. All emotion was banked like a night fire.

"We're going to make love. Aren't we?"

Something was wrong. Very wrong.

He studied the floor. After an eternity, he lifted his gaze to hers. "I'm sorry. I can't do this, Nora."

Honoria's fingers trembled to such an extent that she crossed her arms to hide them. He was going to send her away. She was panting as if she'd raced Marcus across a field. Unfortunately for Honoria, she'd never been a fast runner and had always lost when racing Pelham and Pippa. It was a lonesome, desolate feeling each time. It was the same thing she was experiencing now.

For all her bravado, she felt adrift. He didn't want her. "Why can't you do this?"

"I'm not ready for this type of intimacy or attachment. I have to think of the future. I'll regret it in the morning." The contriteness he wore made him appear like a fallen angel. A beautiful angel filled with remorse and sorrow. "I'm involved in several endeavors that necessitate I do not give my affection without considering the ramifications."

"Are you married?"

He laughed softly. "Not yet."

"Betrothed?"

"No."

Honoria swallowed. Thankfully, her common sense returned in time before she made a colossal fool of herself and begged him to let her stay. Though another man had rejected her, she vowed to hold her head up high.

"I see." She reached into a side pocket she'd sewn on the costume and pulled out a coin purse. "I'll still pay you. It's all here."

He lifted a single eyebrow and openly stared at her. "I'm not for hire, Nora. It was my pleasure to spend time with you."

She graciously smiled determined not to show any emotion until she was outside. "I'm sure we will never see each other again. I wanted to experience something new and special. You've given me that."

He looked at her as if she were a riddle that he was trying to solve. Finally, he spoke, his voice low. "I think you have the wrong impression of me. It's not that I don't want you." He shook his head sadly.

"Is it because I've never done this before?" Her voice betrayed her with a squeak.

"No." He looked up to the ceiling and was silent for a moment. Finally, he turned his gaze to hers. Gently, he cupped her cheeks with his hands. Slowly, his thumbs caressed her cheekbones. "It's not that. It's me."

Five

Marcus cringed slightly when Nora distanced herself from him with a look of shock on her face. When she'd proposed a liaison, he'd never considered she'd be a virgin. However, as soon as their lips touched, he'd known she'd had little experience kissing. Now, it made sense that she had even less experience in bed. He clasped his hands behind his back and forced himself to relax as he contemplated what more to say.

The truth was he didn't want her to go.

For the first time in ages, he wanted a female's company. If he were honest with himself, he wanted a specific woman, Nora. This want—no need—for her company could not be explained. She was a country girl —someone he'd never dealt with before. Somehow, she had invaded his thoughts. He found her fascinating and didn't want to let her out of his sight. He could tell she was well-educated by the way she spoke. She had to be a wealthy farmer's daughter, or perhaps she was the daughter of an estate manager.

Bloody hell. He turned to stare into the fireplace. How inconvenient. She didn't want to know anything about him, and she didn't want to share anything about herself, but she wanted him in bed.

Yet, he wanted to know everything about her for the sake of his charity.

And for his own reasons.

"You're an honorable man for your choice." Her voice dropped. "I understand."

He tore his gaze away from the fireplace and looked at her, really looked at her. Whatever earlier distress she possessed was gone. She tilted her chin in a defiant manner. The woman before him stood tall with a fearless confidence that was breathtaking.

She wore it like a battle shield. His Venus had transformed into Athena right before his eyes. She wasn't simply beautiful or kind, but magnificent.

Nora might walk out this door, but Marcus would do everything in his power not to let her leave his life. At least until he had found out more about her.

What if this was the woman whom he could spend his life with? Share everything he desired? Everything meant a wife, a family, a home, and a legacy that would replace everything he'd lost.

His common sense had just flung itself out the window.

Yet, the only rational thing he could do was not to let her go.

"Don't leave," he murmured.

"I must." She stepped toward the door.

"Nora, I beg you."

With an ingrained elegance, she turned on her heel to face him. "I can't stay here."

"I know you are concerned for your reputation, but I'll ensure..." His voice trailed off as a look of amusement crossed her face.

"My reputation? Hardly," she huffed. "That's the last thing I'm concerned with." She smiled sweetly. "I must go."

"Why not stay here so we can talk?" he asked, then smiled.

She considered him carefully.

"Allow me to tell you a story first. Maybe that will change your mind." He held her gaze, and she nodded for him to continue. "When I first started learning to swim, I discovered I was uncomfortable when the water was higher than my head. I didn't like it at all." He reached for her hand. "That's how I'll feel if we bed one another."

51

JANNA MACGREGOR

"Did you learn to swim?" She squeezed his hand.

"Like a fish," he said confidently.

"Then you realize that once you mastered swimming, you no longer feared the water." She lifted an eyebrow. "Perhaps you just need the correct person in the water with you. I'm more than confident in my teaching abilities."

He grinned. "I can see that."

She playfully tapped his arm like a governess would when scolding a wayward charge. "On my part, it was an honest offer."

His hand shot out and captured hers. Her gaze lifted to his, and that magic that had danced between them all evening returned in full force. Was he making a mistake by letting her go? It took every ounce of sanity he possessed not to pull Nora into his embrace and kiss her until neither of them knew their own names.

"Let us be serious for a moment." He brought her hand to his mouth where he pressed his lips to her knuckles. She trembled at his touch. "Give me two weeks."

"Two weeks? I don't understand..." Her gaze searched his.

"Give me two weeks of your company. I'd like to spend time with you. Become better acquainted." He swallowed before he spoke the next part. If his friends heard what he was offering her, they would fall to the floor laughing. "I just want the pleasure of your company."

She tilted her head, then smiled. "I don't think that's wise."

"Hear me out. Show me your favorite places around Amesbury and what you like to do. I'll show you the same." He pressed his lips to her hands again. "We can share two weeks and then part ways. No expectations or disappointments. Just share your delightful company with me, and I'll do my best as a gentleman to ensure you're entertained." He lowered his voice. "You'll haunt me for the rest of my life otherwise."

She scoffed, but it sounded like a laugh. He grinned in response.

"I didn't know that I was a ghost."

"Just a heavenly body. Say yes. That's all you need do."

She blushed prettily at his words, which was his aim. The light in her eyes danced with mirth. "You pay me compliments, and in return, you want me to escort you to my favorite places around Amesbury?"

"Simple, right?"

52

"I need time to consider it." She looked toward the door. "I should go. It's getting late."

"Let me take you home. We can discuss the details."

A look of horror marred her face as her hand flew to her chest. "That won't be necessary."

"I'm an honorable man. I can't allow you to drive home in the dark by yourself." When she chewed on her lower lip again, he had to suppress a frustrated groan. The woman was a master at tormenting him.

She tapped her tempting mouth with the edge of her mask as she contemplated his offer. Her eyes widened suddenly. "You can escort me outside. My home is not more than a mile or so from the Jolly Rooster."

"Where is your home?"

"That's not really relevant, is it?" She blinked innocently.

By her answer, it became apparent that she was either embarrassed of her home or she was hiding something from him. Perhaps both. Her hesitancy made it more plausible that she was a farmer's daughter. He'd bet his next yearly income on it.

"You cannot escort me home. If you want my company, then that is what I demand." She crossed her arms over her chest. Such a movement gave the appearance that she was offering her luscious and perfectly sized breasts to him on a platter.

He sighed quietly. "Fine. You drive a hard bargain. I'll escort you to your cart. I'd like to stop by the stables and retrieve my mount anyway. I think I'll be going home as well." He'd much rather work on his charity than attend the masquerade. But he knew the real reason he wanted to leave. If Nora wasn't there, then there was little to keep him here.

Within a quarter of an hour, they stood next to one another near her cart hidden behind a copse of trees. His stallion was tied to a branch.

"Is your horse all right?" She pointed toward his pesky stallion who was gnawing on the tree trunk, making a racket, and acting like a diva.

"His name is Bergamot." That earned him the sound of her delightful laughter. It reminded him of crystal goblets meeting in a toast of celebration.

"Bergamot? That's unusual for a fine piece of horseflesh."

She recognized the quality of his horse, another clue that she was accustomed to the country life.

"Most men I know would grant their horse some sort of noble name such as Lancelot, Gawain, or Percival." A light from a coaching inn lamp illuminated the road across from them. As she glanced his way, the glow caressed her skin, giving her the appearance of a fae creature who ruled the woodlands at night.

He ran a hand down his face. *What in God's name was happening to him?* Now, he was comparing her to magical creatures. This was the effect of clean country air. It addled the brain and thinking. It was the only explanation.

"I've had Bergamot since he was a colt. His mother was my mother's horse. So, in many ways, we grew up together. He's a prickly fellow. He can be sweet one minute and tart the next. Hence, the name." He turned from the cart to take a gander at the animal. Bergamot's nostrils flared and his ears flattened when Marcus looked at him. He snorted and stomped in offense that he had been forgotten since his master's attention was completely captured by the beautiful woman who stood beside a cart with a small mare hitched to the front.

There would be hell to pay on the way home.

To make up for the nasty ride ahead of him, Marcus took the opportunity to sweep a stray lock that had fallen across her cheek. Her skin was softer than the finest silk in all of London.

Savoring the simple touch, he closed his eyes for a moment. "What's your mare's name?"

"Florence," she answered. "The star on her forehead resembles a map of Florence I once saw. My brother gave me the cart and Florence on my sixteenth birthday. She's a special horse since I can ride her, but she's also trained to pull a cart.

Another clue that she was a farmer's daughter. Most horseflesh was either trained for work or riding. Only in the country would a horse serve dual purposes.

Nora turned to him with a sweet expression, and he smiled in return.

"Let's meet tomorrow. You tell me where." He played with a lock of her long hair. Interwoven with her hair were red and gold ribbons, giving the appearance that her hair was red, but underneath, he could tell it was various shades of blonde.

"Do you know the old Hampton Road?" she asked.

He nodded.

"There's a bridge about a mile outside the village to the south. Let's meet there at noon tomorrow."

"You must sleep late," he teased. "I'll be up and will have broken my fast by nine o'clock."

Her head whipped to his. "I'll have you know, sir, that I rise at six o'clock every morning."

"A farming girl then." He waited for her response.

"Among many other occupations," she responded, her face a blank slate. "But I can't meet any sooner. I... I have responsibilities that must be met before I can see you."

By the hesitation in her voice, she didn't want to divulge anymore. Well, he'd always enjoyed mysteries and had little doubt he'd enjoy learning everything there was to know about his Venus.

"Noon, it is," he said.

Nora turned to face him directly. "Thank you so much for a wonderful evening."

"The pleasure is mine." Without hesitating, he leaned forward and pressed his lips to hers. It was an innocent kiss. After a few moments, he pulled away. "That was a promise for our tomorrow." Without waiting for her answer, he swung her into his arms. A squeak of surprise escaped her before he gently set her in the bench seat of the cart. "It would be very ungentlemanly not to assist you." He waved a hand at her gown. "Especially in that. You've had a hard time walking this evening."

"Thank you."

He didn't want to let her go, but he took his horse's reins in hand, then in one movement, mounted Bergamot. "Until tomorrow."

"Until tomorrow," she repeated. She studied her reins for a moment before turning her gaze to his. "Promise you won't follow me."

The hint of worry in her voice made him pause. Whatever she was hiding, he'd be damned if he'd abide by her wishes. She wanted him to leave her in front of a gambling hell and allow her to travel by herself dressed in a Venus costume. With his Nora, he wasn't taking any chances.

His Nora?

"I promise"—he paused and waited for her to look into his eyes before he continued— "as long as you promise me you'll be safe."

She nodded once.

"Sweet dreams, Nora."

"The same to you," she said softly.

"Oh, I will," Marcus said confidently. "I'll be dreaming of you...and me."

Without lingering any longer, he urged Bergamot down the lane at a steady trot. Nora clearly needed to return home quickly. When he turned around, the cart was out of sight. He decided to give her another minute or two then he'd follow to ensure she arrived safely home.

But those moments felt like hours if truth be told. He'd never been an impatient man, but tonight that trait turned on its head. It reminded him of that quote by Moliere about slow growing trees bearing the sweetest fruit.

With an audible sigh, he turned Bergamot around and cantered toward the Jolly Rooster.

When he reached the copse of trees where he'd left Nora, he discovered she was gone. There was no sign of her. Something sparkling caught his attention on the ground.

It was her mask. Marcus quickly dismounted then picked it up. The crystals glued to the paper-mache mask glistened in the moonlight. Without hesitating, he stuffed it in a pocket, then mounted Bergamot urging the horse toward his home.

With a smile tugging at his lips, Marcus felt happy for the first time in a long while. And it was all because of a Roman Goddess who was masquerading as a mere mortal.

Six

Since it was past two in the morning, Honoria settled Florence in the stable without being seen, left the cart with the other vehicles, then snuck through the back entrance of Pelham Hall. She entered a small sitting room and changed into the simple day dress she'd worn to the Jolly Rooster before she'd changed into her gown. Silently, she took the servants' stairs to the family quarters. As she depressed the latch of the door to her bedroom, she released a breath. Fate was extremely kind this evening. She had arrived home without anyone the wiser. Plus, the night had been almost perfect.

And Marcus had been almost perfect. Though he wouldn't agree to her request, he did want to spend time with her. It was hard to fathom that a handsome man actually wanted her company, and he didn't even know who she was. This might be her only chance to spend time with a man and not have it end in marriage.

Now, she just had to find a way to meet him privately without anyone knowing her business. She smiled to herself as she walked further into her bedroom. She had never imagined her adventure tonight would last for another two weeks.

"Honoria, there you are," Pippa exclaimed, sitting up on the bed while rubbing her eyes. "Where have you been?"

She froze, unable to move. *Of all the nights to find her sister in her room.*

"Honor?"

"If I tell you, you can't tell anyone. Especially, Pelham."

"It depends." Pippa's voice was calm, her gaze steady. "If you're in trouble or hurt, I can't promise to keep your secret."

"No, it's nothing like that," Honoria reassured her.

"What's happened? What's that under your arm?" Pippa scooted to the edge of the bed.

Honoria sat next to her and kissed her cheek. "It's my costume."

"*You* went to the masquerade?" Pippa cried, pointing toward the costume.

Honoria nodded, then handed the dress to her sister. "How long have you been waiting for me?"

Pippa held the garment in front of her and examined it. "After I couldn't find you, I went to my room and started designing dresses. I figured you might have gone to the library to read. When I tried to go to bed, I couldn't sleep." She smiled sheepishly. "I got up and headed to the library only to discover you weren't there. Then, I became worried." She turned the garment to study the back. "My word. This looks indecent." Her gaze slowly met Honoria's. "Did anyone see you return home?"

"No. I was careful."

"Oh, Honor, why?" The concern in her sister's voice cut her in two.

"I just wanted to meet a man, someone who didn't know me. Someone who..." How to explain that for once in her life, she didn't want to feel isolated? She wanted someone who would see her as being worthy of his complete attention.

Pippa's face lacked any expression.

"It's not what you think. I met a wonderful man there tonight." She sighed, then stood up to take off her day dress.

Pippa followed. "Who?"

"Marcus," she said dreamily as she drew her dress over her head. "He's taller than me with black hair and the darkest blue eyes you've ever seen."

Pippa stilled from the task of folding the costume. "Marcus...? What's his last name?"

Honoria opened her mouth to answer, uncertain how much to share. But if she didn't tell Pippa everything, she might go to their brother. "I don't know. I asked him not to tell me as I wouldn't share mine. But he lives nearby. He's a farmer. We're meeting tomorrow. He wants to show me the countryside."

Pippa returned to the bed. "There's Marcus Kirkland, the Earl of Trafford. He's one of Pelham's friends. I've met him before when I've gone to London."

A cold chill crawled straight up her spine as if someone had walked over her grave. "He can't be the Earl of Trafford. The man I was with tonight is a farmer."

Pippa hmphed slightly. "What is a farmer doing at our brother's gambling den? I thought only his friends from London were attending the masquerade."

"My Marcus spends time in London, but he's from up North. He also lives here."

"Your farmer must be rich. Pelham only invites the wealthiest men to attend so they'll fill his coffers to overflowing." Pippa laughed.

"That's not very flattering," Honoria scolded. "He has many gallant traits."

"Hmm, Marcus or our brother?" Pippa's left eyebrow lifted. She looked just like Pelham when she was challenging someone.

Pippa and Pelham were so alike. It was easy to see the resemblance between her siblings. They both possessed sharp intellects, confidence, manners, and an excellent work ethic.

Not to mention, they both looked like Ardeertons.

Honoria smiled as she sat beside Pippa. "You are wicked, and just like our brother."

Pippa scrunched her brow in contemplation, then nodded. "I'll take that wickedness as a compliment."

"You're much more than that." Honoria pressed a kiss to her cheek.

"Turn around." Pippa started to remove the ribbons that had been braided into Honoria's hair. "Did you recognize anyone?"

"No. The women at the Jolly Rooster had all traveled from London. The men were dressed in dominos. But Pelham did sneak up on Marcus and me." She faced her sister. "Our brother didn't recognize me when Marcus was kissing me."

Pippa's eyes grew wider than the Pelham formal dining plates, which were considerable in size. "Tell me about the kiss."

"It was magical. My first kiss." She closed her eyes as the sensation came over her once again of being in his arms and having his lips touch hers. "It was like, in that moment, I'd found heaven and never wanted to return to earth."

"Did he know that it was your first kiss?" Pippa asked.

"I told him."

One corner of Pippa's mouth quirked upward. "Interesting tactic. Honesty. Keeps them off guard." She nodded. "What did he say?"

"He said it was perfection." Honoria walked to her dressing table and started brushing her hair. "I can't believe he wants to spend time with me." He was the first man besides Pelham who actually wanted her company.

"Oh, I like this Marcus." Pippa chortled. "And I very well can believe it. You're warm, vivacious, and simply wonderful. Darling, any man would be lucky to have you. Where are you going to meet him tomorrow?"

"Old Hampton Road bridge," Honoria said.

Pippa narrowed her eyes. "I have to pack, but shall I come with you and act as chaperone?"

"No, thank you." How to explain to Pippa that she wanted their time together to be private? The memories she made with Marcus would be the only ones of their kind, and she wanted them all to herself.

"I think you should take someone with you. Perhaps your groomsman, John Alton. He keeps secrets."

"He's not needed." Honoria took Pippa's hands in hers. "I'm a good judge of character. Nothing will happen to me. Marcus is honorable."

"I'm sure he is," Pippa explained. "However, what if someone sees you? You'll be ruined and have to marry a farmer."

Honoria stilled at the thought. Truthfully, the idea filled her with a sudden warmth and longing. She'd never felt like this before. Was it possible to fall in love at first sight, or was this a lingering enchantment from his kisses? She closed her eyes, remembering the warmth of his hard body against hers as she stood in his embrace. If she married Marcus, they'd share such kisses every day. Every night, they'd share the same bed. As a farmer mayhap he wouldn't care that she wasn't the old duke's daughter.

Carefully setting her brush down, Honoria dismissed such a fantasy. She was not marrying Marcus. He didn't even want to bed her.

"Besides, how could my reputation be ruined if no one knows who I am or who he is?"

Pippa shrugged. "Just be careful." She took the costume from the bed. "I'm keeping this in my room. Alice won't suspect anything if she finds it. She'll think it's another creation of mine."

Honoria stood before a mirror. She smiled at her sister's reflection. "Thank you for helping."

"You're welcome. Also, I'll keep your secret. You certainly have quite a few. I didn't know you could design and sew gowns. I wonder what else you're hiding?" Her sister's smile grew faint. "Wouldn't it be wonderful if this man of your dreams turned out to be real and gave you the life you deserve?"

Honoria turned from the mirror and regarded her sister. "I don't believe in fairytales anymore." She hadn't ever since her father had declared her and her mother worthless. It had colored everything in her life. "I believe in living in the present."

"We learn valuable lessons from the fairytales. We can take those fantasies and create our own realities. It's taking power and controlling our own destinies."

"What's your destiny?" Honoria asked.

Pippa shrugged. "A dress shop, a man who loves me unconditionally, a dog, and a cat." Her brow furrowed adorably. "Perhaps those are desires."

"Maybe they're both," Honoria said quietly.

"Maybe." Pippa nodded, then frowned. "If I'd known you were going to sneak into the masquerade, I would have accompanied you. But perhaps it's for the best you went alone."

"Thank you for understanding."

Pippa stood on her tiptoes and pressed a kiss to Honoria's cheek.

"I'm happy for you. I've never seen you so excited. You're open to new adventures. This bodes well for you going to London."

"Good night, my fairy godmother." Honoria laughed at such silliness. "Let's leave London be."

"No, I don't think so. If you can sneak into a masquerade ball, then you can handle London. I want to show everyone that I have the most wonderous sister in all the land," Pippa said with a yawn, then closed the door gently behind her with the Venus costume tucked close to her chest.

Honoria finished her nightly ablutions and made her way into bed. Although she should be exhausted by such a late night, sleep was elusive. A handsome gentleman with bold, brazen kisses took center stage in her thoughts.

The next morning, the house was quiet as it usually was when the Duke of Pelham had a party at the Jolly Rooster the night before. Honoria couldn't help but feel a little smug at the thought that she'd breached the doors of such a hallowed place without detection.

She practically floated down the steps from the family quarters to the main living floor. As she made her way to the intimate family dining room, the smells from the breakfast buffet greeted her before she entered the room. Expecting to only find Pippa, she came to an abrupt halt when her brother slowly lowered the letter he was reading and regarded her with a scowl.

To make matters worse, Pelham's eyes traveled the length of her, taking in her appearance. She discreetly smoothed her navy and crimson riding habit, then strolled nonchalantly into the room as if nothing were amiss. But something was off if Pelham was attending breakfast with them this morning after such a late night at the inn.

"Good morning," Pippa said a little too enthusiastically. "Look who decided to join us this morning." Her sister's eyes darted between their brother and Honoria. "Aren't we lucky?"

"Pippa, enough with the excessive cheer this morning. I haven't had any sleep," Pelham murmured. Immaculately groomed in a black morning coat, starched cravat, and buckskin breeches, he looked every inch a country gentleman. He must have just come from a bath as his blond hair had darkened like it always did when wet.

"Good morning," Honoria called out as she proceeded to the buffet and loaded her plate with her favorites—eggs, crisp bacon, toast, jam, and fresh fruit. As she strolled to the empty chair across from Pippa, a footman poured her a fresh cup of tea. The scent wafted her way. She inhaled deeply, hoping the fumes would give her strength.

Pelham never spent time with them the day after such a party unless there was some emergency from London.

Or...he had discovered her activities from last night.

Steady course. There was no cause for alarm...yet.

Narrowing his eyes, Pelham folded the letter with minimal effort. His movements were always subdued. It was the reason for his uncanny ability to sneak up on others. Her skin prickled at the look of consternation in his gaze.

"How was your party?" she asked politely.

"Oh, Honoria, it sounded absolutely grand...." Pippa's voice trailed off as Pelham raised an eyebrow in her direction. She cleared her throat slightly.

"Interesting," he drawled as his gaze skated between her and Pippa. "I don't recall saying a word about it."

"Well, I'm sure it was grand." Pippa blinked rapidly. "Why wouldn't a masquerade be grand. The costumes, the food, the people attending." She leaned back in her chair. "I do wish you'd let me and Honoria attend sometime."

Bully for you, darling. The best way to distract their brother was to put him on the defensive. Pippa's ability to deflect their brother's conversation from the matters at hand had increased dramatically over the years.

"It's not an appropriate place for young ladies like you."

"I wouldn't call either of us young," Pippa pressed, then laughed.

"You're perfect," he replied. His earlier frostiness melted away with an affectionate smile. Then he nodded to the two footmen who were serving them this morning. After the double doors were shut, it was just the three of them. Their brother slowly turned his attention to Honoria. "What do you have to say for yourself?"

Pippa squirmed in her seat.

That made two of them. Honoria took a deep breath. The best way to handle bravado was to dish it out in equal measure. She tilted her chin an inch in the air. "What are you referring to?"

His gaze never strayed from hers. "You're going riding? I thought you were ill."

For the first time this morning, she could relax. Her brother didn't know about last night. "I thought a bit of air and exercise would be refreshing. I'm going to see some of the tenants today. The Middleton's had their new baby. I'm taking food to them."

He nodded, but his gaze didn't leave Honoria. Any second he would tell her that he knew she had attended last night. She tightened her stomach waiting for the announcement.

"An emergency has arisen at my solicitor's office in London that I must attend to. Pippa and I are leaving as soon as possible."

"Really?" Pippa's face transformed into a look of sheer joy. She scooted to the edge of her seat. "I'm not completely packed."

"Since we must leave within the hour, I instructed my valet to have Alice prepare your trunks." He looked directly at Pippa. "You're to pack light. I'm having one of the most popular modistes in London create you a new wardrobe."

"Honoria, Alice will travel with Pippa," Pelham announced. "Ask one of the second-floor maids to attend you while Alice is gone."

She wanted to cheer "huzzah" as it meant she could still see Marcus.

"As soon as I arrived home this morning, Winston informed me that you retired directly after I left for the Jolly Rooster." His eyes narrowed in concern. "Perhaps you should stay inside. You can postpone the Middleton visit until next week." He placed his hand over hers. "You look tired and out of sorts. Before I leave for London, I'll have Winston send word for Dr. Mallory to attend you."

"There's no need," Honoria said quietly. "It's nothing that I haven't experienced before."

It was enough of a hint that Pelham understood Honoria was

discussing her monthly courses. Immediately, his face reddened, and he turned his attention back to his letter. "All right."

Honoria swallowed slightly. She hated to lie to her brother. It always felt wrong. But sometimes, secrets were too precious to reveal. She would not miss this chance to live her life as she chose.

And that choice was spending time with Marcus.

"The next time I go to London, I'd like to take you for a new wardrobe." Pelham squeezed her hand. "I hope you'll allow that."

"We shall see," she said noncommittedly. "I'll miss you both."

"I'll miss you," Pippa said softly.

Before Honoria could reply, Pelham did the honors for her. "Indeed. We'll both miss you. But perhaps it's for the best. I can only handle one Ardeerton sister at a time."

Seven

H onoria waved goodbye as the carriage with her brother and sister picked up speed on the main road. Then with a quick pivot on her foot, she headed straight for the house. Smiling, she exhaled and climbed the steps. She'd had Pelham Hall to herself before, but this time it felt different. She could practically taste the freedom in the air.

Granted, she loved her brother and sister, but Honoria planned to enjoy every minute she could with Marcus. She smoothed her riding habit, then checked the time. As she walked down the black and white tiled hallway, she stopped at a mirror and glanced at her appearance. She didn't need to pinch her cheeks. The excitement of her day provided a pink glow.

Honoria had asked the cook to prepare several baskets for her to deliver to a few of the tenants who farmed the rich land surrounding the ducal estate along with stopping by the Middleton's. There was still plenty of time to deliver the baskets before she met Marcus.

She'd also asked the cook to prepare a basket for her use, which she'd share with Marcus. The cook didn't even blink at such a request. She was used to Honoria spending time by herself, walking the estate or visiting tenants, then having a bite to eat. Honoria was practically bouncing on the tips of her toes to leave.

Jasper Archer, one of her favorite footmen, came from the direction of the kitchen. "My lady, the last of the baskets are being loaded into your cart."

She grinned. "Wonderful. I can be on my way then. Thank you."

"Shall I go with you? Some of those baskets are quite heavy," Jasper offered.

"No need." She smiled again.

"Yes, my lady." The footman bowed.

Before she could walk another step, Winston approached. "Lady Honoria, a carriage just arrived after His Grace and Lady Pippa left. You have a visitor."

"Me?" It couldn't be Marcus. She'd been cautious last night. He didn't know her identity. "Who is it?"

"The Earl of Carlyle." Winston lifted a brow. "Alone." He sniffed in disapproval. "I've placed him in the blue salon."

This was the deuced worst timing in the world. Why was Carlyle even here? He was her brother's friend who lived only a few miles away, which meant she had to see him.

"Will you ask one of the upstairs maids to join me?" Honoria sighed slightly. Perhaps she could make the visit short, then be on her way to meet Marcus.

"I've already asked Mary. She's waiting for you outside the salon." Winston lowered his voice. "No posts from London this morning."

"How disappointing." She said not hiding her irritation. She'd thought by now the investigator would have found something.

Winston nodded, then bowed.

Squaring her shoulders, she made her way to the sitting room where Mary stood waiting for her. The upstairs maid was small in stature, but she more than made up for it in personality. She always had a smile on her face.

"Thank you, Mary," she said softly. "I know you're busy today."

"Of course, my lady." Mary's grin stretched from ear to ear. "It keeps me from having to do the laundry."

Since no one was there to announce her to her visitor, Honoria did it herself. "Lord Carlyle, what an unexpected surprise."

Immediately, the earl rose to his feet and made a curt bow. "Good morning, Lady Honoria." He looked to Mary and nodded.

Honoria took the seat on the sofa and patted the spot next to her, directing Mary to stay close. "Your mother isn't joining us?"

"I'm afraid not," Carlyle said as he took his seat. The earl was looking directly at her as if she were the most fascinating person in the world. It was quite unsettling. She shifted in her seat.

"Would you care for tea?" she asked.

Amusement danced in his eyes. "No, thank you."

She wanted to shout "thank you" to the heavens for small favors. "I'm afraid my brother and sister have traveled to London."

"They're not the ones I wanted to see." He leaned forward, never taking his gaze from hers. "It's fortunate you stayed at Pelham Hall."

"Oh? How so?"

She just wanted him gone. It would be rude to ask him what he wanted. That was the problem when you attended a finishing school for six years. Deportment lessons and manners were drilled into you.

Carlyle finally looked to Mary. "Would you mind if I spoke with Lady Honoria privately?" Before Honoria could object, he continued, "You can move to the next sitting area. You'll still be able to see your mistress."

Honoria nodded in approval when Mary stole a quick peek. As the maid walked to the sitting area at the end of the formal salon, Honoria gripped the arm of the blue velvet sofa. She was going to be late. She only hoped Marcus would wait for her.

"I want to court you."

"You don't even know me," she retorted. *Good heavens, what was the man doing?*

His face reddened, and he glanced at his clasped hands. "But I'd like to."

"Why would you want to marry me?" Her finishing school instructor Mrs. Rutland would have been horrified by her outburst. But what was a lady to do when presented with such a declaration?

"Several reasons. You're the Duke of Pelham's sister. You have a considerable dowry. A match between us would be advantageous for many reasons." His gaze never left hers, and a small grin tugged at his lips. "Aligning our families would be advantageous to both."

With light brown hair and tawny eyes, the earl was one of the most eligible bachelors in London. At least, that's what the gossip rags had pronounced. Probably most women would find him attractive, but Honoria wasn't one of them. She was partial to men with black hair and dark blue eyes. She was also partial to gentleman farmers over earls.

She blew a breath to force herself to focus. "Perhaps you'd really like to marry my brother. His fortune is much larger than mine."

A genuine laugh escaped from the earl. Immediately, his eyes brightened. That was not the response she was looking for.

"Forgive me." He studied the floor, then raised his gaze to hers. He wore a new self-assurance. "I don't want a biddable wife. I want a wife who will challenge me. A wife who has mettle and will fight like a tigress to protect her own. Your brother possesses such traits, and I think you do, too."

"I see." But she really didn't. "Are you aware that I'm coming into a fortune next month?"

"Yes." He didn't even bat an eye at her question.

"Then you must know that I really don't need to marry." She folded her hands on her lap. It was a signal that the discussion would go no farther.

"I disagree," the earl countered. "Every woman of the *ton* wants to marry. It's their goal in life."

"I'm not part of the *ton*," she argued.

The earl leaned back against the chair in shock. Thankfully, a new type of quiet surrounded them, one that she controlled and not him.

Then his eyes brightened. "I can go to London during the House of Lords' sessions, but I'd want you to attend upon occasion." He smiled shyly. "I've shocked you, but I hope you'll consider my offer. We'd make a powerful couple."

She grinned in return but shook her head at the same time so as not to be misunderstood. "I'm flattered, but I'm afraid you're wasting your time."

At the clock strike, she cringed. She was supposed to meet Marcus at this very minute.

Thankfully, the earl glanced at the longcase clock. "Just consider it, I beg of you. I must take my leave."

She stood at the same time he did. As they said their goodbyes, the earl walked toward the exit, then stopped and turned in her direction. His eyes narrowed slightly as he evaluated her. "Did you attend your brother's masquerade ball?"

Honoria froze like a rabbit hunted by a fox. "Why would you ask that?"

"I was there for a short time. A woman who looked remarkably like you attended." His eyes were glued to her face. "Same stature."

"Really? It must be someone else." She clasped her hands together in a dutiful pose, but inside, her stomach was churning. "My sister and I have begged to go every year, but Pelham forbids us. He says it's not proper entertainment for ladies."

"I find your brother has always been astute." The Earl of Carlyle bowed briefly, then left.

Marcus pulled his father's timepiece from his pocket and checked the time again. Venus wasn't coming. As soon as he'd arrived, an acute sense of disappointment had threatened. He'd hoped she'd have been here, waiting for him, as anxious to see him as he was to see her. Last night, he'd sipped a glass of whiskey as he'd stared into the full moon, wondering what it was about this woman that fascinated him so.

The answers had come easily enough. She was beautiful and unique. But more importantly, she was intelligent and quick-witted. Besides, her sensual kisses had kept him up all night. Perhaps it was for the best that she'd decided not to come. Pelham had sent a brief note this morning that he was returning to London on an emergency. He'd invited Marcus to call on him when he returned to London.

Pelham was more protective of his two sisters than he was of his pride and joy, the Jolly Rooster. The very idea that he had proposed a match with his sister Honoria was remarkable. It could only mean he held Marcus in high esteem.

Lady Honoria had to be at least six years younger than Pelham, making her age twenty-four or perhaps older. That was one of the mysteries of the eldest Ardeerton sisters. She had never had a Season. According to Pelham, she didn't want one since she preferred the country. That fact, and the school Lady Honoria had started, boded well that she would be interested in his charity.

He unhitched Bergamot from the tree, and when he took his seat on the bay stallion, Bergamot did his usual dance of agitation. Marcus nudged the horse's side, and the stallion took off. Wherever they went was fine with Marcus. Perhaps a good, hard ride would dispel his disappointment.

Eventually, Bergamot slowed his gait to a walk. Unfortunately, the ride didn't quell the never-ending question of why Nora hadn't met him. He feared she'd changed her mind or, worse, had found another man to take his place. His lips pursed at such a thought.

But what if she was ill or an emergency had occurred? She had been so careful with her identity around him that he had no way to find her. Just as she had no idea how to locate him.

He found himself back at the bridge. What a sap he was to still be looking for her. To his right, several bucolic smaller farms sat nestled in a deep green valley surrounded by hills. He stopped to enjoy the view. There was a peacefulness to the area that was unique to Amesbury. He'd never been able to find the same in London or at his ancestral home.

The jangle of a harness caught his attention. Coming down the road was a very familiar cart with Venus driving. With her regal stance, she looked like the queen of all she surveyed. Yet, as soon as she saw him, a brilliant smile appeared.

At the sight, his heart somersaulted in approval. He raised his hand in greeting, and she did the same.

Bergamot looked up from where he was munching on a particularly green patch of grass, then snorted.

Without waiting for her to meet him, Marcus urged his horse in her direction. Nora slowed the rig to a stop.

As soon as he reached her side, Nora cooed to Bergamot in greeting. His stallion threw his head in answer, then eyed her mare with interest. Marcus knew the feeling. There was more than met the eye with these two.

He slid off his horse to help Nora, but she waved him off. "I can do it. I'm not so constricted in my riding habit like I was in my costume."

"I see that." He absently patted Florence as he took in the sight of Nora. She was dressed in a beautiful crimson and blue riding habit. Though he wasn't an expert in women's fashion, he knew it was stylish and expensive. Another clue she was a wealthy farmer's daughter. He closed the distance between them. "I thought perhaps you'd changed your mind."

"I was detained by an unexpected visitor, and I had to deliver some...items to several friends. I apologize for being late." When she lifted her gaze to his, the sun's rays flirted with her hair, emphasizing the copper strands braided throughout. It was beautiful, just as she was.

He wanted to ask about the visitor and the friends but knew she wouldn't answer. Instead, he waved a hand at the back of the cart. There was a basket, a blanket, two fishing poles, and another small basket.

"You're fishing?"

"We're fishing," she corrected. By then, she had unhitched Florence from the cart and tied her reins to a tree. "You wanted to see some of the unique places in the area. I thought we could start with one of my favorites." She lowered her voice. "This is a secret that I'll only share with you. It's the best fishing in Amesbury."

"I like a woman with secrets." He tied Bergamot to the same tree. He hadn't been fishing since he'd been a lad, but he'd always had a deft hand and usually came home with a catch that would feed himself and the servants. "I also like a woman who fishes. A sight rarer than Venus, I'd wager."

She batted a hand in dismissal. "I've been fishing since a little girl. It was an excellent way to escape..." She shook her head. "What I meant was...we can chat as long as we're quiet."

She had been about to share another secret with him, but then decided against it, which made him extremely curious. Perhaps he could coax it out of her when they were whiling away the hours on the river-bank. "What's in the baskets?"

"Food is in the bigger basket, and in the smaller one are flies." She blushed prettily. "If they're not biting, then I thought we could share a luncheon."

"Where is this magical place?" A wayward lock of blonde hair had fallen from her chignon. Slowly, he lifted his hand and tucked it behind her ear. He cupped her cheek and rubbed his thumb gently across her silken skin. Last night, he'd thought her eyes simply blue. But in the daylight, their brilliance was spellbinding. They were an exquisite hue of blue and green, more akin to turquoise, with flecks of gold adorning her irises.

"That magical place is right here," she answered softly in the same seductive voice from last night.

"You mean between us?"

Her eyes widened at his forwardness, then a worldly grin graced her lips. "The magical place I refer to is right underneath this bridge." She grabbed the poles and the smaller basket. "Come before the breeze dies down. This is perfect fishing weather."

Without waiting for him, she made her way around the bridge, then disappeared under it. He grabbed the basket with the food and followed. About a quarter of a mile upstream, she stopped.

"If you open your basket, there's a blanket on top of the food. Why don't you spread it out for us while I handle these?" She nodded at the fishing gear, then proceeded to the riverbank and set about her work.

Nora was completely comfortable giving directions as Miss Efficient. He chuckled softly as he prepared the area per her instructions. Perhaps her mother was a housekeeper at one of the nearby estates. It would explain how Nora had learned how to supervise people. But there really weren't any large estates nearby except for Pelham's and his. But Marcus hadn't had the chance to call upon any of the neighbors. She could be a daughter of a country squire from a smaller estate.

He knew if he asked her, she would refuse to answer. Was it to protect her reputation or her heart? Perhaps both. He knew the feeling. As he strolled toward her, she was already testing one of the bamboo rods with a fly made with a violet feather.

He sidled up beside her and watched as she cast her lure into the crystal-clean water of the stream. "What are you casting for?"

"River trout," she said without acknowledging him, her concentration keen on the exact location where her lure landed.

"I've never seen a violet fly lure before," he said nonchalantly.

She lowered her voice to barely above a whisper. "I made this one from a bit of extra trim from a hat."

He bit his lip to keep from laughing out loud. The minx's serious demeanor was a far cry from her pleasant company of last night. "Do they work?" When she shot him a look, he waved a hand in the direction of the stream. "Do the fish prefer violet or some other color? Feathers, fur, or horsehair? Perhaps a bit of pink feathers from your costume last night might garner their interests. It certainly did mine."

She cast in another part of the stream. With a comfortable maneuver, she jerked the rod gently in a constant motion to the entice the fish. Once the rhythm was set, she turned her turquoise gaze in his direction. "Are you an expert on angling, sir?" she said sweetly, but her eyes darkened in challenge.

"I've had my fair share of catches in the day." He leaned in and spoke barely above a whisper. "But the fairest catch of all is standing before me now."

His reward was her smile, one that coaxed the sun to shine brighter.

"Shall we wager?" she asked. Though her expression was matter of fact, the sparkle in her eyes gave away her excitement. "Pick out whatever flies tickle your fancy, then let us have a competition on who catches the most. We catch five river trout. Whoever catches the majority will be declared the winner."

"And the loser shall cook the catch for the other," he added to the wager.

She nodded decisively. "Excellent."

He didn't tarry and bent to pick out a standard lure made with several iridescent peacock feathers. It was a beautiful lure and had to have been made by an artisan who knew his craft. He'd never seen such a well-constructed lure. He tied it onto his line and with a deft flick of his wrist cast the lure into the water.

"Which one did you pick?" she asked innocently.

"The peacock one."

She hmphed slightly. "I made that one."

He swiveled his gaze to her. "You?"

Keeping her attention on the water, she nodded. "Last week."

Before he could respond, she tugged sharply on her pole and lifted it straight into the air. With one hand, she gently tugged on the fine horse-hair line. He grabbed the net and secured the trout. Its belly shined in a kaleidoscope of colors.

"What a beauty," she said in awe. "Shall we keep it?"

"It's a good size." He nodded, then stowed the fish in a wooden basket that was submerged in water. "My turn." He brought his rod back to his side and then flicked the line into the water nearby where Nora had caught her fish. After teasing the lure in the water for several moments, he turned her way. The hard set of her delicate chin indicated her pure determination to win this wager.

Pelham immediately came to mind. With Nora's blonde hair and assured stance, she reminded him of the duke. He'd seen his friend with the same resolve when gambling at the Jolly Rooster.

What a perplexing thought, but where did it come from? Nora was nothing like the rapscallion duke.

Again, she jerked her pole straight into the air, hooking another fish. With an innate grace, she efficiently brought it to shore. Marcus dropped his rod once again to assist.

"What is this enchantment you weave over the water?" he murmured.

"It's not magic. It's a skill," she said while laughing merrily. "It's the purple. You should have tried the pink." She lifted a single brow in the air.

"Last night, I thought you a goddess, but today I know exactly what you are." He deepened his voice. "A mermaid."

Her gaze drifted to his. "What are you about?"

"You're one of those mythical creatures like a selkie or a mermaid who control the waters and all the beings around them." Again, he placed the fish in the basket. Brushing off his hands, he stood and regarded her with a smile. "The fish are charmed as much as I am."

Before the words were out of his mouth, she'd caught another.

"Enough," he cried theatrically. "You've won."

She surveyed the river before settling her gaze to his. "You didn't even try."

He shrugged slightly. "I know when it's a hopeless cause." He stowed the last fish and helped her gather up the rods and the rest of the fishing equipment. "I'm hungry."

"I am, too," she said.

As soon as everything was placed in the back of her cart, he entwined their fingers and led her back to the blanket. He'd picked a spot out of the sun. Underneath a tall oak that provided shade, they could watch the water cascade over the rocks as it made its way downstream.

"This is lovely," she said. A beautiful pink fell over her cheeks.

It was on the tip of his tongue to say, "Not as lovely as you," but he held the response. He was bestowing too many compliments. The way Nora responded meant she wasn't accustomed to receiving them. Nor was it obvious whether she enjoyed them or not.

So, he decided to be the consummate host. Since she'd brought the food, he served her a plate of chicken, sliced cheese, the choicest strawberries, which meant she must have access to a hothouse, and a small almond cake. As she poured them each a glass of wine, he withdrew his pocketknife and sliced an apple to share between them.

"Tell me about yourself," he said as he took a bite of the tender chicken. He leaned against the tree and regarded her. She sat regally with her legs tucked under her.

She finished her bite of apple, then daintily pressed her serviette to her mouth. "There's not much to tell. I'm twenty-four and a spinster. I like to read, garden, and do what other women of my ilk do."

"Which is?" he pressed.

A myriad of emotions fell about her face. Uncertainty, trepidation, and regret were all there, but then a miraculous change happened. She pushed her shoulders back and looked him directly in the eye. "Create my own happiness."

"How so?" He sat up and leaned toward her.

"By not relying on anyone else," she said defiantly.

But Marcus could detect a hint of defensiveness about her.

"Did someone hurt you?" he asked gently. If someone had, Marcus would rectify the situation himself. That was a promise.

She was silent for a moment and regarded him, clearly judging whether he was worthy to hear her story. "A long time ago, but he's no longer alive." A strongly forged steel had replaced the normal melliferous lilt in her voice. It was enough to warn him off the subject.

He had to know. "Was he someone you'd taken a fancy to?"

"In a manner of speaking." She fiddled with the chicken on her plate. She'd become so silent that he didn't think she would answer. But she finally looked up, and with a deep breath continued, "My father. He didn't care for me."

His stomach tightened in response. "Why?"

She chuckled slightly, but a sheen of pain glistened in her eyes. "It makes no difference now. He's been dead for years." She turned away and stared at the horizon.

What kind of a father wouldn't love Nora? She was unique in her thoughts, and her observations kept him enthralled. When it was clear that she wouldn't share more, he asked, "Any other family?"

"I have a sister and brother...in London," she said hesitantly, then smiled.

"Are they married?"

"Not to each other." She laughed softly. "No, neither one is married."

He grinned at her. "What are you doing here by yourself?"

"I live here," she said, not offering any more information.

Perhaps she'd been sent to the country for some transgression. But that didn't seem feasible. She was a lovely well-bred woman. He could tell by her manners, the way she spoke, and the way she moved. She had an ingrained elegance to her that could only be from years of deportment training. He could see that now.

"What about you? "Nora set her plate aside and took a sip of wine as she regarded him. "Do you have any family?"

He shook his head and debated how much to share with her. Something unfamiliar surged through him, a need to tell her all about the disappointments in his life. Except for Pelham and Ravenscroft, he'd never told anyone how his parents' death had affected him. It was a snap decision. He would tell her about the pain of his dissipated youth.

"My parents died when I was twelve." He took a sip of wine and tried to collect his scattered thoughts into some semblance of order. Of course, it was difficult to explain since he'd acted as daft as one could when something that horrible happened to a boy. "I had no other siblings or relatives. I was left in the care of the..." He'd almost said the guardians and conservators of his earldom, but that would reveal too much.

Nora had been adamant not to share too much of their identities. Which was probably for the best.

"You were saying you were left in the care of whom?" she asked softly.

He shook his head to clear his thoughts. "The local vicar," he said.

It was a small lie. The vicar in the earldom's local parish had visited him several times a week after his parents had died while the solicitors were working out the details of his father's will. The vicar was a young man with a wife and baby. He had been truly gifted in how he made Marcus forget his sorrow, at least for the hour or so when he'd visited. He seemed to care about Marcus and had always brought him something sweet that his wife had made. He'd been the only one who had taken an interest in him as a person.

However, the vicar had disappeared from his life. The bishop who oversaw the parish had named the young man a rector and assigned him to a larger parish. After he'd moved, no one had come to see Marcus or to talk about his grief.

"Were you happy?" Nora wasn't regarding him with the syrupy sentiment that others did when they discovered he'd grown up alone.

"As much as any boy who'd lost his world." He bit the inside of his cheek. He still sounded like a grieving lad, but it felt right to say this to her. Perhaps he *was* still grieving.

"I can't imagine living with another family," she said ruefully. "I lost my mother shortly after my father, but I still had my sister and my brother. By then, we were practically adults. Are you still close to the family you stayed with?"

"Of course." Immediately, he thought of Pelham and Ravenscroft.

He smiled, trying to lighten the mood. "Such sorrow shouldn't dull our beautiful day."

She frowned slightly.

Slowly, he leaned forward, then angled his head in such a way to make his intent obvious. There was only one surefire way to change the mood between them.

He would kiss her.

Eight

Honoria stood still as Marcus sat up and leaned her way, his intent obvious. Last night, she'd replayed their kisses for hours, growing hot and restless as she lay in bed. Her heart thudded in her chest loud enough he had to hear it.

As soon as his lips touched hers, all thoughts scattered like drops of water on a hot skillet. She moaned slightly and without reservation, her hand fluttered to his chest in welcome. He cupped her cheeks, the warmth of his fingers enveloping her in a sea of sensations.

Every moment she spent with him was finite, and she wouldn't waste such a gift on thoughts of proper deportment. Not during these precious days she had with him. As his tongue stroked hers, she met his fire with her own. When he groaned, she felt a feminine rush of victory. Indeed, she was the siren from last night, Venus in all her glory.

Gently, he settled her on the ground with his body covering hers. As he coaxed her mouth with his, she lifted her arms and entwined her fingers in the soft strands of his midnight black hair. It was softer than she remembered. She pulled him closer and spread her legs, so that he angled his thighs to rest between hers.

She gasped when one of his hands cradled her breast while he continued to seduce her mouth with his. The couple from last night had shared a kiss like this. Last night, she'd been hesitant to lay with him. In broad daylight, she should have been terrified, but there was a hunger building between them that had to be satisfied.

"Marcus," she murmured, "please."

His lips trailed from her mouth to her ear, his warm breath sending a chill through her body. The hard angle of his hips against hers was nothing compared to his swollen member that pushed against her center, lighting a fire that demanded more.

She angled her hips against his hard length and moaned. Without hesitation, Honoria took his hand and placed it on her skirt, coaxing him to lift it.

His hand froze and, suddenly, he leaned away. "I don't know what possessed me to do that. Anyone could see us if they passed by." He gracefully moved to the side and sat up, then ran his fingers through his black locks. "I apologize for my forwardness."

For a moment, she laid there numb, her tingling lips swelling from the sensual machinations of his mouth. She flexed her fingers against the coverlet. They'd broken bread together, then they'd kissed each other senseless. That old fear reared its ugly head and demanded attention. He was a man, and he was refusing to have anything to do her. How many times had she promised herself that she would never allow herself to be in that position again?

She propped herself up on her elbows and tilted her head. "I believe there were two of us in that kiss. If anyone got carried away, it was both of us."

His lips, the very ones she'd just feasted on, tilted up in a half-smile. Her breath caught at the sight. In that rare moment, she saw a glimpse of what he must have looked like a boy. His eyes glistened, and pure joy seemed to radiate around him.

"Indeed," he said sheepishly. He stared at her for a moment, then pressed his lips against her cheek before helping her sit up. "You're a lady. I shouldn't—"

She pressed her hand against his mouth. "I never said I was a lady."

"You didn't have to." He dipped his head to meet her gaze. "I can tell by your manners...and other things..."

She scooted away from him and smoothed her skirt. "What other things might you be referring to? Is it my lack of skill or knowledge in kissing or lovemaking?" She lifted an eyebrow and brushed her skirt of crumbs. "You said last night that we're all virgins once."

"Do you say aloud everything you think?" He threw his head back and laughed, the rich sound filling the air.

It was such a mesmerizing sight she couldn't help but grin. "Well, I try."

"You are pure temptation, Nora." He regarded her with a shy smile, then exhaled painfully.

She leaned her back against the oak tree and plucked a piece of grass. She studied it for a moment, trying to decide whether this meant he'd lost interest in her or had grown bored. Two days ago, the old Honoria wouldn't have dared to press him for an explanation. That woman would have been too fearful of the reason. Once a person was deemed worthless by their father, it was easier to let things slip under the proverbial rug rather than face them head-on. That way you never were reminded how disposable you could be.

"I'm not asking you to be a gentleman," she said quietly. Never turning her gaze from his, she continued, "I'm asking for a lover." The determined set of his square jaw was sharper than a knife, but it didn't sway her. For once in her life, she'd fight for what she wanted, and that was Marcus. "I can only promise you a week or so. I'd like to make the most of our time together."

He tilted his head and stared into her eyes. If he was trying to divine all her secrets, he was wasting his time. She might share her body with him, but she'd not share all her dreams and heartaches. Those were hers alone.

"Why is that?" he finally asked.

"My life will return to my regular routine." Her routine consisted of executing a plan to end her father's reach beyond the grave. If she found that letter, she'd at least have a chance for a normal life, perhaps a family of her own. She studied the piece of grass she held in her hand as if it were a piece of art, which it was in its own way. She could appreciate it because she had so much in common with it. They were ordinary, everyday occurrences that no one really noticed. But each one had a part to play in the larger scheme of things.

Last night had taught her to expect more from others, but also herself. She might not ever have a chance to experience love and all the wonderful things that it entailed, but she'd not forgo this chance to understand the physical side of such emotions.

She drew a breath for fortitude, then exhaled silently. "I'd hoped to spend this time with *you*. However, if you're not interested, tell me immediately. We shall part company as friends. I'll find someone else."

He'd made it clear last night his intent. She should have known better than to have expected anything else. She stood quickly and started to straighten her skirts.

Immediately, Marcus stood also, then took one of her hands in his. "Nora, was that a threat? I don't take well to such warnings."

"No," she said, not breaking her stare, although heat, the kind that told too much, bludgeoned her cheeks. "It was a promise." *Heaven help her.* "I know what I want, Marcus. I'll attain it."

"Stop, sweetheart," he soothed in a voice that reminded her of one of Pelham's groomsmen trying to calm a fractious horse.

She wanted to stomp her foot. Why did he have to play the chivalrous knight at this very moment? A part of her heart cracked at the sweetness in his tone. He truly was a kind and honorable man. It was such a pity that his honor had decided to make an uninvited appearance today.

"If you're worried I'll be hurt, don't," she argued softly, then squeezed her eyes shut. This was not at all how she'd envisioned their day together. Tears burned, but she refused to allow them to fall. Not in front of him. It was another reminder of how ordinary she was. "I must leave." She bent over to pick up the remains of their luncheon. This was beyond mortifying. *Damnation.* A tear fell.

She turned from him and hastily wiped it away. To the devil with packing up the dishes and the blanket. She'd leave everything there as a memorial to this dreadful day.

At least she had already packed away her fishing rods and basket. They were the most valuable anyway.

Marcus came up behind her. Gently, his hands gripped her arms. "Don't go." His voice sounded guttural. "I beg of you." He pressed a kiss to her cheek then squeezed her arms. "I apologize."

She stood frozen, unable to move. But it wasn't from the gentle pressure of his hands on her arms. It was the misery she'd heard in his voice.

"There's no need," she answered.

"There's every need since I've upset you." In an instant, he moved to face her. "I won't tell you my name or where I live since you asked me not to." The muscles in his jaw tensed in aggravation. "But allow me this. I must explain. I can't let you think the worst." He combed his hand through the long strands of his hair as he exhaled. "I started a charity. It means a great deal to me. It's my purpose in life. I don't know what I'd do without it. I look forward to each day because of it. I must rely on others to help me with it. If my reputation is damaged or even tarnished, then the charity will suffer or be shut down." He rubbed the back of his neck. His eyes clouded with worry. "I just can't risk a scandal. No matter how much I want this."

His sincerity reached inside her chest and squeezed. Her heart crumpled, knowing that she had pushed him to the point that he was hurting. "Oh Marcus, I don't know what to say. I understand." Willing him to see that she recognized his worry, she cupped his cheeks with both hands, then searched his eyes. How could she have been so selfish? "I put my needs above yours. Forgive me."

He nodded once and pressed a kiss to the center of her palm.

Her eyes blurred with more tears. "Tell me what type of charity?"

"It's a charity for orphans." He took her hands in his, then pressed a quick kiss against her lips.

"How wonderful." She smiled all the while battling the tears that threatened to fall.

He searched her face. "I want to know everything you are thinking." He brought her hands to his mouth and pressed a gentle kiss on each one. "I want to do everything with you. But we must be discreet. I can't risk discovery, but I can't risk losing you either. So, I'm begging you, Venus, let us start anew." He smiled, but the yearning was clear in his eyes. "I'll give you whatever you want. All I ask is that you spend your time with me."

The hopeful desperation in his eyes stole her breath. He pursed his lips. He was as lonely as she was. Why hadn't she seen it before?

Honoria nodded. "I'd like that. We'll be discreet."

Instantly, Marcus relaxed his shoulders as if the weight of the world had been lifted from him.

"On one condition," she said. "Let us both make the decisions as to how we spend our time together." She smiled slightly. "For whatever days we have to share, let us be equals."

"Agreed." He smiled in return. "Now, have you given any thought as to how we shall spend the rest of the day together?"

She shook her head.

"I have," he said without a hint of boastfulness. Gone was the man who had seemed ready to fall on his knees and beg for her company. "Shall we ride? I'd like to show you my favorite places."

She nodded. "However, allow me to take home the fish and cart, then I'll return on horseback." How she'd accomplish that without a groomsman would require some quick thinking. This morning, when she'd told the groomsman assigned to her that she was visiting several estate tenants, he didn't ask about her poles and baskets.

"Venus," he called out as he walked to the river's edge. "Remember, the fish are mine to prepare for your dinner." He picked up the basket, then suddenly jerked it open. "What the devil," he grunted. "They're gone."

"What?" Honoria came to his side and peeked into the basket.

"I must not have latched it correctly. More likely, those wily fish unlatched it themselves."

She bit her lip to keep from laughing but failed miserably.

The skin around his eyes crinkled when he finally joined in. Once their laughter quieted, he bowed. "Now, I must serve a feast in place of the fish. Meet me back here in an hour, and we'll ride. Afterward, I'll serve you a meal you'll never forget."

"Make it two hours," she answered. That would give her enough time to return the cart, then assign her groomsman a task to keep him away from the stables. She could saddle Florence on her own and leave without any interference or an escort.

"Take all the time you need. I'll be waiting for you." Then, the most miraculous thing happened. He smiled again, but it was different this time.

It was a smile she'd remember for the rest of her life. It tilted her world upside down.

Marcus had taken the time since leaving Nora to ready the hunting lodge on his estate. It was a beautiful three-story stone building that was set high on a hill overlooking the valley below. A small river cut through the valley. The scene was idyllic and completely romantic.

A perfect spot to spend time with a beautiful woman.

He mounted Bergamot, and the horse immediately set off down the hill. He patted the beast's neck and let his mind wander as he surveyed his land.

Every time he thought he understood Nora and her circumstances, she'd say something that made him reconsider his conclusions. When she discussed her father and family, he could see her brightness dim. What could possibly have happened for her to be sent to the country while the rest of her family was in London? Who was she staying with?

He'd never taken a virgin to bed. The thought that Nora had no experience made his chest tighten along with his cock. He shouldn't want her. But the problem was he couldn't get her out of his thoughts. All the fresh country air must have addled his brain, and that wasn't a good thing.

He shook his head as he approached the stream where they'd fished. There was a nervous energy about him that could only be explained by the need to see Nora again.

He dismounted from Bergamot and checked his pocket watch. He smiled when he heard the thunder of hoofbeats approaching from behind. When he turned, Nora was galloping toward him. Her sure seat on her horse was a thing of beauty. She had changed her riding habit to one of browns and greens. It was subdued, much like her from a distance. But the closer she came to his side, the more elaborate the habit became. Made of brown and gold brocades and silk, the garment spoke of wealth and status.

Another piece of the puzzle that that didn't fit with his first impression of Venus.

With cheeks reddened from the wind, she came to a halt before him. "I saw you check your timepiece." She laughed as she caught her breath. "I'll have you know, sir, that I'm never late, or at least, I try not to be."

"I'd have waited for years just to capture a glimpse of you in that riding habit."

At his compliment, she blushed prettily. "Thank you."

"Why did you change?" he asked as he mounted Bergamot, ready to take her to his hunting lodge.

"Well...I thought it might be more comfortable." Suddenly interested in the tree they kissed under, Nora wouldn't look at him.

He took the moment to study her riding habit a bit closer. It buttoned down the front, another example of the superb quality of the garment. It was expensive and would be something she could easily put on herself...or he could take off her without much effort. He gripped the reins tightly at such thoughts.

"It's very becoming, but I believe you'd look lovely in a horse blanket," he said softly.

Her eyes brightened at the comment, and a true grin flashed across her face.

"Come, Venus," he coaxed, "Let's ride."

Without a moment's hesitation, she coaxed her mare into a gallop. He did the same with Bergamot. As soon as they reached his land, he showed her the apple and cherry orchards, then the mill that set next to the river. He explained that they were his favorite parts of the area but didn't say that they belonged to him.

Finally, they reached the hunting lodge. The sun was setting low in the sky. Wisps of pink, purple, and orange clouds decorated the sky like satin ribbons painted across the horizon.

"I thought I knew everything in this corner of the world. But I haven't seen this. What is this place?" Her hand rested above her heart. "It's beautiful here."

He dismounted then reached for her. "It's a hunting lodge that I...I borrowed from a friend. No one will disturb us here."

"Excellent," Nora said confidently as her lithe body slid into his arms.

As her chest met his, her jasmine fragrance twined around him. Immediately, he stiffened, keeping Nora suspended against his chest. A surge of need ricocheted through every particle of his being. This was something completely different from the usual desire he felt when he held a lovely woman in his arms.

"Is something wrong?" she asked, studying his features.

Marcus closed his eyes and pulled her tighter against him. He forced himself to breathe through his nose. *Everything is wrong.*

Yet, it all felt so right somehow.

Bloody hell.

The only way to purge this unique gnawing and aggravating need that held him captive was to have her in his bed tonight.

Nine

With a confident stride, Nora entered the lodge, though her heart pounded with relentless thuds, warning her to be careful. It wasn't that she was afraid of Marcus. Quite the contrary. He was like an addictive elixir, the kind that bubbled and fizzed, making every part of her overflow in effervescence.

But her heart kept beating wildly against her ribs. The blasted organ tried its best to break free and rush into his arms. She had to remember these two weeks were a gift, and she planned to do a lot of unwrapping. But she could not afford attachment. Her gaze skirted to his as he followed her into the quaint lodge. Immediately, he started to build a fire. With an assured expertise, he stacked the wood, took the tinderbox off the mantel, then with a flick of the flint against the steel, he ignited the tinder that surrounded the wood.

He made the task look simple. She'd seen the footmen at Pelham Hall prepare fires for the family thousands of times, but never really noticed how intricate the steps were of such a task. Marcus rested on his haunches, and each movement of his arms emphasized his athletic gracefulness. With a nod, he brushed his hands against one another, then stood with an elegance that would make a prima danseur envious.

His gaze met hers, and he smiled. "Didn't think I could accomplish the task?"

"Of course." A farmer knew all about such domestic tasks. She half-shrugged and gave a playful grin in return. "If you ever find yourself in need of employment, you should seek a position at Pelham Hall. They always need good footmen. Plus, the ducal livery would look quite fetching on you."

His laughter filled the air. The rich, dark velvet sound provided more warmth than the newly built fire. "I'll have to remember that. Have you been to Pelham Hall?"

"Of course. Everyone has around here," she answered as she turned her attention to the window overlooking a small pond. It wasn't technically a falsehood.

"And you like the footmen's livery?"

She gasped softly when she'd realized that he'd closed the distance between them. No matter how many minutes or hours they shared together, she would never grow accustomed to his size. His body and his presence seemed to make the room shrink. What once she'd considered to be a relatively large hunting abode now seemed like a one-room cottage.

His blue eyes sparkled with mirth as he cupped her cheeks. His thumbs brushed slowly over her skin. "What is it exactly that you like about the livery?"

"From what I remember, the attire is very elegant. The coats are of the finest gray silk with gold frogs and crimson cuffs." She waggled her eyebrows. "The black knee breeches with white silk stockings and buckled shoes show a pretty leg. They're a nice accompaniment to the coats. No bright colors. I heard the Duke of Pelham doesn't want his footmen looking like preening peacocks nor does he want them receiving more attention than he does."

"My word, you're a minx." Marcus leaned close to her ear, his soft breath tickling the tender skin. "I've seen those footmen. Their uniforms are very subdued compared to some of the livery used in the fine houses of London. Do you like subtleness in your men?" He pressed a whisper of a kiss against her tender skin.

Like a cat seeking heat, she rubbed her cheek against his. The hint of bristles sent prickles over her skin, strengthening her desire and the need to get closer to him. Even in a crowded country assembly, she'd know his presence even if she couldn't see him. His aura was that powerful.

In response, he pressed an open mouthed kiss against her neck. Immediately, she tilted her neck, giving him greater access to her skin.

"I favor men who know what they want and go after it. I find the trait equally attractive in women as well," she purred. "What do you think?"

"I think I want to taste your lips," he growled. He wrapped her in his embrace and pressed his mouth to hers.

With a slight moan, she melted against him. She trailed her tongue across his lips, and he opened for her. When her tongue swept in, his was waiting. In a duel of sensations, their tongues parried and thrusted against one another. She'd always found the art of fencing to be somewhat erotic with the elegant movement of the fencers battling against each other, much like they were taking part in a physical and mental game of chess, each player trying to outmaneuver the other. But with this kiss, there would be two winners and no losers.

She wrapped her hands around his neck. The hard breadth of his chest welcomed her soft curves. One of Marcus's hands slowly slid down her backside until he grasped her bottom and drew her closer to his groin. She canted her hips against his hard length, trying to ease the ache between her legs.

Slowly, he broke away from her.

If only she had the talent to paint. She would sketch then paint the smoldering desire that gleamed in his eyes. No wonder women fancied pieces of jewelry painted of their lover's eye. Such a vision would guarantee her future would never be lonely if she had such a remembrance of him.

He touched his finger to her lower lip and traced the curves. "What are you thinking?"

She leaned into his touch and nipped his finger, then sucked.

"Christ," he exhaled.

She leaned her head against his chest and laughed. "I was thinking that I wished I had my sketch pad here. I'd draw the desire in your eyes and then I'd take it to someone who paints miniatures and put it in a pin."

The heavy lashes that shadowed his cheeks rose slowly. "Why?"

"As a way to remember our time together."

"Do you think our days will be worth such a keepsake?"

She traced her finger down each silver waistcoat button. "They're priceless to me."

"You said no attachments." His voice had deepened as he said the words slowly. "Have you changed your mind?"

It was difficult to tell whether he wanted more or was warning her away from expecting more from him. He needn't worry. She was adamant about no attachments...for now.

"No." She gracefully stepped out of his embrace and laughed. "I've come to realize in our short time together that I enjoy you. Why shouldn't I keep these memories close?"

He narrowed his eyes and stared at her. "What if I fail you?"

"You won't. All I want is to have a marvelous time these next ten days together." She proceeded into the kitchen, then halted. A table had been set with beautiful fine china, silverware, and food fit for the King.

She whirled around. "Did you do all of this?"

"I did." He bowed slightly. "I wanted this to be special for you. I plan to feed you before..."

"Before we go to bed," she offered helpfully.

"The things you say," he murmured while rubbing a hand on the back of his neck. "I was going to say before we got to know one another better. I've never heard anyone say what they think as freely as you do."

"*It's not a bad thing.*" Honoria straightened her shoulders as the overwhelming urge to defend herself made her pulse pound. While in exile, she'd changed from the docile child she'd been to a spirited young woman who said what she believed. She'd also changed since she left finishing school. She'd decided that she would never allow herself to be at the mercy of another. It was one of the reasons why she was working hard to find the old duke's letter. "My brother taught me never to become a shrinking violet. A wilted violet barely deserves any notice at all."

"Nora." He chuckled as he put up his hands in a defensive manner.

"I'm not judging but making an observation." A half-smile tugged at the corner of his mouth. Nonchalantly, he strolled to her side and took her hand. Slowly, he raised it to his lips. "Truce, darling."

The press of his lips against her knuckles soothed her anger, and the tenderness of his touch made her stomach perform an endless loop of somersaults.

"You, sir, are a master of diplomacy." She gently pulled her hand away.

"I'm simply a man who knows when the odds and facts are stacked against him," he said as he pulled out a chair. "After you."

She sat at the table and placed a serviette on her lap as Marcus served her. There were deviled partridge eggs, sauteed potatoes with parsley, roasted carrots, and roasted chicken.

He poured them both a glass of red wine and lifted his glass in the air. "To you."

"And you." She lifted her glass in return. Together, they took a sip. By the taste, it was an excellent Bordeaux. Her gentleman farmer knew his wines. "You said earlier that you dreamt about me. You've only known me for a day and a night."

"Of course, I dreamt about you." He cut a piece of chicken and popped it into his mouth.

"Of course, you did," Honoria answered, a tad sarcastically. She didn't believe him for a second. She narrowed her eyes and bit her lip to keep from laughing aloud. "I'm so relieved that I'm in your dreams and not your nightmares."

"Hush, woman," he said and leaned close with a piece of chicken on his fork. "Taste."

"You are the very definition of officious," she grumbled slightly, then opened her mouth for the bite. The intimacy of eating from his fork didn't escape her. Lovers shared like this. As soon as the flavors melted on her tongue, she closed her eyes to enjoy them. "Heaven."

"I'm lucky enough to have a cook who knows how to create masterpieces."

"My compliments to him or her." She tilted her head. "I wonder what your cook could have done with the trout?"

Marcus said with a laugh, "I humbly apologize for allowing the fish to escape." He lifted a hand to the middle of his chest. "I'm trying to find a place in your good graces." He waved a hand across the table. "Obviously, the way to a woman's heart is not through her stomach." He leaned close. "Perhaps it's by giving her compliments."

"Only if they're sincere," she instructed.

He winked then took her hand. "You are beautiful."

A man was flirting with her, and she was flirting with him in return. My God, such simple joys she'd missed throughout the years. Marcus sat before her with an expression that made her feel that there was no place in this entire world he'd rather be than sitting at this table, spending time with her.

When she leaned close, he mimicked her movement. He brought his mouth to within an inch to hers. She couldn't resist and leaned a little closer to him.

"You're too bold, sir," she whispered. "The way to *this* lady's heart is through her stomach. Now, please share the deviled eggs."

"A kiss first," he answered with a wry smile.

"All right." She'd softened her voice, hoping to elevate the intimacy between them. She could easily become addicted to sharing evenings with a man.

But not just anyone. Only him.

Before he could press his lips to hers, three sharp knocks sounded.

Her gaze flew to the door. No one was supposed to know that they were here.

Marcus must have sensed her shock and stood quickly. "I'll see who it is and send them on their way."

"Is there a place for me to…wait?"

"Any of the rooms upstairs." He pointed to the staircase.

Without making a sound, she rose from the table and ascended the stairs. Once she reached the top step and out of sight, Honoria stood silent.

Light fell into the main room as Marcus opened the door. He stepped across the threshold and closed it, casting the room in shadows again. By the sound of the muffled conversation, two men had come to visit. She leaned against the wall and concentrated. The word "fire" and "blacksmith" were mentioned.

Within seconds, Marcus walked through the door again and stood at the bottom of the stairs. He tilted his gaze to hers. "I must go. There's been an accident." He ran a hand through his hair.

As fast as humanly possible, she flew down the steps. "What is it?"

"A fire has broken out in a barn at Woodbury Park." Worry radiated from his eyes.

"No one lives there," she said.

Quickly, he looked out the window in the direction the men were heading. "It was sold recently. They need my help." Marcus looked to the door and then back to Honoria. "I can't escort you home."

"Go," she said gently. "I'll clean up here and see myself home."

The lines across his brow and eyes eased. He put on his coat, then brushed a kiss across one cheek. "Thank you. Let's meet here tomorrow at the same time." He nodded his goodbye, then was out the door.

In mere seconds, he was galloping across the meadow toward the estate. She could smell the smoke and there was a dark, menacing haze floating in the sky. The fire had to be massive, particularly, since they came for Marcus's help. Honoria watched until his figure was out of sight. She put out the fire then cleaned up the remnants of their meal. After she'd washed and dried the dishes, she reset the table with the fine china and wine glasses.

If Pelham could see her now, he'd suffer a case of apoplexy. He wouldn't stand for one of his sisters performing domestic chores. However, Honoria had been doing those "chores" for years. When in London, she had stayed out of her father's way by hiding in the kitchen. Their French cook, Claude, had made a special seating area for Honoria where she would read and visit with the kitchen staff. Claude had taken her under his wing and had even allowed her to help him prepare meals. Her father had never found her hiding place.

She glanced out the window. A spiraling tower of smoke was ascending skyward. She quickly said a prayer, asking that no one be injured. Even though their acquaintance was less than two days, she would be distraught if anything happened to him. How had he become so vital to her in such a short period of time?

It had to be infatuation.

With one last look at their meeting place, she stepped outside and closed the door. The mare waited for her with a look of expectation. She pulled the horse close to a mounting block, then hoisted herself into her sidesaddle. With a click of her tongue, they started for home. At the main road, she turned toward Pelham Hall.

Over the rise, an open landau lumbered closer. It was the Earl of Carlyle and his mother. *Of all the rotten luck.* She debated whether to turn the mare around and gallop in the other direction. By then it was too late. The carriage was almost upon her. She drew her horse to a stop and smiled sweetly.

"Lady Honoria, hello." He waved at her with his hat, then turned to his mother. "*Maman*, look whom fate has brought to us."

The earl's mother hmphed loud enough that Honoria heard it. The dowager countess lifted her hand and waved it with a weak flick or her wrist. Whether it was a wave toward Honoria in welcome or to shoo her away, it was hard to tell. By the set of the countess's mouth, it was probably the later.

"Good afternoon, Lord Carlyle. Lady Carlyle." Honoria dipped her head in both their directions.

"Beautiful afternoon for a ride." The warmth in the earl's smile echoed in his voice. "*Maman* and I are enjoying it as well."

The countess sprouted a contemptuous smile. "Riding alone, Lady Honoria?" She glanced around the vehicle. "Not a groomsman in sight."

"No, Lady Carlyle. It's the country. Around here, we try not to put on airs," Honoria answered sweetly.

"In my day, we never went anywhere without a proper escort. Country or not." She huffed her disapproval. The old lady's eyes narrowed. "Does the duke know that you cavort about on your own?"

Feeling her fury start to boil, Honoria made a fist with her hand as she clasped the reins. She wouldn't allow the old virago to needle her any further. "Do you mean does the duke know that I'm calling on his tenants on his behalf? That cavorting?" She didn't allow her treacle-sweet smile to waver. "Indeed, he does."

Finally, the earl spoke up. "Isn't Lady Honoria's mare a beauty?"

"Hmm." The dowager countess peered over the side of the landau and studied the mare, then Honoria. The woman looked at Honoria like she was evaluating a pile of horse dung. Honoria straightened in her saddle as a shiver clambered up her back. Her horse could feel the tension and whinnied. Honoria reached out and patted Florence's shoulder in comfort.

"Isn't that the same horse we saw at the hunting lodge we passed an hour ago?" This time her gaze landed on her son. "Wasn't there another horse there as well?"

Honoria's heart started to gallop for the hills. Just as she longed to do.

The earl shook his head slightly, but then his eyes widened as he finally realized what his mother was insinuating. His gaze slowly turned to Honoria.

"What hunting lodge?" Honoria asked innocently.

The one that belongs to Woodbury Park," Lord Carlyle answered with a gleam of curiosity.

She'd learned from her brother that the best defense was to attack the other party and try to put them off-balance. "Come now, my lord." She leaned forward in her saddle and chuckled softly. "Surely you're aware that bays are one of the most popular colors for horseflesh in all the British Isles. Around Pelham Hall, we have dozens of them."

"Quite right." The earl chuckled.

The countess pressed another treacle smile to her lips. "My mistake." She arched a scrawny aristocratic eyebrow. "However, I could have sworn that the bay we passed had the same star on its forehead as your mare."

The old biddy was taunting her. Florence had been tied to the lodge's lean-to with her rear facing the road. "I'm afraid not, Lady Carlyle. I was visiting the Middleton family." She reeled the mare around. "I must be off. It was so lovely to see you."

Without waiting for the earl or his mother to say goodbye, Honoria clicked her tongue. Immediately, Florence took off. She gave the horse its lead, and soon they were galloping across the fields on their way back to Pelham Hall. She turned her head slightly in the direction of Woodbury Park where the smoke still rose. Thankfully, the swirls were no longer black but had faded to a light gray. That meant the fire was under control. She brought Florence to a stop and gazed at the estate in the distance. So, Marcus had borrowed the lodge from a friend. Whoever owned Woodbury Park was Marcus's friend. She'd ask her brother who had bought it.

The answer would give her a clue to Marcus's identity. Though her curiosity rivaled a cat's, she shouldn't do it. She had demanded that he not tell her who he was. It wouldn't be fair.

By the position of the sun in the sky, she should hurry home.

Tomorrow, she'd find a way to ride over to Woodbury Park. Even if she couldn't see Marcus, she'd feel closer to him just knowing he'd been there. Honoria chuckled to herself. Funny how her hours were devoted to seeing Marcus.

She liked having the freedom to visit whom she liked and for how long. However, she couldn't count on her brother being gone for more than two weeks. He always returned home to Pelham Hall earlier than expected. She had to be prepared.

Which meant, the next time she saw Marcus, she would take him to bed.

Ten

Marcus reviewed the list of materials that had to be purchased to repair the stables. It was an exceptionally detailed list that even went as far as estimating the number of nails that would be required. The young land steward, Dalton Winthrop, sat across the desk from Marcus. He'd been employed at the estate for the last five years.

"Is there anything I missed?" Winthrop asked.

Marcus signed his name to the list and handed it back to the young man. "I don't believe so. Anything that is needed to complete the job as quickly and expeditiously as possible, purchase it. We need the building rebuilt as soon as possible."

The young man nodded and took the list. "I understand, sir. I wouldn't want my horseflesh at another barn. Thankfully, the Marquess of Ravenscroft's and the Duke of Pelham's stables are large enough to accommodate yours."

Marcus stood and so did Winthrop. "They're good men and friends. They won't mind it in the least."

The young steward took his leave. Immediately, Marcus started to put away the journals and accountings for Woodbury Park. It was a profitable place, and the servants and the tenants were loyal. He was determined to keep the property in top condition.

The longcase clock in the study chimed the hour of four. Marcus's eyes widened. He'd completely forgotten about meeting Nora. He ran a hand through his hair, wishing there was a way for him to turn back the hands of time. All day, he'd been working in his study. He'd been consumed with the repairs of his stables. *Damnation.* Nora would have been waiting for him for hours if she was still there.

"Humphrey?" he called out.

Immediately, his butler swept into the study. "Yes, my lord?"

"Will you ask that Bergamot be saddled immediately?" He was the only horse that Marcus hadn't sent to Pelham's stables. It would be like cutting off his right hand. Not only was the cantankerous fellow his best mount, but Bergamot had been through every major life hurdle in Marcus's life. Plus, he was the fastest horse Marcus owned...if he was in the mood to race.

"I'll see to it immediately," Humphrey said with a bow.

"One other thing? Will you ask Cook to prepare another basket for me?"

"Again, for two, my lord?" The butler's face didn't reveal a hint of censure or curiosity.

"Yes." Marcus didn't normally share any of his personal business, but desperate times for called desperate measures. "Have you ever heard of someone living in this area with the first name of Lenora or Nora? Perhaps a farmer's daughter or local gentry?"

Humphrey's brow crinkled as he considered the question. After a moment, he shook his head. "No, sir. I can ask Cook. He's been around a lot longer than we have."

"Thank you." Marcus exhaled a silent sigh.

The butler nodded once, then left.

Hopefully, she'd had the patience to wait for him. If not, then he'd hire investigators in

London to see if they could locate her. How difficult would it be to find Venus? It'd be damned difficult if she didn't want to be found. She might have given him a false name. She'd chosen not to be forthcoming with personal details about her life.

Tonight, he would tell her who he was. Hopefully, she'd tell him the same.

Within minutes, he was on Bergamot, galloping toward his hunting lodge. The sky was turning darker with storms rolling in. The black clouds off to the west were thick and hung low on the horizon. He held his breath as they crested the hill that overlooked the lodge.

He smiled in relief. Nora was still there since Florence was resting in one of the stalls of the lean-to. After he and Bergamot came to a halt at the lodge, he made quick work of placing the stallion in the stall next to Florence. Nora's mare peeked around the corner and neighed. Bergamot returned the greeting, then threw his head. Normally, his horse didn't like other horses near him, but the mare seemed to be the exception. Before he made his way to the lodge, Marcus patted Bergamot then did the same to Nora's horse.

"Take care of each other," he murmured as he untied the food basket from his saddle.

As soon as Marcus entered the lodge, he started to call out, "Nor—" but immediately grew silent when he saw her curled up in a chair fast asleep with a book resting on her lap. He placed the basket on the small wooden table, then knelt by her side.

Her eyes fluttered open, and a soft smile tugged at her lips. "You're here."

When he cupped her cheek, she leaned into his palm. Her warmth cast a peacefulness over him that he hadn't experienced since the fire. "Yes, finally."

With a catlike grace, she stretched her arms over her head. "I thought you'd forgotten."

"Forgive me for being late," he said softly as he took her hand. In tandem, they stood together.

Gently, she placed her index finger on his lips. "No apology."

When he pulled her close, her curves melded against his body. Instantly, he was reminded of his long-forgotten home. The sudden urge to ask her to visit his ancestral seat came from nowhere, but he didn't voice it. He didn't even know her full name.

"I would have expected you to rail at me for my carelessness," he murmured as he rubbed his lips against the softness of her hair. "I should at least buy you a piece of jewelry to make up for the inconvenience."

She leaned away with a puzzled look on her face. "Why would you do that?" A moue of displeasure pursed her lips. "That is what a man gives his mistress."

"I wasn't thinking of you as a mistress," he countered softly. "My father made a habit of giving my mother..." He let the words trail to nothing.

Nora suddenly grinned. "You were about to say that he gave her jewelry if she was peeved at him. I'm not your wife, nor am I angry with you."

His heart stumbled at the lightheartedness in her voice. "What are you?" The question was out before he had time to reconsider what he was saying.

She smoothed her hands up and down his chest, then turned her bright gaze his way. "I'm your friend and, hopefully soon, your lover."

He sucked in a breath. Women had always wanted him but never had one ever claimed to be his friend. But from her, he believed it.

Truth be told, he could see her as his wife.

"Nora," he said on an exhale, "you are the most unique person I've ever met."

"That's a good thing," she said as she stood on her toes and pressed her lips to his. Without removing her mouth from his, she continued, "I very much want to be extraordinary."

He hugged her tight as she wrapped her hands around his neck.

"You are exceptional." He leaned down and took her mouth with his.

When she moaned, he slipped his tongue between her lips. She tangled hers in his in a dance that set his blood on fire. His Nora was a fast learner. Every part of him heated as he explored every part of her mouth. It felt right to be here with her.

He slowly pulled away, and she whimpered in distress.

"Hungry?" he asked.

"For you," she said. "Show me the upstairs." Her lashes fell, then slowly opened. The air around them seemed charged with an electrical current. "That's what I want." She took his hand and studied it for a moment. All the while, her thumb caressed his skin. "I want all of it." She slowly raised her gaze to his. "You're all I've thought about, and I want you to be my first lover."

He squeezed her hand as a lurch of desire made him dizzy. "That implies you'll take another."

She shrugged, and the heat of her gaze revealed a smoldering desire that seemed to make the flecks of gold in her blue eyes dance. It was the most erotic sight that he'd ever seen.

"It might also imply that you'll be the only one I'll ever have. Neither of us knows what tomorrow might bring, but we have tonight." She tugged him toward the stairs. "I want you to teach me everything."

Marcus didn't show her the rest of the lodge. As soon as they had ascended the stairs, he led her into the first bedroom and closed the door. It was more intimate that way. As he started a fire in the fireplace, he realized he was nervous. He'd never been with a woman who didn't have experience. Just thinking he'd be the first to possess her caused his cock to harden even more if that was possible. But as a gentleman, he couldn't go forward without her understanding all the ramifications.

The fire was finally blazing. Slowly, he stood and turned to her. She stood so confident by the bed without a hint of embarrassment or doubt. A flash of lightning lit the room as if a hundred candles were in a chandelier above them. In that moment, she looked like a queen from another world bathed in light from the beyond. He shook his head at the fantastical ideas that were filling his brain. By then, Nora had lit a candle on the nightstand.

"Nora." At the sound of her name, she took a step forward, but he halted her by raising his hand. "Before we proceed, we must have a frank discussion of what's going to happen."

"All right."

"Take a good look at me." As he waved a hand from his chest to his groin, her gaze slid down the length of him.

Her eyes flickered in awareness at the state of his arousal, and her nostrils flared as she took a deep breath. She might be angry with him, but she needed to understand that there would be no going back if they did this.

"When I take you"—he lowered his voice—"you'll leave the bed a different woman."

"It'll be that earth-shattering?" She arched a perfect eyebrow, then laughed softly. "Perhaps you'll leave the bed a different man?"

"I have no doubt." He ran a hand over his face. He sounded like an arrogant arse. "I didn't mean to sound so full of myself. Did your mother discuss what happens when a man and a woman...?"

A blush bludgeoned her cheeks at his words.

He didn't finish. She was shaking her head so hard he thought she might hurt her neck.

"No." She straightened her shoulders and regarded him with a poise queens would envy. "However, I've grown up around farms, and I'm well-read. I know what will happen." Still slightly nervous, she gently chewed her lower lip as she met his gaze.

Every nuanced emotion and movement she made was driving him mad. He let out a frustrated sigh.

"I don't want...there to be a chance of a child." There was a hint of vulnerability in her voice.

"Neither do I," he murmured. "I'll not come inside you. But there's always a chance."

Her eyes grew hooded. "I trust you."

"When I said that you'd leave the bed a different woman, what I meant was that you can never go back after we make love."

A crack of thunder vibrated through the room. It could have been a warning from heaven that it was about to condemn him for even offering such a blaspheme.

"I want all of it." She lifted a hand, an invitation for him to join her. "Help me undress," she commanded softly.

He'd grant Nora her due. The woman wore self-assurance like a perfectly fitted gown or perhaps, it was a shield. She might keep secrets, but he was finished with them. If he showed her a little trust, perhaps she'd do the same.

"All right," he said as he closed the distance between them. "Turn around."

She did as asked, presenting him with a row of buttons down her dress. From the soft silk, the exquisite stitches, and the detail of the buttons, he could tell that her dress was expensive. Her dress would be perfect for an aristocratic lady of London to wear as she made her morning calls.

She shivered slightly as he cupped his hands over her shoulders.

"Nervous?" he asked.

She turned her head to meet his gaze. "Just aware of you." Then Nora rested her hand over his, and Marcus's own body shivered, much like Bergamot before a race. But there was a huge difference. This wasn't a race. He'd ensure that she was well and truly pleasured.

And that took time.

Time he looked forward to.

Eleven

Honoria hadn't been entirely honest with Marcus or herself. She was nervous. She'd never undressed in front of a man before. Of course, she'd undressed in front of Alice and Pippa, but it was like comparing apples to lemons.

Fortunately, she had a hardy constitution, so she'd escaped examinations performed by a doctor. But the idea that Marcus would see her naked was a little daunting, to say the least.

Slowly, he unbuttoned the back of her gown. His nimble fingers brushing against her skin. She hunched her shoulders slightly at the contact of his warm skin against hers.

"Relax," he murmured, pressing his lips to the back of her neck. "You can undress me next."

"You'll have me at a disadvantage, sir. I'll be completely naked while you're dressed."

He chuckled gently, then pressed a kiss to her shoulder. "You see that as unfair? I see it as a gift. It'll be like the best Christmas feast ever, as I'll devour you with my eyes."

The deep rumble of his voice vibrated against the soft skin below one ear. Wrapping an arm around her waist, he brought her body flush to his. Her softness met the hard planes of his body, including his erection. Slowly, she inhaled, reminding herself to memorize this moment and the ones to come tonight. She'd tuck them away, perhaps in a private journal that she could reread on cold nights when she found herself alone.

Marcus skimmed his hands over her shoulders, pushing her dress down where it puddled to the floor in a soft *swoosh* of silk. She turned to face him. "Allow me to undress you now."

"I'll allow it if you pay the toll."

"What toll is that?" She ran her hand down his chest.

"A kiss." With a half-smile tugging at the corners of his mouth, he looked like a schoolboy who'd gotten caught reading naughty books under the stairwell.

"Very well." She stood on tiptoe. When he moved to press his lips to hers, she drew away. "I give the kiss."

"You know what you want," he said with a chuckle. "I've always found that extremely seductive in a woman."

A flash of jealousy roared through her. "Have there been many women in your past?"

"A few," he murmured. "But no one worth remembering. Not when you're here."

"And after our time together is over?" Her years of deportment lessons told her that she shouldn't press him on this unsuitable topic of conversation. Yet, she couldn't stop herself.

He wrapped his arms about her. "I'll always remember you." He tilted her chin slightly until their gazes met. The seriousness in his expression caught her off-guard. "For some unfathomable reason, you're different. I've never wanted a woman the way I want you."

"Is that a compliment?" She didn't take her gaze from his. His dilated pupils hid the flecks of silver that made his dark blue eyes so unique.

"Yes."

Before she could ask more, a blinding flash of light followed a deafening clap of thunder. It was so loud that the walls of the lodge vibrated. But instead of the lightning diminishing, it seemed to be growing in intensity.

"What was that?" she asked.

"I think lightning hit a tree," Marcus said as he strolled to the window, then pulled the muslin curtains aside. "It had to be some distance away. The horses are safe."

His eyes grew hooded as he came back to her side. "Do you know what I enjoy?"

"Tell me," Honoria said.

"Storms. Do you know what I would adore more?" His voice had grown husky. He trailed the back of his hand across her cheek. "Being in bed with you where we will create our own tempests."

She moved closer to him, compelled by her desire to touch him. Tonight was her destiny. She wouldn't waste another minute being missish about spending the night with Marcus.

Honoria presented her back once again. "Let's hurry then."

Marcus pressed his warm lips against her skin. "A woman after my own heart."

For a minute, she stilled as he made quick work of untying her stays. She would not allow herself to examine his words too closely. His heart was guarded by an infantry of hurt. To think she might be the one to break through his invisible fortress was ridiculous. But she could pretend she meant something to him, at least for the hours they had left.

As the last tie was undone, she took a deep breath as her breasts were released from their jail.

Laughing, she turned around to face him. "Your turn."

His eyes slowly swept down her body, marking her, possessing her without even touching her. She couldn't look away. Everything fizzled inside of her like a glass of champagne.

Slowly, his gaze met hers as he discarded his coat. "You're beautiful."

"So are you." She released the silver buttons of his waistcoat, then pushed it off his shoulders. As she examined the breadth of his chest, her stomach swooped just like when she took a high jump on the back of Florence. She inhaled his clean scent. All her life she'd waited for this moment, a spec of time to be embraced by a man who wanted her.

That was what defined life. At least, it was for her. The desire to belong to another, even if it was for only one night. She would not allow herself to consider wanting more, no matter what her greedy heart wanted. She'd made an agreement with herself, and she would keep it.

While Marcus flicked open the top two buttons of his breeches, his eyes never left hers.

However, she dipped her gaze. There was no chance she would miss the unveiling of his body. The swell of his erection was *huge* as it pressed against the falls of his breeches. Her breathing grew ragged as the fall slipped down, and he continued to undo the buttons.

Then the dastardly man chuckled, *actually chuckled*, as he bent over slightly and pulled both boots from his legs. His keen sense of balance would have made a grocer's scale envious.

"Patience, love," he said. "All things come in good time."

"But you've seen a woman before." Her gaze darted to his. "I've never seen a man."

When he whipped off his shirt, her breath caught. The cords of sinew and the contour of his muscles made her fingers itch to reach across the distance and discover each dip and swell of his chest. His small, dark brown nipples were so different from hers, yet firm and hard. Just like hers.

"I may have seen other women, Nora," Marcus drawled softly, "but I've never seen you. That in and of itself is a treasure that none have ever experienced, much like the holy grail." He took a step back and smiled. "So, I'm as anxious as you for our mutual unveiling. Now, shall I help you with your chemise?"

"I'll do it." She gathered her chemise into folds until she grasped the hem. Biting back a moan as the soft silk of the garment brushed against her nipples, she pulled it higher and higher up her body. Who would have ever thought that silk could be a torture device?

If she wasn't mistaken, he growled.

Finally, she whipped it over her head. She glanced down at her body and shivered slightly.

"You're not simply beautiful. Stunning is a better description." He stepped forward and took her in his arms. The touch of his soft lips, and the warmth from his hot body melted whatever remaining reluctance might have been buried deep inside.

Honoria gasped at the sensation, and his tongue swept into her mouth, coaxing her to match his movements. She pushed her center against his cock, desperate to feel more of him. When his length pressed against the wetness that grew between her legs, Marcus groaned. He seemed to be pleased that she was in such a state.

Without their mouths breaking from each other, he swept her into his arms. In two strides, he was beside the bed. He gently laid her across the covers. Then, finally then, he lowered his breeches.

The daze of desire she'd been under suddenly waned as she caught her first glimpse of his hard length and girth. Firm and engorged, it stood proudly.

How would such a thing even fit inside her?

Marcus reached down, grasped it by the root, and tugged. A dot of pearly liquid appeared at the top. She licked her lips. Funny, but the longer she regarded it, the more her desire grew. Without a second thought, she extended her arms. "Please, don't make me wait."

A devilish smile creased his lips, and he slid onto the bed beside her. With an innate grace, he gathered her in his arms and kissed her again. It was simply heaven.

Leaning away, he studied her. "Now, what do you desire, Venus?"

"You," she said confidently, then reached up and took his head between her hands. He deepened the kiss. His weight and the length of his body kept her floating in a cloud of exquisite sensations.

Marcus trailed his lips across her cheeks before slipping down her neck. When his tongue found her pulse at the base of her neck, he pressed his lips there, then tongued it. She arched her hips until her center met his hardness. In that instant, she understood what her body had been craving all those nights when she'd thought about making love with a man. When her own body had grown wet with thoughts of kisses and embraces, it had been preparing itself for this.

With his mouth, he explored her body, down her chest, never taking his eyes off hers. As he moved lower, she whimpered slightly.

"You'll like this, I promise," he whispered. When he reached her chest, he studied her breasts.

While she wasn't endowed like some of the other women her age, she was proud of her body. She was proportioned well, and she was strong. She could ride a horse for hours and never shied away from work of any kind.

"Look at you," he crooned softly. He nuzzled the soft flesh and then tongued her nipple. "Pink and more delicious than I could have ever imagined." His gaze locked with hers, he took one nipple in his mouth and sucked.

She practically flew through the air as pleasure exploded through her body.

With his other hand, he fondled the other breast. She moaned when he gently ran his teeth over the hardened nipple. Still playing with her, he leaned back, his eyes wide. "My God, you have freckles."

She crinkled her brow. She'd always been cursed with them, but she'd never really thought much about the effect they'd have on a man. Particularly Marcus. Trying to hide her consternation, she asked, "Is something the matter with them?"

"Oh, darling," he purred. "They're magnificent and a sight to behold." He traced a pattern with his finger, circling around one nipple, then the other. "They're unique like you."

The smile on his face should be outlawed. He seemed to relish every aspect of her, and anything he wanted to do, she was game for it.

He continued to slide down her body, kissing her stomach, tonguing her navel, and tasting each hip. "Spread your legs." His voice was gravelly, sending a riot of sensations cascading through every inch of her.

She parted her legs and, instantly, he fit his chest between them. It was an odd position, but she wanted to learn everything with him.

"Have you ever read about men kissing women here?" He pressed his lips to her mons.

She shook her head. "No, but I like it when I touch myself there."

"Show me." The darkness in his voice thickened with desire.

Slowly, she slid her hand down her stomach. Every inch of her skin burned.

His gaze turned feral.

She combed her fingers through her nest of curls until they were coated with her arousal. A moan escaped.

"That's it. Show me." He gently spread her legs wider.

She circled the sensitive nub leisurely, teasing him as much as herself.

"Let me try," he said softly. "Watch me." A knowing smile curled one side of his mouth.

Honoria couldn't tear her eyes away as he lowered his head. She lifted her hips as soon as his tongue licked her tender flesh. Instantly, her body buzzed as if electrified. Marcus was enjoying her like a fine wine.

With his mouth, he supped.

With his tongue, he teased.

She grabbed his hair, steering him to the most sensitive spot. He chuckled at her determination, his breath on her skin another delight.

She was close. "Marcus," she begged. She was desperate to reach her climax.

As he continued to please her, he pushed two fingers into her sheath.

Her muscles clenched automatically.

"Christ." His voice was deep as he withdrew his fingers.

She cried out at the loss. Instantly, he entered her again, this time with three fingers. She arched her back, needing more. She was like an archer's bow, taut and ready to fire.

He sucked her tender nub until her body flew apart into a million pieces. Nothing was in her control as she cried out his name.

Finally, her heartbeat and breath slowed. She collapsed on the bed as he pressed kisses along her inner thighs, then up her stomach. He rested his weight on his elbows and regarded her before taking her in another kiss.

She could taste herself on his tongue and lips. It was wicked and sweet at the same time. She wanted more, which meant only one thing.

Honoria was in deep trouble. "What have you done to me?"

Marcus slowly pulled away. Nora's voice had softened like wisps of gossamer floating in the wind. But the shock of her words reverberated around his brain. He'd never hurt her for the world. "Did I injure you?"

By the look on her face, she was terrified, but then coming out of her trance, she shook her head briskly.

"Nora?"

"No...you didn't hurt me. But I didn't expect to feel so much." She blinked slowly and regarded him. "Is it always like that?"

"Not in my experience," he said tentatively.

God, he'd come undone when he'd tasted her. Who was he fooling? He had feasted upon her. He wanted more and more of her. Then he'd shocked her, and perhaps had frightened her. He'd never forgive himself for that.

"Truthfully, I quite liked it. Perhaps a bit too much." She pulled him closer. "Is that bad?"

"Oh, darling, I think that's very, very good." He waggled his eyebrows. "It means we're well-matched."

"We should try it again just to make certain." A coy smile broke across her lips. "But this time, I want..." Her cheeks heated with a delightful blush.

"Tell me," he coaxed. "I'll give you whatever you want."

"Very well. I want you to enjoy it, too."

The sweet sincerity of her smile and the honesty in her eyes made his heart somersault in his chest.

"Please," she said softly. "I want you in me."

They stared at each other for a moment before he could speak again. "We'll take it slow. Anything you don't like, or if you become uncomfortable, tell me, and we'll stop."

"I don't think that will be a problem." She laughed and pulled him down on top of her body. "Please."

He rested on one elbow. "Lift your hips." Taking himself in hand, he drew his cock through her wetness. He closed his eyes as her heat surrounded him. This was torture but heaven at the same time. All he wanted was her. In this bed, they were Nora and Marcus with no need for anything else.

She canted her hips in invitation. He couldn't resist her any longer. He brought his cock to her entrance, then slid inch by inch inside her. He leaned back and tilted her hips higher. It was a better position for her. When her muscles tensed, he stopped. Good Lord, what was the matter with him? He was like a randy untried youth. This was Nora's first time at lovemaking. He should be seducing her with kisses and caresses. Anything to make her more at ease.

He bent at the waist and pressed his lips against hers. "How are you?"

She smiled bravely. "I'm fine."

"You're better than fine, sweetheart." He nibbled at her lips, then slid his tongue across her mouth. When she moaned, he deepened the kiss. As their tongues mated, he pulled her closer. She wrapped her arms around his shoulders and her legs around his waist.

She relaxed. When he fully entered her, she tightened every muscle.

"Good?" he asked.

Her eyes glistened with tears, but she smiled in triumph. "Glorious."

He took her again in a kiss as he slowly pulled out of her, then pushed back in. Purposely gentle, he continued the steady rhythm as he learned what she liked. By now, his brow was covered in sweat, but he didn't care. His only concern was ensuring her pleasure and making this night one that she'd never forget. Every nerve in his body felt electrified. His gaze locked with hers.

When he reached between their bodies and caressed her clitoris, her back arched.

"Please," Honoria pleaded.

She didn't need to beg. He was ready. Marcus started to pump faster as the mindless sensation promising release roared through his body. When she sobbed his name, he pulled out of her with a groan. He held his cock as his seed spilled on her stomach.

Weak as a newborn lamb, he collapsed on the bed beside her and wrapped his arms around her. He kissed her neck and buried his head in her shoulder. Now was the time to tell her who he was. He took the linen toweling on the table beside the bed and cleaned her body with gentle strokes.

She cuddled closer.

He pressed another kiss to the sensitive skin below her ear. It had never been so consuming when he'd made love with other women. He wanted to howl to the moon that she was his, but he couldn't go against her position of no attachments. Perhaps if he told her who he was, she'd change her mind.

"Now that we've shared our bodies, I think we should share our full names." He positioned himself on his side, bending his elbow and resting his head in his hand. "Nora, I'm the Earl of Trafford. I own Woodbury Park." He trailed a finger down the soft skin of her arm. "I know this may sound nonsensical. But I think I'm falling in love with you." She might run at hearing such a confession, but he had to tell her how he felt. "You don't have to share your feelings with me now but tell me who you are."

The only answer he received was her slight snore, signaling she was fast asleep.

"All right, darling." He chuckled while tucking her snug against his chest. "Tomorrow first thing, you can tell me."

Twelve

The cock of a pistol woke Marcus. It had to be a dream. Immediately, the trill of the larks quieted, warning a predator was afoot.

His eyes slid open as he struggled with the sense of the where and why everything felt off.

Of course! He and Nora had slept together last night. They were at his hunting lodge. He inhaled slowly, trying to calm the sudden pounding of his heartbeat.

A low, menacing growl broke through the stillness. Was there a dog in the room? He turned to Nora. She was snuggled close to his side with her hand resting on his chest. The sight was so unbelievably tender he could only stare at her.

"Make peace with this world. Then ask your creator to grant you forgiveness for your sins. Afterward, I'm personally delivering you to Hell."

For the love of God, a butt of a barrel was pressed into his left temple. Suddenly, he recognized the voice.

"Pelham?" Marcus's hoarse whisper broke the morning stillness. "What the devil?"

"The question of the day it appears," Pelham drawled. "What the devil are you doing in bed with my sister?"

"*Sister?*" Marcus shot back in shock. His heartbeat galloped in his chest, probably hoping to outrun the horror unfolding in the room. At that moment, Nora woke up beside him. Her hand on his naked chest immediately tightened, and her eyes widened in horror. "I thought your only sisters were Honoria and Pippa."

"Pelham?" she asked in a whisper.

The pistol dug a little deeper into Marcus's temple. Yet that didn't stop his gaze from whipping between Nora and Pelham. "Are you his sister?"

Both she and Pelham ignored his question. Nora slid across Marcus, placing her body in front of his so she faced her brother.

The fury in Pelham's eyes had darkened the normal blue color to almost black.

"It's not what you think," she said weakly. "Please put away the pistol."

Marcus knew, in that instant, that his minutes were numbered. "You *are* his sister."

"She is." Pelham's gaze turned to Nora. "Honoria, are you naked?" He slammed his eyes shut. "Don't answer. I don't want to know if you're naked or not."

Marcus's first instinct was to protect Nora or Honoria or whoever she was, so he wrapped his arm around her waist. He was signing his own death sentence, yet he wanted to give her reassurance that everything would be all right.

But, frankly, there was nothing reassuring in the situation at all. Confusion and anger blasted through every inch of him. He'd never been in this situation before. The woman he held in his arms was Lady Honoria, the woman who hid from society. According to the rumors, she was supposed to have three heads or three legs or something.

The *ton* was masterful at crafting fabrications that were simply ludicrous. Honoria was exquisite. But this situation was a disaster.

"Don't do anything you'll regret," she said softly to her brother.

"Like you have?"

"Do not talk to her like that." Careful that the bedlinens covered her

JANNA MACGREGOR

body, Marcus pulled Honoria across his body until she was on his other side.

Pelham squeezed his eyes shut. "I saw her shoulder. She's naked." His eyes flew open, and his gaze nailed Marcus in place. "Once I kill you, I'm going to kill you again."

"Pelham." Nora's voice had turned low and guttural, growling in the same manner as her brother.

Marcus closed his eyes, struggling to find a way out of this mess. How could he have been so lackadaisical about her identity? All the signs were there. When Pelham had approached them both that night, she had stiffened like a rabbit caught in the sight of a fox. She even had the same coloring as her brother, blue eyes and blonde hair. But hers was streaked with copper.

When Marcus sat up, the sheet fell to his waist. Instantly, Honoria struggled to keep her chest covered.

"Honoria, what the—?" Pelham stopped suddenly and released a ragged breath. "Just what are you doing here? And with him?" He ran a hand down his face, then scowled at Marcus. "For the love of heaven, you seduced her. Meet me outside." An arrogant eyebrow shot upward. "With a pistol."

"There are rules to a duel. Gloves being slapped in the face. Seconds. Surgeons," she cried. "You cannot shoot him."

"I can and I will. There will be no need for a surgeon." Pelham's clipped voice raised the hair on Marcus's arm.

There had only been one other time when Pelham had been this angry. It was when he had recounted a story about his father berating one of his sisters. He'd told Marcus when they'd returned to school to start a new term.

That sister had to have been Nora, who was originally Venus and now Honoria. This had to be a nightmare. She had too many names. Yet, she'd told Marcus that her father had disliked her. No wonder Pelham was acting this way.

Marcus didn't move his gaze from Pelham. His friend had every right to challenge him to a duel. What he'd done was unforgivable.

"Allow us to dress, and we'll meet you in the study." Marcus could tell by the color of the duke's face he was getting angrier by the minute.

"For your information, he didn't seduce me." Honoria lifted her chin in defiance. "I seduced him."

"*Honor*," her brother exclaimed loudly, then turned to Marcus and sneered. "You have the morals of a tomcat. You've ruined her."

"No one is ruined," Honoria argued.

Now, she had another name. *Honor*? Marcus shook his head, and his stomach clenched in revolt. His entire life had changed in mere moments. He was in real danger of losing his best friend, the only real family he had. He closed his eyes as the truth began to unravel in front of him.

"*Go.*" Marcus pointed to the door. "I'll meet you downstairs, and we'll discuss this like adults.

Pelham sneered in Marcus's direction once again. "You expect me to leave you alone with her after what you've done."

"Please, Dane," Honoria said softly. "For me?"

At the sound of her brother's Christian name, Marcus blinked. He'd never heard anyone refer to Pelham by that name.

Without another protest, Pelham stormed from the room.

"Honor?" Marcus asked incredulously as he slowly turned his attention to her. "Who the hell are you?"

Unease snaked its way up Honoria's throat and held it hostage, for a moment, but then she swallowed and found the fortitude to speak again. "I'm Pelham's oldest sister, Honoria. He calls me Honor for short. Who are you?"

"Trafford." The two-syllable word echoed off the walls.

"The Earl of Trafford? You're not a gentleman farmer?" Nervous didn't even begin to describe her state of mind. She smoothed the bedlinens on her lap, wishing she could do the same with the situation she and Marcus were facing.

"No, and you're not a farmer's daughter." The roughness in his morning voice didn't hide his unadulterated anger. "You're the sister of the Duke of Pelham."

She stared at the counterpane, desperate to find a solution. She had wanted adventure and romance but had always believed she'd have this time without repercussion. "I'll go and talk to him. I promise he'll settle down." Even a knife couldn't cut the silence that loomed between them. "I'm sorry, Marcus."

"Sorry." He huffed out a breath. "Seriously, that's your answer to the quandary we're facing. Sorry?" When he stood, his naked backside was still as mesmerizing as it had been last night. He pulled up his breeches, then threw on his shirt. He raked a hand through his hair and slid a side-eye glance her way.

If only a hole would open in the bedroom and swallow her whole. Then she wouldn't have to navigate this awkward conversation. Her heart still raced from when Pelham had pointed a pistol at Marcus.

"I'm going downstairs to face your irate brother, who happens to have every right to be livid and want to kill me." He closed the distance between them and cupped her chin in his hand. "I don't care for the name Honor. I much prefer Nora or Venus, or perhaps, Noria. Hmm?"

His touch was gentle, but there was no denying the anger that radiated heat hotter than a bonfire. If she were any closer to him, she'd be scorched. "Whatever you'd like."

"Noria it is. It's close to Nora. Now, *Noria*, if I've lost his friendship, I'll never forgive myself." Marcus tipped his head back and ran both hands through his hair before returning his gaze to hers. "I tried to tell you who I was last night, but you fell asleep. I meant to tell you this morning." He shook his head slightly, then regarded her. "Damn me to hell."

With the old duke, it had been quite easy to determine if he was angry with her. But with Marcus, it was difficult to determine if he was disappointed or irritated. There was no screaming or pounding of fists. No threats or banishments were forthcoming.

"Are you angry with me?" Slowly, like the dawn greeting a new day, everything became crystal clear. "You are angry. You blame me for this."

Her accusation flew across the room like a well-thrown javelin, and he winced.

The regret in his eyes was unmistakable. "I've gone about this all wrong. This is my fault. You told me your expectations, and I agreed to them. Forgive me for implying otherwise." He faced the window. By his rugged profile, Marcus had grown distant, lost in his own thoughts. "We'll have to marry." His announcement broke the silence like a boulder dropped in a calm pond.

"No." Honoria pulled the sheet higher and straightened her back. "Remember? We said no attachments."

"This isn't an attachment. It's a knot that can't be untangled. I have a charity that will suffer if we don't marry." Without another word, he turned, grabbed his boots and stockings, and walked out of the room, slamming the door behind him.

For a moment, Honoria didn't move. A hot knife stuck in her chest would have been preferrable to Marcus's words. He'd made it clear that he valued Pelham's friendship and company over hers. Tears welled in her eyes, and she quickly brushed them away. Why should she be surprised? It was exactly as the old duke had spouted all those years ago. What redeeming qualities did she possess that drew people to her? None. But when she'd pretended to be someone else, she had attracted a handsome man, one who enjoyed her company.

She'd be damned if she allowed Marcus and her brother to craft her fate without her being a part of the conversation. As she quickly dressed, the undeniable truth hit her. She'd found a man whom she cared for deeply and had never been too concerned with who he was. She'd repeatedly told him *no attachments*. But just by her actions, there were attachments. Namely, her brother demanding satisfaction. And Marcus declaring they'd marry.

I am an Ardeerton. She repeated the phrase over and over as she fought her emotions. She bent her head and stared at her hands. Her stomach roiled with the thought she'd somehow tarnished Marcus's reputation and charity. Heaven help her. What had they done?

What have I done?

When Marcus entered the main room of the lodge, he found Pelham staring out the window that overlooked the green valley below.

Without acknowledging his entry, Pelham broke the quiet. "Whose sheep?"

"Mine," he answered.

"A gentleman farmer." Pelham chortled, but there was little humor in the sound.

Marcus turned to pour a whiskey for his friend but decided it was too early. Instead, he filled the kettle with water. There was nothing more soothing that a strong cup of tea in the morning to clear the senses. He hooked the kettle over the fire that Pelham must have built up while Marcus was talking to Honor. He shook his head slightly. He'd never become accustomed to calling her that. He turned from the fire and faced Pelham. Whatever it took, he'd try to salvage the friendship. "I'm a better shot than you."

"Perhaps." Pelham turned around and crossed his arms over his chest. The anger in his eyes hadn't abated. "However, I have the necessary rage to take the shot and not even think twice about it." He examined Marcus with a stone-cold fury. "You, on the other hand, have all the guilt of stealing the hen from the henhouse."

"I don't think your sister would appreciate being compared to a chicken." He laughed softly. "What is it with you and chickens? The Jolly Rooster. The hen in the henhouse."

Pelham didn't move. He didn't answer. He just continued to stare.

Marcus ran a hand through his hair as he grappled with what to say next. "Pelham—"

"You should have recognized her. Her portrait is hanging in my London home."

Marcus blew out a frustrated breath. "She was eight years old in that painting. Just a girl."

"A girl with hair so fair that when she reached adulthood anyone would realize she was my sister," Pelham argued.

"She wore a hat in that portrait," Marcus answered in a clipped voice. Under no circumstances could he allow this interaction to turn into a shouting match. He breathed heavily through his nose.

"No excuse," Pelham drawled.

"Noria..." At the severe frown on the duke's face, Marcus corrected himself. "Honoria was at the Jolly Rooster, and you didn't even recognize her. Your own sister."

"I wasn't looking for my sister at my masquerade." The menace in the duke's low voice warned that Marcus was losing more ground.

"The first time I saw her..." He clenched his teeth so hard, that his jaw ached. "I didn't know who she was. I care for her. Perhaps more than care," he said softly.

"You love only yourself," Pelham hissed.

"That's like the pot calling the kettle black," Marcus retorted. He stood tall and faced his friend. "You once asked if I'd be interested in marriage to your sister. The answer is yes. I'm prepared to rectify the situation and do the honorable thing. I'd like to marry Honoria."

Before Marcus could say another word, another voice broke the quiet.

"Over my dead body," Honoria announced.

Thirteen

Honoria smoothed her wrinkled gown, tipped her chin up, and moved forward. It was the only way to hide her pain. She could not marry Marcus. It was best for both of them.

Pelham's gaze shot to his sister's. "Why am I not surprised that you've been listening in to the conversation? How long have you been standing there?"

Honoria descended the last two steps of the staircase and did her best to gracefully enter the room. "Long enough to hear that you both believe you have the right to decide my future."

She'd not feel sorry for herself. Nor would she enter a marriage where she'd be vulnerable to a man's whims and emotions.

"I'll not allow it." She caught her brother's attention with that statement. "By and by, how did you know to find me here? Why aren't you in London with Pippa?"

"Carlyle came to see me at White's yesterday." Her brother's lip curled in disgust. "Couldn't wait to tell me that he saw you talking with someone near the Gilly's house." He lifted his eyebrows. "Said he saw a woman who looked remarkably like you kissing a man that he recognized as Trafford. Then he shared that he saw Florence at the hunting lodge other day. I stayed at the club for another hour or two to give the impression that I didn't care about his rumors, particularly if he decided to tell his story to someone else."

She stood stock-still as she tried to understand the significance of his words.

"Afterward, I rushed home as soon as possible." Her brother came forward and took her hand. "Darling, be sensible about this. Marry Trafford. Give him an heir, then live your life. You don't want a scandal associated with your name. Think of Pippa."

She was thinking of her sister and brother. She was protecting them particularly if there was a chance Marcus would be given that letter and her entire tainted story came to light.

Honoria swallowed a sob and bit her cheek to keep quiet. She stole a glance at Marcus, who was staring out the window with a look of total shock. Even with his wrinkled clothes, disheveled hair, and the bristle of the night's beard on his face, he was a devastatingly attractive man.

She'd laugh if it weren't so sadly absurd. She'd found another man who didn't want her and couldn't even look at her.

Much like the old duke.

"No. I'll not do it to myself or to Marc—Lord Trafford." The words tripped from her mouth. She was rambling now, but there was no way she would ever marry the Earl of Trafford. Her heart skipped a beat at the thought. "I'll live somewhere far away from London"

Pelham shook his head while Marcus turned to stare at her.

"Perhaps...I can sail to Greece and never be heard from again."

"Honoria," Pelham bit out.

Her heart threatened to break through her chest, but she continued, "Don't worry. I promise it will all work out."

Oh, God, she sounded weak. But she'd not be forced into a marriage where her husband would hate her once he found out the truth of her birth. Even if Marcus received that letter disavowing she was the duke's daughter, he'd marry her. His honor would dictate it.

Plus, her brother would insist the marriage take place.

Just the thought sent her mind reeling. She didn't even want to think about what Pippa and Dane would suffer if that letter came to light.

. . .

Marcus extended his hand to quiet her brother. "Allow me to have a private conversation with your sister."

For once this morning, Pelham didn't argue. He said to Honoria, "I'll get Florence ready for the ride home." Then his gaze swung to Marcus. "Make it a good one."

After the door closed, Honoria turned to Marcus. "A good what?"

"Proposal," Marcus answered. "Honoria, would you do me the highest—"

"Stop, I beg of you." She closed the distance between them and took his hand in hers. "Don't do this."

He stared down at her, and for a moment, real emotion blazed from his eyes. Whether it was anger or something else, she didn't want to hazard a guess.

"I have to do this." His voice softened into the same dulcet tone as hers. It was the voice a lover would use with their beloved.

She blew out a silent breath. She'd have a greater chance of being hit by a meteor than having Marcus, the Earl of Trafford, fall in love with her. She couldn't contemplate a marriage without that. Her own parents' vitriol was proof that without love, people suffered in a marriage.

Suddenly, he dropped to one knee and took her hand in his.

"Don't," Honoria begged. "If you ask me, I'll say no. And that will make me the villain."

"Aren't we both the villains in this?" His patience seemed endless. Gone was any anger. "So, let's change the story. Marry me, Noria."

"Perhaps it's already written." She withdrew her hand from his and turned toward the door. As a small girl, she'd always dreamt of the moment when a handsome man would ask for her hand, then whisk her away from Ardeerton House and her father. But this proposal wasn't at all how she'd thought she'd feel. She couldn't marry until she had that letter in her possession. Hearing Marcus's words and fearing that it could never happen was devasting. A knife would cause less pain.

As soon as she depressed the door latch, Marcus's voice reached her. "I'll be at Pelham Hall in the hour."

She turned to face him. "There's no need."

Tears threatened, and she prayed for the strength not to fall apart in front of him. As regally as she could manage under the circumstances, Honoria walked outside where Pelham waited, holding Florence's reins. Without a word, he lifted her onto her sidesaddle.

Pelham easily mounted his stallion, Hercules. In seconds, they were galloping for home. As usual, Pelham took the lead. Instead of taking the road that led to Pelham Hall, they rode across the fields. For a moment, she didn't understand, but the truth dawned. He was trying to hide her and protect her reputation as much as possible.

How he would handle the servants at Pelham Hall was another question.

Within a quarter-hour, they approached the ducal ancestral estate. As soon as they reached the stables, Pelham greeted his head grooms-man, John Ellis, then assisted Honoria down from the horse.

"A moment, Honor."

She stood by as her brother approached John. She couldn't hear the conversation. No doubt, Pelham was asking the man to keep quiet about their early morning appearance.

In mere moments, her brother was by her side and pressed a kiss to the middle of her forehead. "Clean up and meet me in the study in an hour. We'll find a way through this. Don't forget we're Ardeertons."

"I'm not a young girl," she protested.

"You're not," he agreed. "However, you're my little sister and always will be." The redness in his eyes betrayed the depth of his feeling. "Go," he said gruffly, obviously uncomfortable with the emotion. "One hour."

She turned and walked to the back entrance. Even her own eyes watered at her brother's concern. Heaven help her. Why did everything have to turn into such an entanglement? These ten days were supposed to have been her time to experience life on her own terms.

However, her terms also affected more than just herself. If only Pippa were here. Her sister would help her find a solution to this disaster.

Pelham's earlier words invaded her thoughts. If Honoria was ruined, then poor Pippa would bear shame because she was, unfortunately, Honoria's family. The same was true for Pelham. Honoria would never forgive herself if she had tarnished her brother and sister's hopes and dreams for their own future.

If only she'd stayed away from the Jolly Rooster. She drew to a stop and dragged in a sharp breath. Marcus's reputation wouldn't suffer, and his charity wouldn't be sullied.

She had to be the one to figure out a way out of this mess and do the right thing for Marcus and her family while protecting herself. Honoria huffed silently. She'd done a poor job of it so far.

She slipped through the servants' door. Thankfully, no one was around. Breakfast was long past, and morning chores were being completed. Yesterday, before she joined Marcus, she'd sent word to the butler that she was not to be disturbed as she was suffering from another headache.

Winston stood at the back entrance, waiting for her.

"Welcome home, my lady." The smile on the older man's face was filled with grace and a hint of worry.

"Good morning," she said quietly.

"If you wouldn't mind, I suggest we take the servant's stairs upstairs." He bowed slightly. "I have the rest of the staff in the front rooms cleaning for Lord Trafford and His Grace's arrivals."

"How do you know about Lord Trafford?" Honoria placed her hand on her stomach. Did everyone know about her indiscretion?

"Your brother."

"Pelham told you?"

Winston shook his head twice. "He told me that he was going to Lord Trafford's new estate. I'd never seen His Grace so riled in my life. When I discovered that you were not home last evening..."

She buried her head in her hands. "Oh, God."

"Lady Honoria, please look at me."

She lowered her hands, but she was still smarting from the sting of mortification.

"I didn't mean to distress you." Winston smiled kindly. "Lord Trafford is a good man." He clasped his hands in front of him. "I've taken the liberty of having a bath prepared for you. Mary, the upstairs maid, is ready to assist. She's very discreet."

"You're a godsend," she answered. "Thank you."

As the butler escorted Honoria up the narrow steps, she stopped. If she was going to be successful in not ruining Marcus, she had to come up with a plan. She'd thought of the idea a couple of days ago but dismissed it. Now, it seemed brilliant.

"Winston, maybe I could publish a notice of marriage."

The butler slowly turned on the stair to face her. "You mean the announcement to Lord Trafford?"

She laughed. "No. A pretend notice of marriage. I need to find that letter as soon as possible or everyone I care about, including Marcus... Lord Trafford will be ruined." She tangled her fingers together. It helped her think.

Winston's brow furrowed. "Where would you publish it?"

"I can't put it in The Times. Everyone would see it." She squeezed her hands into fists hoping for a miracle. "Are there any publications that cater to the legal profession?"

His eyes widened. "Indeed, my lady. There's the *Law Chronicle*. You have to be a solicitor or a barrister to subscribe. It's for legal notifications such as dissolutions of partnerships and bankruptcies to name a few. My second cousin is a clerk there."

She clasped her hands together. Finally, fate was smiling at her. "That could work. No one will think a thing about it except for the old duke's solicitors. I'll publish it twice to ensure that it is seen."

Winston blinked several times, but it didn't hide his astonishment. "My lady, I hesitate to offer encouragement."

"It has to work."

His bushy white eyebrows shot upward.

"I'm desperate." She blinked back the burn of tears in her eyes. "I'm not going to escape this scandal or marriage, I'm afraid. Yet, I can't marry Lord Trafford without that letter. He'll hate me."

"Why not announce that it's Lord Trafford that you'll marry?"

Her eyes widened in horror. "Absolutely not. If I did then the solicitor might send it to Marcus's residence. What if someone besides Marcus read it? What if Marcus read it? What would he think? He'd hate me. What if he told Dane? I can't take that chance." Tears welled in her eyes. "This is my family. I can't hurt them."

He stared at her for a moment, then slowly nodded his agreement. "I'll do everything in my power to help."

"Thank you." She placed a hand on his arm. "You've been a good friend to me."

Winston placed his hand over hers and patted it. "And you've been one to me. Go upstairs, my lady, before anyone sees you."

Honoria nodded then slowly ascended the stairs.

"My lady?"

She turned and faced Winston.

"If Lord Trafford read that letter, he wouldn't hate you."

"You don't know that." But Honoria didn't have time to argue. She had to be downstairs to face her brother and Marcus. "Does anyone else know that I wasn't home last night?"

"No one in the house, my lady," he answered.

"Good." She sighed silently.

"However, the head groomsman met me first thing this morning and informed me that Florence wasn't in her stall." Winston lowered his voice. "John Ellis is loyal and doesn't spread tales. He's been with the family as long as I have. Your secret is safe with us."

Now her lies were entangling more innocent people in her deception.

Who would have known a simple seduction could lead to so much trouble?

Marcus galloped into the Pelham Hall circular drive where a liveried footman waited for him. He had always suspected that under Pelham's pretentious and flamboyant personality, there was worry, the type of anguish a man would hide by showcasing himself as the exact opposite to the rest of the world. Perhaps with this dreaded discussion between Marcus, Honoria, and Pelham, he could mend this rip between the two of them and find a way to save all their reputations.

He stopped on the marble staircase that led to the entrance of the Pelham Hall, a masterpiece of Palladian architecture. The urge to clench his fists and roar to the heavens grew intense and nigh near impossible to ignore. She'd flat-out refused him. At the sound of the front door opening, Marcus tamped down the compulsion and turned.

"My lord," Winston exclaimed with a slight grin. "How wonderful to see you at Pelham Hall." As Marcus climbed the rest of the way up the steps, the butler continued, "If recollection serves me, this is the first time that we've had the honor of your company here."

Leave it to Pelham's wily butler to ensure that Marcus was aware of the momentous occasion. He was about to set foot into the Duke of Pelham's ancestral seat, a place so guarded and protected that even the sun had a hard time peeking in.

If Pelham thought he'd make decisions regarding Honoria's future without Marcus having an opportunity to participate, then the duke wasn't as nimble minded as he'd once thought.

As he crossed the threshold, Winston snapped his fingers, and another footman came forward and took Marcus's hat and gloves.

"If you'll follow me, sir?" Winston inquired.

Marcus furrowed his brow. "Shouldn't you announce me to the duke?"

"Sometimes the element of surprise is the best strategy," the butler murmured.

"As in war?"

"No, I was thinking of love." Winston stopped in the middle of a long hallway that must lead to Pelham's study. The butler chuckled softly as he clasped his hands in front of him. "There are great warriors and generals who believe that war never ends. I'd like to think the same applies to love. For two such contrasting behaviors, they're very similar."

Ever since his parents had died, he'd never felt such emotion or "behavior."

Except possibly with a woman named Honoria.

Winston gazed fondly at a portrait of a young Pelham, Honoria, and his youngest sister, Pippa.

Winston nodded brusquely and started forward. "I beg you, Lord Trafford, to accept my musings as something to consider when you have a moment." Without saying anything further, the butler knocked on a double set of doors, then swung them open. "Your Grace," he boomed across the open room. "The Earl of Trafford to see you and Lady Honoria."

Marcus's mouth practically fell open. Not once had he mention the woman's name. How in the world would the butler have known unless Pelham or Honoria had made mention of his visit?

Pelham slowly stood and regarded Marcus with a disapproving scowl. "That'll be all, Winston."

Winston nodded. "Yes, Your Grace."

"And we don't want to be disturbed unless my sister shows up."

"Of course, sir." With that, the butler closed the door, leaving Marcus alone—once again—with Honoria's irate brother.

"I realize I've invited myself, but I should be here..." His words died to nothing when the duke raised his hand to silence him.

"I know," Pelham answered resolutely as he walked to an inlaid side table where bottles of whiskey and brandy stood at attention, much like Pelham's disciplined footmen. Quickly, he poured two fingerfuls of whiskey into two glasses and handed one to Marcus.

The duke held his glass in the air. "May we find a resolution to this quandary quickly."

Marcus mimicked the movement. "I'll drink to that. How did Winston know that I was to see Honoria?"

"He has a special fondness for Honoria. He must have deduced what was going on when I arrived home. I may have taken your name in vain a couple of times." He took a sip and then nodded to a pair of sofas that framed a massive fireplace where the flames crackled in welcome. "I've asked Honoria to join us." He glanced at the longcase clock behind him. "She'll be here any minute."

Just then the door swung open, and Lady Pippa entered with another slightly older woman trailing behind her.

"I came as fast as I could," Lady Pippa called out.

Pelham stood immediately. "Pippa? What are you doing here? I left you in London."

Marcus followed suit.

"A lot of good that would do either of us." Lady Pippa turned to Marcus. "Lord Trafford, it's lovely to see you. You must be Honor's Marcus."

"Indeed, my lady." Marcus wondered how in the devil she knew that he was involved with Noria. But the welcoming smile on her face didn't betray any knowledge, or even misgivings, that he'd slept with her sister.

"No need to be formal," Pelham said as he completely ignored the other woman who'd entered the room.

The woman frowned and narrowed her eyes.

Just then, Honoria glided into the room. Marcus's heart tripped in his chest at the sight of her. She must have freshly bathed since there were blonde wisps of wet curls adorning her neck. Her rose-colored gown was trimmed with a dark turquoise ribbon around the waist and neck. She looked like a confection for a starving man.

And he was famished.

"Pippa," she exclaimed and swept her little sister into a hug.

"I'm here," Pippa soothed as she rubbed Honoria's back.

As Honoria held her sister, Marcus was intrigued by the raw emotion on the two sisters' faces. They did not act like a typical aristocratic family, where such outpouring of sentiment was frowned upon.

"I'm in quite the predicament," Honoria murmured.

"I know, darling. That's why I've brought a friend." Pippa broke away from her sister and extended her hand toward the other woman, who wasn't much older than the Ardeerton sisters. "Honor, this is Lady Grace Weston, the Earl of Dansby's eldest daughter."

As the ladies introduced themselves, Pelham's jaw tightened. "Of all the mongrels to bring home, why did she have to pick *her*."

Marcus swung his gaze to the duke but, obviously, the remark had not been meant for anyone's ears.

Pelham was already strolling forward. He stopped, and in one motion turned on his heel to face Marcus. "Come, Trafford. Let me introduce you to the *Governess,* otherwise known as Lady Grace Weston."

Marcus came to his side. "Doesn't she fix scandals? How do you know her?"

"Unluckily, I once fancied her and proposed." Pelham lowered his voice to a whisper as he rolled his eyes. "Thankfully, she refused me." His hand shot out and gripped Marcus's shoulder. "My sisters do not know the tale, and I would be obliged if you don't tell them."

"You have my word." Marcus stole a glance at the lady in question. "But you courted a woman? It's inconceivable that I didn't know."

"It was practically over as soon as it began."

"Who is she?" Marcus asked.

"A person from my past who should have stayed there." Pelham turned his gaze to Lady Grace, then lowered his voice. "She's a governess of sorts. While most governesses navigate children to adulthood, this particular one navigates people out of ruinous situations."

Fourteen

A scorching heat bludgeoned Honoria's cheeks as Marcus approached.

Lady Grace placed a gentle hand on Honoria's arm, drawing her attention. "I know it seems impossible now, but all will be well, I promise." She discreetly glance at Pelham, then turned back to Pippa and Honoria. "Let me handle your brother."

"Lady Grace," Pelham drawled. "Never in my wildest imaginations did I ever think you'd stroll through my door."

Lady Grace performed an abbreviated curtsey. *"What a compliment."* The sarcasm in her voice was as sharp as a newly whetted knife. "I, however, knew our paths would cross again. Wherever you are, scandal is your stalwart companion. Consequently, it was simply a matter of time before my services were required."

Marcus's curious gaze met Honoria's. Never had she seen anyone dare take a swipe at Pelham. Gingerly, she slid her gaze to her brother.

Pelham's nostrils flared, and his eyes practically shot daggers at the woman in from of him. "I see you still have the charm of a wildcat, Grace." He bowed slightly in her direction, then introduced Marcus. "One of my oldest and dearest friends, the Earl of Trafford."

Both Marcus and Lady Grace greeted each other.

Without wasting another moment on pleasantries, Lady Grace motioned to the twin sofas in front of the fireplace. "Shall we? We have a bit of work in front of us this morning." She pulled a dainty timepiece from a hidden pocket of her gown. "I must be in London by seven tomorrow evening. I have several appointments."

"Cancel them. I can send a courier to inform *your appointments*," Pelham ordered, then turned toward the sofas. He stopped when no one followed him. "You all heard the Governess. We have issues that must be addressed."

"Your brother still has the most unique way of charming ladies." Lady Grace laughed slightly, then hooked her arm around Pippa's. "We all want to run in the opposite direction."

As the trio walked across the study, Marcus waited for Honoria. "I think your brother..."

"Has met his match?" Honoria offered. "I think we're about to see something that is a rare event."

Marcus chuckled. The sound lifted some of the dread from her shoulders. "What is that, Noria?"

That familiar excitement started to rise within her stomach at the sound of his nickname for her.

"My brother being put in his place." She laughed softly.

But when Marcus extended his arm for her to take, all the air was sucked out of her. He was being kind.

"Will you allow me to escort you to the sitting area?"

"Yes. Thank you." She wrapped her arm around his.

"It's about time you quit saying *no* to me," he whispered for her ears only.

Whether he was discussing her taking his arm or his proposal, she wouldn't hazard a guess. She'd take whatever he offered as long as they continued as friends—good friends—without any rancor.

By then, they'd arrived at the sofas. Honoria joined Lady Grace and Pippa on one while Marcus took the seat next to Pelham.

"Excellent." Lady Grace nodded her approval. "Lady Pippa explained what has happened, but perhaps it would be best if I know exactly what I'm dealing with here." She smiled encouragingly at Honoria, then Marcus. "Who would like to go first?"

"I would," Marcus announced. His gaze shifted to Honoria. "Unfortunately, there was a case of mistaken identity, and I pursued Lady Honoria, thinking she was a member of the demi-monde."

Before he had even finished speaking, Honoria was shaking her head. Of all the things for him to speak aloud, that was not what she'd imagined.

Her brother arched an eyebrow. "Oh, I can't wait to hear this story."

"I pursued *him*. I was Venus at your masquerade." Honoria waited for his reaction. She expected anger, but instead was met with a look of confusion.

Lady Grace's expression matched Marcus's. "Do you think anyone recognized you?"

Honoria shook her head, but then a scourge of disquiet hit her like a battering ram. "Lord Carlyle called on me after my siblings left for London. He thought he saw me at the masquerade, but I told him he was mistaken."

"Carlyle called on you?" Marcus asked incredulously.

Pelham's mouth twitched in a sneer. "Why the devil was he calling on you? When I'm not in attendance."

"Lord Carlyle didn't know that you weren't home. He said he wants to court me." She twisted her fingers together, hoping she could untangle her thoughts which seemed to be in endless knots.

"*What?*" Marcus leaned forward.

"*Pardon?*" Pelham narrowed his eyes.

Both men exclaimed at the same time.

"I told him no." Honoria bit her lip but their outcries hurt. "Is it so odd that a man might be interested in courting me?"

Pelham ran a hand over his face. "I apologize, darling. That's not what I meant. He should have come to me first, that's all." Pelham's gaze met hers. His eyes flashed with that familiar protective streak. "Just out of curiosity, did Carlyle say why?"

She nodded. "He said he admired you and your ability to make money. He wants to be part of the family. I told him that he should marry you."

A true smile tugged at Marcus's lips. "Brava, Noria."

"Gentleman, please," Lady Grace scolded. "This makes the situation more serious."

Pelham nodded contritely.

Lady Grace pursed her lips. "A member of the *ton*, Lord Carlyle, saw Lady Honoria's horse at your hunting lodge. He also thought he saw her at the masquerade. That same gentleman saw Marcus with her without a chaperone the day prior when you met on a bridge. After he'd expressed interest in marrying her."

"I was visiting one of the tenants when Lord Trafford passed by," Honoria said defensively. "It was completely harmless."

Pelham pursed his lips into a thin line. "Carlyle said he saw you kiss each other."

Lady Grace pursed her lips for a moment. "That is an unfortunate complication."

Marcus's back straightened as if spoiling for a fight. "I said I'd marry her."

"That's the only solution," Lady Grace agreed.

Pippa met Honoria's gaze. "What do you think, dearest?"

This was like a bad dream where she'd been dropped into a crowded ballroom only to discover she was the only one completely naked. And there was no exit.

The heat of Marcus's gaze burned a hole right through her chest, narrowly missing her heart. She released a tremulous sigh. There was no way she could proceed with such a plan without having that letter in her possession. "I can't marry him."

Marcus didn't move except for the twitching of a muscle over his angular left cheek. "For the sake of discussion, may I ask why not?"

"Couples forced to marry are rarely happy. I don't want that for you." Honoria forced herself not to look away from Marcus.

She'd never forgive herself if she married him without that letter. Marcus would feel deceived if it was delivered the day before their wedding. If she received such a missive, she would feel the same. He thought her a daughter of a duke when she was nothing more than her mother's indiscretion. What if Marcus were miserable in the marriage? She'd lived through it once, witnessing her own parents' unhappy marriage. She'd not subject herself to that. Nor would her heart be able to withstand the agony if he turned his back and left her at the altar.

"I'm a man of honor, Honor." As Marcus used the familial nickname, he smiled. "I'll not allow you to bear the brunt of this scandal alone."

Honoria stood suddenly. She walked to the fireplace and started to pace. They couldn't marry. She had that letter to contend with. "Next month on my birthday, I'll receive my trust fund. I'll move to the continent."

"You could," Pelham drawled, "but that means I'll have to kill Trafford." He arrogantly tilted his head.

The Governess's nostrils flared. "That will make things worse for your entire family."

In return, Pelham's eyes blazed in anger. "If my sister leaves in disgrace, then I'll have to clean up the rest of the mess."

"Be serious. Once the scandal dies, then I could return." Honoria wanted to stomp her foot in frustration. "This is my life and his we're discussing."

"And Pippa's and mine," Pelham said gently.

Lady Grace rose from the sofa and came to stand beside Honoria. "My lady, I don't see another way." She turned her gaze to Marcus. "Do you, my lord?"

Marcus shook his head.

A sudden bout of nerves swept through her. How could she marry Marcus without having everyone's reputation ruined. She discreetly clenched her hands into fists. Her plan to place an advertisement in a legal paper had to work. All she needed was for the solicitor who held that letter to read her announcement then deliver that letter to Pelham Hall. Winston would keep it safe for her.

Then her life would be in her control again.

"You have to marry him, but it should be in London." Grace said gently. "If you marry at Pelham Hall, everyone will believe Carlyle's insinuations. I'm concerned that the rumors would never die down." Grace took Honoria's hand in hers and squeezed, then turned to Pelham and Marcus. "You should go to London for the remainder of the Season." With a nod toward Honoria's brother, she continued, "Your

Grace, you'll announce that the earl has set his cap for your sister, and you're in town to announce the betrothal. People will see it as true love, and all the chatter will soon whither."

"I agree on the marriage, but not the rest." Pelham stood and sliced his hand in the air. "I will not allow my sister to become the latest mincemeat of a scandal just so the *ton* can cook up all sorts of rumors and innuendos and serve it as gossip." He stalked over to Grace's side.

"Respectfully, Your Grace." The Governess's voice had taken on a dulcet tone, much like a nursemaid coaxing a wayward charge to take his medicine. "You've been out of society. You haven't a clue as to how it operates." Pelham shook his head, but Grace lifted her hand. "This is the only chance Lady Honoria will have to save her reputation and, as importantly, save Lady Pippa's at the same time. Nor to mention yours and Lord Trafford's reputation as well. Otherwise, if we don't get ahead of this *situation*, it'll be like having a wild boar as a household pet. You'll never be able to control it."

Pelham caught Honoria's gaze. "Do you want to listen to this?"

Honoria glanced at Marcus. "Do you?"

God, she'd fall to the floor laughing if it wasn't so tragic. She was *going to literal hell*.

She was going to London.

For whatever unfathomable reason, Marcus couldn't bear to expose Honoria to loose tongues and gossip. "I still believe it will better if we married and then went to London. I'll ride and procure a special license. Then we go to London, and she'd have my protection as my wife."

The stubborn set of Lady Grace's jaw matched Pelham's.

No doubt, he wore the same expression as his friends. Obstinance rose within him much like high tide. He forced himself to take a deep, calming breath. It was always easier to get what he wanted when he reasoned with people.

"I attend society events on occasion," Marcus offered. "There's always some scandal that is the topic of discussion at one of these events. It usually lasts a week, then another takes its place. If we married here, then the scandal would be minuscule. Lady Honoria wouldn't have to make an entrance into society."

"Perhaps," answered Lady Grace.

Lady Grace took Honoria's hand in hers and led her back to the sofa.

A look of distrust darkened Pelham's face. "Trafford's right. Why go to London if they're not married?"

Once they were all seated, Lady Grace shifted in her seat so she could face Honoria only. "You're the eldest sister of the Duke of Pelham, and you're a ghost." Pelham hmphed in disgust, but Grace held up her hand to silence him. "What I mean is that no one knows who you are. You've never had a Season. To put all the rumors to rest, you need to conquer them with your charm and grace. Show them why Lord Trafford is lucky to marry you." Grace smiled at Marcus. "The earl is a catch, and everyone will want to know who the woman is that has captured his heart. This is the best way to protect your family. Women are the usual victims and must pay the price if the scandal doesn't blow over. They experience cut directs, insults, and are ostracized. It will not make any difference that you are Pelham's sister."

Honoria's gaze shot to Marcus's. "I think she's right."

Marcus was already shaking his head in disagreement. "I do not, my lady."

"I do," Lady Grace said softly.

"What balderdash," Pelham interjected.

Honoria stared at the carpeted floor beneath her feet. "It's true, I'm an enigma to society." She lifted her gaze to her brother.

The look of abject misery on her face twisted Marcus's gut into a knot. "If this is what you want, I will be by your side. You won't face this alone. I wouldn't allow anyone to denigrate you or your family."

Lady Pippa and Lady Grace beamed at him as if he'd just declared that Honoria was the most beautiful woman in the world.

Which she was.

But that was beside the point.

"We don't know the social harm yet. But we must see and be

prepared. Only then can we repair it." Lady Grace placed her hand over Honoria's.

Marcus didn't move a muscle, but he ached to be the one to offer comfort and tell her everything would be all right...even if he didn't believe in such miracles.

Lady Grace released Honoria's hand and turned her stalwart attention to the duke. "I think it best if you all come to London immediately."

"For how long?" Pelham bit out.

"For as long as it takes," Marcus answered stoically.

"I can arrange for Lady Honoria and Lady Pippa to have a new wardrobe made," Grace offered. "Introduce her to some of my friends and announce that His Grace is in town. I can drop into conversation that I believe he's here to celebrate the upcoming betrothal of his eldest sister to his best friend."

"Former best friend," Pelham murmured for Marcus's ears only.

"I feel the same, old man," he volleyed in return.

Lady Grace turned her attention to Honoria. "Invitations will start flooding your London home, and I'll help you pick out several to attend. I think a month should do it. Another engagement or rumor will erupt which will grab society's attention next."

"What if we just ignore it?" Honoria clasped her hands tightly.

"That time has passed." Marcus blew out a breath. "When your brother ran from London last night, the opportunity was lost."

"Trafford is right," Pelham said. "I should have stayed in town and dismissed the bastard's insinuations."

Marcus clapped his friend on the back. "You were trying to protect your sister."

"From the hound next door," Pelham growled.

"They're the most loyal," Marcus growled in return.

Fifteen

After it was decided that they would all go to London the next day, Lady Grace, Pippa, and Honoria went to her room to look at her wardrobe to see what to take for the month.

"Oh, my word." Lady Grace smoothed her hands over a satin and silk sapphire ballroom gown that Pippa had created for Honoria. "Where have you worn this?"

"I haven't." Honoria looked longingly at the fantastical creation.

"Why not?" Lady Grace asked.

"There was never any occasion." Honoria strummed her fingers lightly over the handsewn crystals on the gorgeous fabric. "It would be perfect for a masquerade in Venice."

"Or a London ball during the Season." Lady Grace smiled, but it was one of those expressions that demanded an answer.

Honoria sighed. Every young lady of her position had looked forward to their introduction into society. At one point, Honoria had wanted that also. After completing finishing school with her other friends, she had been determined to push all her previous failures aside. A Season was a chance to meet new friends and perhaps capture the attention of a dashing suitor. But when time had come to discuss it with her brother, Honoria had lost her courage. She'd used the excuse that

143

she wasn't ready, but Dane had pushed her until she'd told him that she'd never step foot in London again. In a gentle but brotherly fashion, he'd cajoled her, but she hadn't budged on her decision.

She didn't want to be the center of attention. That damnable letter hung over her head like a boulder about to drop. It was safer to stay at Pelham Hall and never take the risk of being rejected again.

"Was it because of your brother?"

Honoria glanced at the window. The gray day matched her mood. "Not really, my lady."

"Would you call me Grace?" She smiled earnestly.

At her sweet expression, Honoria felt more comfortable with the woman. "If you'll call me Honoria," she replied.

"It would be my pleasure," Grace said.

"I'll be back shortly," Pippa announced with a smile. "I have several of Honoria's gowns stored in my rooms."

When Pippa left, Grace took one of Honoria's hands. Quickly, she brought them to a small sitting area in the bedroom. "Sit, please." Once they were both settled, she continued, "I know your brother quite well." A confident but knowing smile creased her lips. "At least, I used to. He can be well-meaning but misguided at times."

Honoria rushed to defend him. "No, you misunderstand. He's a wonderful brother." She twisted her fingers together as she tried to explain the sordid story.

Grace's eyes blinked in surprise. "Part of his duty is to introduce his sisters into society,"

Honoria tilted her chin in defiance. "If those sisters want that introduction."

Grace didn't reply.

After a long silence, Honoria continued, "Next month, I'll turn twenty-five and come into a fortune that my aunt left me. Pelham said he will give me my dowry at that time also...if I'm not married." Words tumbled free, but she had to make certain that Grace knew that it was her, and not her brother, who was the reason for her not having a Season. "I can have my own household. Why would I want to give up that type of freedom?"

Grace nodded in understanding. "I can see the attractiveness of such a life." She softened her voice. "But what about love?"

"Love is not something I'm looking for. I'm satisfied with my family's affection." At least for now. "I appreciate you being here for me." Honoria squeezed her eyes shut as she recalled the mess she'd made with Marcus. "I'm just so sorry that Lord Trafford is involved in my scandal. I'm prepared to do whatever is necessary to protect his reputation."

Affection glistened in Grace's eyes. "That's surprisingly kind of you. Most women would be screaming for a ring on their finger. But it's his scandal, too."

Heat licked her cheeks. "He didn't do anything wrong."

"You care for him?"

For a moment, Honoria didn't breathe. It had to be obvious if Grace had discovered Honoria's feelings after only knowing her for several short hours. She nodded slowly.

"That happens," Grace said gently as she patted her hand. "We need to discuss which events you and Lord Trafford will appear together."

"Events?" She shuddered at the horror of being paraded around at such societal affairs. "I thought perhaps we'd just go to one and be done with it."

"No, darling," Grace said affectionately. "You both will need to make several appearances. It's important that you appear with Lord Trafford but still mingle with others. You must appear open to other friendships. But your true affection lies with each other. The *ton* loves nothing more than a romance that sweeps everyone off their feet." She leaned in conspiratorially and lowered her voice. "But they do tire of such sweetness quickly. It's like eating an entire Christmas pudding on your own. Too much, and you never want to eat it again."

Honoria tried to swallow her discomfort. "I see."

Grace nodded sadly. "Men rarely feel the bite of disapproval from the *ton*. They're like pampered pets. Misdeeds are quickly forgotten. It's usually poor women who find themselves out of step with society. Some women aspire to something other than marrying well, and they find they're in trouble over nothing." There was a hint of censure in her tone. She straightened her back and clasped her hands. "Your marriage will repair your reputation once society sees you for who you are."

Honoria nodded once, but her insides recoiled at the brisk business-like discussion of the betrothal. It was the idea of appearing in public that made her toes curl and her shoulders slump like a turtle seeking protection in its shell.

One question had to be asked, and she dreaded it more than anything. "What happens if it doesn't work?"

Grace's eyes hardened a bit as a sympathetic smile spread across her face. "If it doesn't work, then you might never be welcome in London again. Women in your position always have the most to lose. But one thing in your favor is that you're a duke's daughter."

Honoria kept her face blank as her thoughts churned. If he were alive, the old duke would have loved a front-row seat to the mess she'd created.

"And a duke's sister," Grace said then frowned. "You'll have to interact with Lord Carlyle."

Honoria's stomach roiled.

Grace hmphed. "I'm certain when you refused his courtship, he thought to lash out at you and Lord Trafford. Jealously can become a rather sharp weapon." She shifted in her seat and took Honoria's hand in hers and squeezed. "We'll try to keep the interactions with Lord Carlyle to a minimum. It will help if Lord Trafford introduces you to his friends and acquaintances. You must do the same. The wider the social circle, the less likely you'll have to converse with Carlyle alone."

"One thing you should know is that I don't have many friends in London." Honoria cleared her throat and forced her gaze to Grace's. "I'm somewhat of a social...failure. None of my friends from finishing school have kept up our acquaintance except for one or two by correspondence." She bit her lip. How to explain that she was shy and had kept to herself because of her "disgrace?" The truth was that she hadn't opened herself up to anyone but her family. Thus, not keeping her friends around. "Pippa has been much more social than I have. She's invited to house parties that her married friends host."

"Then we'll turn it into an opportunity," Grace said triumphantly. When Honor didn't laugh, Grace smiled gently. "Honoria, you're a kind, gentle-born woman. Not to mention, you're beautiful."

Honoria shook her head, but Grace held up a hand to silence her.

"It's difficult to see our own beauty when we are our worst critics. Trust me. Men will stop and gaze at you when you enter the room."

"That sounds horrifying," she murmured.

That earned a laugh from Grace. "It's a power, and one you would do well to learn to harness. Through my years, I've discovered that women must use every tool to their advantage to earn the respect of the masculine sex. Once you have their attention, it's so much easier to get them to listen." She leaned back and stared at Honoria. A slight smile creased her lips. "It may sound gauche, but I believe it true."

"That might be the case for others, but I'm not certain it'll work for me."

Grace glanced at the delightful gowns Pippa had created, then smiled. "It will. Nothing creates a stir in a crowded room like a woman walking into their midst wrapped in a beautiful gown and an attitude that demands respect and attention. Just pretend you own everything within your gaze. Such strength is riveting, and I'll wager one hundred pounds right now that you possess it."

Honoria bowed her head and laugh. "You make it sound so easy."

"It is once you try it a time or two. You'll be a success. Mark my words." Grace nodded confidently.

Pippa entered the bedroom with her arms overflowing with gorgeous creations of silk, brocades, velvets, and the finest muslin available that made it look like a rainbow had exploded in Honoria's room.

Grace stood immediately on Honoria's sister's entrance and walked to Honoria's bed where Pippa laid the gowns. "This is like Christmas." She smiled in Pippa's direction before she extended her hand to Honoria. "Come and choose what you'll take to London. I'll talk to your brother about finding the perfect modiste who will make the accessories to compliment all this beauty."

As Grace sorted the dresses, Honoria recognized that it was a moment she'd remember always. She'd never done anything this perilous before. It felt as if she were standing on a rocky mountain slope. She couldn't go down the way she came. Otherwise, she'd be leaving Marcus all alone to find his way out of the scandal. Not to mention the harm that might befall her sister and brother. She straightened her shoulders, determined to master her fears, and keep her future under her domain.

The sapphire gown caught her attention again. It had always been her favorite. The deep, rich color represented harmony between lovers and protection against adversaries. Sapphires were also associated with the planet Venus.

Once Honoria donned that sapphire gown, she hoped her patron saint Venus would return. She needed all the help she could find to weather this storm.

And it would all be for Marcus's sake.

Marcus's foul mood did not lighten once he'd arrived at Woodbury Park. How had his life turned upside down and in disarray within a period of hours? Now he had to return to London. As he walked through the front door into the handsome marble and granite entry, he discovered his butler and valet engaged in a jovial discussion.

"My lord," Lester Maddox, his valet, called out. "You're just the person to settle this argument between me and Humphrey."

Though Maddox was slightly younger than Marcus, he had an air about him that was reminiscent of a middle-aged man.

Humphrey chuckled with such joy that he sounded like a little boy who had found the ring in the Christmas pudding. "This will teach you a proper lesson in fashion, Maddox. His lordship has the finest tastes in all of the British Isles."

"Old man, who do you think dresses his lordship?" Maddox said with a sly grin before turning his attention to Marcus. "If you were attending a dinner at the Duke of Pelham's estate, would you dress as formally as you do in London?"

Marcus didn't bat an eye. "I wouldn't be attending."

Both the butler and the valet's mouths gaped open resembling two trout hauled onto shore.

"Whyever not?" Humphrey was the one brave enough to ask. "He's your closest confidant."

"It's irrelevant." Marcus wanted to tip his head back and roar at the debacle of the day. "Pack for London. We'll leave at first light on the morrow."

"London?" Maddox murmured. "We just arrived at Woodbury Park."

"A situation has arisen that must be addressed," Marcus bit out. As the two men stood there with expectant faces, Marcus lifted one eyebrow. "That'll be all."

He turned on his heel and continued to his study. As soon as he'd entered, he poured himself two fingerfuls of brandy. He tipped the glass back and finished the liquor in one swallow. It took some of the edges off, but his disappointment at himself was still sharper than a stiletto blade. He sat behind a painted beechwood Robert Adam desk decorated in the Etruscan style. The piece was a little too dramatic for his tastes, but after today, drama seemed to be his middle name.

Everything he'd worked for in the last five years was in jeopardy. His charity and his desire to open Woodbury Park to orphaned children couldn't survive a scandal of the proportions that he had flirted with today. And his friendship with Pelham had been damaged.

It shouldn't needle him so, but those old feelings of abandonment came roaring to the surface. Everyone who meant anything to him in his life, he lost.

Not only was he in danger of losing Pelham's friendship, but if Noria had her way, he'd lose her also. He had to convince her that they would make an excellent match. He had no doubt that with her empathy and gentle nature, she would be a perfect partner for him as they ran the charity together.

Lady Honoria Ardeerton.

Though he didn't know her very well, he could sense that she was worth the effort. He'd do everything in his power to protect her reputation, thereby protecting his. He wanted a wife and family and could easily see a contented life with her. He'd make her happy. He was sure of it.

His heart lurched as her adamant denial echoed in his thoughts. She didn't want to marry him. But when they'd been alone together, he hadn't imagined the warmth and affection that had shown brightly in her brilliant blue eyes.

She had wanted more with him just as he'd wanted more with her. But he still didn't understand her hesitation to marry or her contradictory ways.

He exhaled loudly and slumped in his chair. He could see Noria hosting his dinner parties and soirees. She could even sponsor balls, all in the name of growing more funds. More importantly, they'd gain patrons who would spend time with the young peers and develop kinships that were sorely needed.

It was all so simple yet so difficult, especially when the woman you wanted to marry didn't seem all that thrilled with the idea of marrying you. Who knew that a simple mask could lead to so many complications?

A knock sounded on the door.

"Enter." Marcus didn't bother to straighten his stance in his chair. The only person that would dare approach him when he was in such a mood was Humphrey.

"Your lordship, a note has arrived from Pelham Hall." Humphrey stood before the desk and lowered his voice to a conspiratorial whisper. "The wax seal is the Duke of Pelham's insignia."

Marcus took the letter from Humphrey's outstretched hand and ripped the seal in two. He quickly scanned the contents. "I've been summoned for dinner."

The butler raised both eyebrows. "Aren't you pleased, my lord?"

"Simply overwhelmed," Marcus distractedly answered.

Humphrey rocked back on his heels. "I'll ask Maddox to set out your clothes. Never fear, sir, we'll have everything ready for your departure tomorrow so you can enjoy your evening."

With that, the butler took his exit, leaving Marcus alone.

A very familiar feeling.

He caught his face in the mirror, and for a moment didn't recognize himself. The reflection gazing back resembled him, but he looked older and wearier. He stood from his desk at the same time he pushed aside such thoughts. He was still the same man, even if his troubles had tripled since this morning.

He shut the door behind him and started down the hall toward the staircase. He'd just taken a proverbial road in life that had no return path. Whatever Pelham had to say, Marcus would listen and wouldn't react.

However, the same couldn't be said if he saw Honoria. As God as his witness, he craved her. Much like a tree craved the sun. When he was around her, he felt centered and anchored in a way he'd never felt before.

He huffed out a silent breath. Whatever this was between them, he had to ensure that she knew that when they married, she would be his foremost priority.

And he'd do his damnedest to see that the marriage happened.

Sixteen

Honoria pinched her cheeks in the hallway mirror before descending the stairs. Pippa stood waiting for her at the bottom of the steps. Grace had left late in the morning to return to London for her appointment. No amount of cajoling by Pelham would change her mind.

Honoria smoothed a hand down her skirt in a desperate attempt to settle the butterflies that were currently gavotting in her stomach.

As soon as she reached Pippa, her sister slid her arm through hers. "Your Marcus is already here. He and Pelham are in the library."

Honoria tugged her sister closer to her side. "Keep your voice low when you say that."

"*He is your Marcus.*" Pippa's eyes widened mischievously. "I meant to say that in a whisper."

"What did you mean to say in a whisper?" Pelham was strolling toward them with a confidence that Honoria envied.

"Nothing." Pippa smiled beguilingly. "Come to fetch us?"

"Yes. Only because I'm hungry." Her brother laughed at his own joke, and Pippa joined in.

Would she ever be as poised and assured as her brother? Pippa carried herself with the same confidence. It was another thing for

Honoria to accomplish while she was in London. Grace had told her people who believed themselves self-important typically were granted such status within the *ton*. Everyone loved self-assuredness in others since it made them comfortable with themselves.

She had to remember that.

Pelham turned his gaze to her. "Honor, you look lovely tonight."

She nodded. "Thank you."

"Be careful with our guest. I don't trust him as far as I can throw him." Pelham shot a glance over his shoulder. "The man arrived a half-hour early for tonight's dinner engagement." He turned his attention back to her. "Why do I feel that I've invited the fox into the hen house?"

"Because you own the Jolly Rooster," Honoria answered.

"That's a perfect answer, Lady Honoria," a masculine voice laughed behind her brother. Pelham stepped aside and allowed Marcus into the conversation. His attention was directed at Pippa. "My lady," he said with a bow.

"Good evening, Lord Trafford," she said cheerfully.

Slowly, Marcus turned to her. "Lady *Noria*."

The use of her pet name made her insides bubble just like a sip of the finest champagne. Her pulse pounded as all eyes came to rest upon her. "My lord, how delightful you could join us this evening."

"So, you were the one who invited me this evening?" The huskiness of his voice did little to calm the riot inside her.

"I invited you." Pelham huffed a disgruntled breath. "Do not make a nuisance of yourself."

Ignoring her brother, Marcus took a step closer and held up his arm. "May I escort you into dinner?"

She tilted her gaze to his and answered the slight grin on his face with one of her own. "That would be lovely."

Pelham watched them for a moment, then turned to Pippa and held out his arm. "May I?"

As her two siblings led the way into the dining room, Marcus held her back for a moment. "I didn't want to say anything in front of your brother in case it would start a war that rivaled the one with Napoleon, but...you are beautiful tonight."

"Thank you." Her cheeks instantly heated at the sultry sound of his deep voice. Heavens, it was the one he'd used when they'd made love last night. It had reminded her of the softest suede, smooth on the outside but as strong as well-worn leather.

By then, they'd arrived in the informal dining room. It was the smallest of the two rooms used to entertain guests in the ducal home. As a family, they used it exclusively since Pelham never entertained here.

The table was set with the best bone china, the one used for holidays, birthdays, and other special occasions. Two footmen dressed in the formal Pelham livery stood at attention, ready to serve.

Marcus elegantly held out her chair and assisted her as he and Pelham chatted about a new piece of legislation about to be introduced into the House of Lords. In any other house, it would have been an ordinary dinner between friends, but this wasn't an ordinary house or an ordinary dinner.

Marcus leaned close. "Is something amiss?"

He was so near that she could smell his cologne. It was the same bergamot orange that he'd worn last night. An awareness blossomed and slowly warmed her from head to toe. She adjusted herself in her chair and turned his way.

Honoria froze. His gaze seemed to caress every inch of her. Her hand fluttered in her lap as an ache made her insides clench. This was what desire felt like. It had the force of a turbulent river that swept you away, then captured you in a swirling eddy that you couldn't escape from.

And didn't want to.

"What did you say?" she asked softly.

"I asked if something was amiss?" His eyes drifted to her mouth.

It would take so little effort to lean close and press her mouth to his.

"My lady, may I serve you?" Breaking the spell between them, Atwell, a new footman stood behind her chair with a soup tureen.

"Yes, please." Honor allowed a shallow breath to escape. Jasper, the other footman serving them tonight, dipped a ladle into the tureen and filled her bowl with leek and potato soup. She smiled slightly. It was her absolute favorite. "Thank you."

Both men nodded then served Marcus. As the footmen moved

around the table to Pippa and Pelham, Marcus murmured under his breath, "It's not like your brother to serve such plebeian fare."

"I decided the menu tonight." She kept her inflection even, but there was a chill to her tone. Since she turned the age of eighteen, she'd planned the menus for Pelham Hall and had heard nary a complaint.

Even from Pelham.

Honoria folded her serviette into a neat square and rested her hand on her lap. It gave her a moment to tame her chagrin. As a good hostess, she had to ensure that her guests, or rather, her brother's guests, were happy. It was one of the first things she had learned in finishing school.

"If it isn't to your liking, I'll ask for something else to be served." She smiled politely.

His eyes sparkled in awareness, and a slight, teasing grin tugged at the corner of his mouth. "I can tell by the shape of your lips, that I've made you angry. It wasn't my intent. Normally, at the Jolly Rooster, his French cooks serve a ridiculous amount of heavy fare with thick, rich sauces."

"Is that your preference?" she asked.

"No," Marcus confided. "I prefer food like this." He waved a hand at the soup. "Hot, wholesome, and delicious. Much like you."

"Pardon me?" Though she kept her voice low, her incredulity was apparent to her dinner companion.

"Shall we?" Pelham picked up his spoon, signaling that the meal should begin.

Soon, they were all partaking of the excellent soup that the Pelham Hall cook had prepared. Mrs. Collins had been with the family for over two decades, and her skills in the kitchen were exceptional. Any criticism of Mrs. Collins's food would receive a sharp dismissal from Honoria.

With his eyes widened in mirth, Marcus addressed Pelham, "Excellent meal. My regards to your chef."

Pelham nodded. Marcus turned her way and discreetly grinned. The handsome rogue was flirting with her.

"Honoria plans the meals and supervises the pantry," Pippa offered. "She's excellent at keeping the house in order." She turned to their brother. "Wouldn't you agree?"

"Yes," Pelham said warily.

"She ensures that Pelham's secretaries are timely in sending out correspondence."

Honoria blushed at the pride in her sister's voice. "I thank you, but we don't want to bore our guest."

"Not boring at all," Pippa answered, then turned her attention to Marcus. "She also visits the tenants monthly, delivering baskets and inspecting their properties to see if there are any repairs that are needed. She loves to visit their children. She started a school for them and visits regularly. She's always ordering books from London for the students. You should visit with her sometime." Pippa's voice warmed. "The children adore her, just as we all do. Plus, Honoria's amazing at how she keeps Pelham Hall running efficiently along with the estate books. She's masterful at it, really." She dipped her spoon in her soup, then glanced playfully at their brother. "Pelham couldn't spend so much time at the Jolly Rooster otherwise. Isn't that right?"

The befuddlement on their dear brother's face wasn't something you saw every day. Then, like the sun breaking through the clouds, his eyes widened, and he scowled. "What are you doing?"

Smiling, Pippa straightened in her chair. "Something that you should be doing. Extolling the virtues of our glorious sister."

"*Pippa*," Honoria exclaimed. If she could have sunk into the floor and escaped, she would have done it without hesitation. This morning had been one of the most humiliating moments of Honoria's life. Yet, her sister's boasting of her accomplishments came in a close second.

Marcus grinned at Honoria, then turned his attention to Pippa. "I'm enthralled. I beg you to continue."

"After dinner," Pelham ordered, then motioned for the footmen to proceed with the rest of the meal. The next course was perch in hollandaise sauce, followed by sauteed pheasant in a delicate cream sauce. The last course was a cream cake served with sliced apples.

After the footmen had cleared the table, they brought a tray with brandy and four glasses, then left. As soon as the door closed, Pelham poured four glasses and passed them out.

"Let's get down to business, shall we?" their brother announced as he stared at Marcus. "I want to hear everyone's expectations for London." He looked around the table. "Who shall go first?"

Pippa sat on the edge of her seat. "Allow me. I think Grace's plan is sound." She took a sip of brandy and then silently set it on the table. "But the most important thing is that I want to see my sister happy and settled in the life she wants. Not one that has been foisted upon her." She glanced at Honoria with tears welling in her eyes.

The sight instantly made her own eyes water. Her darling sister was her biggest champion and her best friend. "Thank you."

Pippa nodded. "I'd do anything for you."

Pelham strummed his fingers on the table. "We all want Honor happy. But the problem is how to protect her." He lifted a single arrogant eyebrow and gestured toward Marcus. "The same with you."

Marcus leaned back in his chair with an ease that resembled a lion who'd just finished his latest kill. Honoria's stomach tightened at the awkward silence that descended between them all.

Finally, he turned his steely gaze toward Pelham. "I still think we should marry quickly." Then he turned to face Honoria and that familiar slight smile appeared again.

For some unknown reason, she felt comforted by his gesture.

"Lady Noria and I are the ones who shall face whatever happens in society. I haven't had an opportunity to discuss London with her."

"If you think I'll allow you to be alone with her again..." Uncharacteristically, Pelham fell silent when Marcus lifted his hand.

"I'm not asking that. But I would like the opportunity to have a private conversation with her. Perhaps you and your sister would be kind enough to act as chaperones as we take a stroll about the courtyard." He turned to Honoria. "If you're agreeable, my lady?"

Honoria smiled and nodded. Indeed, she'd relish the opportunity to discuss the happenings of the day and how they would interact with each other in society—without any interference from her brother.

"Chaperone," Pelham huffed. "That's like closing the barn door after the cow is out."

"Do not compare our sister to a cow," Pippa scolded.

"I agree," Marcus said in support. "I believe the saying involves a horse instead of cow." He stared at Pelham. "Perhaps you should not have put the horse in the barn in the first place. Some creatures are destined to be free of captivity."

"Hear, hear," Pippa announced.

Good God, Marcus is referring to me. He presumed she was treated like a prisoner here. Her brother had never treated her that way. She was the one who had restricted herself. All because of her fears that the old duke would hurt her.

Marcus stood from the table and extended an arm in Honoria's direction. "Come, my lady. Your night awaits."

Seventeen

~~~

A s soon as Marcus descended the steps into the formal courtyard of Pelham Hall, he could breathe. It was the first time all night that he didn't have to watch every word he uttered.

Pelham and Lady Pippa were chattering like magpies behind them.

"I must apologize for my family." Noria slid him a side-eye glance as they strolled toward a large marble fountain surrounded by Greek statuary. "You see, they're unique."

"And obnoxious," Marcus offered. He was rewarded when one of her rare, beautiful smiles fell his way. "You should do that more often. It makes me not want to pummel your brother into dust."

By then, Pippa's and Pelham's voices had grown softer. They had stopped following them when one of Pelham's retrievers loped into the courtyard, begging for attention.

"Your brother makes a horrible chaperone." Marcus drew her into the circular path that surrounded the fountain where they stopped and faced one another. The soft bubbling of falling water accompanied the sweet call of a nightingale. The air was still. No one could see them as they were on the other side of the massive fountain. All he wanted to do was kiss her, but he needed to keep his wits about him.

"He can get a little carried away," she said with a slight shrug. "Perhaps he trusts you more than you think." She tilted her gaze to his.

If he even thought about kissing her, then things would spiral out of control just like they'd done this morning.

"When you said I'd leave that bed a different person, I had no idea how different. It's hard to believe that it hasn't even been a day...since we were together." A delectable pink darkened Noria's cheeks.

"I've had that same thought." Practically every hour. He was consumed with the idea of having her again. By all rights, he shouldn't even contemplate spending time with her since she threatened his self-control. Yet, he could not stop thinking of her cheeks, or God forbid, her rosy lips. He'd never tasted anything as sweet as her.

He tightened his gut, determined to keep his mind on his purpose, but for a moment, he forgot what his purpose was. "Where was I?"

"Now, our entire futures have changed," she said. "I'll do whatever is necessary to protect your reputation and help your charity."

"Thank you." He brought her hand to his lips. Her statement was simple but heartfelt. It meant the world to him. He continued to press his lips against the soft skin of her knuckles. "There's something else. You never answered my question."

"What question?"

"Will you marry me?"

"I...I" Her eyes widened at his questions.

"Your expression leads me to believe that perhaps I'm going about this all wrong." At least, she wasn't telling him no like she had done earlier. Perhaps she was starting to believe that they could be together. Determined to put her at ease, he grinned. "I want to give you the life that you want. Tell me what that is."

As he was about to reassure her, she laughed. The soft sound melded into perfect harmony with the nightingale and the gurgling fountain. His heart tripped in his chest when her gaze met his, and he remembered everything about their time together—her astonishing wit, her laugh, her kindness, and...her reluctance to marry him.

"I'm not certain you can give it to me. What if it's not the life for you?" She grinned, then stared at the fountain. Slowly, she lifted her gaze to his. "You love the city. I want to live here." She shrugged slightly.

There was more than nonchalance in her tone. It was almost a defensiveness. Finally, he could ask some of the questions that had been rumbling in his thoughts ever since he'd discovered her identity. "Why did you come to the Jolly Rooster that night?"

She dropped his arm and meandered to the other side of the fountain. He followed her, and soon they were surrounded in darkness except for the brilliant moon that hung in the sky above her shoulder. It provided enough light that he could see a myriad of emotions cross her face, including resignation. Marcus needed to be near her, so he closed the distance between them. It was the only way to keep his equilibrium.

"For once in my life, I wanted to know…"

She lowered her voice, so he leaned close to hear her better. The slight scent of her jasmine perfume wafted his way, and he inhaled deeply to capture it and her essence. "You wanted to know what, Noria?"

"Passion. Affection." Her gaze never strayed from his. "Please don't misunderstand. My siblings are wonderful to me. But I wanted someone who wasn't family. Someone who didn't know me and wanted *me* and not a duke's sister. Someone who wanted my affection and would give it to me in return even if it was only for one night." Her pulse pounded in the hollow of her neck, betraying how hard this was for her. "I sound silly."

"Not in the least," he answered softly.

She bit her lower lip and turned away.

What happened to you in the past, Noria, that makes you believe you don't deserve those things in life? Thankfully, he didn't say it. "And I happened to be the lucky man who found you first."

"Or the unlucky one," she quipped. "You were the one who had to stare at Pelham's pistol this morning."

He took her hand in his and squeezed. The coolness of her skin surprised him. "There was no harm done. I'm still here."

"Thank heavens." She tilted her head and stared at the sky. "I just wanted that one night with you, and then I could live my life with no regrets. You have my sincerest apologies if I've caused unnecessary complications and problems for you. I'll talk to Pelham and ensure he understands that none of it is your fault."

He pressed a finger to her lips. "I value your brother. I always have. For years, he's been like my family. Family forgives family." He delivered his most charming smile.

She smiled in answer.

In that moment, things changed between them. For the better. He could feel it.

A crushing need to nuzzle her neck and press his lips against her pulse roared to life, but he focused on her. "Would you want that passion and affection every day of your life?"

"Hmm." She swallowed, then forced her gaze from the study of the sky to his. "I've learned that it's more conducive to a happy life if I focus on expectations instead of wants."

"Don't you believe that we would have that?" He'd not leave Pelham Hall until he understood why she was hesitant to marry him. "I believe we would."

"It's not that." She placed her hand on his arm, offering comfort. "What if we married and you discovered we didn't suit one another?"

"We'd work to make it better," he answered a little too quickly.

"That's an easy answer. What if something happened to make you realize you'd made a mistake?" she asked.

Was she referring to herself marrying another but used him as an example? His nostrils flared as a sudden wave of jealousy swept through him. "Is there another you want to marry?"

She sighed but didn't answer him. Her silence was enough to warn him away from the subject. She had enjoyed his company just as he'd enjoyed hers. He was convinced of it.

"Help me understand."

"I'm doubtful that marriage to me would be right for you and your future." Her soft voice was laced with a steely conviction.

"Some things would require work, but I think that gives a person purpose. I'd want you to be by my side as we work on my charity." He took both of her hands and squeezed her fingers gently. "We could build something spectacular. It would be our legacy to our children if we were so blessed. I don't want to waste this life. Come, be my wife. Stand by my side."

She turned away but squeezed his fingers just as he'd done to her.

In that moment, he grew weary.

Weary of her dismissing what they had shared last night.

Weary of denying himself the pleasure of her lips.

"It's not a hard choice," he argued gently. "Easy doesn't always mean it's the wrong decision. Let me show you."

"How?" Her eyes searched his.

He put his arms around her waist and pulled her close. "By kissing you." Slowly, he lowered his mouth to hers. A slight moan escaped her lips. If it meant she craved him as much as he wanted her, then they could converse for hours without saying a single word to each other.

When her lips parted, he deepened the kiss. As he swept his tongue into her mouth, hers was waiting in welcome. The sensation of holding her this close and showing her everything he felt in that moment made him believe they were doing the right thing. He just had to convince her.

As they grasped each other tighter, their tongues moved in a sensual dance. He pulled her against him. Whatever desire that had ignited last night paled in heat and fire to what was happening between them now.

He was ravenous for her. It was an insatiable hunger that could only be satisfied by her, but she broke apart from him and inhaled deeply. She was practically panting.

He was the same. He trailed his lips across her cheek and kissed the area directly below her ear. He'd discovered how sensitive it was last night when she'd moaned in encouragement.

"Noria, you said marriage would be too easy. Does it feel that way to you now?" He ground his hard cock against her as he raked his teeth gently down her neck. "I could take you now," he whispered. "I want to give you the passion and affection you crave. I crave it too."

"I could take *you* now," she countered and bit his lower lip. Not hard enough to draw blood but hard enough to garner his attention. Then she kissed him without any hesitation, reminding him she was his equal and as essential as the air he breathed.

"I won't stop until I get a yes."

"Kissing me?" she parried. "I'll always say yes to that."

"I'm serious," he said.

"So am I." She grinned.

"Marry me."

Her eyes danced with delight. Then the minx kissed him again.

"I'll take that as a yes." He laughed as he pulled away from their kiss. "However, we must stop." Marcus rested his forehead against Noria's as he struggled to tame the fiery desire that threatened to incinerate them both. "Else we'll find ourselves naked on the grass."

"For the love of my head gardener and the rest of mankind, please refrain yourself," a masculine voice growled behind him.

Noria's gaze shot to her brother. "Pelham."

"Damn him," Marcus muttered, then pressed his lips against hers again in a promise that they hadn't finished the conversation.

"Honor, perhaps it would best if you go inside. Pippa is looking for you."

She nodded at her brother, then turned to Marcus. "Good night, my lord." She curtseyed to Marcus then swept down the path toward the portico where Pippa waited for her.

Marcus nonchalantly turned and studied the duke.

Pelham's face had never been so dark and austere. The only time Marcus could recall him as menacing was when he'd had to revoke a membership to the Jolly Rooster for bad behavior. The fact that it was directed at Marcus should have unnerved him. Instead, he found a rising fury within him.

"There will be hell to pay for this, Trafford." Pelham took a step forward. "If you think I'll allow you to maul my sister in public—"

"Enough," Marcus bit out. "I'll deliver the same. What the hell have you done to her?"

"Meaning?" The chill in Pelham's voice would have sent an ordinary man scurrying away to escape the duke's wrath.

Thankfully, Marcus had never been intimidated by the man. "Why won't she accept my hand in marriage?"

"I thought she had," Pelham answered curtly.

"No. I want to hear her say it." His jaw tightened. Why was she being so obstinate? "Is there someone else? Did you tell her that I was a bad match?"

Pelham's eyes widened in shock. "Of course not. Are you serious?"

"Deadly. What is she scared of?"

"To my knowledge, there is no one else." Pelham scowled slightly.

"She would have told me. Besides, I would never characterize Honor as fearful." He tapped his index finger against his chin regarding Marcus. "Perhaps she knows of your reputation as a rake."

Marcus had never been so frustrated and angry in his life. "I may have had loose morals in my youth, but we both know that's no longer true of me." He ran a hand through his hair, desperate to control his frustration. "I have no experience with any of this, and I'm in a quandary as to how to proceed."

"Take my advice. Woo her in London. Perhaps she feels forced into a corner. Let her learn more about you. She'll warm to the idea of marriage to you. But know this if she doesn't"—he shrugged—"I won't force her."

"Fair warning. I won't leave her alone," Marcus answered.

"I understand," Resigned, Pelham nodded once.

"I have a piece of advice for you." Marcus took a slow gander at the powerful duke before him. "You should spend more time with your delightful sister. I plan to."

Without waiting for Pelham's reply, Marcus turned on his heel and proceeded to leave Pelham Hall. He couldn't wait to return to London. It would give him some needed distance from his aggravating friend.

More importantly, it would give him an opportunity to woo his Venus.

After blowing out all the candles in her bedroom, Honoria drew back a curtain along the wall of windows that overlooked the formal courtyard. Pelham and Marcus were still in a conversation. Abruptly, Marcus turned and strolled through the garden toward the house, then stopped and stared directly at her window. Though there was no earthly way for him to see her, she held her breath. After a moment, he continued into the house. In moments, she heard his carriage pull away.

"His stare sent chills down my spine," Pippa whispered. "He knew you were there."

Honoria placed her hand over her heart, hoping it would slow the galloping beat. "He couldn't have seen us."

Pippa shook her head. "He is certainly intense. What did you two discuss in the courtyard before Pelham discovered you?"

"You mean the Duke of Busybodies?" When Pippa laughed, Honoria smiled at her own joke. "If you couldn't see us, then you don't know. He caught us in a kiss."

"A kiss?" Pippa's face brightened as she walked to Honoria's bed then scooted onto the purple brocade bedcovering. She patted the spot beside her. "Come and tell me all." She sighed slightly. "How romantic."

Honoria sat on the bed and drew her legs underneath her skirts. "At first, we were arguing, then, before I knew it...we were kissing and arguing at the same time." She could still feel the touch of his mouth against her. His firm but soft lips had been unrelenting and had drawn forth all her pent-up wants and needs. He made her feel cherished and wanted in a way that she'd never experienced before.

"Arguing about what?" Pippa tilted her head and narrowed her eyes. It was as if Honoria were an intricate-locking puzzle, and her sister was determined to bend and shake every piece until it unlocked.

"He asked me to marry him again." She picked at the bedcovering, hoping to discourage her sister's inquisition.

"How did you answer this time?" Pippa's voice was laced with hope.

"Perhaps." Just saying the word felt foreign. Was she actually considering his proposal? He was a wonderful man and if she were any other woman, she would be thrilled. Ecstatic even. But she'd rather stab herself in the back than hurt him or her family. "Sometimes, I wonder if it would've been better if I'd never gone to that masquerade ball. I'm caught in a web, and I can't find a way out. A wonderfully nice man thinks I lied to him about my identity, and he is correct. Yet he still honors me by asking for my hand."

"Look at me, Honor," Pippa commanded gently.

When Honoria tilted her gaze, she found her normally jovial sister wearing a serious expression.

"You did nothing wrong." When Honoria opened her mouth to object, Pippa put her hand up to keep her from objecting. "Yes, I know a duke's sister shouldn't be attending such parties in disguise. Nor should they be finding a man to make love to. But these were special circumstances. You wanted to experience the company of a man, a wonderful one at that." She scooted closer to Honoria and took her hand.

Honoria entwined their fingers together. "I'm the creator of this scandal. It isn't Marcus's fault." She squeezed Pippa's fingers and lowered her gaze. "Do you know what I feel the most horrid about?"

Pippa shook her head.

"If our scandal destroyed his friendship with Pelham or hurt his charity, I'm fearful Marcus would never forgive me." Her heart stumbled in her chest as tears welled in her eyes. She, above all others, knew that a family was more precious than wealth. "Our brother is the closest thing to a family Marcus has."

"Oh, darling," Pippa softly murmured in comfort. "You didn't know."

"That doesn't make me feel any better. I know how I would feel if I ever lost either you or Pelham. It would be devastating."

Pippa's brow wrinkled, marring the smoothness of her skin. "Would it really be the end of the world if you married Marcus. You wouldn't have to move away."

"Pippa..." She didn't want to keep her sister out, but it was difficult to talk about. "My worst fear is that we go to London, and the rumors are worse than we expect. If that occurs, you, Pelham, and Marcus will suffer. All because of me." Her throat swelled, and tears burned her eyes. She was so tired of the old duke reaching a bony arm out of the grave to steal her happiness.

"What if Marcus falls in love with you and you with him? Isn't it worth the risk to take a chance on love?" Pippa asked innocently.

"That only happens in books," Honoria argued. Not in real life when you're not who you say you are.

"Nonsense. Look at King George III and Queen Charlotte. They were a love match." Pippa crossed her arms.

"In counterpoint, I offer the Prince of Wales and the Princess of Wales. They hate each other."

"Darling, stop." Pippa leaned over and enveloped her in a hug. "It must be frightening to have your life upended. Let alone being tossed into London society when you want no part of it. But you should look at it from a different perspective." She leaned back and took Honoria's hands in hers. "Be open to new experiences. You should look upon this as a grand adventure. It'll be like the London Season you never had. We'll go to the theatre, the opera, musicales, shopping, and gorge ourselves on Gunther's ices." Pippa exclaimed while clapping her hands. "Allow yourself to be open to...involvements of the heart with Marcus."

"Pippa," she warned.

"I saw how you both looked at each other tonight. I'm only suggesting that you not destroy this chance for happiness. Let Marcus show you what's in his heart." She pointed to the middle of Honoria's chest. "And you should consider what is in here." She yawned. "I must retire. We're leaving early for London tomorrow." She kissed Honoria on the check and left.

Honoria's gaze drifted to the window where Marcus had stood. He was resolute that they'd marry. She closed her eyes.

Without a second thought, she went to her desk and pulled out a sheet of parchment. There would be little chance her siblings or Marcus would see it. Let alone anyone else. It only took a moment to write the notice of her pending marriage to her pretend fiancé. She folded the parchment, melted wax over the closure, then pressed her personal seal in the middle.

Did she dare take this risk?

She must. Otherwise, she'd never forgive herself.

She wanted to marry Marcus Kirkland, the Earl of Trafford. For the first time in her life, she felt hope and wanted her future to be tied to his.

Eighteen

A s the black ducal coach neared Ardeerton House in Mayfair, Honoria vowed that this time when she entered the family's London home, she would not allow memories of the previous duke to haunt her. Last night, after she'd addressed her letter to the publisher of the *Law Chronicle*, the legal newspaper published weekly in London, she'd taken it to Winston. He had promised to post it the next day. Everything was set in motion. If fate was kind, the letter would be sent to Pelham Hall within two weeks.

Perhaps she could marry Marcus. But until she had that letter in hand, she wouldn't allow her fantasies to venture too far afield.

She looked out the carriage window. Nothing in London seemed familiar or even friendly. If Marcus were with her, she wouldn't even care how gray or lonely the city appeared. All her attention would be devoted to him.

She sat in the forward-facing seat. Pippa and their lady's maid, Alice, sat in the rear-facing seat. As soon as they'd left Pelham Hall, Pippa had compiled lists of places to visit and shop. Frankly, it did little to relieve Honoria's worries. They would still be in London, and it still would be the place she had been banished from.

"We're almost there," Pippa announced. She gracefully stood and slid onto the bench next to Honoria.

"Indeed." She squeezed her sister's hand.

"Perhaps we insist our brother throw a party on our behalf." Pippa smiled. "No matter how much he protests, we won't give in. Together, we'll conquer."

Honoria laughed at such silliness, but she didn't really want such entertainment either. Yet, the excitement on Pippa's face made her want to share in her sister's happiness. Perhaps she could tolerate a small dinner party or two.

"My ladies"—Alice looked out the window—"I believe Lady Grace is waiting to greet you outside Ardeerton House."

Like two children, she and Pippa stared out the window at the late Palladium home that was Ardeerton House. Indeed, it was Lady Grace in a beautiful peacock blue gown with a matching bonnet.

"Is that our brother with her?" Honoria said in wonder.

Pippa nodded. "I do hope he's acting a bit wicked. A mild flirtation would lighten the mood considerably for all of us. If he acts too ducal, she might just throw up her hands and desert us."

"I believe she's made of sterner stuff than that." As the carriage rocked slightly turning into the drive, Honoria pulled on her gloves and straightened her hat. Perhaps being in London wouldn't be as bad as she'd imagined.

Mayhap if she kept saying that to herself, she'd believe it.

When they stopped, a liveried footman unfolded the steps and opened the door. "Welcome home, Lady Honoria."

She instantly recognized him as James Grant, one of the footmen from Pelham Hall who had been promoted to head footman at Ardeerton House. "Hello, James. It's lovely to see you. I hope you've been well. How's your mother?"

The exceptionally trained footman's eyes widened briefly before he replied, "She's much improved, my lady. It's been over a year since she was ill."

Honoria smiled at the news as she stepped down. "I'm so happy to hear that."

"Thank you for remembering. My mum will be so pleased when I share that you asked about her." He lowered his voice so the others wouldn't hear. "I've worked in many households before coming to Pelham Hall and Ardeerton House. Not many of your peers would think to ask about a footman's family."

"My family is fortunate to have you as part of the staff here." She meant every word of it. James sent most of his salary home to his family in Sussex. He valued family. "I just wish you would move home to Pelham Hall."

"If I may be so bold, perhaps you'll consider residing in London." A slight smile creased his lips, then he turned to help Pippa and Alice.

"You've finally arrived," Grace announced and linked her arm around Honoria's. "Your brother and I were just chatting."

"I hope he was behaving." Honoria glanced in her brother's direction. Pelham rolled his eyes, but a tell-tale flush reddened his cheeks. She'd surely interrupted something.

"As best as His Grace can," Grace acknowledged, then laughed. "Excuse me while I greet Pippa."

"Honor," he said with a nod, but his gaze followed Grace as she made her way to meet their sister. "You've made excellent time."

"We never stopped except for the time when highwaymen shouted, 'stand and deliver.' Of course, they ravished me," she said matter-of-factly. "Repeatedly."

"Excellent," her brother answered, not looking at her.

"I must have interrupted something important between the two of you?" Honoria poked him in the arm. "Did you even hear what I said?"

"There's nothing going on between the two of us. She's a menace and a curmudgeon." He pursed his lips in the same manner as when he ate a tart lemon. "Yes, I heard every word you said. You never stopped. Glad to hear it. That damnable woman is giving orders like she's the duke."

"Meaning?" Honoria glanced at Pippa and Grace. Alice had already gone inside to see about unpacking their trunks. Grace had a beautiful smile on her face. With her black hair and green eyes, she was stunning.

Pelham finally turned his attention to her. "The Governess has set up appointments at several modistes, haberdashers, and"—he frowned in annoyance—"cobblers and perfumeries."

"It all sounds exquisite to me," Pippa said as she joined them. "Grace was telling me that you volunteered to escort us."

"More like I was commanded," Pelham murmured.

Pippa leaned in and kissed his cheek. "You're such an amazing brother."

By then, Grace had joined them. "He's amazing in so many ways. Come, my ladies, we have a luncheon prepared, and I'd thought we'd sort through the invitations that you've received."

"Invitations? People already know we're in town?" Pippa asked incredulously as she hooked her arm through Honoria's.

"Seems the Governess made certain every single person in the *ton* knew we'd arrived." Pelham didn't hide his churlishness.

"Your Grace, it was my utmost pleasure," Grace said with a sickeningly sweet smile.

Their brother had turned to go inside the house when Honoria called out, "Pelham?"

"Yes?" He stopped. His gaze shifted between the three of them.

"Would you escort Grace inside," Honoria asked.

In response, he held out his arm.

"Always the epitome of decorum," Grace cooed.

Pippa burst out laughing as did Honoria. With a huff, Pelham ignored them, then escorted Grace up the front steps.

"How do you think they met one another?" Pippa wiped a tear as the remnants of one soft giggle escaped.

"I have no idea. Perhaps we'll uncover the truth while we're here." Honoria tugged her sister's arm, and soon they were inside the house.

When their elegant elderly butler saw them, he called out, "Welcome, Lady Honoria and Lady Pippa." When he bowed deeply, his head of bushy white hair didn't move an inch.

As a little girl, she'd thought it a scientific marvel that a hair was never out of place on his head. "Ritson, it's wonderful to see you."

"I feel the same, Lady Honoria." He beamed at her, then turned his attention to Pippa. "And, my lady, welcome home again."

"It feels good to be back." Pippa held out her pelisse, and an attending footman took it.

Honoria held her tongue. If only it felt the same for her.

"My ladies, Lady Grace thought you might enjoy partaking in the refreshment offerings in the small breakfast room." Ritson bowed.

"Thank you." Pippa tugged Honoria along. "Tea sounds marvelous. I'm famished."

As they wove their way to the family quarters where the private breakfast room was located, the walls seemed to narrow. Honoria felt every inch of the place was primed to crush her with the old duke's belittling voice haunting her. She could practically hear him bellow, *"Get her out of my sight."*

Honoria abruptly stopped and placed her hand over her chest as her heartbeat accelerated. She would never survive London.

"Are you all right?" Pippa asked. Her gaze narrowed in concern.

For a moment, Honor tried to form a response, but she was trapped in the old duke's machinations. Finally, she took a deep breath and composed herself. "I'm lost in memories. I swear I heard the old duke's voice."

Pippa squeezed her hand. "He can't hurt you anymore. If you want to go upstairs, Dane will understand. I'll tell everyone else you're tired."

"No. I want to do this." She was acting like a ninny scared by ghosts. It was time she pushed aside her memories of the old duke. Without hesitating, Honoria led the way. As they were about to enter the dining room, the smell of mushroom tarts and fresh tea greeted them. Honoria stepped through the threshold, then stopped.

Marcus stood in the middle of the room. His gaze collided with hers. But it wasn't an ordinary glance. He practically stared straight through her as if this were the first time that he'd ever seen her. Immediately, her gaze fell to her skirts to see if something was out of order. She was a bit wrinkled, but that was to be expected with her travel from Amesbury.

"My word, he can't take his eyes off you," Pippa murmured softly.

"Perhaps my hair is out of place," Honoria whispered as she patted her coiffeur to ensure it had not fallen sideways.

"No, darling. You're beautiful," Pippa said with sweet affection in her voice. "It just proves what I said last night. He's taken with you."

By then, Marcus was strolling to their side. As soon as he reached them, he delivered a courtly bow. "Welcome to London."

Pippa curtseyed in return. "It's wonderful to see you, Trafford. If you'll excuse me?" She didn't wait for an answer but headed to the refreshment table, leaving Marcus and Honoria alone.

"Your trip was uneventful, I presume?" he asked with a slight grin.

He was *actually happy* to see her.

"Thank you for asking. It was a pleasant trip." She leaned close and lowered her voice. "I told Pelham that we were set upon by highwaymen. Do you know what his response was?"

Marcus shook his head. "Do tell. But I imagine he went into a blind fury and vowed to capture such a treacherous lot and string them up by their toes."

"Hardly." She laughed. "He said, '*Excellent.*'" She glanced at her brother, who was still scowling at the Governess. "He was staring at Lady Grace at the time. I've never seen him so out of sorts before. Have you?"

Marcus followed her gaze. "He does seem inordinately preoccupied with her, doesn't he?" He chuckled slightly, and the whisky-dark sound vibrated against her chest.

Each time she saw him, the pull between them grew stronger.

She should not dwell upon that. Everything they had shared at Amesbury was left behind. They were here to repair their reputations. She sighed at such a daunting task, but she was determined to succeed for her family's sake and, as importantly, Marcus's sake.

"What are you doing here?" she asked him.

"I wanted to see you." A corner of his mouth hitched upward in a grin.

"Oh." She smiled in return. Only he could make London bearable for her.

"You can tell me later how wonderful it is to see me." He leaned close, and his warm breath caressed her neck. It was almost a kiss. "In private."

She leaned near him, craving his scent, his warmth, but most of all craving him.

When he pulled away, his face darkened slightly. "Are you sure you want to do all of this?"

She nodded. "We must. There's no turning back now."

He took her hand and raised it to his lips. "As long as we're together, we'll succeed."

The gleam in his eyes reminded her of a hungry predator. Good heavens, he was even more handsome than she remembered.

Grace was by their side then. "Honoria, won't you escort Lord Trafford to the buffet and serve yourselves? Once we're all seated, I'll tell you what I have planned."

"Of course," Honoria said. Grace turned and walked back to the table where Pelham and Pippa were already seated and partaking of their tea and tarts.

"She would have made a brilliant strategist for Wellington, don't you think?" Marcus laughed slightly and took her arm.

As they approached the buffet, Honoria couldn't help but tense a little at the fact that her arm was entangled with his. Though he wore a fine woolen morning coat with a linen shirt beneath it, she could easily imagine the feel of his naked skin against hers. She drew in a deep breath, ready to tame her errant flights of fancy.

Instead, she was teased by his scent of bergamot and orange and pure male. Her breath hitched at the raw sensuality that enveloped her.

"Something wrong?" he asked as he gave her a plate so she could serve herself.

"No," she replied but her voice trembled a bit betraying the effect he had on her. It helped to have something to focus on besides him. She picked up a mushroom tart, a miniature cream cake, and spooned several fresh strawberries on her plate. Shortly, they were seated side by side.

Once they'd eaten, it was quickly decided that Honoria would attend outings in Hyde Park, strolls along the Serpentine, and rides in the fashionable places around town. The first ride was with Marcus and Pelham.

Grace smiled as her gaze darted to Marcus. "Will that be acceptable to you, Lord Trafford?"

"No." The curt word sailed around the room. "I hardly think that Noria being seen with me and her brother will stop the gossip. If we were married and seen together, it would be a different story."

Pippa sighed and turned to Grace. "Every time he calls her Noria makes me believe in true love."

"Pippa, please," Honoria said quietly. Her cheeks flamed hotter than a farrier's fire. Just then, a hand touched hers under the table.

Without anyone seeing a thing, Marcus had laid his hand over hers and squeezed. Just from the sureness of his touch, she relaxed.

Pelham ignored everyone except for Marcus. "Ack, old man." He tutted dismissively. "Let Lady Grace do her magic. She has more experience with such matters than all of us put together."

This time it was Honoria's turn to squeeze his hand. She prayed that he understood that it wasn't worth fighting a battle over her.

With her free hand, she fidgeted with her serviette. "I'm not established in society, so hopefully, they won't even notice." She tried to laugh. "They'll probably forget all about me by the next ball."

Grace narrowed her eyes. "It's not that easy, Noria. Consider this like a twelve-course meal. This is only the first course."

Honoria stilled at Grace's use of Marcus's pet name for her.

"You seem to be forgetting that you're a duke's daughter and the sister of the current Duke of Pelham. You are a major part of society whether you have attended events or not. Everyone wants to see Pelham's elusive sister. With Lord Carlyle's rumors about you and Lord Trafford, you'll be even more popular. Wildly so."

Honoria blinked slowly. "Surely, you jest."

Grace slowly shook her head. "I'm afraid not. Rumors can make a person popular, then the scourge of society next." She smiled kindly at Honoria. "Don't worry. We'll navigate you through these rocky shores without capsizing. I promise you."

A footman entered and gave a letter to Pelham. He thanked the servant, then read the note. Pelham stood and straightened his morning coat. "I apologize. I must meet with my solicitor. As soon as I'm finished, I'll return." He turned to Honoria. "Then, I'll be completely at your service for the rest of the day." He executed a bow, then left the room.

Marcus let go of her hand, then leaned so close that his breath tickled her ear. "I need you...alone."

Nineteen

Marcus turned to Grace. "I need to speak with Lady Noria. If you or Lady Pippa would stay with us, I'd be much obliged."

"Of course," Grace answered. "Shall we make our way to the family sitting room? A change of scenery would do us all a world of good."

"What is this about?" Honoria whispered to Marcus.

"Excited, are you? Excellent." He offered his arm.

Noria slipped her arm through his. "Do you know where the family sitting room is?"

He nodded. "I'm normally in London the same time as your brother. I know where he keeps his rare bottles of whisky. If you ever want one, I'll sneak you down there."

"You've been in the basement?" As they climbed the steps to the second floor where the family's sitting room was located, Honoria slid him a side-eye glance. "You know this house better than I do."

For a moment, he didn't know how to respond. For all the years of his friendship with Pelham, Marcus had never asked the circumstances of why Noria never visited. "Don't you care for this house?"

She smiled, but it didn't reach her eyes. "It never felt like home." She pulled him into the sitting room where Pippa and Grace had already arrived. They sat in front of a table with fabric samples spread across the stop.

Both nodded when he and Noria entered, but they quickly went back to inspecting the samples.

"Let's walk around the room," Noria offered. "Sitting in a carriage all day, I prefer to walk."

He kept his pace slow but, thankfully, it was a large room, and they could conduct a conversation without drawing the others' attention. "Why did you never come to London? I'm not talking about a Season. I'm talking about with Pelham and Lady Pippa."

He could practically see the mask that slowly slid down her face.

She waited a moment before she responded. "I prefer living in the country."

"Most women I know can't wait to come to the city. They love the shopping, the theatre, the arts, and the freedoms and adventures it allows."

"I'm not most women," she retorted. "Why do you enjoy London?"

"Friends. My charity mainly. I must be here to meet with people and encourage them to help the children. I try to match them with adults who can be a friend and a confidant as they grow into adulthood."

"I'm sure you're marvelous at it." Her eyes sparkled.

An unfamiliar heat bludgeoned his cheeks at her kind words. "Thank you." He slowed their walk. "I want you to meet one of the small boys that I mentor. He's the Duke of Dartmore. He's a shy lad, and I think you might be the one to bring him out of his shell."

"Me?" She drew back in mock horror. "Why me?"

Because you're the one who makes me believe that life isn't as lonely as I once thought. I can be myself without pretense. You can do the same for a lonely nine-year-old boy. You'll be in his heart forever.

Just like you might be in mine.

What bloody nonsense. Thankfully he didn't say any of that aloud.

But the more time he spent away from her, the more he realized that he was missing something very important in his life. He had Pelham's and Ravenscroft's friendships, and they were priceless to him, but now, he wanted something more. Something more with a woman.

A specific woman named Honoria.

For as long as he lived, he'd never forget that night in the lodge with her and not feeling he had to entertain her every minute of the hours they'd spent together. They were comfortable with each other. For him, it was a heady experience and one that had always proven elusive with other women. Yet, how to say it without scaring her away?

"Underneath it all, you are a true friend to others. The time you spend with the tenants, the school, and with the staff at Pelham Hall is a testament to your good deeds. But your friendship and love for your family is exemplary."

And he was a lucky devil to be included in her close circle of friends. Or at least, he hoped he was in her circle of friends.

But Marcus wanted Dartmore to see what real friendship meant, and a visit from Noria and Pelham would be a wonderful preview of friendships between male friends and siblings.

Marcus wanted the young duke to find his fortune in friends since he'd lost everyone except his little sister. The friends that the young duke would make in school might very well become his new family in some way. Much like Pelham and Ravenscroft were Marcus's family. More importantly, it was imperative that the young duke have something to look forward to besides the dullness of his everyday life. Other than a nursemaid and governess, the boy and his sister had no one.

He reminded Marcus of himself.

"No one needs a group of friends more than that lad. He lost his parents to a carriage accident on the continent. His only family is a little sister."

"How horrible. Those poor children." Tears welled in her eyes.

That's what he loved—admired—about Honoria. She was empathetic. That's what had caused such a response. Most society women said the right things, but for many, there were never any real feelings behind their words. But with the naked emotion in her eyes, he knew that Noria spoke the truth.

"My father died when I was fourteen and my mother a short time later, but I was practically an adult," she continued. "They're so young, and such a loss is devastating."

He paused at her words. Who thought a fourteen-year-old was close to being an adult? "When I was fourteen, adulthood was some distant future. I was more worried about a new cricket bat and buying my first horse." He leaned close until his mouth almost touched her ear and whispered, "I still have that mare. Her name is Athena."

"But you were riding a stallion when I met you. Where's Athena?" The sparkle was back in her eyes, and he was determined to keep it there.

"She's at Woodbury Park, retired and out to pasture. She's a little grayer and a little slower, but she's a beauty. The next time we're in Amesbury, I'd love for you to meet her."

A melancholy look flashed briefly in her eyes, and she took a step back. "I'd be honored to meet her...someday." Unsolicited, she continued, "I had a pony when I was a girl." She peeked at him through her lashes. "She was my best friend. When I lost her, I...well, you can imagine the pain. You're lucky to still have Athena."

"Will you come?" he asked. Whether it was to seek her promise in seeing Athena or Dartmore, he didn't clarify. Perhaps if she just said yes, he could hold her to both promises.

"Yes," she said.

He wanted to shout in jubilation, but he just smiled. "Excellent."

"What time shall we meet Dartmore and his sister?"

"Her name is Lady Julia Banbury. Perhaps directly after you finish at the modiste." By now, they stood at the end of the long rectangular room. Pippa and Lady Grace were still engrossed in their conversation. "I wager I could kiss you now, and neither of your chaperones would object."

She smiled at such an outrageous suggestion, then leaned in until only inches separated them. "I dare you."

Her ruby lips were so close that he could practically taste them. His gaze slid to her mouth at the exact moment she bit her lower lip. Like a magnet's pull, he couldn't resist such temptation. He leaned closer until less than an inch separated his mouth from celebrating the heavenly taste of hers. He lifted his gaze to hers. "We're playing with fire," he whispered.

"Do it," she commanded softly before a booming voice echoed in the room.

"My ladies," Ritson called out.

Instantly, they pulled away from each other.

"Lord Carlyle to see Lady Honoria."

Honoria's gaze flew to his, then the butler. "Here?"

"Indeed, my lady. I took the initiative and put him in the formal salon downstairs." The butler sniffed loudly revealing his displeasure. "His mother is with him."

"Oh, dear." Pippa stood. "Grace can accompany me. I'll meet him and Lady Carlyle. We'll tell them that you're resting."

Marcus and Honoria crossed the room to stand next to Lady Grace and Pippa.

Lady Grace put her hand on Pippa's arm to stop her. "Darling, that won't work."

"I agree. He probably saw my carriage outside and decided to investigate," Marcus added. Just like a damnable boggart, Carlyle was already trying to intimidate Noria. "I have a suggestion. Why don't we all greet them in the salon?"

Lady Grace's eyes widened. "An excellent idea. It'll be our first salvo in introducing you and Honoria to society as a couple."

Honoria shook her head slightly. "I'm not ready."

"Yes, you are," Marcus soothed. "I'll be right by your side. I won't allow him to spew any innuendos, nor will I allow him to say anything that will make you uncomfortable."

Lady Grace and Pippa nodded in agreement.

Noria took a moment and smoothed her hand down her skirts, a bit unsure of herself. Then she did what he had come to expect from her over the short time they'd known each other. She tilted her chin, perfected her posture, and claimed a bit of haughtiness that would be expected from the sister of a powerful duke.

"Shall we?" she asked with an assuredness about her that was absolutely mesmerizing.

And completely seductive.

"Come, let's not keep your guests waiting." Marcus glanced at Noria and smiled. It was one of reassurance and, thankfully, she returned the smile. He vowed then and there that he'd help fight whatever battle she faced. He'd never leave her side as long as she needed him.

He hoped she needed him forever. Just as he hoped she knew how much he needed her.

Together, they followed Ritson to the salon. The butler nodded at the two footmen who stood at the double doors. Simultaneously, they opened the doors, and Ritson, in his most arrogant butler voice, announced the ladies first, then Marcus.

As soon as they entered the room, Carlyle stood, but there was a hint of challenge in his demeanor.

If the *bloody earl* was here to stir up trouble, Marcus promised to deliver it.

As the eldest sister, Honoria moved forward. "What an unexpected surprise to see you both."

Marcus chuckled slightly at her "unexpected surprise" phrasing. It was a surprise to see a rat in the house. It was completely unexpected to see two.

As Lady Carlyle struggled to stand, Honoria held out her hand. "No need for you to stand, my lady."

The old woman collapsed onto the black and white striped formal sofa with a look of gratitude.

Lord Carlyle smiled fondly at his mother and waved a hand in her direction. The movement flicked the lace at his wrist into an extravagant wave of decadence. "*Maman* suffers from a bit of rheumatism today, but she wouldn't have missed this visit for all the world."

With his cream pantaloons, crimson waistcoat, and black silk morning coat, Carlyle easily could claim the title of the king of dandies. What a waste of time and energy. The man surely had responsibilities and duties besides aggravating Noria.

The earl turned and greeted the other ladies before swinging his attention to Marcus. "Trafford."

"Carlyle," Marcus addressed the earl, then turned to the dowager countess. "Lady Carlyle." He performed a succinct bow. As soon as the necessary greetings were completed, he returned to Noria's side. It was a clear sign that she was with him.

"Shall we all sit?" Noria asked while waiting for everyone to take their chosen positions on the two matching sofas that faced one another. Pippa and Lady Grace sat on the sofa facing Carlyle and his mother. Noria took a seat on a chair close to both sofas. Marcus took the remaining seat next to hers. "I'm afraid His Grace had to call on his solicitors. "But he's expected to return shortly."

"We're not here for him."

The earl's sly smile sent a rush of disgust through Marcus.

"We wanted to be the first to welcome you to London and to offer our escort," Carlyle announced with a gentlemanly tilt of his head.

"You're a tad late," Marcus offered. "As you can see, I'm first. Besides Lady Grace."

Lady Carlyle's eyes widened slightly at the brusqueness in his tone, and Marcus arched an eyebrow in challenge.

"Word has it that you traveled together," Carlyle offered in a sickly sweet voice that didn't hide the growl in his voice. The man was definitely annoyed by the fact that Marcus was present.

"Lord Trafford traveled with our brother. We came separately," Noria answered.

"I see," Carlyle said. "If we'd known you were coming today and that the duke wouldn't accompany you, I would have been delighted to offer my escort as you traveled."

"But you're already here in London," Noria pointed out.

"Still, the earl is correct," Lady Carlyle chimed in. "Ladies shouldn't travel alone. It's unseemly."

Marcus opened his mouth to object, but Noria did the honors for him. "The duke always ensures our safety is his top priority. We had an entire battalion of ducal outriders with us."

Carlyle reached over and patted his mother's hand. "You're always so kind. Looking out for others."

At her son's praise, any hint of Lady Carlyle's disheartened disposition evaporated. The lady practically beamed. "Thank you."

Carlyle swung his gaze to Lady Grace. "I'm delighted but astonished to see you here. Surely, you're not here to repair any ruined reputations."

Noria bristled beside him. Marcus wanted to roll his eyes at the insincerity that practically oozed from Carlyle. He sat on the edge of his seat ready to give the earl the tongue lashing he so deserved. But Lady Grace was one-step ahead of him.

"Lud," Grace exclaimed curly. "Anyone who knows me knows how close I am to the Ardeerton family. Of course, I'm here to welcome them."

Carlyle nodded knowingly. "We all know your past with the illustrious family, particularly with the duke." His hint of disapproval was clear to all of them.

Lady Pippa huffed quietly. "Lady Grace and I are dear friends."

But when he turned his attention back to Honoria, Marcus's gut clenched as he waited for the next round of poison to spew from the earl's mouth.

"Have you decided what events you're likely to attend this week? It would be an honor if I could escort you and, of course, your sister, to Lord and Lady Merriman's ball the evening after next."

Noria smiled politely. "I'm not certain of our social calendar yet, my lord. But thank you for your interest. I'm certain that we'll see each other at the various events."

Marcus wanted to clap his hands and shout "huzzah" at her gracious response, which deflected the earl's obvious attempt to wheedle his way into her social life.

"Besides, my brother and Lord Trafford will accompany us to any event we choose to attend," she offered with a smile.

"Of course, my lady. In case your brother or the earl can't accompany you, my offer still stands. We all know how busy the duke is with his business pursuits, particularly the ones in Amesbury. And Trafford has other *interests* in London, I've heard."

Marcus fisted his hands at the thinly veiled insult. "What interests are you referring to?"

"Wine, entertainment, and other nighttime frivolities. Everyone knows your history, Trafford." Without waiting for a response, he stood and assisted his mother. "We must be off. We have several other calls to make."

Carlyle walked to Honoria. When she stood, the cad took her hand and bowed over it in a show of respect and smiled weakly. Then, he turned on the ball of his feet and took his leave of the other ladies before escorting his mother to the door.

It was the devil inside of him, but Marcus called out, "Carlyle? I must point out that it's best to know the historian before you accept the history. Always entertaining to see you."

The earl waved a hand in the air but continued walking out the door with his mother.

Everyone could hear the dowager countess exclaim a bit too loudly, "Such manners. They didn't even offer us tea."

They all sat still for a moment, then everyone spoke at once.

"What in the world was that?" Lady Grace ventured.

"His mother is certainly forthcoming in her thoughts," Pippa said.

"That's a nice way of expressing it. The woman is rude and opinionated," Noria said.

"As is her son," Marcus added. When all eyes swung to him, he put his hands behind his back. "I assume you all recognized what he was maneuvering to do."

Lady Grace slowly shook her head. "Except to insinuate that the Ardeerton sisters are in some kind of trouble that I'm helping them with."

Noria reached over and patted Lady Grace's hand. "You were brilliant and truthful."

"But then he laid down that insinuation about me and your brother." Grace looked at each of them. "I never even thought about our past and if it might complicate things, including your situation."

"What is your past with our brother?" Pippa asked.

Grace froze as her face lost all color. She tried to smile, but it looked like a grimace. "Didn't he tell you?"

Both Noria and Pippa shook their heads.

Grace gazed at her clasped hands in her lap, then regarded them with a ramrod straight spine. "It was a long time ago, but your brother and I had developed an interest in one another." Her voice didn't betray any anguish, but her eyes dimmed. "Unfortunately, we weren't free to act upon our feelings—I mean, interests."

Pippa's mouth fell open.

Noria's expression clearly communicated a question. *Did you know about this?*

Marcus shook his head slightly. All of this was as new to him as it was to Noria. As one of Pelham's best friends, it would be expected that the duke would share this history with Marcus, but he never had. "Noria is right, Lady Grace. You handled it perfectly. But you all saw what his ultimate goal is, didn't you?"

They all shook their heads, including Noria.

"Isn't it obvious?" Marcus had always been able to ferret out other people's motivations. "He's trying to ingratiate himself to the Ardeerton sisters. It made little difference to him that Lady Grace and I were here."

Noria's gaze locked with his.

"He has every intention of courting you." Marcus didn't look away from her when he said the next words. But it was a vow, and she needed to understand that he never broke a promise. He lowered his voice. "I'm not going to let him."

"I have already told him no." Noria's brittle smile softened slightly. "I'm not interested in him no matter what he says or does."

But Noria didn't know Carlyle. He was like a honey badger when he wanted something.

By the gleam in the earl's eyes, that something was Noria.

Then and there, Marcus vowed he'd not let Carlyle have a moment alone with her. The bastard had purposely set out to ruin her. That way he could have her all to himself without any competition. More fool he.

Marcus thrived on competition.

Twenty

H onoria stood still as Mademoiselle Mignon, the owner of the most exclusive modiste shop in all of London, took the final measurements for a new emerald silk gown trimmed in white lace. It would be ready in two days, and Honoria would be wearing it to the theatre.

Amazingly, Grace had managed to finagle an appointment with the widely popular modiste. People normally waited months for an opportunity such as this. But since Grace was friends with Lady Somerton and her mother, the Duchess of Langham, the duchess had asked the modiste if she'd fit Honoria into her busy schedule. Consequently, they'd all been welcomed with open arms.

Pippa was absolutely entranced with the shop and Mademoiselle Mignon. She was currently examining every bolt of fabric that was on display for today's clients. The look of awe on Pippa's face was a true sight to behold. Honoria had never seen her so happy.

This was exactly the type of business that Pippa dreamed of having someday. Thankfully, she had the creativity and the business sense that would ensure her success when she owned her own shop.

"There." The modiste smoothed her hands over Honoria's shoulders. "With your coloring and the turquoise of your eyes, along with that gown, everyone will be begging to make your acquaintance."

"If only that were true." Honoria laughed. "Thank you for all your hard work on my behalf."

Mademoiselle Mignon picked up her pincushion. "It's my pleasure. Now, I'll personally come to Ardeerton House when the gown is finished and complete the final fitting." She turned to gaze at Pippa. "Your sister's excitement is infectious. If you'll excuse me, I promised her a tour of the workrooms and storage area."

"Pippa is in heaven," Honoria said as she turned around from the three mirrors and gazed at the modiste.

Mademoiselle Mignon smiled. "If she decides to open a shop, I'd welcome it. I turn away twice as many customers as I accept. I can't wait to see her designs. She creates gowns for herself and you?"

Honoria nodded. "She's amazingly talented."

"That's why I'll do the final fitting at your home. I'll be able to see her designs." The modiste pointed to an area by the fitting room. "If you'd like, I can have one of my seamstresses make you some tea."

"No, thank you, but I'd love to take a peek at that crimson velvet on the counter," Honoria said.

"Such a color on you would be magnificent. I'll save enough for you." The modiste left Honoria's side and made her way to Pippa.

As Honoria walked to the front of the shop, she could hardly believe that she was even contemplating more dresses. After all the gowns that Pippa had created for her, and now this beautiful creation from Mademoiselle Mignon, her wardrobe was overflowing. Yet a beautiful red velvet gown would be perfect for Christmastide.

Immediately, she could imagine Marcus's eyes when he saw her in the emerald gown. They'd widen in appreciation, and he'd whisper something in her ear. After his declaration yesterday that he'd thwart Carlyle's plans, Honoria's imagination had taken flight. It was easy to believe that he did care for her...as more than a friend.

She stroked the nap of the velvet, upsetting it, then smoothing it flat again. That was exactly how she'd felt when she'd arrived in London yesterday. Unsettled, but today everything seemed brighter.

The bell over the shop door jingled, and a trio of women entered, chatting gaily. She smiled at them but returned her attention to the rich velvet.

"Lady Honoria?" called out one of three women.

Honoria pasted on a smile. It was her nemesis from finishing school, the one who had teased her incessantly about being too tall and gangly. Lady Beatrice Sutton was still as gorgeous as ever.

"What a surprise," Honoria said. The skin on the back of her neck tingled much like if a spider crawled on her skin. Frankly, that was a much preferable torture than the current one of facing Celeste.

"Allow me to introduce my friends, Lady Anne Vickery and Miss Celeste Worsley. Lady Anne's brother is the Marquess of Haverford. Miss Worsley's grandfather is the Duke of Exley." Celeste turned to her friends. "Lady Honoria is the eldest sister of the Duke of Pelham."

"Perhaps you've forgotten, but I also went to finishing school with Lady Honoria." Celeste turned to Honoria with a genuine smile. "It's lovely to see you again."

"The same for me."

Before Honoria could elaborate, Lady Beatrice cut her off. "We simply must call on you. I must meet your brother."

Lady Beatrice had brought a maid into the store. The poor woman looked embarrassed at the heavy-handed way Lady Beatrice maneuvered to meet Pelham. Honoria bit her lip to keep from laughing. It would be like inviting mice into the lion's den. Her brother didn't suffer fools or marriage-minded ladies. Thankfully, Celeste Worsley had never badgered her about her brother.

Honoria smiled at the maid. "Hello."

The maid dipped a quick curtsey. "My lady."

Though Lady Beatrice didn't think it important to introduce the maid, Honoria knew what it was like to be reduced to someone invisible when ignored. The old duke had treated Honoria the same before she'd known the truth about her birth.

Celeste had suffered the same. Though a mere "miss" since her father was a viscount, people believed she had an inflated sense of self from her grandfather the duke. But she'd once confided to Honoria that her grandfather was a tyrant and expected perfection from everyone.

Celeste's suffering reminded Honoria of her own. Men always had power over the women in their family.

Lady Beatrice smiled. "Word around the drawing rooms has it that the most eligible earl in all of England has shown an interest in you."

"It's more than an interest, isn't it, Lady Honoria?" Lady Ann chortled. "You've nabbed a fine one. I say whatever it takes, a lady must do what she must to attain a husband." She sniffed the air. "Even if it's a source of gossip." She lowered her voice. "I'm sure the rumors will wither sooner rather than later."

"Pardon?" Honoria was careful not to divulge too much. Lady Beatrice and Lady Ann might appear friendly, but she'd learned early in life that friendships, and especially familial relationships, weren't all that they seemed. Anything she said today would spread like wildfire throughout the drawing rooms and salons within London.

"No need to pretend otherwise. We know you've been diligent in your pursuit. To think you nabbed him in plain view of a bridge in the countryside. And with a kiss." Lady Ann laughed. "I heard that he's fallen hopelessly in love with you," Lady Beatrice confided. "Reformed rakes make the best husbands."

"Nonsense," Celeste said with a wave of her hand. "They're just rumors."

"Pardon me, but whom are you referring to?" Honoria pasted a polite smile on her face, hoping to hide her trepidation at having to speak with Lady Ann and Lady Beatrice. At least Celeste was trying to squelch such divisive clatter.

"Trafford, you goose," Lady Beatrice scolded. "He's a different breed. He's picky about the female sex in general. He's made it known throughout London that he's only interested in a paragon of a woman —the most attractive, the richest, and the most biddable in all of the British Isles. He wants someone whose character and good breeding are exemplary."

"Above reproach?" Honoria asked guardedly. She was anything but that. These women most likely had shared every piece of gossip they had heard about what had happened in Amesbury. Lady Beatrice had been the biggest rumormonger in finishing school.

Lady Anne nodded in agreement. "Last Season, he showed a mild interest in Lady Susan Tinswood, and she made no secret he was her choice of a husband." She lowered her voice. "Irritating chit after being declared a diamond of the first water. She could have had any man, but she wanted Trafford. He turned her down cold. All because she'd been seen riding with another man. That's why she'd set her cap for Bertie."

Suddenly, wild horses couldn't pry Honoria away from the conversation. They were talking about *her* Marcus.

"Excuse me?" asked Honoria incredulously.

Beatrice nodded. "She stole my Bertie away then dropped him like a hot potato."

Celeste shot a sympathetic look at her friend.

"Darling, he wasn't your Bertie," Lady Ann said. "However, I must agree that Lady Susan is fickle." She patted Lady Beatrice's hand. "The only person more so is Lord Trafford. He's very judgmental from what I gathered."

"Lord Trafford could do no better than you," Lady Beatrice declared. "Besides, you were caught together. Compromised."

"*Ann*," Celeste chided incredulously. "Where are your manners?"

Lady Ann turned to Honoria and shared a sheepish smile. "Forgive my bluntness. I should apologize if I've upset you. Lord Trafford will come up to snuff. You're rich and a duke's sister. What more could he want?"

Someone who's not an imposter like me.

"Has he come up to snuff?" asked Lady Anne.

"Hush, Anne," Celeste scolded. She turned to Honoria. "Just don't allow those matrons to bother you. They love a good rumor. They bandy them around like a ball in a tennis match."

Lady Anne smiled as she turned to Honoria. "Eventually, someone misses the shot. Just hope they lose interest quickly. Forewarned is forearmed."

Just then, Grace and Pippa exited Mademoiselle Mignon's office. Grace stopped momentarily, and by her narrowed gaze, she'd assessed the situation quickly and didn't like what she saw. "Come, Lady Pippa," she said with the authority of a general taking command of the troops.

As soon as she reached Honoria's side, she dismissed the trio with a tilt of her nose in the air. "Good morning, ladies. I do hope you'll have as much luck finding a perfect gown as Lady Honoria did. She'll be devastatingly beautiful in Mademoiselle Mignon's creation." She linked her arm around Honoria's and nodded at the Pelham footman who'd been waiting inside to assist the ladies with their purchases.

He gathered the packages that had accumulated beside him and then opened the door with his free hand.

"Goodbye," announced Grace, and Pippa waved a hand.

"It was a pleasure meeting you," Honoria said to Lady Anne and Lady Beatrice. She turned to Celeste and squeezed her hand. "It was lovely seeing you again. I hope we see each other again soon."

With that, she summoned her best ducal sister bearing, then walked out the door with her head held high. Pippa and Grace were in the carriage by the time she reached it. Without a look back, she took the footman's hand and purposefully entered the coach.

As soon as the door shut, Grace put a finger to her lips. Once the carriage was in motion, she leaned over and placed her hand over Honoria's. "Lady Ann and Lady Beatrice remind me of a Greek Chorus. They know everything, and they tell everything they know. But like that chorus, they aren't reliable storytellers."

Honoria shook her head, still stunned by the conversation. "They said Lord Trafford only wants a paragon for a wife." She twisted her fingers together. She should have never left Pelham Hall. "I'm hardly that."

"You're everything he wants," Pippa said without hesitation. "Ignore what they said. Celeste did challenge them when they said something reckless. Did you see Marcus yesterday? Really see him? How valiant and brilliant he was? He only had eyes for you. Trust your own instincts."

Her instincts were telling her to run as fast as she could away from all of this.

"There's no need to defend him to me," Honoria said as she knocked on the roof of the carriage. But what would he think if he knew about her parentage? Good breeding was a laugh. She couldn't even claim she knew her father. She was merely a cuckoo in the nest.

She, above all people, knew not to believe in fairytales, and she'd been weaving one right before those women approached her in the shop.

"Those women said Marcus is highly desirable as a potential groom." She fisted one hand by her side. It was the only thing she could control at that moment. It was beyond foolish to believe that she could have him as her husband. "I've never liked society or competition, and I won't compete for Marcus's attention."

Just then, the carriage slowed to a stop. Pippa grabbed Honoria's hand. "What are you saying? He cares for *you*. As an Ardeerton, you don't cower," she scolded.

"Indeed," Grace cried out much like a soldier prepared for battle.

Which was what London was turning into...a war.

And inside, Honoria felt she hadn't been taught properly how to shoot.

"We shall see," she replied to Pippa and Grace. Though she wasn't trained in how to handle well-placed innuendos and gently veiled threats, she promised herself that she would not bring shame to her siblings or Marcus.

The footman opened the door, and Honoria exited. Earlier, she'd asked the coachman to stop at a children's toy and book shop before she visited the Duke of Dartmore and his sister.

She walked to the shop with a newfound sureness. Indeed, she wouldn't compete for a man's attention. But she would succeed in other ways. She'd always had a way with children. Like her, they could easily be dismissed when others were in the room.

But today, she would ensure that did not happen with the little duke and his sister.

She'd also vowed that she'd find her own path.

She only hoped that London wasn't her downfall.

Twenty-One

M arcus stood next to an impatient Pelham as they waited for the ladies to return from their shopping trip. They were expected over at the home of the Duke of Dartmore to meet the duke and his sister Lady Julia. When another emergency meeting arose between Pelham and his solicitor's office, Grace had kindly offered to escort Honoria and Pippa to the modiste.

He was also a little impatient to see Noria. Marcus believed the children would warm to her instantly. He couldn't wait to see the duke and his sister's reaction to Noria. He'd never brought a woman to see these orphans, only his most trusted friends, and he considered Noria one of those and more.

How would she react to the fact that he considered her special? Would she allow herself to accept such regard? For the brief time that they'd known each other, he suspected that she didn't trust her feelings. His hunch was that she didn't believe what he felt for her was real. If that was the case, then he'd just have to show her and ensure she enjoyed those efforts.

At the sound of the carriage turning into the drive, Pelham nodded his satisfaction. "Finally. I'm anxious to meet this little duke. The way you sing his praises, he must be a genius."

"He's anxious to meet you. He's never met one of his peers."

Pelham's mouth turned down into a frown. "I knew his father well. I always found him sensible and a man who knew his own mind. It's a shame that he and his duchess left two small children behind."

"Their situation reminds me of you and myself. We had to navigate similar situations, but there was one main difference." Marcus opened the door and motioned Pelham to go first.

"What's that?" Pelham was right beside him as they descended the granite steps of Ardeerton House.

"We had each other," Marcus answered.

By then, the carriage had stopped in front of them. The footman opened the door, and Pelham assisted Lady Pippa down. He released her hand and motioned for the footman to retrieve the packages piled on the back of the carriage. "Did you buy everything in sight?"

"Practically. Mademoiselle Mignon is an absolute artist when it comes to gown creation." She turned her attention to Marcus. "If you don't mind, I think I'll stay home. I'm so inspired, gown designs are percolating in my head."

"It's our loss," Marcus replied with a smile. But honestly, it meant that he'd have more time alone with Noria and Lady Julia. He'd already planned for Pelham and Dartmore to spend time together.

Marcus entered the carriage and sat beside Noria while Pelham said farewell to Pippa.

"Hello," he said softly to keep it intimate between them.

Her eyes twinkled as she smiled. "Hello, yourself."

He smiled at the playfulness of her voice as he threw his beaver hat to the empty bench opposite of them.

Pelham entered the carriage. His gaze swept between the two of them before it landed on the empty bench and the hat.

"Where's Grace...Lady Grace?" Pelham inquired in a bored voice.

"She was feeling a little under the weather."

"Nothing serious?" Pelham asked with concern.

"No." Noria smiled. "The megrims."

He huffed slightly. "That's the excuse you used to stay at Pelham Hall and attend the masquerade." His haughty gaze landed on Marcus. "We all know how that turned out."

Marcus ignored his friend's comment and pointed to Noria's packages on the floor of the carriage. "Would you like for me to give those to a footman?"

She shook her head. "Those are for Dartmore and Lady Julia."

"That's kind of you." Marcus couldn't stop looking at her. She was gloriously beautiful today. The smile on her lips told him that she was happy to see him.

"I imagine they don't receive many gifts," Honoria offered. "They're really nothing. A few books for each of them, a cricket bat for Dartmore, and a doll for Lady Julia."

He knew then that he'd made the right decision to invite her today. "They'll be thrilled. Thank you for thinking of them."

"Sounds like a bribe of some sort. Beware a Greek bearing gifts." Pelham chuckled at his own joke.

"Behave," his sister admonished.

"I'd gladly climb into a Trojan horse with you," Marcus murmured.

Unfortunately, Pelham heard him. "I should challenge you to a duel right now."

Noria's sudden pink blush was a fair exchange for Pelham's feigned wrath. When she witnessed first-hand what he was passionate about, would she feel the same as him? With every fiber of his being, he wanted that. He wanted that with her. In that moment, he could see this outing as a regular excursion for them to see such children every week. She'd be wonderful and nurturing with any child she met.

He'd wager his estate on that.

It was becoming easier to imagine their future together. His only problem was convincing her to take a chance on them. To trust that whatever hurt lay in her heart, he'd do everything in his power to make it better.

Or at least, he hoped she'd let him try.

The day was sunny, and they had the curtains pulled up in the carriage. Several bystanders watched the carriage pass and pointed at the seal. Since Noria and Marcus were in the forward-facing seat, they were easy to see. Several women of the *ton* stopped their stroll to gaze at the coach. Immediately, they started talking and gesturing. Hopefully, word would get back to Carlyle quickly that they were together again. Perhaps the earl would finally believe that they were a couple. Then, Carlyle would have no choice but to leave Noria alone.

The earl reminded Marcus of a barnacle. A person couldn't shake them without using blunt force.

Noria turned to him. "I meant to ask earlier. How did you become involved with Dartmore and Lady Julia?

Pelham's gaze swung to his. "Yes, tell her." The teasing in his voice was unmistakable.

Marcus cleared his throat. How would she take the news that he used informants? It really wasn't that scandalous. Men in his position used their wealth and influence to change things they didn't like. He didn't do it for his benefit, but for the benefit of the children who found themselves in the same circumstances he had faced growing up.

"I'm friends with a clerk who has employment in the Court of Chancery. He takes notes for the judges who appoint the conservators and guardians." He shifted slightly in his seat so he could watch Noria's eyes as he explained the rest of the story. "I pay him to watch for children like Dartmore and his sister. Specifically, children who have lost both parents."

Her face froze with a smile at his confession. All grew quiet except for the clank of the wheels against the cobblestone streets. As the carriage slowed, she finally nodded. "I would do the same thing. How can you help if you don't know who is in need?"

"Exactly." Marcus grinned like a besotted fool, which defined him perfectly.

Pelham lifted a eyebrow. "Trafford has been doing this since he left university. He started with a boy who is in the millionaire's club. That was ten years ago. The young man recently reached his majority, and I'm happy to say that, through his involvement with Trafford, he hasn't lost his fortune. In fact, he's increased it substantially by setting up several new businesses."

"Is he a peer?" Noria asked Marcus.

His heart pounded in encouragement at the gentleness in her dulcet voice. "No. His father was a wealthy landowner in Sussex. There are over a hundred families that farm on his land besides his own operation."

"Wouldn't the conservators of the estate have protected the farmers?" Noria asked.

"Undoubtedly. But they wouldn't have taken the time to teach him how to manage the property or how to help the tenants who rely on him." If her brother wasn't present, Marcus would have swept her into his arms that instant and confided how much her interest meant to him.

The carriage pulled into the circular drive of Dartmore's home. The house itself was an excellent representation of Baroque architecture. Though handsome in appearance, the house lacked any real warmth. It was Marcus's opinion that any personality the house had possessed when Dartmore's parents were alive was missing now.

Once the coach had stopped, a liveried footman opened the door. Pelham descended first, then Marcus. He immediately turned and held out his hand for Noria. When she placed her gloved hand in his, he couldn't resist squeezing it, a sign of intimacy just between the two of them. "Thank you for your kindness."

"I want to be here," she said softly. "Our wealth and position should be used for such noble causes."

"Not everyone believes that philosophy," he answered. "Many of our set only think of themselves." He was being too serious for such a lovely day. "May I help you with your packages?"

"That would be lovely." Noria picket up the cricket bat and the box with the doll and gave them to Marcus. She picked up the books herself.

As the three of them climbed the marble staircase to the front door, it opened. A butler stood waiting for them. There wasn't a smile of greeting or even a sign that the man recognized who they were.

Marcus was the first to speak. "I'm the Earl of Trafford with the Duke of Pelham and his sister, Lady Honoria Ardeerton, to see His Grace and Lady Julia."

The butler nodded and stepped aside so they could enter. Inside was as beautiful as the outside, but there were no signs that anyone really tried to make it a home. On the massive oak entry table stood a vase without any fresh flowers. There were no footmen waiting to lend assistance. There weren't any signs of the normal hustle and bustle of servants who cared for a great house such as this one.

Marcus lifted his gaze to the young duke and his sister. They stood at the top of the circular staircase. The boy clutched his sister's hand. Both wore a stark expression that Marcus recognized all too well. As a young boy, he'd felt that same sense of loneliness.

Their governess stood several feet behind the children, but by her sharp stare, she was evaluating the visitors.

"Your Grace," Marcus said and bowed slightly. "Lady Julia."

At the greeting, their cautious gazes landed on Marcus, and they both grinned.

"My lord," Dartmore exclaimed. "Come, Julia." Dartmore hurried down the steps with his sister on his heels.

"Your Grace," the governess scolded. "Running will lead to you both falling and cracking your heads open."

The boy didn't acknowledge the rebuke, but he did slow down so his sister could keep up with him.

Marcus waved to the governess. "Mrs. Mortimer, I'll return your charges to you when our visit is over."

The governess nodded, then disappeared down the hall.

Once the children reached their sides, the boy's gaze shifted from Marcus to Pelham.

"I've brought some friends I'd like for you to meet," Marcus said. "The Duke of Pelham and his sister, Lady Honoria Ardeerton."

"Hello." Noria knelt so that she was at eye level with them. "Your Grace and Lady Julia, the pleasure is mine."

Pelham didn't kneel, but he did smile. The skin around his eyes creased into fine lines as his gaze fell on the young duke. "Dartmore." When his attention fell to the little girl, she tried to hide behind her brother. "Lady Julia, it's a pleasure to meet you also."

The boy didn't suffer any shyness. "Hello, sir. My lady." But his attention was focused on Marcus. "Trafford, I've some new soldiers that you should see. I've been in the nursery all morning setting up various battles."

"No navy ships?" Pelham asked.

The boy's expression turned serious. "Mrs. Mortimer doesn't allow me to set up an ocean anymore." He lifted his gaze in the direction where the governess had last stood. He sighed remorsefully, then turned back to Pelham. "The last time, a gale storm hit. I'm afraid the water grew choppy."

Julia popped her head around her brother. "He tried to swim in the tub with the ships. Water spilled over on the floor and ruined the ceiling in the second-floor salon."

"There was a man overboard." Dartmore shrugged. "How else was I to rescue him?"

Noria laughed. "Quick thinking, Your Grace. Not many would have gone into the water in the first place. You were very brave."

Dartmore beamed at her.

Pelham's lips twitched. "Clearly a heroic deed under the most trying of situations." He turned to the little girl. "I'm glad you weren't swept away in the storm."

"I was swept away for a nap." Julia stood beside Pelham and tilted her head to look at him. "You're tall. My papa was tall."

Noria's eyes softened, and Pelham's gaze shot to Marcus. The duke's eyes widened with an expression of "What do I do now?"

It had been two months since the children had lost their parents. The first time Marcus had visited the pair, neither would discuss their father or their mother. Today was a good sign that the children were becoming more comfortable talking about their parents. Few recognized that children needed to grieve. Most thought that if the children didn't talk about them, they'd forget the pain of what they'd lost.

Marcus knew better.

Noria clasped her hands together. "How tall was your father?"

"As big as a tree," Lady Julia proclaimed proudly as she stretched her arms into the air high above her.

"My word, that is big," Noria answered. "What else do you remember about him?"

"He was handsome," the little girl offered. "And kind."

Dartmore joined in the conversation. "He was a good father," the boy said solemnly.

Marcus knelt beside Noria and clasped the boy's shoulder. "He was the very best father."

The boy nodded. "The best."

"I'm going to lose a tooth." Julia opened her mouth and wriggled a bottom front tooth.

"Julia," Dartmore scolded. "Mrs. Mortimer says you're not supposed to show people your mouth."

The little girl hid her face. "I forgot."

"It's all right," Noria offered as she stood. "I was very excited when I lost my first tooth."

Julia smiled. "I like you. You look like a fairy princess."

Noria's hand flew to her chest in mock surprise. "You look like a princess also. And I like you."

"What are those?" Dartmore pointed at the packages in Marcus's hand.

Julia frowned. "Mrs. Mortimer says you're not to point."

Pelham released a long-suffering sigh, but a smile teased his lips. "Lady Julia, dukes can do whatever they please."

Julia tilted her head and stared at him. "Really?"

A charming but arrogant smile tugged at one side of his mouth. "It's the ducal rules of conduct. They're not written, but everyone knows them."

"What about me?" she asked as she stared unabashedly at Pelham.

"Well, there are sister-of-dukes rules of conduct also," he said softly as his gaze landed on Noria.

Noria narrowed her eyes playfully. "Pelham, tell them the truth about those rules."

Pelham finally leaned down close to Julia. "Lady Honoria should be the one to tell you the special rules."

"Indeed." Noria slid her brother a side-eye look then turned to Julia. "We have a very special power. We can revise the ducal rules of conduct anytime we please to overrule our misbehaving brothers."

Marcus laughed at such a sight. These two were perfect for Dartmore and his sister. "Let's find somewhere to sit and discover what's in all those packages."

Pelham took a package of books along with the cricket bat from Marcus. "Dartmore and I are off to his study to do ducal things. Come find us later." He turned to the young duke. "Lead the way, Dartmore.

You'll discover that the majority of your business transpires in your study. It's a room you should become well-acquainted with."

For the rest of his life, Marcus would never forget the sight of the two dukes strolling down the hall to the study. Pelham stood over six foot three inches tall, while the top of the Duke of Dartmore's head barely reached the Duke of Pelham's waist.

But they shared one thing in common.

They each walked with an identical swagger, one that only a duke could possess.

Noria glanced at Marcus and then at Julia. "Where shall we go? I'd like for you to open the package that Lord Trafford is holding."

"Really? I've wanted to ask what's inside the box, but Mrs. Mortimer says I ask too many questions."

Noria shared a knowing look with Marcus. She must have been thinking the same thing as he was. Mrs. Mortimer seemed to tell the children everything they couldn't do but didn't seem to offer much of what they could do.

By then, Julia was practically bouncing on the balls of her feet. The giddiness of discovering the contents of the box was infectious. He wanted to see what treasures Noria had brought, almost as much as young Julia.

"It's such a beautiful day. Do you have a garden?" Noria asked.

"We do. It's ever so lovely. Let's go there. We have a seating area with a fountain." Julia tugged on Noria's hand. "Come, my lady."

Noria grinned at Marcus as the little girl pulled her along. "Come along, my lord. You don't want to be late to the party."

Indeed, he didn't. Not when Noria was the main attraction.

Twenty-Two

"I wish I would have had someone like you when I was a girl," Noria whispered as Lady Julia tugged them outside.

"You could have me now," Marcus answered. His eyes dared her to accept.

That's not long enough. I want forever. Thankfully, she didn't say it aloud.

He stopped mid-stride, and Noria did the same. She let go of Julia's hand as the child practically skipped down the steps.

"I'm being a little glib." He lowered his head and caught her gaze. "Tell me what you mean by you wished you'd had someone like me when you were a girl."

"Someone interested in me and my thoughts." She shrugged slightly, then turned her attention to the beautiful courtyard in front of them. Every flower seemed to be in full bloom. The perfume of roses and lilies filled the air. Julia was chasing a butterfly.

"Come, Trafford," Julia called out. "You too, Lady Noria."

"In a moment," Marcus called out in answer, then turned his attention back to her. "Didn't your parents or governess..."

She shook her head and smiled. "Forget I said anything."

What would he think if she told him that Pelham and Pippa's father had banned her from his sight?

He leaned a little closer. "I want to know all about you and your life. I find the real Honoria fascinating." He lowered his voice. "I'll always see you as Venus, but I think underneath, there's a very intriguing person. But she doesn't like to show others who she really is. No masks, Noria. Not with me."

"Lord Trafford. Lady Honoria." Julia stood in the middle of the garden with her hands propped on her hips. "Please do come on." She huffed as only a six-year-old could do.

He held out an arm for Honoria to take. "We're being summoned. Let's finish our conversation later." A grin spread across his face.

Honoria stood as still as the cluster of oak trees in the far lawn. She couldn't stop staring at him.

Happiness radiated all around him because he was with these children, and they weren't even his. Though they were delightful, Dartmore and Lady Julia weren't his responsibility. Most men wouldn't have taken the day for such simple pleasures as reading and having a conversation with these young people. Her father was a prime example of that.

Yet, Marcus was here because he cared about Dartmore and Julia. Pelham was here because underneath his gruff exterior, he relished Marcus's friendship just as she did.

Honoria let her mind wander as she imagined what marriage and family would be like with Marcus. But then a prick of unease swept through her. It was a reminder to keep a clear head on her shoulders and only think about the upcoming release of her announcement and the freedom it would grant her.

"My lady," Julia called. "Please, let's open presents."

She nodded and took Marcus's arm. She forced a smile to her face, then descended the steps to join the little girl. As soon as they had all sat down at a garden table, Marcus piled the presents in front of Julia.

"Which shall I open first?" Lady Julia's gaze bounced between Marcus and Honoria.

Marcus tilted his head and gave Honoria a questioning look. "My lady?"

"These books are for you. Your brother also received some. But this"

—Honoria pushed the box that contained the porcelain doll in Julia's direction—"is only for you."

Julia sat on her knees in the chair and reached for the box resting on the table. She untied the ribbon and lifted the lid. The little girl's eyes grew wide, and an *O* formed on her lips. "She's beautiful. What's her name?"

"We were hoping you could tell us?" Marcus asked.

The man was simply too charming, and Honoria couldn't help but smile in return.

"Winifred," Lady Julia announced as she hugged the doll close to her chest. "Thank you ever so much, my lord."

"It's all Lady Honoria's doing. Not mine," he said gallantly.

Julia turned and smiled in her direction. "Thank you, my lady. Winifred will sleep with me and Jane tonight."

"Who is Jane?" Honoria asked.

"The doll my mother gave me last Christmas. She's so beautiful. Mrs. Mortimer says I'm not to sleep with Jane. She's afraid Jane will remind me of my mother." The girl reverently touched Winifred's cheek with her fingers. "Sometimes, I have a hard time falling asleep at night. But Jane tells me she'll keep me safe." She looked up at Honoria. "Jane is nice like my mother."

"Oh, darling," Honoria said softly as her heart crumbled in her chest for all this precious little girl had lost. "I imagine your mother receives so much joy, knowing that Jane gives you comfort. I think your mother must like it very much that you remember her and how much she loved you. I'm sure she wishes she could be here with you."

Julia stared at her with wide-eyed wonder. "I imagine that too, my lady." She pulled Winifred close. "Now, while Jane watches over me, Winifred can watch over Jane." Julia climbed down and stood beside Honoria.

Honoria pulled Julia onto her lap, then hugged her. She chanced a glance at Marcus, who had his gaze trained on them.

"You smell nice." Julia hugged her. "Winifred thinks so, too.

Honoria laughed at the announcement. "So do both of you."

"Does your nursemaid hug you?" Marcus asked.

"I don't have one," Julia said.

Honoria blinked. It was unheard of for a child Julia's age not to have a nursemaid to help her dress, stay in the nursery at night, and ensure that the child was eating the proper food.

"The men who take care of Dartmore fired her last week. I cried."

Honoria shared a glance with Marcus. Lady Julia was too busy with Winifred to see their concerned looks.

"I'll not let this stand," Marcus murmured for Honoria's ears only. The sharp angle of his jaw could cut stone. But it was the determination in his eyes that stole her breath.

Just then, Mrs. Mortimer came outside and held out a hand. "Lady Julia, it's time for your nap."

Marcus stood and waved the governess over. "Mrs. Mortimer, if you'd be so kind as to allow me to ask a question."

"Of course, my lord," she said politely as she clasped her hands in front of her.

"What happened to Lady Julia's nursemaid?"

For a moment, the governess looked stunned at his bold question. "Mrs. Albin was let go." She blinked twice. "I heard that they gave her an excellent reference since she'd been with the family for so long."

"Exactly how long had she been with the family?" he growled.

"For over thirty years, my lord. Mrs. Albin was the duchess's nursemaid," Mrs. Mortimer said softly.

Honoria took the opportunity to show Julia the books, but she overheard Marcus's next question.

"And how long have you been with the children?"

"For three months," she said quietly.

"I see. The one servant who had years of service to the family and was trusted by the late duchess was let go. Before my anger runs away from me, perhaps you can answer another question. Do you know the reason why?"

"To save money, my lord." She dipped her head rather sheepishly. "There is a new guardian. Come, Lady Julia."

Julia hugged the books and dolls close to her. "One moment, Mrs. Mortimer." She turned her gaze to Honoria. "Will you come visit me again?"

"I would like that." Honoria knelt by the child's side, then gazed at Mrs. Mortimer. "If it's all right?"

"Of course, my lady." Mrs. Mortimer escorted the little girl back into the house, leaving Marcus and Honoria outside.

"Whomever the guardian is, I'm going to string them up by their..." He clenched a fist, then exhaled. "Pardon my language."

"No apologies necessary. I'm appalled myself. I couldn't help but overhear the conversation." Though it was a small white lie, it was still a lie. For some odd reason, she didn't want to hide that part of herself from him. "I'm not being truthful with you."

His gaze whipped from the house to hers. One perfect eyebrow arched.

"I purposely heard the conversation. I like to listen to conversations between others. I know that I shouldn't, but as a little girl, I discovered that I was quite talented at being ignored in company."

"But I wasn't ignoring you," Marcus protested.

"I know." She shrugged. "Old habits, you see."

He nodded, but his eyes narrowed as if trying to discern her thoughts.

"Marcus, we must do something. Mrs. Albin could help the children with their grief. She could tell them stories of their mother when she was a little girl. The nursemaid could also tell them how happy the duke and duchess were with their family." Tears welled in her eyes for all that Julia and Dartmore had lost when the nursemaid was let go. "You and Pelham should find her and convince the men responsible to rehire her."

"My thoughts exactly. This shall not stand." The smile that lit his face instantly warmed her from the inside out. "You are surprising in so many ways." He held out his arm again. "Let's find the dukes."

Without hesitation, she took his arm. "How am I surprising?"

"Flirting with me, now?" he teased. "Asking for compliments?"

"Never." She stopped, and he had no choice but to draw near.

"You should," he said softly. "Flirting is very becoming on you. We should do it daily. Perhaps hourly with compliments. I love your blushes."

The roguish smile on his face should be outlawed. It made her desire things that she shouldn't and couldn't want. "Come, let's find my brother."

In minutes, they arrived at the young duke's study. Marcus rapped on the door, then opened it. As soon as they were both in the room, they came to an abrupt halt.

"What the devil, Pelham?" Marcus asked, clearly annoyed.

"Oh, Pelham." Honoria shook her head. "We should have never left you both alone."

Sitting on the wooden floor next to Dartmore, her brother swatted the air. "Don't be bothersome." Just then, he rolled a pair of dice, then released a long-suffering sigh.

The young duke clapped his hands. "I win."

"You're teaching him dice?" she asked in disbelief.

"It's more than that," Pelham answered somewhat crossly. "I'm teaching him things that only a man can teach another."

Honoria wanted to roll her eyes, but somehow managed to keep her face composed. "Really?"

"Yes, really," Pelham answered with a drawl. "Right, Dartmore?"

The young duke nodded vigorously. "Pelham explained that there are things a man must know." He stuck out his chest. "Next week, he promised to teach me fisticuffs and how to watch for others cheating at whist."

Marcus ran a hand through his hair. "Pelham, Dartmore is a child."

Pelham stood quickly and offered a hand to the young duke. "Not really. Dartmore informed me they're sending him to Eton next term."

The young duke nodded his head.

Pelham stuck his chin in the air. It was a gesture he used when he was riled. Honoria had seen it before, particularly when their father had done or said something that was horrible. "He's a bright young man."

At her brother's words, Dartmore gazed at the duke as if he'd hung the moon.

Pelham put his hand on the boy's shoulder. "The duke can't attend that noble institution without having a grasp of games of chance or how to protect himself. I'll not allow older students to bully or take advantage of him."

Marcus strolled to the boy's side and knelt. "When was this decision made?"

"Last week." Dartmore held up the dice to Pelham. "These are yours."

"You keep them," Pelham answered.

"Do you want to go to Eton?" Marcus asked softly.

The boy shook his head. "I don't want to leave Julia. I'm her big brother. I'm supposed to protect her."

Honoria's heart clenched at the conviction in the young boy's voice. It was exactly how she remembered Pelham treating her as a young girl.

"That's very commendable." Pelham placed a hand on the boy's shoulder. "You must take that responsibility to heart. Our sisters are treasures and must be protected at all costs."

Dartmore nodded then turned to Honoria. "Thank you, my lady, for the gifts. I've never seen such a fine cricket bat. And I shall enjoy the books."

"You are most welcome," she said with a smile.

The duke told me that he has always protected you and your sister." Dartmore grew serious. "I want to be just like him with Julia."

Marcus nodded at the young duke. "An admirable trait, Dartmore."

They said their goodbyes to the young man, then headed to the waiting carriage.

Marcus slowed his steps as Pelham walked in front of them. "Did your brother protect you at all costs?"

"Yes."

His whisky-dark voice grew smoother. "What did he protect you from?"

"From everything when I was a little girl. Spiders, snakes, rats." She pasted a slight smile on her face. "But when I became older, I learned to protect myself. Yet Pelham always made me feel important."

Without offering further explanation, she walked to her brother's side and took his hand. Carefully, she climbed into the carriage.

Twenty-Three

~

Marcus handed his hat and walking stick to the attendant at White's Gentlemen's Club. The smokey smell of cheroots, whisky, and brandy filled the air. After returning home yesterday from visiting Dartmore and Lady Julia, Pelham had sent over an invitation for Marcus to join him and Ravenscroft. The purpose was unknown. But Marcus wouldn't put it past his old friend that he was strategizing how to protect Noria and Lady Pippa at Ravenscroft's ball.

The marquess was hosting his annual family event that evening.

Pelham tipped his chin in Marcus's direction as soon as they made eye contact. Ravenscroft raised a hand in greeting as Marcus strolled through the crowded club to his friends. As soon as he eased into one of the chairs, a footman arrived with his usual drink, two fingerfuls of the finest whisky that could be found in all of the British Isles. Marcus inhaled and sighed contentedly at the smokey scent.

"I was wondering when you'd arrive." Pelham leaned back in his chair and took a sip of brandy.

"Indeed." Marcus turned to Ravenscroft. "How goes the preparations for tonight's event?"

Ravenscroft let out a dejected whoosh of breath. "I suppose, if you inquire of my mother, she'd say everything is in order. If you're asking me, I'd say it's a sad situation when a man can't even rest in peace in his own home."

Pelham's lips pursed. "That's why I never host a party. I don't want my house overrun by imbeciles."

"Wish my mother thought that way, but she says tradition dictates I host this ball. Alas, I've agreed under the condition that I'm not involved in making the house ready. She gladly accepted my terms." Ravenscroft pounded Pelham on the back. "Good luck with not hosting parties with two sisters around."

"I've told them that they can host a dinner party before the theatre sometime," Pelham said glumly. He turned to Marcus. "That's enough of a concession, isn't it?"

Immediately, his mind went to the last conversation he'd had with Noria when she'd declared that Pelham had always protected her and made her feel important. There was more than met the eye with his friend. "Before I answer, what did Noria and Lady Pippa have to say?"

Ravenscroft's eyes widened. "Noria? Who is that?"

"Honoria," Pelham answered, then lowered his voice. "Your friend here has been calling her that pet name since I caught them together."

"He's your friend, too, if I remember correctly," Ravenscroft retorted quite jovially. "One of your best besides me."

"That was before I found him naked—"

"Enough!" Marcus leaned forward and stared his old friend in the eye. "You should be supporting me instead of threatening to shoot me at every opportunity."

Pelham arched a wicked eyebrow. "Tell me why you want to marry her, and don't say it's the honorable thing to do."

Ravenscroft chortled softly. "A clever turn of the tables. I approve. If she were my sister, I'd want to know the answer, too."

For a second, his mind couldn't form a single coherent thought. It was easy to spout that the scandal would disappear if they'd marry. Though it was the truth, it wasn't the whole truth. He did enjoy her company, and the empathy that she had shown yesterday with the young duke and his sister made him even more determined to marry her.

He felt a kinship, a bond, with Noria that he'd never experienced with any other female. When they'd made love, it had been different. There was true affection. But for the first time in years, he felt whole.

Did it mean that they'd be happily married? No one could predict that. But Marcus would do everything in his power to make her happy.

He traced his finger around the edge of the glass. He hadn't taken a sip of the whisky yet. Finally, he looked up at his two best friends. "I have deep affection for Noria. I wouldn't be here if I didn't."

Pelham's gaze turned as sharp as a freshly cut diamond. "Tell me more."

"This sounds serious," Ravenscroft murmured.

Marcus ignored the marquess and stared straight at Pelham. "There's more than honor involved. Sometimes, it's hard for me to fathom how much I enjoy her company. I want to know her better and give her the chance to do the same with me." He dipped his gaze for a moment. "I'm determined to make her happy."

Pelham narrowed his eyes, taking stock of Marcus's words and of his person. After a while, the duke exhaled, relief falling across his face. "I believe you."

"*Bloody hell*," Ravenscroft muttered under his breath. "My mother has sent one of my footmen to retrieve me. I can tell by the pleading look in his eyes. The woman is a menace to my sanity." He slowly stood and nodded at his footman dressed in the Ravenscroft navy livery. "I'll see you both this evening?" The marquess's brow wrinkled into neat lines.

"Wouldn't miss it for the world." Marcus stood also.

After they had exchanged farewells, Pelham finished his brandy and, with an elegant air, placed the tumbler to his side, a sign for the footman to refill his glass. "Let me ask you a question," he queried softly. "Weren't you and Lady Susan almost betrothed last year?"

As usual, the staff at White's was accustomed to serving the members as quickly as possible. Marcus waited until the footman left so they could have privacy. Ironically, though, White's was normally crowded with members at all hours of the day, so it was the perfect place to share a confidential conversation. There was always a loud hum of voices or boisterous laughter filling the rooms. There certainly weren't any servants with loose tongues about the place. Otherwise, they'd never keep any members...no matter how prestigious the membership was.

"No, we weren't. I think she might have set her cap for me, but the feeling wasn't mutual." He leaned across the table. "What the devil, Pelham? You know everything about me. If I was courting anyone, it was her father. He has first-hand information on the Chancery Court's daily docket. His cousin sits on the bench."

"So that's your informant. His cousin's clerk." Pelham nodded in approval. "Very sly to become friends with Edgeheath. It keeps the focus off the clerk." Pelham leaned back in his chair. By the smile on his face, everyone would think they were having a pleasant conversation.

Marcus knew differently. "Why are you concerned about Lady Susan?"

"I do not, and I repeat, *do not* want my sister harmed any more than she already has been. If you have feelings for Lady Susan, you should tell Honor now." The smile on his friend's face didn't reach his eyes.

"I do not have feelings for Lady Susan. But I will tell Honor what happened last year so there is no doubt or confusion about my intentions." Marcus stared at the duke, so he understood how serious this pledge was. "I can't control what others say."

Pelham nodded and released a stoic breath. "Thank you."

"You've never really shared much of your sisters. Noria said that you were protective of her." At the pet name, Marcus expected Pelham to growl, so it was the perfect moment for Marcus to take a drink. The whisky burned his throat as the smokey taste filled his mouth.

"I was the first family member to hold her after she was born. I was six years of age. My father wasn't at the birth, and our mother...well, she couldn't be bothered to see about the child. Our nursemaid found me in the library and brought her to me."

It had to be the dim light in the room but, for a second, it appeared the duke's eyes glistened with tears.

"Noria was lucky to have had you welcome her into the world."

Pelham took another drink of brandy. "She was completely bald. The ugliest thing that I'd ever seen in my life." He laughed softly, but the sound didn't hide the true emotion. "When she looked up at me with her blue eyes, my chest tightened. I knew in an instant that I'd lay down my life for her." He studied his glass. "Our parents didn't take an interest in her or even much with Pippa. So, I made certain if they ever needed anything, I was the one who provided for them."

"You've never really said much about your parents. I thought perhaps it was to save me the grief of remembering my own." For all their years together, Marcus had never had such a frank conversation with the man who sat across from him.

Pelham shook his head. "They were horrible parents. They both were unfaithful and used it as a weapon against one another. Sometimes, my sisters and I were caught in their selfish affrays." He lifted his hand to stave off any objections to his statement. "I know that in the *ton's* circles, it's widely accepted that couples have affairs, especially after an heir is born." His eyes narrowed as he became lost in thought. Finally, he turned his attention back to Marcus. "Their regard for one another was caustic to be around." He shook his head. "Christ, it was like walking on eggshells more times than not. They hurt Honoria with their venom."

"How did they hurt Noria?"

Pelham stared straight through him. "Our father never thought her good enough."

"Do you know why he hurt her?"

Pelham shook his head. "It's not my story to tell. I've said enough."

An uncomfortable revelation hit him square in the chest. For a split-second, he considered keeping quiet. But then he'd always wonder about his friends' true regard if he didn't ask. "Do you think I'm the type of person who would marry your sister then have an affair or keep a mistress?"

"No," Pelham answered softly. "Never you. You're the most loyal friend I have. I believe you'll be that way with a wife you care for." He sighed gently. "I'm still smarting over Carlyle. I never wanted her hurt, or you for that matter. But Carlyle has revealed a side of himself that I'd never seen before. I thought him a bit staid and totally unadventurous. Never manipulative. You can tell by his investments that he doesn't care for risks." He slowly fisted his hand. "Now you understand my direct-ness. If I'd had any inkling that he'd harm Honor, to force her hand in marriage, I would have sent him to Hades when he approached me in London."

Marcus leaned back in his chair. "Perhaps you're too hard on yourself. Even a stopped clock is right twice a day."

"You're good for me." A mischievous half-grin tugged at the duke's face. "Most of the time." Then he turned serious again. "My sisters are my family. I try not to make any decision that would affect them without thinking of all the ways it could go wrong."

Marcus still wasn't satisfied with the duke's answer. "Let's get back to the original subject. I don't care about money. You know that about me." Marcus shook his head at the duke's raised an eyebrow.

"I am always serious about money," Pelham quipped.

"Do you think I would hurt Honoria?"

Pelham leaned back in his chair with a startled look on his face. "I thought you called her Noria?"

"For you, I'll call her Honoria when we're alone." He rested an elbow on the table.

"You'd hurt her if you ever caused her to doubt herself."

"Pelham," Marcus chided. "I'd never do that."

"Perhaps not." The duke finished his brandy and placed the empty glass in front of him. "If she falls in love with you, and you don't love her in return"—he slowly stood—"that would be cause enough for me to shoot you in the back."

With those cryptic words, the duke turned and walked out the door.

Marcus pushed his unfinished whisky away and fell back against the chair. He'd protect Noria with his own life and everything he possessed.

A knot formed in his chest when he remembered the night they'd made love. He'd willingly gone into that bedroom with her. He'd once thought he was halfway in love with her. He still felt that way.

Maybe it was more than halfway.

Twenty-Four
❧

"The Duke of Pelham, Lady Honoria Ardeerton, and Lady Phillipa," the Marquess of Ravenscroft's butler boomed at the crowded ballroom.

Honoria flinched slightly at such an ostentatious announcement. Everyone stopped what they were doing to gawk at them. She slid a sideways glance at her brother. Thank heavens, he was beside her. Hopefully, all the guests would be looking at him instead of her. With his silk evening coat and breeches, Pelham cut a dashing figure. He'd grown up being fawned upon, and this was probably an everyday event to him.

By then, the entire crowd had turned their gazes to the top of the steps where they stood. Pippa stood beside her with a self-assurance that rivaled their brother's.

"Darling, you must either smile or look bored," Pippa said softly while keeping her own smile in place. "That's what Grace advised. Remember?"

She smoothed a hand down the dark blue gown. It was the one that Pippa had designed and sewn for her. It was a stunning creation and would be the envy of every woman there. She swallowed the army of frogs that currently resided in her throat. Perhaps she should have worn something else. She'd never liked to be the center of attention.

An older woman, escorted by a handsome man, was walking up the curved white marble staircase to meet them.

"That's Ravenscroft and his mother," Pelham murmured. "It's an honor that they're greeting us here instead of down below."

By then, the marquess and his mother had arrived.

"Good evening," the dowager marchioness said to Pelham with a kind smile. "We're delighted that you're introducing your sister at Ravenscroft's ball." She turned to Honoria and smiled.

"Lady Ravenscroft, may I present my sisters. This is Lady Honoria," Pelham said. "And you already know Lady Pippa."

Honoria curtseyed deeply, as did Pippa, both murmuring, "My lady."

Ravenscroft came forward and shook Pelham's hand. "Don't forget me."

Pelham rolled his eyes, and the dowager marchioness laughed.

"You're always so entertaining when you attend Ravenscroft's event," the marchioness said playfully and batted Pelham's arm with her fan.

"That's always my aim with you, my lady." Pelham pressed a kiss to her hand, then turned to Ravenscroft. "Well, I suppose I must be polite this evening since it's your ball. You remember Lady Pippa." He affectionally took ahold of Honoria's elbow. "And this is my eldest sister, Lady Honoria Ardeerton."

Again, they curtseyed in tandem.

Ravenscroft came forward and greeted Pippa before he took Honoria's hand and bowed over it. "Lord Trafford's description of you didn't do you justice. Welcome to Raven's Splendor. May I have the pleasure of your first dance?"

As tall as their brother, with hair as dark as night and sparkling green eyes, the marquess was a handsome man. For a moment, she froze. This wasn't at all what she'd expected. To have the first dance with the marquess, their host for this evening, would give the impression that she was a special guest. She'd hoped to only dance with Marcus and perhaps Pelham, then stay out of sight.

The marquess continued to smile as she debated her choices. There was only one. She had to dance with him. "I'd be honored."

Pelham sighed slightly in visible relief.

He turned to Pippa. "My lady, may I have your third dance? I must dance with my mother next."

"How delightful," Pippa answered cheerfully.

"Shall we, then?" the marchioness answered and waved a hand for them to descend the steps into the ballroom.

The three of them followed the marchioness and the marquess. Honoria kept her gaze ahead of her, although the urge to seek out Marcus grew nigh impossible to ignore.

Just as she was about to steal a glance, Pippa laughed softly, the sound filled with unfettered glee. "Look. There's Grace."

Honoria stopped on the third step from the bottom. Indeed, Grace was waiting for them with a brilliant smile on her face. Immediately, Honoria felt the pressure in her chest relax.

Just as she started to take the last step, the unthinkable happened. Her left heel became entangled in her hem. She stumbled slightly. Her hand shot out desperate to find the marble baluster before she fell flat on her face. Like a flash of lightning, someone moved beside her, then took her arm.

"I have you," a rich baritone murmured. The scent of orange and bergamot surrounded her as a masculine arm wrapped around hers.

He was here. Her thrashing pulse quieted at the deep rumble of his voice. His movements had been so graceful that no one would have noticed that she had lost her balance. Dressed in a black silk evening suit with a black brocade waistcoat, he exuded elegance. In his perfectly tied cravat, a sapphire in his gold stickpin glittered in the chandelier's light. Her breath caught when she glanced at his white stockings that didn't hide the flawless lines of his defined calves. The man was a perfect male specimen.

And she had been intimate with him. Good heavens, if I don't get my unruly emotions contained, this night might be my downfall.

"Thank you," she murmured. When she glanced up into Marcus's face, his dark blue eyes shimmered in intensity. "You would make an excellent knight errant," she quipped with a smile, trying to appear at ease.

He chuckled slightly and drew her arm around his. "I know my place now." He slid his gaze to hers. "By your side."

"Trafford," Pelham called out. "Glad you're here. We need to discuss the logistics of the evening."

"I have that well in hand," Lady Grace said demurely. She turned and gave Honoria a dance card. "For you."

As soon as Honoria took it, Marcus was peering over her shoulder. Before she could say a word, he was shaking his head. "This will not do. Why is Carlyle's name even on here? He's a menace. Besides, why does he have a dance before I do? I'm her betrothed."

Her heart fluttered at the agitation in his voice and the menacing tick of his jaw. Was he jealous or just trying to protect her this evening?

Grace skirted around Pelham, who watched her every move. "I'm sorry, my lord. I asked several of the duke's friends to fill in some of the spots on Lady Honoria's dance card. Carlyle was watching me and came forward." A look of contrition fell across her face. "I couldn't refuse him. He signed for the second dance." She turned to Honoria. "You and I discussed this. You'll have to interact with him in public."

Honoria nodded.

But Marcus's face had reddened with anger. "You didn't discuss it with me." He turned to Pelham. "What are your thoughts?"

"The same as yours," Pelham agreed. "This can't stand, Grace."

Pippa, who'd been in a discussion with Ravenscroft and his mother, glanced their way. She put a hand on the marchioness's arm and said something. Immediately, she turned to Honoria. "Is something wrong?"

Pelham nodded. "Carlyle wants to dance with Honoria."

Pippa scrunched her brow, then smiled. "I have a solution. When the first dance ends, I'll come forward and explain that he signed the wrong sister's card."

Marcus visibly relaxed at Pippa's clever solution. Even Pelham nodded in agreement.

"That will work as I had both cards in my hand." Grace took out Pippa's card and penciled in Carlyle's for the second dance. "It's settled then," she said with a smile.

Pippa leaned close. "An excellent sign that he called himself your betrothed. He's still your Marcus."

"Hush," Honoria murmured.

Before she could say more, Ravenscroft was beside her. He lifted his hand in the air signaling the orchestra. As the opening number of a waltz began to sound, he turned to her. "My lady, I believe this dance is mine."

With her most brilliant smile pasted on her lips, Honoria placed her hand in his.

He led her out to the middle of the dancefloor. In seconds, he was twirling her around. Her stomach dropped as she caught glimpses of faces in the crowd as they danced. Yet, something felt wrong. People were murmuring. It sounded like the buzzing of bees. She forced herself to glance at the crowd. Some of the guests were pointing at her. When she caught the gaze of a silver-haired matron, the woman turned her back to Honoria. An older couple did the same.

Were they delivering a cut direct? Good heavens, what if they were? All she wanted to do was walk out the terrace doors behind her and never return.

Honoria forced herself to calm down. It was probably just a coincidence that people were turning their back on her. She was imagining such a slight. Though their pace was not for the faint of heart, the beat in the center of her chest slogged through its movements. She took a deep breath and latched her gaze on Ravenscroft.

The marquess smiled, unaware of the tumult in her thoughts. "What if I told you that right now, Trafford is staring at us." He lowered his voice. "His gaze reminds me of freshly sharpened knives."

"I'd say you're hallucinating," she answered.

A rich laugh sounded, and everyone turned to stare at them. The marquess ignored them. "You are quick-witted. Trafford warned me about you." He smiled fondly. "Your brother should have introduced me first."

"He didn't introduce Marcus to me." When she realized what she'd said, her cheeks caught on fire.

"Oh, I'm intrigued now." The marquess's eyes brightened to a rich green that reminded her of the fields around Pelham Hall. "You have to tell me how you two met."

As humiliation swirled through her, she shook her head. "We met at an event."

"At Amesbury? The masquerade?" His brow furrowed. When she didn't offer any additional comment, he continued, "I see." He winked like a rogue. "Tell me about your sister. Is she as unique and as charming as you?"

"My lord." Marcus shook the Marquess of Edgeheath's outstretched hand. "I'm delighted to see you here." He turned to Lady Susan with his best smile. "My lady, it's always a pleasure to see you."

The marquess chortled and his round stomach jiggled in rhythm with his laughter. "As soon as Susan heard you were attending, she insisted on attending Ravenscroft's ball."

"Trafford," Lady Susan said with a genuine smile. "I'm so happy you're here."

He took her hand and bowed over it.

Lady Susan's gaze flew to the dancefloor. "Is that the elusive Lady Honoria Ardeerton?" A hint of smugness colored her voice. "My word, I'd say she's exquisite, but that dress is in another category. It's stunning."

"It is her," he said proudly. And I will say it. She is beyond exquisite."

She pretended to smile.

Two things could be said about Lady Susan. She was beautiful. And she was well aware of that fact.

But even if the majority proclaimed her the most beautiful woman in the room, she couldn't hold a candle to Honoria. Not in Marcus's eyes.

Susan lacked the warmth that Noria had. If he'd asked Susan to attend him when he visited Dartmore and Lady Julia, she would have refused. Not because she couldn't sympathize with them, but because it wasn't a popular charity that would keep her in the limelight.

Another lord attending the ball waited nearby to speak with Lord Edgeheath. Marcus nodded in the man's direction, then took his leave of the marquess and Lady Susan.

By then, Ravenscroft had escorted Noria to her brother and Grace. Like an unwanted specter, Carlyle appeared. Marcus wanted to curse at the ceiling.

"Lord Trafford?" Lady Susan was by his side and intimately touched his arm. "Is it really true that you've set your cap for her?"

He pulled away, creating enough distance between them to indicate that he had finished with her and the conversation. "Yes."

A grin tugged at her thin lips, but disappointment clouded her eyes. "Until the banns are read, others will believe they have a chance to turn your head."

He smiled slowly and shook his head. "They would be wrong."

"We shall see, won't we?" she said with a hint of flirtation, then turned to her friends.

Marcus didn't spare her another glance. His gaze swept the ballroom for a sapphire gown. When he found it, he wanted to curse the heavens.

Noria was taking a turn around the perimeter of the dance floor.

With Carlyle.

Twenty-Five

"I did not write my name on Lady Pippa's dance card. I looked twice to ensure that it was Lady Honoria's card I signed my name to. See?" Lord Carlyle huffed as he pointed to Honoria's card. "This dance is mine."

Grace's face slackened. "But your name is on Lady Pippa's card."

"I'm afraid, my lady, that there's been some mistake," he answered with a sniff. "I only signed Lady Honoria's card."

Pippa's gaze shot to Honoria. She turned to Lord Carlyle. "What a disappointment," she said coyly. "Unfortunately, I guess none of us will be on the floor as the dance has started. The couples have already lined up in formation."

"Indeed," Lord Carlyle replied without inflection. "Lady Honoria, allow me to escort you around the room then."

As Lord Carlyle extended his hand, Pelham's lips tightened in response. Before her brother could give the man a dressing down, Honoria took the earl's arm. "I'd be honored."

Carlyle nodded in approval. Because he had outflanked her brother and Lady Grace, a hint of pleasure brightened his eyes. "Shall we, my lady?"

She nodded and prayed that they could make it back to the group before the dance ended. With the orchestra playing, it was difficult to talk.

But Carlyle was two steps ahead of her. He walked slowly and smiled at the other attendees. He reminded her of a preening peacock making a claim. Finally, they reached the end of the room where a refreshment table filled with delicacies and a champagne fountain stood waiting for them.

"Would you care for something?" Without waiting for her reply, he motioned for a footman. In seconds, the scarlet and black liveried servant appeared, carrying a tray with two filled glasses. Lord Carlyle took one and gave the other to Honoria.

She studied the glass in her hands. Her white satin gloves were in direct contrast with the slightly pink liquid filled with escaping bubbles. She'd never been so jealous of a glass of champagne in her life. If she were one of the bubbles then, in a poof, she could escape the earl's company.

"Lady Honoria, I think perhaps we've gotten off to the wrong start."

"In what way, my lord?" Instantly, her throat relaxed as she swallowed the cold liquid. If only the rest of her body could follow suit.

"When my mother and I saw you ride, I wished she hadn't been so direct in her questions. I took her to task for that, but she can be a little set in her ways. She only wants what's best for me." He chuckled slightly. "But only I know what that is. And how to get it."

The truth was she didn't care, but she had to be polite. "What is that?"

"I would very much like to court you. I hope you will reconsider." With a gleam in his eyes, he smiled.

Perhaps if she was another lady, she'd have been charmed by such a gesture. But he was the reason that she was currently attending this ball and feeling rather miserable. If he hadn't gone to her brother with his suspicions, no one would have been the wiser.

"We aren't suited. It was apparent as soon as you found my brother at Whites," she said demurely while her stomach was tied in knots. It reminded her of the times when she'd disrespected the old duke. Of course, Carlyle had no hold over her. The damage had already been done.

He sipped his champagne. "I was looking out for your welfare and reputation."

"How kind," she murmured sarcastically. "There's no need. I can look out for myself." She lifted her chin at his insincere smile.

All her life she'd wondered what her first *ton* event would be like. Frankly, she'd looked forward to it more than she'd ever let on. She'd always assumed that at these events, she'd find a way to cure her hurt at being banished by her father. Foolishly, she'd expected people to be nice and welcoming.

But tonight, she'd quickly learned that she hated these events. The music was too loud. The people were even louder. The way that the men and women strutted around each other reminded her of roosters and hens vying for attention. She would have enjoyed the evening more if she had found herself in a viper's pit.

"Lady Honoria, I don't mind that you were seen with Trafford unchaperoned." Carlyle looked down his nose at her. "He's one of your brother's best friends. However, I do mind that you kissed him. When we marry, I expect him to stay clear. You understand?"

Of all the gall. The man was an unmitigated ass.

"This really isn't a suitable conversation for us to be sharing," Honoria narrowed her eyes as she delivered her rebuke. "I'll say it once more. I'm not interested in marrying you."

"Carlyle," a voice called out.

The earl's body stiffened. She smiled, not knowing who it was but thanking the heavens for the divine intervention.

A gentleman stepped forward. "Carlyle, won't you introduce me to the lady?"

The earl sniffed. "Lady Honoria, this is Mr. Malcom Hollandale."

Mr. Hollandale's smile grew, and his brown eyes warmed immediately. The curly dark blond locks of his hair brushed his shoulders. He looked like a fallen mischievous angel. Perhaps he was and would rescue her from the earl and his machinations.

"My lady, it's a pleasure to meet you." Mr. Hollandale took her hand

and bowed slightly. "I'm a friend of your brother's. I call on him every time he's in London."

"Do you know my brother from your days at university?" she asked and took a step closer, creating distance between her and Carlyle.

"Yes." He leaned closer. "I'm also part of his millionaire's club. Would you care to dance?"

"I would enjoy that very much," she answered.

"See here, Hollandale," Carlyle objected, "this dance is mine."

Marcus's deep voice was behind her. "Actually, it's mine."

Mr. Hollandale grinned as he extended his hand. "Trafford, I didn't know you were here."

Marcus shook the man's hand. "Hollandale, it's good to see you." He didn't even acknowledge Carlyle.

"How long are you in town for?" Mr. Hollandale asked.

Marcus shook the man's hand. "Until I marry." Then without a word, he placed his hand on the small of her back. The warmth of his touch brought a much-needed comfort. He pointed to her dance card. "May I?"

Without a word, she handed him the card. He reached into his waistcoat pocket and took out a small pencil, then scribbled his name in the third dance space. Her eyes widened when he continued writing. He filled out the fourth dance, then the fifth, sixth, and finally the seventh. With a satisfied nod of his head, he returned the card.

"It's mine now along with the rest of the dance sets for the evening." He extended his arm. "Come, darling. I've been waiting for this moment all night."

"Now see here, Trafford," Carlyle hissed.

Without wasting a moment, she wrapped her arm around his, and together they walked onto the dancefloor.

Instead of leading her to the center, Marcus chose a spot on the far side where he turned to face her. "We'll have more privacy here, but still be in your brother's direct line of sight."

Honoria turned to see. Indeed, Pelham was looking in their direction. He smiled and nodded once as if approving what they were doing.

The notes for another waltz danced in the air along with murmurs from the crowd. She wanted to stay in his arms all night and never let go.

Tears welled in her eyes. She blinked to keep them from falling, then glanced at the floor so Marcus couldn't see. She hated this night. First, it was the crowd, then Carlyle. She'd never survive if she had to keep attending these events. Her foolish heart tripped in her breast when Marcus took her into his arms.

"What's wrong, love?" He pulled her a little closer.

He called me love. Perhaps it was a slip of the tongue. Most probably, he could see how upset she was. It was scandalous how he was holding her. Her chest brushed against his. But at this moment, she didn't care. She needed comfort, and he was providing it.

"Nothing." She spoke so quietly, she didn't know if he heard it or not.

"Noria, look at me," he said gently.

It took every ounce of strength she possessed to raise her eyes to his. The warmth and concern in his eyes caused another rush of tears to come forward. Only these were tears of affection and gratitude. "Thank you for rescuing me." She squeezed his hand.

"From Hollandale?" Marcus squeezed her hand in return.

She shook her head. "Carlyle. He told me that he'd informed Dane about our kiss to protect me. He says once he marries me, you and I must not have anything to do with each another." She grinned but it probably resembled a grimace

Marcus's gaze never left hers, and his voice turned into a guttural growl. "I'll kill him."

"There's no need. I was rather rude to him." Her breath caught when the anger in his eyes melted into pleasure. "And sarcastic. And direct." She presented a real smile this time and lowered her voice. "My finishing schoolteachers would be appalled at my behavior. No doubt, they'll insist I come back for a remedial lesson or two. Perhaps they'll demand ten."

He tilted his head back and laughed. She could feel the rumble in her chest. Several couples looked their way and smiled. They smiled at her and acknowledged her with a nod. Marcus's delight was infectious, and she laughed with him.

"I'd say you graduated with honors." He twirled her gently, his movements fluid and elegant.

"You're a marvelous dancer," she said with a smile.

"I thank you for the compliment and offer the same," he said as he expertly turned her.

He would make an excellent partner and husband. When she'd seen him angry, he'd been calm and affectionate. He was so unlike her father.

She meant the old duke. She grinned. Marcus had the ability to make her forget. The man was a miracle worker. Never in her life had she ever grinned or felt a shred of happiness associated with her father. Nor had she felt as free as she did now in Marcus's arms.

"You're beautiful," he said. "But when you smile, you make the entire world magnificent."

Her heart wobbled in her chest at the heartfelt tenderness in his gaze.

"I should kiss you now. I want to shout to the entire world that you're mine." He pulled her tighter. Her breath caught at the sudden electricity that flashed between them.

The dance drew to a close. Couples clapped in appreciation for the orchestra. But Honoria couldn't take her eyes off him. Nor, could she let go of his shoulder or his hand. She would remember this moment forever.

"Fate brought us together, Noria. You were meant to be at that masquerade just as I was." He stepped away slightly, then brought her hand to his mouth. His warm breath caressed her, and she closed her eyes.

"I'm the luckiest woman in the world," she answered. She should be in a panic over saying such a thing, but her heart wouldn't let her deny or diminish what they shared. He was perfect.

And he wanted her as much as she wanted him.

"Let's go outside and stroll through the courtyard," he whispered against her hand. "Let me tell your brother."

"Don't," she murmured. "Pelham will never agree to it."

"I'll die if I don't kiss you." He stole a glance over at the ballroom entrance. "Tell him you're going to the retiring room. There's a hallway that leads to the outside terrace. I'll meet you there."

Her pulse quickened at the promise of seduction in his eyes. "All right."

"I'll be waiting, darling." Marcus led her back to her brother's side. He took his leave by saying that he needed to speak to someone. She purposely didn't look at Marcus, though her skin tingled in awareness.

"Are you enjoying yourself?" Dane asked. He bit his lip to keep from smiling. "I've never seen Trafford so happy." He reached for her hand and squeezed. "It's all because of you." He took a step back and evaluated her. "Come to think of it, I've never seen you so happy."

"Extremely happy," she answered with a grin. "I might not hate London now."

Her brother took her hand and squeezed. "Trafford's good for you, then. I should have introduced you to him sooner. I always knew the two of you would be an excellent match."

"You have amazing foresight and hindsight," she teased him. "I must visit the retiring room."

His gaze met hers. "Shall I send Grace or Pippa with you?"

"That's kind, but it's not necessary." Generally, she appreciated his fussing and worrying over her, but not tonight when Marcus waited for her.

Pelham nodded and then was drawn into a conversation with Ravenscroft and Pippa. They'd just returned from the dancefloor as well.

Without delay, she headed toward the doors. A woman abruptly stepped into her path.

Honoria's hand flew to her chest as she drew to a halt. "Lady Carlyle." The woman's face was three different shades of red. Next to her stood two other ladies similar in age. They crowded around Honoria, completely blocking her exit.

"You should be ashamed of yourself. Deliberately making a spectacle with that man on the dancefloor. Are you trying to make my son jealous?" Lady Carlyle seethed. "Flagrant dancing with your paramour."

Honoria's spine stiffened at the directness in her accusation. "How dare you insult me and Lord Trafford. For your information, madame, your son is not my concern."

Lady Carlyle trembled in outrage causing the ostrich plumes in her headdress to quiver. "Why, you ungrateful chit. My son wants to court you and save what little remains of your reputation."

Her two friends, who better resembled a couple of old crows, nodded in agreement.

Lady Carlyle puffed out her chest. "When the good *ton* turns their back on you, remember *my son is not your concern.*"

Honoria was getting angrier by the minute. "Lord Trafford and I have an understanding."

Fury flashed in Lady Carlyle's rheumy eyes. "I'm sure you do. A good mistress ensures that she's paid for her services."

She had to escape before she said something she regretted. She turned to leave, but Lady Carlyle grabbed her arm.

"With you by his side, most of the *ton* will snub him. That charity of his will burn to the ground."

She pivoted on the ball of her foot, ready to deliver a dressing down, but the flash of fury in Lady Carlyle's eyes stole Honoria's words.

"I don't care if you're the Duke of Pelham's sister or not. He's a gambling hell owner for God's sake. By the time I'm finished with you, the entire British Isles will know of your reputation. You should have stayed in Amesbury," Lady Carlyle sneered. "You're nothing but a whore."

"I am not a *whore.*" She was practically screaming but she didn't care. She would not be treated in this manner. The last time she'd seen the old duke Honoria had promised herself that she wouldn't tolerate such treatment by another. She'd be damned if she allowed Lady Carlyle to spout such vile things about her. "I'm also not a dried-up hag whose main pleasure in life is to make others miserable."

As soon as the words were out of her mouth, she slammed her eyes shut. The music had stopped once more, and unlike Lady Carlyle, Honoria hadn't kept her voice down. Flecks of hot humiliation licked her cheeks. Everyone within earshot would have heard her furious tirade. Out of the corner of her eye, she could see the look of concern on Marcus's face. He was standing with Lady Susan, who was clearly shocked by the expression on hers.

Why in the world was he with her? Of course. She was beautiful.

Lady Carlyle would never dare accost Lady Susan. She was the epitome of beauty, grace, good manners, and proper etiquette, which the *ton* valued. Everything that Honoria was not. Tears welled in her eyes as hot licks of humiliation heated her cheeks. Marcus should have never left her side. Lady Carlyle wouldn't have had the audacity to call her a whore or say any of those nasty things if he'd been with her.

Tonight was an excellent reminder of why she hated London with a passion. She also hated Lady Carlyle. All she wanted to do was melt into the floor and find herself back at Pelham Hall. Why did she ever agree to come to this godforsaken place? Her cheeks felt like they were on fire.

By then, Grace was at her side. "It's all right. I don't think many heard what you said."

"Oh, Grace. I'm horrible at all of this. I don't know how to act or behave. If Marcus had been by my side, she wouldn't have said a word." She clenched one hand into a fist, hoping to keep the rolling tide of her emotions under some type of control. "She called me a whore."

"What?" Grace whispered, but she was clearly in shock.

Marcus took her arm. He must have followed her.

"Leave me be." Honoria practically spit the words without glancing his way. She continued to smile in case anyone was watching.

She couldn't remember the last time she was this distraught. The overwhelming urge to escape grew fierce. She couldn't even look at Marcus as she pulled away from him. "If you'll excuse me."

Honoria hurried through the nearest exit and found a vacant hallway. Without a destination in mind, she just started walking. Grace followed. Thankfully, Marcus had stayed away. The noise from the ballroom had turned into a soft murmur.

"Grace, I appreciate you being with me, but I need time alone." She lifted her hand as Grace opened her mouth to object. "I have to get my thoughts in order, and I can't do that if you're with me."

Grace shook her head. "Unmarried women aren't left alone at an event such as this. You know that."

Honoria had no choice but to use the heavy artillery. "Then I'll tell my brother I'm ready to return home. I'll leave for Pelham Hall tomorrow."

"Oh, darling," Grace said softly as she took both of her hands into her own. "I'm sorry this happened."

"I wouldn't wish tonight on my worst enemy," she confided. "I'm miserable in so many different ways, if that makes sense." The worst one was because of Marcus. She had no right to lash out at him, but she'd felt worthless. Lady Carlyle had reminded her of the old duke. Now, Lady Carlyle was going to ruin Marcus's charity because of Honoria's behavior in that ballroom.

Oh God, what had she done.

She wished her recalcitrant heart hadn't given itself to Marcus. She could leave London in the morning and never return. But she'd not leave him with this mess she'd created.

Grace looked in both directions. The passageway was eerily quiet. "Through there is a small library that the dowager marchioness uses." Grace pointed at a room two doors away. "It has a terrace that overlooks the courtyard. No one can see you in that room." Grace smiled gently. "Lock the door behind you. Don't let anyone in. I'll come for you in a half hour."

"Thank you," she said softly.

Grace stood on tiptoes to press a kiss on Honoria's cheek. "Just so you don't forget, I'm on your side." She squeezed Honoria's hands. "Being thrust into society like this is not for the faint of heart. You're managing it remarkably."

"Remarkably poorly," Honoria replied.

Twenty-Six

Honoria pulled the latch to the library door. As soon as she entered the room, she turned the lock to keep the rest of the world away. There weren't any candles lit, but the light from the full moon cast its glow through the windows. She could see that the furnishings and the desk were decorated to the marchioness's tastes. Everything was upholstered in floral and stripes. Without a candle, it was difficult to see the colors.

Honoria strolled to the French doors and opened them. The scent of fresh grass and blooming roses greeted her along with the chill of the night air. She breathed deeply and then released her breath. She repeated the pattern several more times then walked forward and allowed the night to surround her.

She'd never thought much of love in the past. For her, it was almost too abstract, best understood when expressed within a book or a poem. It was something of a fantasy and only happened to other people.

Of course, her siblings loved her. They'd expressed such feelings in their thoughts and actions. She didn't need to hear the words to know they cared deeply for her. Yet, she wondered if it was enough.

Sometimes, late at night when she was alone in her bedroom, she'd fantasize about finding a love that was all-consuming, that would meld her heart with another. In the morning, she would dismiss such dreams.

She'd spent the last ten years scraping together a life that she could be happy with. Though she wanted to be a part of a couple who pledged their troths to one another and promised to live out all their days together, that wasn't her future. Certainly not after this evening when she'd made a fool of herself in front of the entire ballroom and in front of Marcus. He would have no choice but to run from her.

The truly sad part was she wanted him. She'd put the notice in the legal paper trying to draw out the letter. All because she wanted that future with him. Now, she'd ruined that.

An errant tear skated down her cheek. Angrily, she swiped it away. It was self-indulgent to feel sorry for herself. She released a shuddering breath as another tear fell. If she didn't get her unruly emotions under control, she couldn't return to the ball.

Strong, warm hands gently grasped her arms from behind. "Don't cry."

Instantly, she recognized the voice and the feel of his body and scent. She shook her head in denial, not wanting him to see her when she was so heartsick.

Marcus pulled her closer until she was leaning against his chest. Slowly, he wrapped his arms around her body. She closed her eyes and allowed herself the luxury of just feeling. The constant motion of his chest inhaling and exhaling allowed her own breath to calm. The strength of his arms around her waist promised a haven that she desperately needed in that moment.

"I apologize for my behavior. I've brought you shame, then I blamed you for Lady Carlyle." She sniffed. "I was jealous when I saw you with Lady Susan."

"I apologize too. I'm sorry I wasn't by your side when that witch swooped down and berated you." He squeezed her tighter. "Lady Susan is merely a friend."

Honoria made a move to pull away, but he held her close. "I told Lady Carlyle she owed you a public apology. I said if I ever hear her say one unkind word about you again, I'll challenge her son to a duel."

"Over me?" She turned until she could face him. "No. Marcus."

He pressed a chaste kiss to her lips. "Yes. For dogging you to marry him."

"No, you can't."

"He would never accept such a challenge."

"But he'd spread more rumors. I can't stay in London. I'll ruin you and the rest of my family." Honoria straightened and stared into the courtyard. "You should walk away. Otherwise, I'll make your life miserable. Mine as well." Tears threatened again. "But I want you to know that I've never been so happy as when you held me in your arms, and we danced in front of everyone. I wanted people to know you were mine... all mine. I'll never forget tonight."

"Just let me hold you." He pressed his lips to her neck. "I don't want to let you go. I *need* to hold you."

Those words were the sweetest she'd ever heard. "And I *need* you to hold me."

"Then let us give each other what the other desires." This time he pressed an open mouth kiss to the tender skin below her ear.

She relaxed into his embrace and tilted her head, encouraging him to kiss her again.

"You're mine."

She trembled slightly at the rumble of his words.

"Cold?"

"Just the opposite."

"Then I shall continue confessing my thoughts and showering you with kisses until we both combust." His lips pressed against the hollow of her neck as he smiled.

"Promise?" she teased softly.

"I promise if you'll allow me to kiss you."

She turned in his embrace. "I promised Grace that I would lock the door so no one could find me. How did you get in?"

"I know Ravenscroft's house as well as my own." Reverently, he pressed a kiss to her forehead. "There's a small chamber that connects the marchioness's library to her private sitting room."

"Hmm, you're a man with hidden talents," she murmured. A quiet laugh sounded in the distance. "That sounds like Mr. Hollandale."

Marcus slowly raised his head. "He's with Miss Celeste Worsley for a private rendezvous."

"Hmm." She turned toward the couple. They were hidden from the preying eyes of the ballroom, but the marchioness's library terrace gave her and Marcus a clear view. It was more than a rendezvous. Hollandale and Celeste were embracing, and by the look of things, they were sharing quite a bit more than a simple hug.

"Let's watch how far they allow themselves to be carried away in passion. Would you like that?" Marcus dragged his mouth across her skin, then lightly bit her earlobe. "God, I hope they have no restraint."

"Why?" She tilted her head giving him greater access to her skin.

"Because you enjoy watching others. Just like you did with that couple at the Jolly Rooster." There was laughter in his voice as he nestled his nose against her hair and inhaled deeply.

"I can't believe you said that." But there was no real reprimand in her voice. "This is wicked," she whispered and leaned her back against his chest. His arms were around her waist. A gentle breeze blew, sending a cascade of sensation through her body. Her exposed skin prickled, and her breasts grew heavy. Her nipples ached for attention. With every breath, her stays rubbed against the hardened nubs, sending a delicious swirl of desire straight to her core. "I do want to watch," she said quietly.

"Good," he answered. "Because I want to watch with *you*."

The desire in his voice sent another shiver through her. She was already wet with arousal, but this made her want him even more. She began to turn around, but he held her still keeping her back to his front.

"Watch, Noria." He bit her neck. "Don't be impatient."

With a groan of frustration, she tilted her head back and did as he demanded. The couple appeared to be devouring each other.

"Kiss me like that," she demanded.

His lips lowered to hers, and his tongue swept inside her mouth, coaxing and caressing her before she could even move. When she moaned, he responded with one of his own. His arms tightened around her waist.

No one made her feel these things except Marcus. His kisses were like a feast, and she a starving woman. She tangled her tongue against his, relishing the strength she felt in her own passion and his.

Marcus slowed the kiss, turning it from a wild release into something tender. He pulled away and stared at her.

The desire in his eyes made her even more aroused. He wanted her. How would she ever find this with any other person?

The truth was that she wouldn't.

"Look." He nodded toward the couple.

Hollandale kissed Celeste as his hand cupped her breast through her dress.

Instantly, Honoria smiled. Celeste was a lucky woman to have such attention devoted to her. And she wanted the same. Honoria placed her hand over Marcus's and brought it up to her breast. "Feel."

He chuckled as he gently squeezed her flesh. "I was wondering if you'd like this."

"No," she answered with a straight face, then smiled. "I love it."

"How about this?" He licked her neck as he continued plumping her tender flesh. Slowly, his fingers skimmed the skin along the edge of her dress's decolletage. The warmth of his hand caused her to gasp at the sensation.

"Too much?"

"More," she groaned. She arched her back allowing him greater access.

"Noria," he whispered before dipping his fingers into her bodice under her stays. "What shall I find here?"

They both knew what he would find—a pouting nipple, and she wouldn't be happy unless he gave it his utmost attention. His fingers teased the upper slope of her breast then finally caressed her nipple.

She whimpered slightly, encouraging for more.

"I'll be careful not to leave a mark." He trailed his lips against the line of her neck, then bit down lightly on her collar bone as he squeezed her nipple between his fingers. It was such exquisite torture, and she didn't want him to stop. His breath brushed her skin. "Don't close your eyes. Watch them."

She struggled to open her eyes and keep them in focus. Hollandale had abandoned Celeste's breast and had pulled up her dress. Through the darkness, she could hear his groan.

"Do you know what that moan means?" Marcus rubbed his lips against her neck, taking a nibble and then kissing it. "He's discovered she's wet and needy for his touch. His cock is hard because of it. He wants to take her right there," Marcus murmured. "If I touched you there...what would I find?" He skated his hand down her stomach and pressed his fingers against her sex.

Only her gown separated his fingers from touching her bare skin. She bit her lip to keep from crying out.

Wetness coated her thighs, and she widened her stance to give him better access. "You'll have to discover that on your own," she whispered.

"Such a demanding piece," he teased as he grasped her dress and unhurriedly dragged it up her stockings.

She helped him by holding her skirt in her hands. The sensation of being naked in the night air sent a shiver through her.

He slid his hand up her thigh and hip. She moaned again, practically begging him to touch her *there*.

"Quiet, darling."

She gasped when his fingers slid through her wetness to find her clitoris.

"You're so swollen and wet." His voice deepened. "God, you're as sweet as a Gunter's ice. I could eat you whole."

"It's only for you." The breathlessness in her voice surprised her.

"Good," he whispered. Thankfully, he kept sliding his finger against the sensitive nub, all the while playing with her nipple.

Sensations swirled throughout her body. She'd learned how to make herself come with her own hand, but it paled in comparison to sharing herself with Marcus. He was playing her as if she were an instrument and he the virtuoso who knew exactly how to extract an orgasm that would make her sing to the heavens. Her breath caught as he continued to circle his fingers against the sensitive flesh.

"Your breast is heavy in my hand. Your quim is swollen. I'd wager it's turned a lovely shade of dark pink." He nipped her ear, then lowered his voice. "My God, I could feast upon you and never be satisfied." He canted his hips against her bottom, his hard cock pushing against her backside.

What she wouldn't give to make love to him right now. Another needy moan escaped, and, for a moment, she didn't know if it was from Marcus or her.

He nipped her ear again and then tongued it. If possible, she wanted him to fill every empty space and never let her go. Such a realization should have scared her senseless, but she didn't care. Not now. Not tonight. And not tomorrow.

Her breath hitched as the sensation became too much. Everything within her was desperate to reach the peak. She closed her eyes.

"I—I—" she whispered. Honoria closed her eyes as everything within her exploded at once. Stars burst behind her lids as swirls of pleasure radiated through every inch of her body, curling her toes.

"Marcus." She clasped her hand over his, holding him tight against her core. "Don't let go."

"Never."

"Who's there?" a masculine voice called out.

Instantly, Honoria opened her eyes. Hollandale was looking directly at them.

In one quick movement, Marcus pulled them behind the marble pillar out of view. He took Honoria in his arms and rested his forehead against hers.

A rustle sounded in the courtyard before it turned quiet.

"Do you think they saw us?"

He shook his head then pulled away from her. Closing his eyes, he sucked his index finger into his mouth. "You taste divine." When his gaze fell to hers, his eyes blazed in the moonlight. "Just as I remembered."

She didn't hesitate and pulled his head down. She licked his lips, tasting her own arousal on his mouth.

"I will always share with you," he murmured with a chuckle as he brushed a finger across her cheek.

The touch was incredibly tender, and he quietly regarded her. His gaze was so intense she had no doubt that he saw every desire and dream she'd ever had. Before she'd always wanted to shield herself from such scrutiny. But with him tonight, she wanted to share everything.

"When I first saw you this evening, I thought you were the most beautiful woman in the ballroom, but I was wrong."

She widened her eyes in mock surprise because she knew by the affection in his voice that whatever else he would say would be sweet and dear.

"Tonight, in the moonlight, after touching and tasting you, you are incomparable. No woman in the world could be more magnificent than you."

She stood on tiptoes and wrapped her arms around his neck. "You make me feel beautiful."

He pulled her tight against him and pressed his lips to hers. "Put me out of my misery. Tell me you'll marry me."

"What?" she asked incredulously. She searched his eyes. He had to be teasing her. "After my performance in the ballroom."

"Darling, it was an act of stunning bravery. You were protecting me." He touched his forehead to hers, but his gaze was still locked with hers. "You were magnificent. It was sinfully attractive to me. Now, marry me."

She closed her eyes. "If only Lady Susan hadn't seen me."

"Why does that have any sway over your answer?" He leaned away and stared into her eyes.

For a moment, she felt choked by the mortification that rose in her throat. She swallowed. "You said she was your friend. She and the rest of your friends will think I'm not worthy of you."

"My best friends are Pelham and Ravenscroft. They adore you, but not as much as I do."

"Be serious," she scolded.

Marcus placed his hands on her shoulders. "I am being serious. Trust me. I want to share everything with you. You're perfect."

"Marcus, I'm not. I'm shy. I'm quiet except when I'm accosted by a certain dowager countess."

He laughed softly and reverently pressed a kiss on her cheek. "When you're shy, I'll run through the crowd naked so that people will look at me instead of you. When you're quiet, I'll be the one to take command of the conversation. Or we can enjoy the quiet together. If you don't want people's attention, then I'll stand on a chair and give a sermon. I'll do anything to make you happy."

At that moment, she fell in love with him all over again. "You'd do that for me?"

"Always." He brushed a finger across her cheek. "Marry me. Please say you'll have me."

Her eyes searched his. The emotion in his gaze made her want to take what he was offering. It would be a risk, but she'd have that letter soon. She was certain of it. Everything that she wanted was in front of her. A husband who cherished her and wanted to share a life with *her*. And she wanted the same with him.

He thought her worthy.

It was like jumping off a cliff into the ocean and not knowing if the water was deep enough. But with Marcus by her side, she would take the leap. As long as he was hers.

His large hand cupped her cheek. "Darling, I want to hear you say yes."

"Yes," she said softly. "Yes," she said with more strength in her voice. "I would be honored to be your wife."

With a huge grin spread across his full lips, he swung her into his arms and twirled her in a circle. "Oh my God, I can't believe it. I'm the luckiest man in the world." Gently, he set her down. She quivered when his lips touched hers. There was an intoxicating newness between them. Deep in her heart, she knew that she would feel this way forever. His tongue slipped between the seam of her lips. It was a kiss that melted her loneliness. Slowly, he pulled away.

"Thank you for saying yes." He cupped her cheeks with his hands. "I need to get you back to the ballroom before anyone notices our absence." He lifted a playful eyebrow. "And before I make love to you right here."

"I wouldn't mind that." Even in the moonlight, it was apparent that his evening breeches were tented from the strain of his hard cock. "I could put my mouth on you."

"For God's sake, Noria." He slammed his eyes shut and took a deep breath. "That image of you will be all I think of tonight. You'll make me come just like an untried youth."

"Is that a good thing?" Heat crept up her cheeks.

"An amazing thing. One I will never forget," he murmured affectionately.

She released him and smoothed the wrinkles that had taken up residence on her ballgown. Marcus helped her with several locks of hair that had become unpinned.

He took her hand and lead her to the library door. Silently, he unlocked it. Before he opened the latch, he stole another brief kiss. He smiled with genuine affection.

She answered his smile with one of hers and smoothed a hand down his lapel. "I wish we could spend the night together. You could sneak up the servants' staircase at Ardeerton House. My room is at the top of the stairs." As he shook his head, she continued. "I'll keep my room unlocked tonight...in case you change your mind."

"When did you become so naughty?" he said with a teasing grin.

"When I seduced you," she answered.

Silently, he unlatched the door then ushered her into the hallway. "Go, my little siren. I'll follow until you return to the ballroom."

Reluctantly, she made her way back through the labyrinth of halls that made up Ravenscroft's home. But all her thoughts were on the man behind her. No matter what, she couldn't resist him.

A dark shadow came toward them. It was Pelham. By his expression, he wasn't too pleased. Though her heart pounded with excitement, she schooled her features into an expression of calm.

"There you are," her brother announced, coming to a halt in front of her. "Your sister and I have been looking everywhere for you. We're leaving."

She bowed her head. It was best to address the naked elephant in the room. "I apologize for my behavior."

Pelham lifted an arrogant eyebrow. "You have nothing to apologize for. I gave that woman a cut direct."

She'd never seen Pelham so out of sorts. He had the unique ability to disguise his emotions no matter what. But not tonight. She was the reason he was out of sorts. Her heart stumbled in her chest at the thought of her sister. If Pippa was embarrassed, she'd never forgive herself. "Is Pippa all right?"

"Your sister is fine. More than fine. Her dance card was full. There will be quite a few disappointed dancing partners," he groused.

"Your carriage is here." Ravenscroft had escorted Pippa to them. He took Honoria's hand and bowed over it. "I apologize for what happened. If it's any comfort, Lady Carlyle was practically shunned after you left."

"I'm the one that should apologize to you." Honoria dipped a slight curtsey.

The marquess's mother came forward. "I'm calling on my friends tomorrow. By the end of the week, all of Lady Carlyle's invitations will be revoked."

Honoria shook her head. "Please, not on my account."

Lady Ravenscroft lifted her nose in the air. "I won't tolerate anything less." She took Honoria's hand in hers. "Don't worry, my dear, everything will be fine."

Marcus came around the corner just then. "I'm leaving as well." Once he reached Honoria's side, he took her hand and kissed it. As the others chatted, he leaned close and whispered, "You've made me the happiest man on the planet." With a gentle squeeze of her fingers, he released her hand, then turned to Pelham. "We have much to discuss."

"Come over to Ardeerton House tomorrow," her brother said.

After thanking everyone, Honoria and her siblings were soon in the Pelham ducal coach headed home.

Honoria took off her gloves. The truth was it was for the best that they'd left. Her lips felt swollen, and her dress was extremely wrinkled. Anyone with half a brain would have figured out that she had been someplace she shouldn't have been. But neither Pippa nor Pelham were the wiser.

"I have news," Honoria announced. She had to be the one to tell her siblings what had occurred. "I agreed to marry Marcus."

"Congratulations," Pippa cried as she hugged Honoria.

"My turn." Once Pippa released her, Pelham took her into his arms and squeezed tight. "I'm very pleased." He released her, then arched an eyebrow. "And if I may say it, relieved." He chuckled slightly. "Good tidings to you both." Pelham relaxed against the back of the black leather squab. He opened a door in a side compartment and brought out a small bottle and three glasses. When he uncorked it, the smell of whisky spilled into the air. He poured three glasses and handed them to her and Pippa. He lifted his glass. "To Honor and Trafford."

Pippa lifted her glass. "Huzzah!"

They all took a drink.

He took another swig, then put the bottle away. "I'll see you home, then I'm off to the club. I'll ask Trafford to meet me there. We can discuss the settlements."

Her stomach swooped just then. She was going to marry.

And for once, there was nothing the old duke could do to steal her happiness.

Twenty-Seven

The next morning, Marcus stood in front of the bay window that overlooked the terrace and formal garden at Ardeerton House. Earlier, Pelham had shown him and Ravenscroft the portrait of a young Honoria with Pelham and Pippa when they were children. Honoria must have been a delight as a young girl. She'd no doubt have had many adventures with her sister and brother as they grew up.

"What was Noria like as a child?" he called out over his shoulder in Pelham's direction.

"Noria? I keep forgetting that's what you call Honoria." It was still early after his late ball, but Ravenscroft was always one who never needed much sleep.

Marcus was the same. However, Pelham looked like something dead that the dog had found in the garden and rolled over. He had to have been up all night.

When Pelham turned his attention to Marcus, his face wore a mask. "Happy, I suppose." He nodded as if convincing himself. "Of course, she was happy."

"Why do you ask?" Ravenscroft stood and joined Marcus by the window.

Marcus exhaled and turned to look at his friends. "I want to know more about her. She's in higher spirits at Pelham Hall, more so than in London."

She was also happier in his arms last night than he'd ever seen her. But so was he. When she shared herself with him, he'd experienced a connection that he'd never tire of. Thank God, she'd said yes to marrying him.

When Marcus had met Pelham at White's, the duke had demanded that they settle Noria's future last night. He'd been extremely generous in the marriage settlement. The only proviso was she be allowed to live where she wanted, and her inheritance stayed in a trust for her benefit and any children born of the marriage.

Marcus turned to Ravenscroft. "I'm marrying her."

Ravenscroft slapped him on the shoulder. "Congratulations, old man," he said affectionally. "Where is she?" Ravenscroft turned to Pelham. "I want to warn her about Trafford's bad habits."

"She and Pippa went shopping with Grace." Pelham huffed a breath as he straightened some papers on his desk.

"Thank you for the kind words. But for your information, I don't have any bad habits." Marcus went to the side table near the duke's desk and poured a cup of tea. It gave him a chance to examine Pelham's easy acquiescence to the marriage in another light. Last night, the duke had been jovial and quite anxious for the two of them to marry. He'd even offered to pay for a special license.

Pelham stood and walked around his desk, then sat on the edge. "Seriously, Trafford, I've never seen her happier than she was last night after meeting in the marchioness's library with you. My advice? She'll agree to a special license. Ask her if tomorrow is too soon. Once you're married, any and all gossip will stop. It'll make Lady Carlyle look foolish."

Ravenscroft roared with laughter. "This is rich. Pelham is giving courtship advice and instructing you how to marry his sister. My dog could do a better job."

"You don't have a dog." Pelham's iron gaze swung slowly to the marquess. "Grace suggested it after last night's confrontation with Lady Carlyle."

"You've made my point." Ravenscroft chortled. "I do have a dog. Remember? You gave her to me."

Marcus's eyes widened as he realized what Pelham had said earlier. "How did you know about the library?"

"Do you think that I don't keep track of my sisters?" He laughed. "Always. She was with you last night right before I found her." Pelham shrugged. "She was actually smiling and coming from the direction of the library. She only does that when she's with you. That's why I agreed to the marriage." His brow drew together in narrow lines. "I want her happy."

"She will be." Marcus didn't even have to consider it. "I'll get a special license, but if she wants some time before we marry, that's fine with me. Making her happy is my top priority."

For the first time in his life, he felt as if everything he wanted were about to come true. More than anything in this world, he wanted a wife and a family. His loneliness would become a thing of the past. He vowed then and there that he'd dote upon Noria and any children that they were blessed with.

Ravenscroft sighed. "If I was the romantic sort, I might have a few tears in my eyes."

"You haven't a romantic bone in your body," Pelham said curtly. "That's why you'll never marry one of my sisters."

Ravenscroft looked at Marcus and winked. "I woke the bear." He turned to Pelham and grinned.

Pelham ignored him and picked up a document.

Ravenscroft rocked forward on his toes. "You told me once that we all must marry sometime. Since there's one sister left, perhaps—"

"Don't even consider it." Pelham threw the document back on the desk. "I won't."

Marcus laughed. Leave it to the marquess to always lighten the mood around the duke.

"What are your plans?" Pelham asked Marcus. "I can send around a note when Honor returns home today."

"I'd appreciate that." Marcus settled into one of the matching sofas that ran parallel to the massive fireplace. His friends joined in on the other sofa. "I'm seeing Edgeheath this morning. He sent an inquiry to his brother, asking who was named the new guardian for Dartmore."

Pelham nodded. "I'm glad you're pursuing it. As one of the millionaires in my club, his interests are my interests. His father was adamant that he be protected if anything ever happened to him."

"It seems a little too convenient that the longtime family servant was sent away." Marcus thrummed his fingers on the arm of the chair. "The question is, what can I do about it?"

"What servant?" Ravenscroft asked.

"A nursemaid who had been with the duchess since she was a little girl." Marcus stared at the ceiling, trying to put the pieces together. "Most guardians and conservators want to keep the status quo. It's less work. But this new guardian is changing everything. The governess is still there, but for how long?"

"Well, if anyone can figure out the lay of the land, it's you," Ravenscroft said. He rose from the sofa. "I'm off. Mother will want to rehash the entire evening's event."

Pelham winced. "Sounds like torture."

"It is. This is her way of subtly nudging me to the altar. Once I marry, my wife will be the one hosting the ball and making all the plans." Ravenscroft clapped Marcus on the shoulder. "Good luck, old man. I wish you and Lady Honoria happy."

After everyone said their goodbyes, Marcus finally was alone with Pelham. "I *will* make her happy."

"I know." Pelham smiled ruefully. "I should have introduced you to her earlier. I made two mistakes with Honor."

"What are those?"

"I introduced her to Carlyle." The duke shook his head in annoyance. "The other is that I left for London with Pippa and left Honor at home."

"Because I was still at Woodbury Park?" Marcus would never forget his friend's anger that morning when he'd discovered Marcus in bed with Noria. "I'm sorry you found us that way."

Pelham shook his head. "You misunderstand. I'm sorry that I left her at the mercy of Carlyle's company and the subsequent rumors that he spewed. One thing you'll discover about Honor. She's tough on the outside, but inside, she hates this."

Though he'd known Noria only a short while, he could tell from her expressive eyes exactly what she was feeling. At Pelham Hall, she was confident and steadfast in what she wanted. He loved that about her.

But in London, she was unsure of herself. Tonight, he'd do everything in his power to make her feel comfortable being with him and being out in society. She was intelligent, kind, and caring. Anyone would want her for a wife.

Thank God, she was his.

After Honoria had arrived home from her shopping excursion with Pippa, she'd stood for her last fitting with Mademoiselle Mignon. The emerald creation had been more than she'd ever hoped for. Mademoiselle had said that with her height, it had turned into a masterpiece. No one could have worn such a daring gown except Honoria with her slight curves. The modiste had been a genius in cutting the material. Honoria didn't even recognize herself in the mirror. She looked like a princess. Her pulse sped up at the sight. She couldn't wait to see Marcus's reaction to the gown.

"I can't thank you enough for this." Honoria carefully stepped out of the gown. Alice stood by helping her. As soon as the maid had the gown in her hands, she left the room, leaving the modiste and Honoria alone.

"There's no need to thank me. I should be the one giving you my thanks. It's a pleasure to dress you." Mademoiselle Mignon blushed slightly at the praise, then lowered her voice. "You will be the center of attention."

Honoria's eyes widened. "But I don't like attention."

"My dear lady"—the modiste chuckled—"let them gaze upon you. All the men will be salivating when they see you in that gown."

There was only one man she wanted salivating over her.

Mademoiselle Mignon took her leave. Alice had returned from carefully storing the gown for tonight's event and was helping Honoria dress again. It was a beautiful floral silk in pinks and creams that Pippa had made her. It complimented her coloring.

Of course, it didn't hurt that she also dressed with a certain gentleman in mind. It was becoming a habit. She always looked for Marcus to appear, either in Pelham's study or coming through the front door.

A knock sounded. Alice answered it, then was back at her side.

"My lady, you have a gentleman caller."

"Who is it?" she asked a little too breathlessly. She crossed her fingers behind her back. She was acting like a schoolgirl with her first crush, but she didn't care. They hadn't seen each other since last night.

Alice shook her head as if she knew Honoria's thoughts. "It's Lord Carlyle. He said he wouldn't leave until he saw you."

Her stomach twisted itself into a knot that she didn't think would ever untangle. The man was becoming a pest. "Is my brother home?" she asked calmly while thousands of butterflies took flight in her chest.

Alice shook her head. "And Lady Pippa is napping after shopping this morning. Shall I wake her up?"

Her poor sister had worn herself out last night. After they'd returned home, she'd gone to her bedroom and sketched dresses for hours. You could ask Pippa about any lady's dress at last night's ball, and she could recite everything about it.

Including what was wrong with it and why. Not that she was cruel, but Pippa could take one glance at a lady and tell if she wore the wrong kind of stays, had chosen a style that was unbecoming, or wore a color that didn't complement the woman's complexion. Besides designing dresses, it was her sister's talent.

"Will you come with me?" Honoria asked.

"Of course, my lady."

Honoria took one look in the mirror and patted her hair. Satisfied, she turned to the maid. "Shall we?"

As they descended the stairs, Alice stayed right beside her. When they reached the bottom, the maid stopped. "I'm not liking this, my lady. Why would he come now? It's a little early for callers." She glanced at the formal salon where Carlyle waited for her. "I hope it's not about his mother. The flowers he sent weren't even the biggest."

Honoria studied the table outside the salon where Ritson had instructed the footmen to display all the flowers and posies Honoria and Pippa had received this morning. Honoria had been thrilled with the deliveries, but Marcus's red roses had stolen her breath. The card had said red was for passion, and the roses reminded him of last night.

She was going to marry Marcus. Honoria had pinched herself this morning at her good fortune. It was a fairytale, and one that she would protect. She'd already sent a note to Winston this morning asking if he'd received the letter from the old duke's solicitor yet. She would sigh in relief once it was in her possession. Then she planned on burning it on the old duke's grave as retribution for how he had treated her.

"If it is about his mother, I'll make the visit short." When another worried expression crossed Alice's face, Honoria put her hand over the maid's. "I know how to handle myself."

"Do you know how to handle *him*, my lady?" the maid asked.

Honoria delivered her best reassuring smile. "We shall soon see." With that, she went to the salon door where a footman stood waiting. At her nod, he opened the door, and she and Alice stepped inside.

Carlyle stood and slowly prowled forward. "Good afternoon, Lady Honoria." When he stood next to her, he took her gloved hand in his and kissed her knuckles. He ignored the slight growl of warning from Alice. "It's a little early for social calls, but I'd hoped we have a chance to talk privately." He smiled politely.

"Of course, my lord." She signaled to Alice.

The maid nodded then took a seat at the far end of the room closest to the door. A tea service had already been brought in by one of the downstairs maids. Honoria sat and prepared the cups as Carlyle studied her.

"Thank you for the flowers." She handed him his tea.

"Your manners are impeccable," he said. "Even with what happened last night."

It was such an odd thing to say. He was evaluating her for some reason. She didn't have a clue and shouldn't care, but that nag of worry that she was never good enough came crawling to the surface. "Why would say that?"

"Always direct, aren't you, my dear?" He chuckled softly.

She sat ramrod straight at the endearment on his lips. "I've discovered that it's always better to be direct when one can. It saves time."

He took a sip, then carefully set the tea down. "Let me come to the point then, Lady Honoria." He leaned back in his chair and regarded her. "You should marry me."

Honoria slowly put down her tea. She would put a stop to this right now. She lifted her gaze to his. "No, Lord Carlyle. I'm marrying Lord Trafford."

He propped his elbow on the arm of the chair and rested his chin in his hand. From the smile on his face, he wasn't discouraged in the least. "I don't think that's a good idea."

"Pardon me, but I don't care."

"You should." He leaned forward in this chair. The challenge was clear in his voice. "You and Trafford both disappeared from the ballroom at the same time." He smiled when he saw the shock on her face. "Did you think no one would notice? Don't be naïve, my dear. You're one of the wealthiest heiresses in the British Isles. Your sister is another. Do you honestly think that the men of the *ton* aren't watching your every move?"

"I was with Lady Grace," she countered. "I'm not really certain what you're attempting here, but it's not working."

He lifted both eyebrows at her abruptness, then relaxed. He reached into a pocket on his waistcoat and pulled out a sheet of paper. Without a word, he handed it to her.

She unfolded it and immediately gasped. It was her announcement from the *Law Chronicle*.

To whom it may concern: Miss H. Ardeerton will marry Mr. Giuseppe Antonio Forliti of Florence in a private ceremony to be held at Pelham Hall in Amesbury. Miss Ardeerton's brother gives his best wishes to the couple.

. . .

All her bravado disappeared in a puff of smoke. "Where did you get this?"

"My solicitor brought this to my attention early this morning." A smug grin appeared. "I mentioned to him that I was interested in marrying you. He thought I could use this to get what I want. He is always looking out for my best interests. Clever of you to refer to yourself as 'Miss H. Ardeerton,' but alas, Pelham Hall is a dead giveaway that you were referring to yourself and Pelham."

Instantly, chills ran down her spine. The bloody bastard was taunting her. Honoria lifted her chin. "And what do you want?"

"I want your wealth. I want the attachment to your brother." He pointed to the announcement. "You and the rest of your family will face utter ruin. I've posted a letter to that Antonio chap at Pelham Hall. I've also asked my solicitor to send one to Trafford. They're basically the same. I informed them that you want to marry both of them. Neither will want you once they discover you're collecting fiancés." He tapped a finger against his chin, feigning that he was deep in thought. "It's against the law to marry two men."

She clenched his fists as she tried to control her anger. "How dare you interfere in my life. How do you even know that I was responsible for that announcement?"

"Dear, dear Honoria. The paper kept the original note. It was your brother's personal wax seal." He tutted softly. "I don't know this Antonio, and I've never heard your brother mention him. Is he another paramour of yours? Why would your brother try to undermine his best friend's engagement with his sister? This is the scandal of the century. Do you really think Trafford can afford another of your scandals? All these questions lead me to one answer. It was you."

As emotions swarmed within her, she kept her expression calm. If she didn't admit anything, he couldn't prove it.

"Right now, Trafford is at his *good friend's* house calling on Lady Susan. Her father isn't at home. I just left him at Whites." A pitying look fell across his face. "She still wants him. It's readily apparent to everyone who knows them."

"Everyone is entitled to their own opinion. Marcus will marry me." Her voice had weakened. For a moment, she thought she was going to be sick. She stared at her lap. Marcus would be devastated when he discovered what she'd done. Even when the old duke had berated her, she'd never felt such anguish in her life. Tears pooled in her eyes. She'd never wanted to hurt Marcus. For God's sake, she loved him.

He tsked. "What a pity. You've humiliated him. He's a proud man, and this will put a dagger through his heart."

"Why are you doing this?" she asked softly.

For a moment, he stared at her then smiled. "I'm not doing anything. You caused all this."

She lifted her chin an inch. "Lord Trafford is a man of honor and is greatly esteemed by my brother and family. He will marry me."

"Like your friend from Florence?" Carlyle scooted to the edge of the chair and leaned slightly forward.

Honoria tilted her chin in defiance. "None of this is your concern, my lord." The tone of her voice could have frozen the Thames in midsummer.

Carlyle chuckled slightly. "I believe it is my business. Lady Honoria, let me be blunt. Why would Trafford marry you? You've made a fool out of him. Once word of this notice is printed, you'll be banished from society. Your brother's status won't help you. Your poor sister's reputation will be shattered along with the Ardeerton name."

She inwardly flinched, and her newfound assurance evaporated.

"You can't keep him. It makes no difference whether he's Pelham's friend or not." He flashed an empathetic smile. "Trust me. He won't marry you. He loves his charity. I must emphasize that he won't stay with you. But I will."

"*You can't keep him. He won't stay with you.*" The words echoed off the wall, and she wanted to put her hands over her ears to stop the garish sound.

But it was the truth. Once Marcus received Carlyle's letter, it would ruin everything. How could his charity survive once the scandal broke? He'd have to walk away from her. She rested her hand on her forehead.

"I'm sorry if I caused you to become distraught." Carlyle smiled with such benevolence that she wanted to throw a teacup at him.

"I'll never sleep with another woman. Nor will I even look at one. My wife will always be my highest priority. Which means *you'll* be my highest priority." He glanced at Alice and lowered his voice. "Does Pelham know about this?"

She couldn't answer. Her entire world had just been destroyed.

He stood slowly and took her hand. "I'll give you a few days to accept my proposal. Take a week if you'd like."

He saw himself out.

Honoria couldn't move. This was everything she'd feared might happen, but foolishly thought she could protect herself from it. Not only did she face real disaster, but so did Pippa and Pelham.

Marcus would hate her.

And she couldn't blame him. She hated herself in this moment.

Twenty-Eight

M arcus's visit with Edgeheath led him straight to Carlyle's residence.

The marquess had agreed to find out who was Dartmore and Lady Julia's new guardian and acting conservator. Since the man had just been named last week, it wasn't public knowledge yet. But he'd done enough damage in that single week to last a lifetime.

Marcus had had a suspicion who it was through his clerk friend, but he'd wanted verification before he confronted the man. While Marcus waited, the marquess had immediately sent an inquiry to his brother who sat on the Court of Chancery. The newly named guardian and conservator was the Earl of Carlyle.

"Trafford, what brings you to my door?" Carlyle chuckled as Marcus entered his study. With a determined step, the earl closed the distance between them and extended a hand.

Marcus quickly shook it and let it go. "Business. I hope we'll be able to resolve it rather quickly." He could feel the muscles in his jaw flex. There had always been something about Carlyle that didn't sit right with him.

Carlyle waved a hand for Marcus to sit down, then went around the desk to sit at his chair. With a deliberate insouciance, Carlyle rested his elbows on the desk, then steepled his fingers. "Tell me how I can help you."

Marcus smiled slightly. "I've come to inquire about the Duke of Dartmore and his sister, Lady Julia Banbury. I understand that you've been appointed as a new guardian and conservator of the estate."

Carlyle nodded. "I joined the other guardians and conservators to take care of the children and protect Dartmore's duchy. The previous duke was my first cousin. There are no other male relatives except for me. There's a female cousin on the duchess's side that the solicitors are trying to find, but they haven't located her." He slapped the desk lightly, obviously wanting the interview to proceed. "Is Dartmore and Lady Julia to benefit from your little charity?"

Instead of being angry at Carlyle's demeaning tone, Marcus leaned back in the chair to appear comfortable with the man's company. It would be easier to sway Carlyle's actions. "Indeed."

"The duke and his sister don't need any assistance, but I thank you for the offer. The other guardians and I are more than capable of dealing with their interests." He smiled, but it didn't reach his eyes.

"They have no one. It's my understanding that you fired their nursemaid." Marcus waited to see Carlyle's expression, but there wasn't a hint of remorse. "She'd been with the duchess since she was a baby."

"Is there a problem?" the earl asked, sounding bored.

Marcus had enough experience with men of his ilk to know to tread carefully. Perhaps if he shared a bit of himself, Carlyle would understand how his actions could harm the children.

"If you know anything about me, then it shouldn't be a surprise that I value these children and want what's best for them." At Carlyle's puzzled look, he continued, "I lost my parents when I was slightly older than Dartmore. It was devasting for me as a young boy. I'd lost my family and I relied on my governess and my vicar. The vicar received an assignment in another parish, and my guardians fired my governess on the grounds that I was too old for one. In the space of a year, I'd lost everyone."

Now that he had Noria in his life, he could do even more to help those children.

"Tragic tale," Carlyle said sympathetically, "but that's not the case with Dartmore and his sister. Their governess is still employed."

"But their nursemaid isn't," Marcus pointed out.

Carlyle leaned back in his chair. He appeared relaxed, but the tic under his eye gave away his aggravation. "Not that it's any of your concern, but they're too old for a nursemaid. The other guardians and conservators believed it was the right decision to let the woman go. It's our duty to protect the children and the coffers of the duchy."

"But their nursemaid had been with their mother when she was a girl. She'd specifically employed the woman as she considered her part of the family." Marcus sat on the edge of his seat and leaned forward. He locked his gaze with Carlyle's. "You see how devastating that could be for Dartmore and Lady Julia."

"My nursemaid was let go when I was Dartmore's age," he argued.

"But you had your mother." Marcus arched a single eyebrow. "You still have your mother."

Carlyle chuckled. "If you want her, I can make arrangements."

Marcus shook his head. "No, thank you. I saw enough last night."

Carlyle smiled. "Sometimes my mother is her own worst enemy."

"I'm not here to talk about Lady Carlyle. The point is the nurse-maid could help the children grieve. She could help them remember their parents. How can I convince you?"

"Pay her wages," Carlyle said without hesitating.

There it was. The true motivation for firing the nursemaid. Money. It was always money with Carlyle.

"I would do that," Marcus said keeping his voice even, "on the condition that Dartmore's studies at Eton be postponed for at least two years."

Carlyle was already shaking his head. "Under no circumstances. The boy needs to be ready to run the dukedom when he reaches his majority. I'd be derelict in my duties if I didn't prepare him."

"Pelham is willing to help. He's already promised to visit Dartmore monthly." Marcus's anger smoldered as Carlyle shook his head.

"Pelham earns his money through gambling. I've earned mine through inheritance and wise investments. Though Pelham's a friend, he's more likely to teach the boy how to cheat at cards." At the widening of Marcus's eyes, Carlyle shook his head. "Don't take that the wrong way. Pelham is a paragon of a man." He stopped for a second and glanced out the window. Slowly, a smile broke across his lips, and he turned his gaze to Marcus. "All right. I agree with your proposal. Truth is that I've always admired Pelham. Though his duchy was wealthy when he inherited, Pelham has become wealthy in his own right through the Jolly Rooster. He could teach Dartmore quite a bit."

That had been relatively easy. Too easy as a matter of fact. Marcus drew in a deep breath and released. "You'll rehire the nursemaid and keep Dartmore and Lady Julia together for at least two years. And allow Pelham and me to continue to call on them."

Carlyle had nodded up to that last point. "There was never any discussion about you."

"I've been calling on them since I heard their parents passed away." Marcus's voice had deepened with anger. If Carlyle thought to keep him away from Dartmore and Lady Julia, he'd go to the other guardians and ask for assistance. "It would mean a great deal to me. Lady Honoria has already formed a friendship with Lady Julia."

Carlyle stilled at the mention of Noria. "I want to discuss her with you."

"I'll not apologize for my future wife's behavior. She did the correct thing. No person should have to listen to the vitriol that your mother spewed."

Carlyle narrowed his eyes. "When I suspected that you'd ruined Lady Honoria, I went to her brother. With your outlandish behavior, you and she have caused those rumors to breed like mayflies."

"You're talking about my future wife," he challenged.

Carlyle pinched the bridge of his nose and closed his eyes. "She's not yours." His hand fell away from his face, and his gaze shot to Marcus.

For a moment, Marcus weighed how best to respond. "You are incredible." Meaning Carlyle was incredibly difficult, obtuse, and downright cruel.

"I'm trying to make this easy for you." Carlyle sighed. "Rumors are swirling about the two of you. They're going to get worse."

"Rumors that your own mother started." Marcus wanted to reach across the man's desk and pummel him, but miraculously, he didn't. "Lady Honoria is under my protection."

Carlyle's eyebrows shot up to his hairline. "It's over, old man. She's mine. My solicitor sent you a letter. It should be delivered soon. It'll explain everything."

"Over my dead body, you unmitigated, naïve." Marcus didn't care that he was practically roaring. Noria's feelings for him were as strong as his for her. Carlyle would not take her from him. He'd lost everyone that he'd loved before, and he'd not lose again.

"Quarreling with me won't resolve anything. One of the reasons I've agreed to your requests regarding Dartmore and Lady Julia is so you know I will not hold a grudge. I want everyone's best interests served."

Marcus stood and turned on his heel. "You're delusional." Marcus stood and turned on his heel. Without breaking stride, he took his hat from the footman who guarded the front door. He made his way to the street. Only then did he feel as if he could breathe. He silently cursed himself.

The rumors were all his fault. He shouldn't have snuck out of the ballroom and followed her into the marchioness's library last night. But he couldn't live with himself if he hadn't apologized and comforted her.

Now, there was only one thing to do. Without wasting a second, he headed to Ardeerton House. He'd tell Noria what had happened with Carlyle.

Then he'd kiss her senseless. He would not lose her to any man. He didn't care what poison Carlyle's solicitor had written.

Honoria sat in Grace's comfy sitting room. Decorated in florals of pink, red, and white, it was feminine and suited Grace perfectly. What would suit Honoria would have been if the room was decorated in black bombazine. She was mourning the loss of Marcus and their future. The only thing she could do was return to Pelham Hall and wait for the letter. Once she had it, perhaps she'd go to the continent. She took a sip of tea. She could as well have been drinking mud. There was no taste or joy in anything for her.

"Take a deep breath," Grace soothed.

Honoria set down her cup and saucer and then started to pace. She had been dreading asking Grace the question, but now was the time. "With my confrontation with Lady Carlyle at the Ravencroft's ball, along with all the rumors that I'm a woman of loose morals, I'm ruined." She slowly stopped and faced her friend. "I'm here to ask if you'll help Pippa when she attends society events...in your role as the Governess."

Grace carefully set down her teacup, then gave her full attention to Honoria.

"Will you do it for Pippa and Pelham? Please," she begged.

"Of course, darling. Pelham needs all the help he can muster, but your sister doesn't need my help," Grace chided. "And you're not ruined. Lady Carlyle is rude, bombastic, and a bore. Everyone knows it. All you need is for everyone to see who the bigger person is. Just smile at her tonight when you arrive at the theatre. All will be forgotten."

How Honoria wished she'd never accepted Marcus's proposal. She should have stayed at Pelham Hall and waited for the solicitors to respond to her correspondence. She wanted to curse at the heavens. She never dreamed that a solicitor would share her simple announcement with a member of the *ton*. For God's sake, only solicitors were supposed to read those announcements.

Grace bowed her head for a moment, then lifted her gaze to Honoria. "Is there something you're not telling me?"

Honoria stopped pacing and turned to face Grace. "What do you mean?"

"You were happy today when we were shopping. You were giddy as you told me you were marrying him. Why the change of heart?"

Honoria bit the inside of her cheek. She'd best tell Grace as much as possible. Burning tears welled in her eyes. "Lord Carlyle came to visit me today. He discovered something in my past that would shame Marcus and my family." When Grace opened her mouth, Honoria placed her palm out. "Please don't ask me. I'm trying to keep it a secret for as long as I can. Unfortunately, you'll find out soon enough."

She wiped a lone tear that escaped. Her heart couldn't take much more of this.

"Honor, what's happened? Does Pelham know about this?"

"Not yet. I'll tell him tonight after the play. I must return to Pelham Hall."

Grace stood and, in two steps, took her in her arms. "What can I do to help?"

"Nothing." She hugged Grace tightly. "The onus is mine."

"I'll meet you at the theatre." Grace stepped back and took Honoria's hands. "Any time you want to chat, I'll be there for you."

Just thinking of tonight brought forth memories of the previous duke mocking her lack of talent. She grew quiet. "I just want to go home, Grace."

"I know, darling, but you can't right now. It'll look like you're running away with your tail between your legs." Grace squeezed Honoria's hands. "Go to the theatre tonight. Give the old battleax a genuine smile in her direction, then turn to your brother and me. We'll instantly start to chat. Everyone will see who the better person is."

"Will they see that my heart is breaking too?" A tear slipped free.

Grace reached up and brushed it away. "I know you love Trafford."

She stilled like a scared rabbit. "I've never heard the word 'love' or used it in my entire life," she confessed. "I don't know if I'd recognize it with Marcus."

It was a lie that she didn't love Marcus, but she couldn't say it aloud. Perhaps it would be easier for him to walk away from her if it appeared she didn't love him.

"Darling, look at me," Grace commanded gently. "No one has ever told you that they loved you?"

A deep ache that felt like a newly formed fissure took up residence in her chest.

"Your father or your mother? Your sister?" Grace asked. "Pelham?"

"Marcus one time addressed me as love. But he didn't say he loved me." Her breath caught at the words.

All the hurt and longing she'd felt in her life seemed to spill from her broken heart into every crevice of her body. It was seeping through her eyes as another burning tear fell. She angrily brushed it off, then sniffed. Tilting her head back, she fought to compose herself.

"I've always told myself it didn't matter. And it doesn't," she declared.

"Doesn't it?" Grace challenged with a smile. "I think everyone wants to hear that they're loved. What if Marcus said he loved you?"

"I couldn't imagine him saying that." He told her wonderful things and gave her compliments that made her blush, but they'd never discussed their feelings. Nor would they ever, especially now.

"You might not imagine him expressing it, but I do. When he looks at you, everyone else disappears." Grace took her hand and squeezed. "I know that to be true."

Honoria bowed her head and studied their clasped hands.

Grace softly tut-tutted and then lifted Honoria's chin so she could look her in the eye. "What do you feel for him?"

She sniffed her tears, then with the Ardeerton backbone she'd learned from her brother, she regarded Grace. "Marcus is my first thought in the morning and the last before I sleep. I feel alive when I'm with him"

"That sounds like love to me. I've watched both of you together." She smiled gently. "It might not be love yet, but it's true affection. You must have affection before you find love. He's the type of man who would stand by your side as you weathered this storm."

Honoria shook her head. She couldn't let this continue any longer. Other interests were at stake, namely her family, Marcus, and his charity.

"I'll do as you say for tonight. I will attend the theatre for everyone's sake."

Grace nodded with a smile. "I want everyone to see you in that stunning gown. Thank you."

"Like the ugly duckling who turned into a swan." She smiled, but her heart wasn't in it. "Grace, one more thing."

"What's that, darling?"

"I'm leaving London at the first opportunity. As you can imagine, it's lost its luster."

Twenty-Nine

Honoria stood at the entrance to Pelham's box.

After the play, she was telling her brother that she was leaving in the morning. Marcus had sent a note to her earlier saying that he had to address a matter regarding Dartmore and Lady Julia. He would miss the first act. Perhaps it was best that he not come. He'd know something was wrong.

Her heart was breaking at the reality that tomorrow Marcus would be free of her. But there was no other choice. If she married him, she'd ruin him along with Pippa. Pelham might suffer some, but he was still a duke and wielded power.

Of course, if she married Carlyle, perhaps all of her troubles would end. He wouldn't publish her announcement. But if the old duke's letter wasn't at Pelham Hall, that might mean Carlyle would receive it.

For the love of God, this was a nightmare that would never end.

But this trip hadn't been wasted. Honoria realized her future wasn't in London and never could be. Though Pelham had been marvelous to her over the years, claiming she was an Ardeerton through and through, it was a lie. She'd write and tell Marcus the truth about who she was. He was an honorable man and would keep her secrets. Once he heard the truth, he'd be glad to be rid of her.

It had been her destiny all along. Marcus would be free to pursue another.

Her heart stumbled in her chest at the thought of leaving him, but it was the best for everyone.

Honoria's breath caught. She loved Marcus more than she'd ever thought possible. His calm acceptance of her and all her flaws had made her fall into love painless. She smiled at the irony of it. Never once did she think she'd experience such a grand feeling. Though he'd never know it, she found comfort in that simple truth. She loved a man and would do anything to protect him, even give him up.

She'd always thought love elusive, but this overwhelming feeling shone a brilliant light on that misconception. It had overtaken her when she'd least expected it. Her last night in town, she'd finally realized it. Perhaps she didn't hate the city after all since it was the place where she had learned about love. It had allowed her this time with Marcus.

How could she be anything but blessed to have her heart full?

For as long as she lived, she would honor what she had shared with him. She'd start her own charity for children. Near her school, she could build one. She could welcome and take in the orphans and the children whom no one else wanted. Who else but she could understand their needs? She suffered the same as them. She could bear the heartache of losing Marcus, but still love him through her actions.

With her new resolve, Honoria took her brother's arm, ready to take that last step. A part of her was happy that she was here. She glanced behind her where Grace and Pippa smiled in encouragement.

Pippa stood beside her with flushed cheeks. They'd all agreed that she would feign a headache after the first act.

Ravenscroft was part of their party, and he smiled her way. It didn't escape Honoria's notice that he hadn't left Pippa's side since they'd departed for the theatre.

"You look beautiful tonight." Pelham leaned over and kissed her cheek. "Are you ready?"

She nodded as she bit the inside of her cheek.

When Pelham nodded at the footman, he pulled back the curtains.

"I'm lucky to have you," she whispered.

"I feel the same about you."

"You should mend your differences with Grace." Honoria's voice was low enough that only Pelham could hear it.

He slowly turned his full gaze to hers, but he patted her hand as they stepped into the box. "She may have charmed you, but I'm afraid I'm immune."

"Life's too short, Dane."

When she arched an eyebrow, he smiled. "I'll try. But no promises."

The chatter of the patrons echoed through the large auditorium exhibiting the wonderous acoustics of the building. As soon as the crowd saw Honoria with her brother, the noise slowly died like a Shakespearean actor during the final scene of a tragedy.

She stood tall with her shoulders square and smiled. She swept her gaze across the crowd but didn't focus on anyone.

"I'm known for my entrances," Pelham said.

"It's not you. It's your lovely sisters," Ravenscroft admonished.

Honoria glanced at their party as everyone laughed at the marquess's joke. It felt wonderful to be surrounded by family and friends. Her heart swelled at the sight. They were here for her benefit, and she loved them for it.

Grace sidled up to her side. "Everyone is waiting with bated breath to see how you'll react to Lady Carlyle. Her box is directly opposite Pelham's on the other side. Remember to just smile. I'm here if you need me."

"I'll be fine." She tried her best to smile..

"I know you will." Grace squeezed her hand, then turned to Pelham. "Will you escort your sister to her seat."

"Of course." Her brother nodded, then ushered Honoria to the front row.

It was designed to put her at the center of attention. Though she hated it, she could do this. Performers were trained to make the audience believe in their emotions while pretending to be someone else. Tonight, she would prove that she was a master at it and had prepared her entire life for such a night.

She took a deep breath while the rest of the group took their seats.

Pelham leaned close. "Trafford came by while you were out. He wanted to see you." He squeezed her hand. "He secured a special license."

"That's lovely," she murmured and closed her eyes. A special license was expensive, and he'd secured it to help protect her.

She decided not to say a peep about her marriage announcement until the morning. She didn't want Pippa or Pelham worrying about her all night. She allowed her gaze to drift across the open space. Her stomach was twisted so tightly that she doubted it would ever untangle. Now was the time to find Lady Carlyle. She would watch her for a few seconds, then smile with approval. She could do this.

When Honoria found her, Lady Carlyle was sitting beside her son. Honoria didn't glance his way. Her gaze took everything in at once. Lady Carlyle was dressed in the same color as Honoria. But the similarity ended there. Honoria's was far more elegant and daring.

For a moment, she lost track of the people staring at her. She lost track of time, too. She couldn't seem to tear her gaze from hers. She had to smile, but she couldn't seem to accomplish the feat.

Yet, she found the strength when she remembered this was for Marcus's benefit. She forced herself to turn to Lady Carlyle. When the woman stared at her with a questioning look, Honoria smiled.

The crowd grew quiet for a moment, but then the patrons' chatter rose in volume after they witnessed Honoria's warm reception to the older woman.

She released a breath. She could finally turn away. With the smile still on her face and her heart breaking at the same time, she leaned toward Pelham. "Let's toast something."

"Something like what?" he answered.

"Anything."

Her brother grew still and examined her. "Are you all right?"

"As you say, I'm an Ardeerton. Of course, I'm all right." She laughed, but her insides were suddenly empty. "Champagne?"

With a single nod to the footmen who attended them, Pelham signaled that his party be served. Soon, they were all toasting the event. Finally, she relaxed. The crowd was no longer looking at them.

After she finished her glass, the curtain was drawn, and the play began. It meant that her performance was finished. They would soon go home.

Finally, it was the end of the first act. Grace elegantly strode to where they stood and whispered in Pelham's ear. "Your Grace, Lady Pippa isn't feeling well."

Pelham nodded and addressed his youngest sister. "Pippa, we'll go home now."

It was finished. She had made her peace with Lady Carlyle.

Which meant her time with Marcus was over. How could something she wanted so badly hurt so much?

When Marcus arrived at the theatre, the hallways were filled with theatergoers seeking refreshments and catching up with old friends signaling the end of the first act.

"Trafford."

When Marcus looked to see who had called out, a man dressed in a burgundy evening coat and breeches stepped in front of him, blocking his path. It was Lord Burrell, a young viscount who'd recently inherited his title. Many called him Lord Midas. He'd made a fortune on his own from odd investments. Everything he touched turned into gold.

"Burrell, I must meet someone. Let's chat tomorrow." The crowd seemed to have magically parted for him. With surprising ease, he stepped around the young man and headed toward the Duke of Pelham's box..

Someone else called his name, but this time, he didn't acknowledge them.

He had to find Noria. Pelham's entire party had stood at the end of the first act. If Pelham was offering champagne, Marcus wanted to be there and give the first toast. He wanted to toast Noria again and again until she blushed. Then, he'd sweep her away to someplace quiet and steal a kiss before he told her that he'd secured a special license at Doctors' Commons. They could marry any time she wanted.

Finally, he'd made his way through the crowd and stood outside the duke's box. It was a bit unusual as there were no footmen standing guard, keeping unwanted visitors away. Pelham always brought several footmen with him, two to serve and one to keep watch of the door.

Without giving it another thought, Marcus pushed through the closed curtains. Instantly, he stopped. There wasn't anyone there. The entire box was empty and devoid of any signs that they'd been there that evening at all.

He turned on his heel and raced outside. Normally, the theatre was jammed with carriages that would still be letting out guests and others delivering supplies.

He pushed open the double doors. Cries from street vendors filled the air along with the scent of meat pies, roasted nuts, and ale. As he made his way to the street, he studied the black carriages lined in front of the theatre. Pelham's was absent.

A groomsman dressed in theatre livery stood at the corner, directing traffic. Without delay, Marcus approached. "Have you seen the Duke of Pelham's coach?"

The man didn't take his eyes off the slow-moving traffic, but kept on waving them on as called out, "The duke left less than a quarter of an hour ago. He directed his coach be made available after the first act. I guess he didn't care for *The Merchant of Venice*."

Marcus heaved a sighed as his shoulders sank. "When was this?"

"As soon as he arrived, sir." Immediately, the groomsman yelled at a coach trying to turn the wrong way. "Whoa. You can't enter there."

The driver of the misdirected coach waved a hand in apology and slowly steered his team down the right direction.

"The Marquess of Ravenscroft was with him."

So, they'd planned to leave after the first act. Why didn't Pelham send a note?

"Thank you," Marcus said. "Will you fetch a hackney for me?"

"Must be a horrible performance if everyone wants to leave," the man muttered under his breath. "The tips are never any good on those nights." He shrugged slightly, then motioned down another street. "You'll have better luck catching one on the next corner, sir."

Marcus nodded and gave the man a guinea for his troubles. With a nod of his head, the man thanked him.

Marcus turned and made his way to the next street. As the groomsman had indicated, there was a line of hackneys for hire. In minutes, he was seated in one and off to Noria's house.

The driver expertly navigated the busy streets and soon delivered Marcus to Ardeerton House. After leaving a healthy tip for the driver, Marcus took the steps two at time and knocked on the door.

Ritson answered. His eyebrows skirted up when he recognized it was Marcus. "Good evening, my lord." He waved Marcus inside the entry. "If you're looking for His Grace, he's at his club if you'd like to join him."

Marcus shook his head. "I'm here to see Lady Honoria." He held out his hat and gloves to a nearby footman, but the man stood at attention, not glancing Marcus's way. He let out a breath.

"I'm sorry, but Lady Honoria is not receiving callers." A perfect look of contriteness fell across Ritson's face. "If you'd like to leave a note, I'll ensure that she receives it first thing in the morning."

The butler waved a hand at the massive beechwood table that guarded the entry where a silver salver gleamed in the light from the chandelier.

"She's retired for the evening?" he asked innocently.

The butler nodded vigorously.

It was half past ten at night. Something smelled off, much like a day old fish. "Is she ill?"

"Oh no, sir. But she normally keeps country hours even when she's here." Ritson looked to the footman, who nodded once in support.

"I see. Thank you." Marcus took his leave. Once outside, he walked down the long drive, then circled back around the house. He'd wager every pence he owned that Noria wasn't asleep. She might not even be home. But Marcus was determined to find out what was going on.

It helped that he knew the house as well as he did his own. He'd find a way to sneak in. He remembered what she'd said about her room being at the top of the stairs next to the servants' staircase.

Thirty

H onoria lay on her bed, her mind swirling with thoughts and feelings best left alone. This was her last night in London. Though Honoria longed for Pelham Hall and her old life, she'd leave her heart in London.

Or wherever Marcus resided.

A soft knock sounded at the door.

It couldn't be Alice. She knew Honoria had gone straight to bed after her trunks had been packed for the return journey. There was only one person who would knock on her door after she'd retired. Pippa.

Without donning a dressing robe, Honoria slipped out of bed. It was odd that Pippa would knock instead of walking into the room as was her usual custom.

"Darling, can't this wait until morning?" Honoria said as she opened the door.

"No, it can't, *darling*." Marcus swept into the room as if she'd conjured him from her dreams.

Honoria shut the door quickly then turned to face him. "What are you doing here?"

"I need to talk to you." He took a step closer while his gaze slid down her body inch by inch. When he lifted his gaze to hers, her breath caught at the intensity in his eyes. "Did you dress for me?" He reached out and trailed his finger across her bare skin from her neck down to the edge of her bodice.

Her breath hitched when he circled one of her nipples with his thumb. The friction of the material against her skin sent goosebumps all along her arms. Perhaps it was best for him to appear. She could finally tell him the truth. She owed him that.

"Why did you leave the theatre?" The seduction in his voice wrapped around her, holding her captive.

"Pippa had a headache." All Honoria's earlier emptiness had disappeared. She closed her eyes and let his hot touch fill her with delicious sensations.

"I came to the box, and you were gone." He slowly took her into his embrace. With one hand under her chin, he tilted her gaze to his. "You planned to leave after the first act."

It was a simple statement with no accusation in his tone. Yet the intensity in his eyes would have frightened the devil himself.

But not her.

"Yes."

"Why?" he asked softly.

"I can't do this anymore," she confessed.

"Can't do what?" he demanded softly.

"London. You. Me." She couldn't turn away as his gaze searched every inch of her face. It was a caress of sorts, like he was collecting a memory of her just as she was of him.

"I can't do it either."

He pressed his mouth to hers in a kiss filled with tenderness and yearning. Then, like lightning, it turned into something wild and insatiable. When he groaned again, she took advantage by sweeping her tongue inside his mouth. He pulled her tighter against him, grinding his hard body against hers.

She tilted her hips and tangled her leg with one of his, capturing him. If she was going to have to let him go, then she wanted one last night with him. They were frantic for one another as the world with all its worries fell away. Aching with need, she pushed against him. She needed him inside her.

She broke the kiss, but when he went to take her again, she pressed her fingers to his lips. "Come to bed."

"No. That will come later." He took her hand and led her to her full-length cheval mirror that stood in the corner.

"What are you doing?" she asked.

He kissed her then trailed his lips ever so slowly across her cheek. "I want you to watch." With infinite care, he slowly raised her gown over her head. Then dropped it to where it puddled into a cloud of silk on the ground.

He came to stand before her as she stood naked. He kicked off his evening slippers, then bent down and pulled off his stockings. He drew off his evening coat, then unbuttoned his waistcoat.

When he lifted his shirt over his head, her breath hitched. The contours of muscles and sinewy cords were masterpieces. She reached out and ran a hand down his chest. With her fingers, she explored each rib, one by one. He could easily be the embodiment of Adonis, and he was in her room.

He stepped away. His gaze never left hers as he unbuttoned the placket of his breeches and let it fall. His erect cock sprang forward, it's crown glistening in anticipation. He pushed his breeches over his narrow hips then kicked them away.

"I need you." She was pleading, but she didn't care.

"Be patient." All the while, his gaze never left her face. "Just watch me."

Her breath caught when he fisted his cock and tugged.

"Ever since I've met you, I take myself in hand at least twice a day. You haunt me in my dreams. I wake up aroused, reaching for you."

Every part of her tingled, primed and ready to explode. "You haunt me, too."

"Do you dream of me?"

Her breath quickened at the dark, seductive sound in his voice. "Yes."

"Do you dream of this?" He gracefully fell to his knees and framed her hips with his hands. He kissed her stomach, then trailed his mouth down her body. He glanced at her and smiled. Then, he licked the crease of her folds.

273

She felt her knees about to buckle so placed her hands on his broad shoulders. The muscles rippled beneath her touch.

"Widen your stance," he instructed softly. When she did as he asked, he smiled with pure wickedness. "Now, I want you to watch yourself in the mirror. I'm going to make you come on my mouth, and I want you to see the beauty I behold every time we're together like this."

Marcus started to lick her slowly, He moaned against the sensitive bud. He circled it with his tongue over and over and then grazed it lightly with his teeth.

She cried out at the sensation.

"Look in the mirror," he ordered.

She was panting as her body pushed for a resolution to the keen ache. Her gaze lifted from Marcus to the mirror.

His head moved slightly as he continued to pleasure her. He moved his arm, and in seconds, two of his fingers entered her sheath. In response to the fullness, every muscle in her body tightened.

The wicked man withdrew slowly, then entered her again. This time with three fingers.

She let go of his shoulders and gripped his hair with both hands, directing him to the sensitive nub that demanded his skillful tongue. He chuckled slightly, then licked her again, this time a little harder.

"Please." Honoria didn't recognize the dark sultriness of her own voice.

He continued as pleasure twined through every inch of her, laying claim to her body. She stood on tiptoes and tilted her head back. She closed her eyes as a thousand shards of light exploded beneath her lids, taking her over the edge. With a guttural moan of his name, she surrendered to her climax.

Marcus took her in his embrace and kissed her as if he were a starving man. She adored the taste of her own arousal on his lips and tongue. It was something only they shared.

She whispered his name again as her body came under her control. She slid her fingers through his soft hair as he held her. He pressed a kiss to her temple, then swept her into his arms.

"How did you like watching yourself?" He smiled down at her while laying her gently on the bed.

Heat kissed her cheeks, but she refused to look away. "I might have a new hobby."

He laughed softly. "I might have the same."

She lifted her arms in invitation, and he covered her body with his.

"Do you know how much I want you right now? It's a *need* that will never be satiated. I think I'll want you like this every day of my life." He shifted his legs between hers.

In answer, she bent her knees, welcoming him.

He took her hand and placed it around his cock. "What do you want."

She positioned him at her entrance. "You."

"I'll always give you what you want." He pressed a gentle kiss to her mouth as he inched inside of her.

She didn't know if she'd ever get used to his size, but the pleasure he gave her was something she'd crave for the rest of her life as well. Once he was firmly seated inside of her, she wrapped her legs around his hips. He rested his weight on his arms and stood poised above her. Studying her.

Slowly, he lowered his head and claimed her mouth, then started moving. He withdrew slowly, then eased back in. He repeated the motion again.

She lifted her hips, encouraging him to take what he needed from her. Whatever he wanted from her tonight, she would gladly give.

His hips met hers again and again. "Noria," he whispered in her ear. "Do you feel this? This is heaven."

"It is," she answered.

He shifted so he could look at her as he moved faster and faster. His hips became pistons against hers. The sound of flesh hitting flesh filled the room, the movement sure and quick.

His brow was wet with sweat, but his eyes devoured her. He slammed his mouth against hers and kissed her like a possessed man, as if she were as vital to him as the air that he breathed.

Suddenly, he pulled her tight into his arms. "Noria," he cried.

Then, he pulled out of her, and hot liquid coated her stomach. He collapsed on top of her, resting his head between her shoulder and her neck. Gently, she combed her fingers through his hair. His heart pounded against hers, and hers answered with the same beat.

Finally, his breathing slowed. "Noria?"

"Hmm?" she answered. The sound of her name on his lips was something she never wanted to forget. She nestled her head a little closer to him.

"Let's marry tomorrow."

Marcus slid off Noria's body as soon as she started to push him away. "I apologize. I must be heavy."

He didn't want to let her go, especially after he'd asked her to marry him. Yet, he could tell by the stark expression on her face, she was troubled.

"What are you thinking?" He brushed her cheek with the back of his hand and scooted closer. Once again, she wore a mask, hiding her emotions from him. He had no earthly idea what thoughts were churning in that beautiful head of hers.

Slowly, she turned to face him. Her eyes glistened with tears as she studied his face. "I can't marry you."

"You can marry me." He rested his head with his elbow bent and gazed down at her. Lovemaking made her even more breathtaking. With the flush of her cheeks and the dark pink of her swollen lips, she was once again his Venus.

He wasn't the same man from a week ago. She needed to understand that simple fact. He had faith in his heart, and right now, it told him never to let her go. He'd not leave this room without her accepting his proposal.

"You can trust me," he said as he cupped her cheek. "I'll never hurt you."

She placed her hand over his then closed her eyes. When she opened them, the intensity nearly blinded him.

"What is it?" Marcus debated what to do when she rose from the bed and grabbed her dressing robe. She didn't say a word as she went to the washstand and dampened two linen toweling. With one, she cleaned her stomach. Then she silently walked to his side of the bed where he had changed positions until he was sitting up and resting against the headboard.

She extended a toweling to him.

"You do it," he said softly, then lifted the sheet away from his body.

He was ridiculously pleased when her breath caught. But his proud Noria didn't turn away. She gently washed his chest, stomach, and cock. It would take little for him to become aroused again. God, he wanted all their nights to be like this. Nothing would ever keep them from sharing such intimacies with each other.

When finished, she lay the cloth aside, then peered down at him. He had no clue what she was thinking behind her hooded eyes.

"You said you wouldn't hurt me, but I can't say the same." One tear skated down her cheek.

He gently wrapped his hand around her wrist, then pulled her close. When she didn't resist, he lifted her onto his lap and held her tight against his chest. He kissed her cheek still wet from her tear. "You would never hurt me."

She leaned against his chest. Needing to comfort her, Marcus rubbed small circles on her back.

"Do you remember when Pelham left the bedroom at the lodge?"

He nodded. He'd never forget. It wasn't every day a man stares down the barrel of his best friend's pistol.

"You asked me who I was." She blinked and another tear fell.

Same as before, he kissed it away. Just as he would do with every single one shed today and tomorrow and the rest of their days together.

"I wish I knew." She played with the tie on her dressing gown. "I have no idea who I am. What I mean is..." She swallowed, then took a deep breath. Her gaze locked with his. "I'm not an Ardeerton."

The air suddenly became charged with a force as potent as a storm about to be unleashed.

"My father was not the previous Duke of Pelham."

"Who is your father?" Purposely, he kept his voice low so as not to upset Honoria any further.

She shrugged but didn't turn her gaze from his. "A man by the name of Thomas Frawley." She tried to smile, but it was more of a grimace. "You'll keep this in confidence?"

He pressed his lips against hers. "Always. But how do you know he's your father?"

She released a painful sigh. "I've told you that my father hated me. When he'd call for my mother to attend him, I'd follow her. I'd enter the study from the second floor so neither knew I was eavesdropping."

"Go on." He stroked her cheek where another tear had fallen.

"One day they didn't have their usual argument about her dress allowance. They argued about me." Her hand fluttered in the air betraying how distraught she was. "Her affairs and the fact that I wasn't his." She struggled to continue, then swallowed again. "The next day he sent me away to a finishing school in York. I never saw him again."

He didn't breathe. Quickly, he performed the calculations. "You were sent to school at the age of eight. Pelham inherited when he was twenty-two years old. That meant...you didn't see your parents for six years?"

She nodded and another tear fell.

"What about holidays?" he asked gently and pushed back a lock of silky hair. He caressed her cheek in encouragement.

"I spent all of them at Mrs. Rutland's Finishing School." She lowered her head and stared at the coverlet. "I didn't want to see my parents either."

Her own parents didn't want her. He closed his eyes, wishing he could shoulder Noria's pain for her.

"What about Pelham? Didn't he come see you?"

"When he could sneak away. The duke had threatened to cut off his allowance if he visited." She slammed her eyes shut as she tilted her face to the ceiling, unwilling to let the tears fall in front of him.

"I don't care, Noria." He bent his head and pulled her close. "Look at me, darling. I know who you are. You're the woman I've given my heart to. All that matters is that you feel the same."

"But you see, I can't." She scooted off his lap and stood.

"Why?" Her words echoed around him. "You can't tell me you feel the same?"

By now, her tears were in a free fall. "That's what I said." Angrily, she wiped her face.

"I don't believe you." He tamped down the growl of frustration.

"I'm sorry if you're hurt," she said without any emotion. "I wanted no attachments, and I meant it. You'll feel differently tomorrow." She wrapped her arms around her waist. "You should leave."

Marcus rested his head in his hand and tried to make sense of what was happening. Indeed, he was hurt and baffled at the same time.

He stood and collected his clothing. As he put on his breeches, he kept coming back to the same thought over and over. He couldn't have been wrong that she felt the same for him. With every breath, his conviction grew. After he dressed, he stood and faced her.

"I don't understand." His voice broke with huskiness as emotion welled in his eyes. Outside of losing his family, he'd never hurt like this. "There's nothing more in this world I want than to make you happy. Come, be my countess. I love you."

Silently, she walked to the window and stared out into the night.

"Noria?" When she didn't answer, he started to walk to her side.

"Don't come any nearer." Her voice trembled, but she didn't turn his way. "This is hard enough as it is without you touching me."

At her statement, every thought and feeling he possessed suddenly turned unreliable. "I don't understand why you're doing this." By the determined set of her shoulders, she was ready to be rid of him. Before he left, he'd have her say it. "I only ask one thing."

"What is it?" Noria glanced over her shoulder.

He threw out the proverbial gauntlet at her feet. "Face me and tell me you don't feel the same for me as I feel for you."

Marcus wasn't wrong. She loved him. He believed that truth with all the strength in his heart.

Honoria turned on the ball of her feet. She lifted a perfectly arched brow and regarded him as if he were the dirt under her feet. "I can't tell you I love you. Now, please go."

Thirty-One

"My lord, the morning posts and *The Times* have arrived." Humphrey approached and placed the items on the breakfast table next to Marcus. "Will there be anything else?"

"No, thank you." Marcus lifted his teacup to his mouth as he examined the mail. He quickly put aside his teacup as he saw the letter from Carlyle's solicitor. He tore open the letter and another smaller piece of paper fell out. He put aside and read the short note from the earl.

Trafford,
    Thought you'd be mightily interested in this announcement posted in the Law Chronicle. Seems she didn't want to marry you after all.
    Carlyle

Marcus slowly placed the letter aside and picked up the other piece of paper. It was an announcement that had been published in the *Law Chronical* three days ago. Carlyle had to be referring to Noria.

He tightened his gut as waves of trepidation washed over him. With a deep breath and fearing every word, he forced himself to read it.

To whom it may concern: Miss H. Ardeerton will marry Mr. Giuseppe Antonio Forliti of Florence in a private ceremony to be held at Pelham Hall in Amesbury. Miss Ardeerton's brother gives his best wishes to the couple.

He couldn't form a coherent thought. He tried to read the announcement again, but the words tangled together before his eyes. The blood in his veins turned to ice.

"Giuseppe Antonio Forliti," he whispered. Who the hell was this man?

Marcus couldn't breathe. He ran his hands through his hair. How could she have changed her mind? How could Pelham do this without a word?

"Humphrey!" Marcus stood from his desk and gazed at the letter and the announcement again.

"My lord?" The butler stepped into the room.

Marcus walked around the desk. "Have Bergamot saddled immediately."

For what seemed like hours, Marcus waited for his horse, then made his way to Ardeerton House. At the ungodly hour of six o'clock in the morning, Marcus pounded on the front door. After pacing the night away in his study, he still couldn't make sense why Noria had changed her mind about marrying him. Now, she was marrying another after making love with him last night.

Something wasn't right about the story. The way she'd held him last night after they made love wasn't a goodbye. He knew that deep in his bones.

When the Ardeerton House butler Ritson opened the door, Marcus was immediately ushered into the breakfast room. As soon as he entered, Pippa stood. "Thank God, you're here."

Pelham stood as well and pulled out the chair next to him. "Come sit. I was going to send word for you to join us at your earliest convenience."

"I need to see her. I won't take no for an answer." He widened his stance, signaling that he had no interest in sitting down for a discussion. He threw Carlyle's letter and the announcement on the table. His heartbeat pounded in his chest as he stared at the duke. "Why are you allowing her to marry this fellow?"

Pelham collapsed in his chair. "I'm not. I was taken aback as much as you are when I read it."

"What?" He glanced at Pippa, who had her head bowed, before turning back to Pelham. "You didn't place that announcement in the *Law Chronicle*?"

Pippa glanced at her brother. "Are you going to tell him, or shall I?"

"I will." Pelham extended a hand to the chair beside him. "You need to sit for this."

"No." He shook his head vehemently. "Where is she?"

"On her way to Amesbury," Pippa murmured.

"And no, I didn't place that notice in the paper." Pelham stood and started to pace. "Honor had a copy of the announcement and gave it to me today.

Trying to get a lay of the land, Marcus slowly walked to the table and sat down. His gaze darted between the two siblings. Pippa's cheeks were flushed and her eyes bloodshot. The same as Pelham's.

Perhaps Marcus was hallucinating from a lack of sleep. He sat in the chair, then rubbed his face, wondering what was about to unfold. The stubble on his chin reminded him that he hadn't bathed or changed his evening clothes from last night. He was still wearing Noria's jasmine scent on his skin.

Marcus met Pelham's gaze. "Just tell me."

His best friend didn't look away, but his anguish was apparent. "Early this morning, she told us that she wasn't marrying you. Then she told us why. Without saying a word, she left the breakfast room, and soon thereafter, the carriage took off. She didn't even tell us goodbye. I was giving her a few minutes to compose herself, then I was going to talk to her. But she was two steps ahead of us." He wrinkled the paper and shook it. "I had no part of it."

He swallowed his disbelief. Noria had left him.

Pippa tried to smile but failed. "Tell him, Dane."

"Where to start? She hates it here." Pelham looked to his sister and nodded. "Specifically, she hates Ardeerton House."

"I need coffee for this." Marcus poured a cup, then stared at it. "I presume this has something to do with her father?"

"And us." Pippa patted Pelham's seat. "Dane, please sit." She released a pained sigh.

Pelham took the seat at the head of the table. He moved slowly as if the wind had been taken out of his sails. When he turned to Marcus, his eyes glistened with tears. "When Honoria was eight years old, we were here at Ardeerton House. She snuck into my father's study. He was arguing with our mother over..."

"She told me," Marcus said gently.

"Told you what?" Pelham asked.

Marcus softened his voice. "Your father said that she wasn't his daughter."

Pelham's shock slowly melted. "Of course, she told you. She trusts you." He bent his head and squeezed the bridge of his nose. "Did she tell you about my father's letter?"

"What letter?" he asked cautiously. By the look on the siblings faces, he wasn't going to like this story.

Pelham fisted his hand. "The bloody bastard," he murmured. He took a deep breath, then focused on Marcus. "Mind you, this is the first I've heard of this. That day in his study, the old duke had announced that he'd written a letter disavowing Honoria as his child. He told our mother that it would be delivered to her bridegroom the day before her wedding. He wanted to ruin her in front of her future husband and hoped it would ruin her in front of society as well." Pelham let out a tortured breath. "I didn't hear him say it, but on that miserable day, I'd never heard him so cold and angry before. Our mother tried to talk him out of banishing Honor, but he wouldn't listen. The following day, he sent Honor away from all of us."

"My God," Marcus whispered. "She never said a word about her father's...the old duke's letter."

"Nor to us either," Pippa said mournfully. "My poor darling sister. I don't care who her father is, she's my sister."

Pelham studied his clasped hands then raised his gaze to Marcus. "The old duke wouldn't allow anyone to say goodbye. I was so furious I didn't care what happened. I saw her off and gave her money."

"Tell him about the horse, Dane," Pippa said softly. "He deserves to know."

"Elsbeth." Pelham ran a hand down his face. "The duke was devastatingly cruel to Honor. Every time she received a gift she adored, the duke had it destroyed." Pelham bit his lip, but a tear escaped. "He sent her pony to be slaughtered."

"What?" Marcus asked incredulously. "What kind of a monster does that?"

"Our father." Pippa sat in her seat, softly sniffling. Tears rolled down her cheeks. Pelham reached into his waistcoat pocket and gave her his handkerchief.

"I'm sorry, darling." Pelham reached over and cupped his sister's cheek. "I'm so sorry. I'm sorry I couldn't stop him."

Pippa looked into his eyes and placed her hand over his. "It's not your fault. Truly, you did everything you could. Honor told me that repeatedly." She shifted her gaze to Marcus. "There's more."

Pelham leaned back in his chair and stared at the ceiling. "When I tried to comfort her and tell her that I loved her the day she left for York, Honor wouldn't let me." When he slowly lowered his gaze to Marcus, the pain was etched in the lines around his eyes. "She said she'd never say the words to anyone since the duke always took away everything she loved." He exhaled painfully. "Hence, her opposition to marriage...and to you. So, she thought to thwart the old duke by never marrying until she had his letter in hand."

Pippa smiled gently. "But when Dane caught you at the hunting lodge, Honoria had to marry without possessing the letter. She told us that was the reason why she fought so long against the idea."

The incredible story explained so much about the woman he loved. Why she had objected to the marriage. Why she couldn't tell him she loved him when her eyes told him something different. Even her soft expressions told another story.

"Oh, God," he murmured. His heart ached for all the pain she'd suffered over the years at her father's own hand. Slowly, anger began to unfurl in his belly at the previous duke who had cruelly tortured Noria from his grave for over eight years now. "I'd like to dig up your sire and kill him again."

"As would I," Pelham answered.

Silence enveloped the room as he tried to put his thoughts in order.

"I take it that there is no Giuseppe Antonio Forliti?" Marcus leaned back in his chair.

Pippa nodded solemnly.

"Why a legal newspaper?"

Pelham leaned forward and placed his elbows on the table as he clasped his hands. "Apparently, she's enlisted the help of my butler, Winston. She's been writing to solicitors across London trying to find that damnable letter. She even hired a private investigator. She wanted to flush it out with the announcement. She thought that only solicitors would read it." He shook his head. "She wanted to marry you, and this was the only way she could have you."

"It's all a ruse to find the letter." Pippa hunched her shoulders. "I don't want to betray my sister."

"Darling, tell Trafford. He cares for her." Pelham squeezed her hand.

"I love her," Marcus said softly. "I need to know everything."

Pippa nodded. "Honoria confided that she came up with the idea when it was decided you and she would go to London." Pippa bit her lip. "She'd have the letter so she could marry you and beat the duke at his own game."

"Of all the ludicrous ideas." Pelham's voice was weak as he shook his head, but then he smiled. "Bully for Honor. She was always a fighter."

"It's actually brilliant if you ask me." Relief had swept through Marcus at Pippa's confession. His darling Noria did things her own way. Even if he didn't like her methods, he loved her even more for it. She didn't let life define her. She had defined it herself. "She returned to Pelham Hall to wait for the letter?"

"Yes," Pippa answered.

Marcus nodded. It truly was a brilliant piece of strategy on Noria's part. For the first time since last night, hope began to unfurl in his heart.

"Carlyle sent the announcement to me. Does all of society know about it?" Marcus asked.

"Carlyle." Pippa's mouth twisted into a sneer.

It was the first time Marcus had ever seen her look cross.

Pelham rubbed a hand down his face. "I'd like to challenge that arse to a duel. Carlyle's solicitor found the announcement and gave it to him. Seems the solicitor knew Carlyle wanted Honor's hand and thought he could use it as leverage." Pelham tilted his head to the ceiling and fisted his hands.

"What?" Marcus asked. By his friend's expression, the story was about to become more unpleasant.

Pelham leveled his gaze to Marcus. "Carlyle threatened that if she didn't marry him, then he'd publish it himself so all of society would know. He's blackmailing her. That's why Honor's frantic."

"What a snake," Marcus hissed.

"My thoughts exactly," Pelham agreed. "I've sent word to my solicitors. Together, we'll be able to figure this out."

"Thank you," Marcus said. Pelham had the best legal minds in the country working for him. If anyone could find a way to keep Carlyle from saying a word, it was Pelham's solicitors. "It seems like a year ago when I met her at the Jolly Rooster."

"The real reason she attended Pelham's masquerade?" With a weak smile, Pippa met his gaze. "She wanted someone to want her."

Pelham cleared his throat and stared at the table. He was obviously trying to control his emotions.

Pippa played with the handle of her teacup. "You should find her and tell her you know everything."

"That's my plan." Marcus stood immediately. "I'm off to Amesbury."

"Trafford, perhaps you should stay here. I'll bring her to you." Pelham stood in tandem. "She's my little sister."

Marcus was halfway to the door, then turned to face his best friend. "She's my future wife. You can come with me if you'd like. If you think I'm going to let Noria go through this without me, then you don't know who I am."

Winston knocked on the door of Honoria's study. "My lady? Here's the morning's post. Two letters from London. One of them is from a solicitor's office."

Honoria looked up from her black lacquered Louis XV desk to see a silver salver in the butler's hands. She'd just arrived from London. Ironically, instead of exhausted, she was consumed with energy. Slowly but purposefully, she stood and took stock of the room. The pink and gold floral wall hangings were always a comforting sight. Hopefully, they'd continue to bring her joy after she received her mail.

Her hands didn't tremble. She'd been waiting for this letter since she was eight years old. Her betrothal announcement must have succeeded in drawing out the person in possession of the duke's final diatribe against her.

"Thank you, Winston." She walked around the desk and put on her gloves. She didn't want to touch the hateful thing with her bare hands. The sympathetic look on the family butler's face made her want to flinch, but she was stronger than that. There was no earthly reason to be afraid of what the duke had written.

Winston bowed as he extended the salver with the faded letter resting innocently on top of another.

"Do you know who brought it?" she asked, keeping her voice calm.

"The first letter was delivered by a runner from London," he said quietly. "I believe he said he'd been dispatched from Lathrop & Sons, Esquires."

Gingerly, she picked it up. "Do you think this is it?"

"I wouldn't hazard a guess, my lady.

"Before I allow myself to read it, will you answer a question? If you know I'm not the duke's child, then why have you been so nice to me?"

His brow furrowed in confusion. "Why wouldn't I, Lady Honoria?"

Heat licked her cheeks, but she refused to turn away. "I'm not really a part of the family," she said bluntly.

"May I be candid, ma'am?" Without waiting for her reply, he continued, "Of course, you are. More so than the previous duke and duchess. They were anomalies. Completely absorbed by their own selfishness. Neither took any interest in this great home, its legacy, or its people." Winston smiled gently. "But you and your siblings have. That makes you more of an Ardeerton than either of them. So, yes, in my opinion, you are family."

Her eyes burned with unshed tears. "Thank you, Winston."

"Thank you, ma'am, for everything you've done." He extended the silver salver again, and this time she took the second letter. By the wax seal, it appeared to be the crest of the Duke of Dartmore.

Winston bowed again. "Please ring if I can be of any assistance." With a proper flourish that her brother Pelham would be proud of, the wily butler left Honoria with her letters.

She placed the old duke's letter on her desk, then carefully opened the letter from the little duke without breaking the wax seal.

Dear Lady Honoria,

Thank you for the gifts you brought Julia and me. More importantly, thank you for visiting us. Will you come again? No need to bring more gifts. We'd like your company.

Dartmore

P.S. Bring Trafford and Pelham if you don't mind.
P.S.S. Julia would like to introduce Jane to you on your next visit.

She trailed a finger across the neat and precise script. Mrs. Mortimer was teaching the duke manners and good penmanship. She smiled, but it was bittersweet. They'd enjoyed her company. The lightheartedness she felt was tempered by a lonely melancholy. Would they even be allowed to see her when the truth of the announcement was revealed?

Would Marcus still want her to be involved in their lives? The answer was doubtful after the lies she'd sown with the announcement. She couldn't blame him for believing the worst of her.

She glanced at the window. The sun was bright overhead. She would not delay. It was time to visit the old Duke of Pelham's grave. Afterward, she had to figure out a way to protect Marcus and her siblings. Perhaps she should leave England. People would assume she married her pretend fiancé.

She picked up the letter and her basket by the door. She'd packed it this morning in preparation for when she received the letter. She'd had no idea it would come so quickly, nor did she know if she was ready for what lay ahead.

Without telling anyone her plans, she exited the mansion then climbed into her cart. She nodded at the liveried footman who held Florence's reins. With the last look at Pelham Hall, she straightened her back. With a cluck of her tongue, Honoria urged her loyal mare toward the village where all the previous Dukes of Pelham and their families were laid to rest.

The cemetery was next to the village church where she had always attended services. She'd only visited the old duke's final resting place once when she'd finally returned from finishing school. Her darling brother had accompanied her. He'd promised in a low, soothing whisper that the old duke couldn't hurt her anymore.

That had been the misstatement of the century.

As the Pelham family private cemetery came into view, she pulled the cart to a stop. For all her adult life, she'd waited for this moment when she'd finally free herself of the duke's disdain and his wrath. She would finally exorcise the duke's loathing that she'd always worn like a cloak.

When Marcus had told her he loved her, they were the most beautiful words she'd ever heard. She could feel his love push aside all the cold darkness she'd been subjected to over the years. She could see everything he felt from the warmth in his eyes. But she had no right to subject him to her ruin.

A strange numbness enveloped her as she climbed down, leaving Florence to munch on the green grass. Yet, an even stranger sense of bizarreness enveloped her, its energy pushing her toward the cobblestone path to the massive black marble tombstone. It was ironic that a grieving angel rested its head on the top of the stone. It was the only being that mourned the old duke.

Her mouth grew dry, and her heartbeat accelerated. She felt herself shriveling in front of his grave. It was eerily reminiscent of the times when she was a girl and had done the same. He should be gone forever, yet she held in her hand his last attack against her, his infamous letter.

Slowly, she glanced around her. There wasn't a single soul in sight. With a deep breath for courage, she examined the front of the letter. *To the Groom of Lady Honoria Ardeerton, Mr. Giuseppe Antonio Forliti.* Quickly, she broke the seal and unfolded the parchment.

Her eyes burned, but she quickly scanned the words. His familiar script made her blood run cold.

To the poor, misguided, foolish swain who thinks to marry the cuckoo that landed in my nest.

Your bride is not my daughter. She's the spawn of some arse whom my unfaithful wife decided to fuck.

Her stomach roiled. She forced herself to inhale to keep from casting up her accounts. She could hear his wrath and disgust in every word she read. For a moment, she thought to throw the letter away, but she would never rid herself of his vitriol unless she finished it.

Consequently, there is no dowry or settlement. If I'm dead and gone, it makes no difference. My will specifically states that Dane Ardeerton, the fifth Duke of Pelham, cannot give any of my money to this woman or her family.

How it pains me to even write this, but Honoria Ardeerton has no talents or achievements to speak of for a lady. A trained dog is better accomplished than she. She lacks the talent to draw forth true affection from others. Most merely tolerate her.

If you think you should marry her as a sign of honor, let me disabuse you of that thought. Even if her name is Honoria, there is no honor in her. Take heed. I am saving you from a life of mediocrity and lies. It's a heavy load to bear. Trust me. I suffered it for years when the girl was in my presence. She is the epitome of weakness and scandal.

My best advice? Do not hesitate to renege on the marriage. No one would blame you.

If you decide to marry her, I've instructed my solicitor to publish this letter in The Times. *You shall have to face the aftermath by yourself.*

Are you confident she's worth it?

I've always said that a whore begets a whore.

Pelham

She couldn't breathe. She couldn't move. His taunts and insults still had the ability to bring her to her knees. She foolishly believed he couldn't hurt her anymore, yet the wily duke had reached from beyond the grave to destroy her.

For the love of heaven, the bastard didn't even care if he ruined his own son and daughter if Honoria had found someone to marry. That's what would occur when that letter was published. The duke simply wanted to destroy her. Only a monster would obliterate everything in his path, including his own family, for revenge. A painful sob rose in her throat, and tears filled her eyes. The *bloody man* had still planned to wreak more havoc if she wasn't jilted. It wasn't enough to ruin her life. He wanted to ruin her brother and her sister.

"Noria," Marcus's voice called out.

She turned slowly, dreading the confrontation that loomed before her. She didn't want to tell him about the letter. But how could she explain her actions otherwise without hurting Marcus more than she already had? For the world, she'd only wanted him to be happy and have the life he wanted and deserved.

And it wasn't with her. She'd ruin him just by association.

Like a specter from another world, Marcus was dressed in all black. His long legs ate the distance between them. When he drew close, she barely recognized him. Black stubble covered his face, and his hair was out of sorts. But it was eyes and the flare of his nostrils that made her suck in a breath.

Her knees buckled as a sense of dizziness overtook her.

He was furious.

Thirty-Two

W hen Honoria stumbled, Marcus started to run without second-guessing himself. She took an awkward step as if a weight had been thrown on her shoulders, but she caught herself from falling. He stopped two feet before her. The lack of color on her face and the flutter of her hands betrayed how distraught she was. All his anger toward her for leaving him disappeared in an instant. Slowly, he reached out to take the parchment from her fingers.

"No." She whipped around and faced the old duke's grave. "You can't see it."

"I don't want to see it. There is nothing in that letter that means anything to me. The only reason I'm here is you." He closed the distance between them and pulled her close so that her back rested against his chest. For the first time since he had left London, he could breathe. "You shouldn't have left without talking to me."

When she exhaled, her shoulders slumped. All the fire and fight within her had vanished.

"I heard you're marrying someone else. Carlyle sent the announcement to me." Marcus kept his tone even much like a simple conversation between friends. He took one of her hands and linked their fingers together. It was a good sign when she squeezed his hand with hers.

Marcus pressed his lips against the crown of her head. Stray wisps of her light hair tickled her nose. Her jasmine scent teased him, and he inhaled deeply. The relief in holding her in his arms erased his weariness. "I'll fight for you."

She shook her head. "You're wasting your efforts."

His heartbeat stumbled at the pain in her voice. He'd never heard her so troubled. "No, I'm not."

Her voice trembled. "I'm not worth it."

"I beg to differ. You're worth everything."

She hung her head. The trembling in her shoulders revealed she was silently crying. After a moment, she lifted her head and stared straight at the grave. "The day before my wedding, my bridegroom was supposed to receive a letter from the previous duke, stating I wasn't his and that he didn't claim me. He called my mother a whore and me one as well. I posted that announcement to have it sent to me." She held up the parchment as proof. "I didn't think anyone would see it." She shook her head. "I was so stupid."

"No, you weren't. You were trying to find a way to be with me." He pulled her tighter against him and rested his arms around her waist. He didn't say a word. It was for her to tell him whatever she wanted him to know.

Finally, she spoke. "He said I was mediocre, and a trained dog was more accomplished than I."

"I'm sorry." He pressed another kiss to the top of her head. "I'm sorry about Elsbeth."

"I loved her, you see." She sniffed. "So, he took her away and destroyed her. He took away everything I loved, including my siblings."

Tears burned his eyes at her sorrow. What kind of a man would harm a sweet child who had no blame for his wife's transgressions?

"He wrote that if my fiancé doesn't renounce me, he'll have his solicitor post the letter in *The Times* so everyone knows the truth about me." An anguished sob escaped. "I knew he hated me, but he didn't care that his actions would hurt Pelham or Pippa. All he cared about was destroying me. Society would be in an uproar for months over the scandal." She covered her face with her hands and wept.

Her body shuddered with agonized sobs. He'd never in his life seen sorrow like she was experiencing.

"Oh, darling, look at me," he pleaded.

Slowly, she turned around and faced him. "What hurts the most? He didn't care if he hurt the man I love. This letter is proof."

"Tell me who the lucky man is that you love?" He closed his eyes and willed her to say *I love you.*

"Don't ask me." Though her voice was soft, she was adamant. "That's why I can't say it. He destroys everything I care about and everyone I love."

His heart broke at the misery in her voice. "Oh, darling," he murmured, then pressed a kiss to the tender skin beneath her ear. He pulled her closer and wrapped her in his embrace. "I promise he won't destroy me or you or us. I said I came here to fight for you. But I came to fight for us, too. And the first person I'll confront is you."

"Me?" A hint of incredulity tinted her voice, and he smiled against her hair. Her grief had dissipated for a moment, and she was thinking about him.

"Yes, you." He cupped her cheeks, then carefully wiped away the tears as he caressed her soft skin with his thumbs. "Why didn't you tell me your plans?"

Another tear streamed across his thumb when she closed her eyes and shook her head. "I didn't want you to be ruined by associating with me. I didn't think you'd want me after the letter was delivered."

"Ye of little faith." He chuckled. Tilting her chin, he stared into her eyes. "I'll always want you."

"I knew his letter would be delivered. It was a noose around my future." She grabbed ahold of his lapels. "I couldn't allow him to destroy you or your work, or even your chance for a life with Lady Susan."

"Not Lady Susan again," he murmured.

She only blinked twice, but abject misery was written across her face. "Carlyle discovered the published announcement. He told me that if I didn't marry him, that he'd publish my announcement so all of London would read it. He also threatened to send you and Antonio a copy of the announcement as well. He said you wouldn't marry me because of it." She sniffed. "I went to the theatre so there would be no hard feelings with Lady Carlyle. The earl said he'd give me a week to make my decision." She shook her head. "I can't marry him. But if Carlyle publishes that announcement, then no one of good standing will have anything to do with me. I'm afraid for you and my siblings."

"Oh darling, we'll stop him. Your brother is already working on it. I'll go see Carlyle. He won't hurt you. He doesn't matter. Only *we* matter." He bent down until he was staring into her bloodshot eyes. "Understand? You're the one I lov—"

She placed her fingertips against his lips. "Don't say it. The old duke will..."

"He'll what, Noria?" He pressed a light kiss to her fingers, then drew her hand down. He kissed her mouth. "I'm kissing you in front of him. He can't hurt you anymore."

She shook her head. "I thought...perhaps if I went away for a year, I could return and be free of the scandal."

"Hmm," he hummed non-committedly. "And now?"

She shrugged slightly, but her eyes filled with tears again.

"Oh, my love," he said tenderly. "Prove the old duke wrong by marrying the man who loves you to the end of the earth. Marry the one who believes you're everything. Marry the man who believes you're the definition of perfection. Marry me," he said gruffly, holding her tighter to him. "I'm begging you. I can only find the best within myself when I'm with you. Be my partner, my lover, and...my wife. I want to give you everything. Don't let him steal your happiness. Don't let him steal mine either."

She let out a shuddered sigh. "Marcus..."

"Do it," he growled.

"I can't," she said softly.

"I know you can. You're an Ardeerton." He pressed another kiss to her lips. "I'll be right by your side now and every single day we have on this earth together."

"I'm afraid." She handed him the letter.

Marcus sneered at the faded piece of parchment but didn't take it. "No. His erroneous opinion won't color the truth of who you are. *I know who you are.* Destroy it."

With a guttural cry, she ripped the letter in half. Then she did it again and again until all that remained were small squares of paper. She stared at him and then stared at the shredded letter. "I can't believe I destroyed it."

"Burn it," he encouraged her with a smile.

Noria wiped her tears away with her arm and smiled weakly. Then with an arrogant air that would have made her brother proud, she placed them in a pile that resembled a funeral pyre, on the old duke's grave. Retrieving a tinderbox from her basket, she started a fire with the remnants.

As the flames charred the bits of paper into ashes, Marcus took her hand in his. "You're free of him now."

With a shaky smile, she nodded. "Thank you for being here. I...I will be free once I think of a way to stop the duke's letter from being published."

"We shall figure it out together. But you've cast the old duke aside, and I'm proud of you. You're the one who did it." Without giving her a chance to pull away, he took her arms and pulled her in tight. His mouth crashed onto hers in a kiss that would leave no doubt how much he loved her. When she opened her lips on a gasp, he deepened the kiss. She wrapped her arms around his neck. Her whimper made every protective instinct he possessed rise to the surface. Never again would he allow her to be hurt or doubt that she deserved love. Every day she would know how deeply he cared for her. He broke the kiss, and her head fell to his chest.

Gently, he pulled away and gazed into her familiar turquoise eyes. "What shall we do with Antonio."

"There's no Antonio," she said softly. She placed her hand over his pounding heart.

He placed his hand over hers. "I know. Pippa told me."

"You must think it silly," she said sheepishly.

"Actually, I think it's brilliant." He kissed her nose. "I'll deal with Antonio next, but first, tell me you love me." But before she could say another word, he continued, "You're an Ardeerton. You have the strength and fire to do it."

"I was an Ardeerton." A slow smile, brighter than a sunset flirting with the ocean's horizon, lit her face. "I want to be a Kirkland because...I love you. I love you," Noria repeated, her voice gaining strength. She turned to the old duke's grave. Staring at the black marble monument, she raised her voice and tilted up her chin. "I love him, and nothing will change that."

"This is music to my ears." He took her in his arms and pulled her tight. "I love you, and nothing and no one will change that." He kissed her with the gentle reverence she deserved. "Whatever happens, we'll get through it. Together."

"What about your charity?" she asked. "I don't want you or it to suffer."

"I have Pelham, Ravenscroft, and many more peers who are good friends. They'll stand by me. More importantly, I have you."

She stood on tiptoe and kissed him. As they explored this newness between them, Marcus had no doubt their lives would ever again be haunted by the dead duke. Noria had turned once again turned into a force who would not be defeated. It was the most seductive sight he'd ever seen.

"Oh, God," Noria groaned. "You made me forget about Carlyle. This will never work."

"It *will* work." He cupped her cheeks. "On my way, I thought about Carlyle. He's going to be my third confrontation. If the *Legal Chronicle* withdraws the announcement, then his threat loses its teeth. There will be no scandal. You and I will go see the editor with my solicitors."

She nodded as she contemplated his answer. "If I was your first confrontation, and Carlyle is your third. Who is your second confrontation?"

"Oh, darling," he said with a chuckle. "Antonio is my second confrontation. As soon as I read the announcement, I rushed back to Pelham Hall and found him in the formal gardens admiring the wisteria. I told him that I fell in love with you the first time I saw you, and I would fight for you. Even if fighting for you meant a duel between us." Marcus's eyes widened playfully. "Though he was aghast, Giuseppe Antonio Forliti understood and acted as a true gentleman. He said his heart would never recover, but he would never stand in the way of true love. He told me I was a lucky man, then he kissed your hand and bid us adieu. Afterward, you fell into my arms, declaring your eternal love." He waggled his eyebrows. "Isn't it romantic?"

Noria rolled her eyes. "That's not what happened. "You fell to your knees and begged me to marry you after you chased away my fiancé." She grinned. "I agreed."

"Or perhaps, I pulled a special license from the hidden pocket of my waistcoat..." Marcus reached into his pocket. "And did just that."

Noria's eyes widened.

He took her hand in his, then fell to his knees. "Marry me. Make me the happiest man on this earth."

Her mouth formed a perfect *O* as the sun wrapped its rays around her. "Yes," she said softly. "I would be honored." A brilliant smile tilted her lips upward. "Who knew walking into the Jolly Rooster would deliver me the man of my dreams?"

Marcus stood and took her in his arms as he laughed. "Would it be crass if I said that I did?"

"It would be perfect." On tiptoe, Noria leaned close and pressed her lips to his. "When do you think we should marry?"

"Immediately," a voice sounded behind them.

They both turned to see Pelham with a huge smile on his face. "No more scandal. I bought the *Law Chronicle*. They're retracting the announcement. Seems one of the staff writers was a bit inebriated when he wrote the story. Got the facts all wrong." Pelham chortled, clearing pleased with himself. "The solicitors who sent that letter don't work for my dead father. They work for me now."

Marcus laughed. "That's brilliant."

Honoria hugged Pelham. "You're the best brother in the world."

Pelham took her hand and gave it to Marcus. "The vicar is inside the church, waiting for both of you."

A carriage pulled up to the churchyard. A groomsman jumped down from the box and opened the door. Pippa, Grace, and Ravenscroft emerged.

"Are we too late?" Pippa asked as she rushed forward.

"Just in time," Noria said. "Will you stand with me?"

Pippa nodded. "I was hoping you'd ask." She sighed happily. "I love weddings."

Marcus turned to Pelham. "Would you stand with..."

Before Marcus could finish his question, Pelham nodded. "I wouldn't miss this for the world."

Noria turned to Ravenscroft and Grace. "Will you both be our witnesses?"

"Honored." Ravenscroft bowed.

Grace nodded with tears in her eyes wearing a huge smile.

Marcus grabbed Noria's hand and pulled her to him. "Let's go. Within ten minutes, you'll be a Kirkland."

"She'll always be an Ardeerton," Pelham proclaimed.

As they all laughed and headed inside the church, Noria stopped and pulled Marcus into a private vestibule hidden from the others. She pressed a kiss to Marcus's lips, then gazed into his eyes. "I can't wait to call you 'the love of my life, my husband' for the rest of my days. Thank you for not giving up on me."

"Thank you for not giving up on us, my lady wife, my love." He brushed his nose against hers and smiled.

"Let's not tarry then." Noria wrapped her arm around his. "Who knew a simple seduction would lead to a simple marriage?"

Epilogue

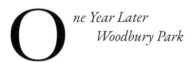

"You can open your eyes."

Just hearing that deep gravelly voice of her husband made waking up in the morning a joy. But Honoria had already been up once this morning to check on Dartmore and Julia. They were staying with Marcus and her for the summer at Woodbury Park. Mrs. Mortimer and their nursemaid, Mrs. Cassidy were here also.

Dartmore said Julia slept better at night now that Miss Cassidy was with them. Honoria had a suspicion it helped the young duke sleep better as well.

Slowly, she opened her eyes and discovered she was surrounded by presents.

"Happiest of birthdays, my darling." An irresistible smile pulled at his lips, but it was the wicked gleam in his eyes that prompted her heart to pound a bit harder. He'd woken her up at midnight with the most exquisite kisses saying happy birthday. Then, tenderly, he'd made love to her. Honoria had never felt so cherished in her life.

Every day, she fell in love with her husband all over again.

She'd also fallen in love with him again when he had confronted the Earl of Carlyle about publishing the announcement. Marcus had boldly and brilliantly threatened to take legal action against Carlyle for defamation if he published that announcement. Pelham had accompanied Marcus. He told Carlyle that he had revoked his membership in the Mayfair Millionaires Club and the Jolly Rooster for his bad behavior. Apparently, the earl fell to his knees begging forgiveness. Both Pelham and Marcus had walked out with another word.

"Good morning." Honoria sat up and rested her back against the brocade upholstery headboard of their bed.

"Well, I wanted us to celebrate privately before your family arrives." Marcus picked up a small black lacquered box, then presented it to her in the palm of his hand.

"What is it?"

"Patience, wife. If I told you, it wouldn't be a surprise." A roguish grin tugged at his lips. He leaned in and gave her a kiss that made her toes curl. She wrapped her arms around his neck and tried to pull him to her.

But he would have none of it. "Darling, I will gladly make love to you as many times as you like, but there's important business that must be attended to first. Now, don't be difficult and open it."

"Such a tease," she groused but smiled.

He was more excited than she was by the sparkle in his eyes.

"All right." She flipped the latch and opened the small box. Her breath caught at the sight. Inside was a lover's eye pin. The miniature of Marcus's left eye was surrounded by small sapphires alternating with turquoise stones. "It's beautiful," she said reverently touching the exquisite piece of jewelry.

"When you first talked about it, I took note." Marcus took her left hand and squeezed. Gently, his thumb caressed her skin. "The stones remind me of our eye colors."

"I adore it." She leaned closer and pressed a kiss against his mouth.

He smiled, then picked up another present wrapped in paper.

"You're spoiling me." She laughed but proceeded to untie the ribbon that held the paper together. When she pulled off the paper, her heartbeat tripped in her chest. It was an art box just like the one Aunt Harriett had given her. "Oh Marcus." Tears gathered in her eyes. "How did you know?"

"Pippa described it to me, and I...I had it made just for you." He lightly tapped the wooden top. "It has everything." Happiness danced in his eyes. "Plus, I have an artist coming next week to give you painting lessons." He took her hand and raised it to his lips. "If that's all right with you?"

She pulled him closer and kissed him again. "I love it."

"Not as much as me, though?" He winked at her.

"Never as much as you." She grew serious and stared into his eyes. "I love you. I never knew I could love a person as much as I love you."

Marcus cupped her face and trailed his thumb across her cheek. "It's your birthday, but I'm the one receiving a gift," he said softly. "All my life, this is what I've wanted. "You." He rested his forehead against hers. "I have one last present for you that I want to give you privately. But I need you to dress."

He whipped off the covers, then helped her stand. A riding habit and all the accompaniments were laid out. In record time, she performed her morning ablutions, then put on her stockings, a chemise, stays, and her riding habit.

"Are you taking me to the hunting lodge?" She pulled on her half-boot.

"No." Marcus playfully batted her hand away. "I'll be your lady's maid today." He made quick work of tying her boots.

Once Honoria was completely dressed, he took her downstairs. He pulled a clean necktie from his waistcoat pocket. "No peeking."

"Seriously? She demanded playfully.

"Surprises are always the best way to receive a present." He stole a kiss.

Honoria laughed and let him cover her eyes with the neck clothe. She inhaled the scent of clean linen, starch, and the unmistakable scent of her husband. No one had ever made such a fuss and bother over her before. It was addictive, and she couldn't wait to return the favor when it was his birthday.

He wrapped her arm around his and led her outside. His body seemed to vibrate with excitement. She couldn't exactly tell, but it appeared he was taking her to the folly across the formal garden.

She inhaled deeply. The sweet scent of honeysuckle wafted through the air. The songbirds were in full chorus this morning as if helping her celebrate her special day.

After a while, they stopped. Marcus wrapped his arm around her waist. "Are you ready?"

Honoria leaned her head against his chest. "You've already spoiled me with presents."

Suddenly, his lips pressed against hers. "I want to give you everything."

The depth of emotion in his voice brought tears to her eyes. Only this man could make her feel like a queen.

"I love you," she said.

"And I you," Marcus answered as he escorted her into a building. The sweet scent of fresh hay filled the air. He stopped and she did as well. "Ready?"

She nodded.

Gently, he untied her blindfold. When she opened her eyes, he stood before her, his eyes red with emotion, but a smile lit his face. "I'd like you to meet someone special." With his hands on her shoulders, he gently urged her to turn around.

Her breath caught at the sight of the piebald pony. "Oh, my goodness," she said softly. "Who is this?"

"Well, darling," Marcus said pulling her close to his side. "He doesn't have a name. I thought you'd like to name him."

"When I first saw him, I thought it was Elsbeth." Her voice quaked with emotion as Marcus pulled her closer to the stall that held the black and white pony. The top of the stall was low enough that she could easily pet the pony's forelock. The pony snorted slightly, then nodded as if he enjoyed her touch.

Marcus patted the pony's shoulder, then took her hand and squeezed. "It's Elsbeth's colt."

For a moment, she couldn't quite fathom what he was saying. "I don't understand." She shook her head in denial and a tear fell down her face. "She's gone."

"She is gone...now." He pulled her close and wiped her tear away. "But she had a happy life with a farmer a couple of counties away."

"How can that be?" She turned her gaze to the pony, who seemed as intrigued with her as she was with him.

"Ritson and Winston," Marcus answered. He laughed softly. "Those wily butlers of your brother's managed to steal her out from underneath the old duke's nose and sent her to live with Winston's second cousin near Hearthshire."

Honoria gasped in relief and in wonder. It was incredible that her beloved pet hadn't been hurt by the old duke. But how appropriate. Just like Honoria, Elsbeth had escaped his destruction. She reached out and petted the pony again. Just like his mother, he nestled his nose against her palm.

Honoria laid her head against her husband's shoulder. "Why didn't they tell me?"

Marcus pressed a kiss against the top of her head. "I asked the same question. When I'd decided to find out exactly what had happened to Elsbeth, I went to Winston. After cajoling him for a good fifteen minutes, he finally confessed. He apologized profusely and said there were more family secrets that shouldn't be unearthed, but he thought it was time for you to know that you weren't without advocates within Ardeerton House."

Tears fell in rivulets down her face. "I don't know what to say. I can't believe that for all these years I thought she'd died because of me and my actions."

Marcus took her into his embrace and pulled her close. "Winston and Ritson apparently felt so guilty, they offered their resignations to your brother. He waved them off and told them to get back to work immediately."

"That sounds like Pelham." She laughed through her tears. "This is the best gift I've ever received. I'm so grateful."

"Where is this miraculous pony that has caused major havoc in my household?" Pelham called out.

Marcus growled softly against her lips. "Your brother still has the worst timing. Perhaps we should move so he can't drop in whenever he wants."

Honoria smiled as she knew that her darling husband relished his friendship with her brother. She pressed a kiss against her husband's cheek and turned to her brother with a smile.

"Come and take a look at this handsome fellow," she called out.

"She's talking about me." Marcus laughed.

Pelham waved a hand in the air as if dismissing his best friend. When he reached his stall, he peered over the railing. "What's his name?"

Honoria looked at her husband and winked. "Antonio."

"He looks like Antonio," Marcus whispered.

By then, Pippa and Ravenscroft had entered the stable. After greeting Honoria and Marcus, they went to meet the pony.

Honoria took the opportunity and pulled her husband into an empty stall. She pulled the lapels of his coat and tilted her gaze to his. "This is the best birthday ever. I'm so grateful to you. I never knew that I could love this much, and it's all because of you. "

Marcus cupped her cheeks. "Darling, we're both grateful. Without you and your love, my life would have been bleak. You're the love of my life and always will be. Anything I can do to bring a smile to your face, is my pleasure. Speaking of pleasure..." Marcus pressed his lips against hers. The swirl of passion that always surrounded them began to take flight.

If you're not ready to say goodbye to Honoria and Marcus, turn the page and scan the code for a bonus scene!

A Simple Seduction Bonus Scene

Get ready for **A Simple Marriage**, *the next book in the* **Millionaires of Mayfair** *series.*
Turn the page for a sneak peek.

Have you read **The Duchess of Drury Lane**? *It's free for KU subscribers. It's also the unofficial start of the* **Millionaires of Mayfair** *series.*

A Simple Marriage

Chapter One

London, 1819

Only the thought of dresses could compel Lady Phillipa 'Pippa' Ardeerton to consider marriage. More specifically, a dress shop was the reason Pippa stood in Hyde Park, pretending to admire the lush trees before her as she waited for the first gentleman she had invited to meet her so they could discuss marriage.

The dress shop in question belonged to Mademoiselle Mignon, who was soon to marry. Like a fairy godmother, she had offered to sell her dress shop to Pippa. It was an opportunity of a lifetime. Mademoiselle Mignon's dresses were legendary. Women from all over the British Isles traveled to London to visit the talented modiste. To don one of her gowns for a *ton* event ensured that the wearer would be the center of attention. It was an understatement to say that her dresses were works of art.

But so were Pippa's creations. To own this shop was her destiny.

To buy it, she needed her trust fund. To receive it, she had to reach the age of thirty and still be unmarried. Since she was twenty-four, that option was out of the question. But the trust provided that if she married, the funds became hers on the day she said her vows. And she'd only consider marriage to a gentleman *if* he'd agreed to leave her trust fund alone after they exchanged "I

Her lady's maid, Alice Robertson, stepped closer and looked over her shoulder. The movement reminded Pippa of a spy, one in the midst of some clandestine affair waiting for the enemy.

Well, this was a clandestine affair, but Pippa didn't want to marry her enemy. All she wanted was one man, and she wasn't picky. Practically, any man would meet her requirements if he agreed she would control her trust fund.

And he must not mind that his wife was involved in a trade.

"My lady, your first appointment should have been here by now," Alice murmured.

"There's no need to whisper. No one can hear us." Pippa bit her lip to keep from laughing. Alice was a little sensitive at times if teased about being too dramatic. She patted her maid's arm in comfort. "He's only five minutes late."

Alice pointed to her elbow. "You know how my elbow can predict things. Right now, it's stiffening up on me. That's a warning, my lady. It's telling me that your idea to fetch a husband by writing him a letter isn't going to work." Alice shook her head in disapproval.

Pippa normally adored her lady's lady maid's antics. It helped keep the loneliness at bay, an affliction that had only become worse when her older sister, Lady Honoria Ardeerton, had married Marcus Kirkland, the Earl of Trafford, and had moved to his estate in Amesbury.

However, today was not the day for Alice's elbow to start acting out. Uncannily, it regularly predicted when it would rain or if there was a change in the weather. But Pippa very much doubted that it could predict when things were set to go awry.

"Sweet Alice, it's a perfectly conceived plan." Taller than an average woman, Pippa smiled down at her maid.

The maid shook her head and looked about the park again. "Don't

JANNA MACGREGOR

you think your brother will think it's a little suspicious that you're going to Hyde Park for the next five mornings for exercise? His Grace is a wily thinker." Alice tapped her finger against her temple. "His mind is always working. He'll smell it. Mark my words."

"Well, it's a good thing he has the sniffles, then," Pippa retorted. Her brother, Dane Ardeerton, the Duke of Pelham, was a *problem*. Uncommonly astute, he was the one who had sole discretion over her trust funds. She'd already asked him to release her funds early, but he declined.

While her brother was the biggest supporter of her art, he didn't particularly care for her going into trade. He'd always declared, "A duke's sister was a rare creature. To lower oneself into mixing with the masses and handling money was unseemly. It would be unheard of for the Duke of Pelham's youngest sister."

However, Pippa considered his thinking to be a tad myopic. His focus was running his millionaire's club and his gambling hell disguised as a coaching inn, the Jolly Rooster. Pelham created the millionaire's club one day at Eton to develop a group where men and women with self-made wealth had a place to discuss business.

In Pippa's opinion, there wasn't much difference between a modiste shop and a gambling hell coaching inn. All were created to deliver a fantasy of sorts. The gambling hell promised a man might win a fortune if Lady Luck sat beside him for the night. A dress offered something just as thrilling. The perfect dress could turn even the most ordinary event into something spectacular. It could also turn that same event into something magical just by how it could make a woman feel.

Pippa's plan was flawless and rather ingenious if she did say so herself. She'd picked five men from her brother's millionaires club to meet and discuss her marriage proposal. Once she picked a man, her brother wouldn't object. He'd personally approved each of the members. It made little difference if they were titled or not. The only requirement? They had to have assets worth over a million pounds. They also had to be trustworthy and honorable. Pelham didn't allow riffraff into his club even if they did possess a fortune. If the men were part of the club, then Pelham would approve them as eligible men to marry. She was certain of it.

"My lady, look over there." Alice threw a furtive nod in the direction of the paved walkway. "He's coming."

Pippa lifted her gaze. The man walking toward them wore a striking blue morning coat that fit him like a glove and emphasized his broad shoulders. She had little doubt that underneath his apparel, his body was fit and trim. Her eyes swept over his buff-colored breeches, another immaculate fit as they framed his muscular legs. Even from this distance, his clothes were expensive and of the highest quality. She could always recognize such clothing. It was her special power.

Yet, Pippa couldn't tell if it was Lord Bedford or not. She'd invited him to be her first bachelor to interview. She'd always found the viscount to be delightful. But she'd never remembered him being that muscular or tall. However, when they'd danced together at an event, he'd always found a way to amuse her. Humor was important in a marriage, more so than love.

As the man came closer, her confidence wilted like a cheese soufflé. The viscount possessed hair a tad darker than Pippa's blonde mane. The man strolling toward her had locks the color of obsidian. Too long, it fell across his brow and brushed his shoulders. It was so dark that it blended into the black of his hat. She still didn't recognize him as the brim shaded his face.

Alice clapped her hands together in glee. "Look, Lady Pippa, it's Lord Ravenscroft."

Pippa gasped in horror as her maid laughed in pure, unadulterated joy.

Of all the men to meet in the park, it was just her luck that strolling toward them was Hugh Calthorpe, the Marquess of Ravenscroft.

He was her brother's best friend. He was also confident, intelligent, and funny. When he shared something with you, he'd lean close and lower his voice. His green-eyed gaze always held yours. He made you feel as if he were sharing something extraordinary only with you. That made him dangerous. Pippa didn't need intimacy with a man.

She needed friendship, and that was all.

Pippa patted her hair to ensure everything was in place, then smoothed her dress. She would not let the appearance of the marquess deter her. She had every right to be in this park. Women of her stature went for walks every day.

She stood tall and tilted her chin slightly when Ravenscroft stopped before them.

"Good morning, my lady." His gravelly voice reminded her of a cat's tongue against the skin, an unexpected sign of affection.

Or a taste before a bite.

"Good morning, my lord," she answered as he bowed.

A man in possession of consummate manners, Ravenscroft turned to Alice. "Good morning, Miss Robertson."

"Oh, my lord, good morning," Alice cooed. "Imagine meeting you here."

That was the problem with her fifty-year-old maid. She adored Lord Ravenscroft. And she always tried to find a way to see him when he visited Pelham which was practically an everyday occurrence. For heaven's sake, the man had even bought an estate close to the Jolly Rooster just to be near her brother and their other best friend, the Earl of Trafford, her sister's husband.

"Yes, imagine meeting me here." Ravenscroft slowly turned his gaze to Pippa's, then smiled. The mirth in his eyes made them twinkle. It reminded her of pure mischief, the aggravating kind. The earl was a master at provoking her brother. Simply throwing out a barb disguised as an observation was his modus operandi.

Whatever he said, she'd not take the bait. She smiled in return. "Are you just arriving?"

"Indeed," he answered, never taking his gaze from hers.

"That's such a shame. We're leaving." She nodded again in a show of manners. "Enjoy your walk, my lord."

"My lady, how unfortunate that you're leaving. I wanted to join you." A wicked smile that emphasized his full lips tugged at one corner of his mouth. Fine lines fanned the skin surrounding his striking green eyes.

No doubt they were a direct result of his constant exultant temperament. Indeed, she'd never seen him angry or bored. Everything seemed to amuse him, which suited him. It enhanced his extraordinary handsomeness, if that were possible. In all her life, she'd only seen a few beautiful men. The Marquess of Ravenscroft was one of those rare individuals. His features were masculine and attractive. Sharp angles framed his cheekbones and square jaw. The only thing that wasn't sharp about his features were his full lips.

Making her wonder if they were as soft as they appeared. She shook her head slightly to clear such thoughts. She had no business considering the man's mouth. He was her brother's best friend.

"How do you know I'm here for a walk?" His voice broke her out of her reverie. "Perhaps I'm here for an assignation of some sort...or another."

The scoundrel winked at her.

"Seems to be the popular thing today," Alice added unhelpfully.

Pippa drew a deep breath and released it. She'd learned early in life that it was best to put your adversaries on the defensive. "We don't want to keep you from your appointment." She waved a gloved hand in the air. "Or tryst or rendezvous," she said under her breath.

"It's my lucky day. It just happens that my assignation is with *you*." He held up his arm. "Walk with me."

"I can't..." She turned toward the entrance of the park. Bedford was nowhere in sight. Where was the blasted man? It wasn't a good omen. Perhaps he wasn't interested in her proposal.

The subtle fragrance of sandalwood mixed with a heavenly masculine scent wafted her way. Ravenscroft always smelled divine. That's why he was one of her favorite dance partners at an event.

He leaned near, almost close enough to kiss her. Then, his whisky-dark voice teased her ear. "He's not coming."

* * *

It was a wonder that Lady Pippa didn't injure herself when she whipped her head to face him.

Hugh didn't mince words this time. "You should walk with me. I think you'll find it highly enlightening."

Her eyes narrowed in wariness, then blazed into anger. She wasn't pleased. Usually, he never involved himself in others' business, but this wasn't any one ordinary. It was Lady Pippa Ardeerton, his best friend's little sister.

Honestly, she was also one of the most interesting people he'd ever met. Uncommonly beautiful with a rare wit, she could make anyone feel at ease, even Bedford, who was a nervous nelly.

Simply put, Lady Pippa was perfect. She'd make a perfect wife and partner.

If someone were looking for such a thing.

Slowly, she took his arm. As they strolled down the path, he chuckled to himself. They must appear as if they were two friends who, by happenstance, met at the park for an early bout of exercise. How wrong that observation would be. He'd purposely arrived at the exact time she was supposed to meet with Bedford.

When Hugh stole a glance at Lady Pippa, her eyes met his. They were royal blue, the same as her older brother's. But he'd noticed that hers had flecks of gold sprinkled throughout the irises. When he'd first met her, he'd been taken aback at her beauty. Even today, she could steal his breath. In a silken green morning gown with a jaunty little hat with peacock feathers, she was confident, assured, and carried herself with a grace others only wished to possess.

As much as he enjoyed counting her attributes, now was not the time. They had business to discuss.

With a quick glimpse, Hugh ensured Lady Pippa's maid was behind them. She was still within proper chaperoning distance but couldn't hear their conversation. With his free hand, he pulled Bedford's letter from the inside pocket of his waistcoat. "The reason your beau isn't coming is because your letter was delivered to me."

She stumbled for a second, and he tightened his arm around hers to keep her steady. They'd stopped their casual stroll, and Pippa's defiant chin was lifted as she stared straight into his eyes. How uniquely refreshing for him. He didn't have to strain his neck when conversing. Typically, women peered up at him, but Pippa was only a half-foot shorter than him. The censorious look in her eyes was also refreshing. Most women, particularly ones looking for a husband, simpered and whispered around him as if he thought such behavior was enticing.

They were all utterly dull. But he would never consider Lady Pippa as such, particularly when sparks of outrage flashed in her brilliant blue eyes.

"For your information, he isn't my beau." She snatched the letter from his hand and examined it. Her eyes widened in horror. "The seal is broken. You opened it?"

He winced at the incredulity in her voice.

"Not on purpose." He closed the distance between them until a mere six inches were between them.

Alice loudly cleared her throat in warning that he was too intimately close. He nodded his acknowledgment and stepped away until a respectable foot separated them.

"When my mail arrives, my butler organizes it on a silver salver and then places it on my desk. All the correspondence is presented with the wax seal facing me. It makes it quicker to open the stack." He shrugged slightly. "When I opened your letter and read it, I realized it wasn't addressed to me."

"You even read it?" Heat bludgeoned her cheeks, and her voice had softened.

"I did." Honestly, it didn't feel as if he had anything to apologize for. She was on a fool's errand that could end in her ruin.

She flinched slightly before a mask of indifference fell across her features. With a stalwart gaze, she slowly surveyed the park, completely ignoring him for a moment. Ramrod straight and with a determined demeanor, she reminded him of Diana, the goddess of the hunt—a good comparison since Pippa would probably like to shoot him with an arrow about now.

Eventually, she turned to him with a pleasant smile on her face. It was as bogus as the calves of the men who wore padded stockings to give the impression that their legs were a thing of beauty.

"I trust that you'll be discreet and keep the information in that letter secret." She chewed on her lip, and her delicate brow furrowed into perfect lines. "As an honorable gentleman, you should do that."

He wanted to roll his eyes at that statement. As an honorable gentleman, he should have gone straight to her brother.

But out of respect for her, he decided to keep the appointment this

JANNA MACGREGOR

morning. As an honorable man, he had to warn her about Lord Bedford. More importantly, as an honorable man, he couldn't allow her to ruin herself.

Bloody hell, she'd asked the man to marry her.

And if that weren't enough, she'd written to four more men asking the same.

A Simple Marriage will be available June 25 at your favorite retailers. For more info, scan below.

For the latest news and freebies from Janna, scan below to sign up for her newsletter.
Visit https://www.jannamacgregor.com for more information about Janna's books.

If you want to spill the tea with Janna, scan below and join her Facebook Readers Group, the Lords and Ladies of Langham Hall.

About the Author

Janna MacGregor pens romance novels with "Austen's spirit" (*Entertainment Weekly*) from her dual residences in the fast-paced Twin Cities and her native home in Kansas City. But she spends most of her time in Regency England, the setting for her beloved Cavensham Heiresses and the Widow Rules series. Her new series is The Millionaires of Mayfair.

For the latest news and freebies from Janna, <u>sign up for her Newsletter</u>.
Connect with Janna MacGregor Online
<u>Facebook</u>
<u>Ladies of Langham Hall Facebook Group</u>
<u>Instagram</u>
<u>BookBub</u>
<u>TikTok</u>

Made in the USA
Columbia, SC
07 September 2024

41911430R00195